Her Cold Blood

Tanya Stone FBI K9 Mystery Thriller

Tikiri Herath

Rebel Diva
ACADEMY PRESS

Her Cold Blood

Tanya Stone FBI K9 Mystery Thriller Series

www.TikiriHerath.com

Copyright ©2023 Tikiri Herath

Edition: 2023

Library & Archives Canada Cataloging in Publication

E-book ISBN: 978-1-990234-15-6

Paperback ISBN: 978-1-990234-16-3

Hardback ISBN: 978-1-990234-17-0

Audiobook ISBN: 978-1-990234-18-7

Large Print ISBN: 978-1-990234-45-3

Author: Tikiri Herath

Publisher Imprint: Rebel Diva Academy Press

Copy Editor: Stephanie Parent

HER COLD BLOOD

Back Cover Headshot: Aura McKay

Tikiri

A Gift For You

Thank you for picking up my latest novel. There's a gift for you for picking up this book!

HER DEADLY END is a 250-page twisty thriller about an unusual murder-suicide case that Tanya (Tetyana), Asha, and Katy accidentally stumble upon while vacationing in Paradise Cove.

It's a pulse-pounding, nerve-shredding mystery of a devious serial criminal stalking a small seaside town in Washington State.

You'll learn about the characters in the Merciless murder mystery series which features private detectives, Asha Kade & Katy McCafferty, and those in the new Tanya Stone FBI K9 series which features Special Agent Tanya (Tetyana) & Max, her K9 German Shepherd.

Join the VIP Red Heeled Rebels Club and receive your exclusive book gift. Click the link below to join.

HER DEADLY END: A gripping thriller with a twisty end

https://books.tikiriherath.com/ts-b0-fbi-herdeadlyend

There is no explicit sex, heavy cursing, or graphic violence in my books. There is, however, a closed circle of suspects, many twists and turns, fast-paced action, and nail-biting suspense.

NO DOG IS EVER HARMED IN THESE BOOKS. But the villains always are.

Tropes you'll find in this mystery thriller series include: female protagonist, women sleuths, detective, police officers, police procedural, crime, murder, kidnapping, missing, creepy cabins, serial killers, dark secrets, small towns, plot twists, fast-paced action, shocking endings, revenge, vigilante justice, family lies, intrigue, suspense, and psychological terror.

The Red Heeled Rebels Universe

The Red Heeled Rebels universe of mystery thrillers, featuring your favorite kick-ass female characters:

⁕

Tanya Stone FBI K9 Mystery Thrillers
www.TikiriHerath.com/Thrillers
NEW FBI thriller series starring Tetyana from the Red Heeled Rebels as Special Agent Tanya Stone, and Max, as her loyal German Shepherd. These are serial killer thrillers set in Black Rock, a small upscale resort town on the coast of Washington state.
Her Deadly End
Her Cold Blood
Her Last Lie
Her Secret Crime
Her Perfect Murder

Her Grisly Grave

Asha Kade Private Detective Murder Mysteries
www.TikiriHerath.com/Mysteries
Each book is a standalone murder mystery thriller, featuring the Red Heeled Rebels, Asha Kade and Katy McCafferty. Asha and Katy receive one million dollars for their favorite children's charity from a secret benefactor's estate every time they solve a cold case.
Merciless Legacy
Merciless Games
Merciless Crimes
Merciless Lies
Merciless Past
Merciless Deaths

Red Heeled Rebels International Mystery & Crime - The Origin Story
www.TikiriHerath.com/RedHeeledRebels
The award-winning origin story of the Red Heeled Rebels characters. Learn how a rag-tag group of trafficked orphans from different places united to fight for their freedom and their lives, and became a found family.
The Girl Who Crossed the Line
The Girl Who Ran Away
The Girl Who Made Them Pay

The Girl Who Fought to Kill
The Girl Who Broke Free
The Girl Who Knew Their Names
The Girl Who Never Forgot

⸺

The Accidental Traveler

www.TikiriHerath.com

An anthology of personal short stories based on the author's sojourns around the world.

⸺

The Rebel Diva Nonfiction Series

www.TikiriHerath.com/Nonfiction

Your Rebel Dreams: 6 simple steps to take back control of your life in uncertain times.

Your Rebel Plans: 4 simple steps to getting unstuck and making progress today.

Your Rebel Life: Easy habit hacks to enhance happiness in the 10 key areas of your life.

Bust Your Fears: 3 simple tools to crush your anxieties and squash your stress.

⸺

Collaborations

The Boss Chick's Bodacious Destiny Nonfiction Bundle
Dark Shadows 2: Voodoo and Black Magic of New Orleans

Tikiri's novels and nonfiction books are available on all good bookstores around the world.

These books are also available in libraries everywhere. Just ask your friendly local librarian or your local bookstore to order a copy via Ingram Spark.

www.TikiriHerath.com

Happy reading.

HER COLD BLOOD
AGENT TANYA STONE FBI K-9 MYSTERY THRILLER

Escape to Death

His heavy footsteps thundered on the concrete floor.

Laura's blood chilled.

Her small naked feet propelled her forward like they had a life of their own. She didn't realize she was leaving trails of blood in her wake, like breadcrumbs for him to follow.

His footsteps got louder.

Terror coursed through her veins. Her heart beat so hard she was sure it would explode.

She wasn't going back to that dank basement, where she'd get strapped down like an animal to be butchered.

No!

Laura raced through the whitewashed corridors of the eerie underground maze. It smelled like a slaughterhouse in there. She passed the ominous red door, but didn't dare look that way.

Behind that door was where the nightmares began. Ones you could never escape from. Her mind spun like the head of an exorcist doll, mad memories exploding like fireworks.

Keep running.

The fluorescent light fixtures on the bare ceiling flickered and buzzed. It was like they were signaling her position to her captor.

Faster!

He was stomping down the stairs, calling her name. A second familiar voice hollered after him. Laura's heart sank.

Is she coming after me, too?

A loud plop sounded on the wall beside her. White plaster exploded into a thousand pieces and sprayed the corridor, stinging her bare arms and thighs.

She ducked and covered her head.

Another plop.

The wall plaster sprayed over her like gun shrapnel.

He's shooting at me!

She glanced back, her eyes wild with horror, expecting to spot him at the other end, but the corridor was empty.

He's shooting blindly. He doesn't know where I am.

She opened her right palm and looked at the crumpled paper she'd been clutching.

Quick.

She stuffed it into her mouth.

If they find me dead, they'll know who did it.

Laura spun around and rocketed through the corridor, trying hard not to make a sound.

Almost there.

She reached the door at the end of the tunnel, grabbed the handle, and turned it.

The force of the heavy basement door hurled her backward. Bright sunlight streamed through the narrow stairway, blinding her, but she didn't have a second to lose.

She raced up, her chest heaving, barely hearing the steel basement door clang shut behind her.

She halted on the top step and blinked, disoriented.

Rows of roses burst in colors next to a manicured cedar hedge. Tall, stately trees lined the perimeter, like giant sentinels shielding the house from the rest of the world.

From afar, she could hear waves crash against the shore below. She wasn't far from the Black Rock cliffs.

Her eyes darted back and forth, desperate for an escape. That was when she noticed the wall that ran along the property line.

Her heart sank.

She was trapped.

Again.

There was only one thing to do now.

She leaped toward the closest tree and grabbed the lowest branch. Holding on, she scrambled up the oak trunk like a monkey.

She clambered higher and higher on her wobbly legs, ignoring the rough bark scraping her bare skin, propelled by her will to live.

She was halfway up when the basement door banged open. She froze and squinted through the leafy foliage.

They're here!

She turned and peered over the wall.

Freedom.

The hiking trail was down below. The path she'd walked only a few days ago, before he seized her and....

Think! What do I do now?

The massive oak tree spread over the enclosure, giving shade to the trail outside. Clinging to a branch, she inched toward the wall.

"Laura! Come back right now!" came a furious male voice. "Get down or I'll punish you!"

But Laura wasn't listening to him anymore. She kept moving, clutching whatever she could. Her entire body was trembling so hard, she was scared her hands would slip.

"I'm warning you. Get down or I'll shoot to kill!"

He's lying.

He hated spilling even one ounce of precious blood. He needed her alive. That's why he had fired his weapon near her. Not at her.

She teetered over the wall, ignoring the furious shouting below.

The bough bowed dangerously. It was too thin at the end.

The branch snapped with a loud crack. Laura fell through the air, barely feeling her T-shirt rip against a sharp twig.

The cold air rushed against her face. Then she heard an ugly thump, followed by a searing pain that scorched through her frail body. Her head hammered like an army battalion had stormed inside and was firing machine guns.

She tried to open her eyes, but all she could see was a blur of blinking stars. She felt something crumbly next to her cheek.

Dirt.

A dog barked nearby.

Someone was shouting. She didn't recognize the voice.

Help. Please. Help me. Her cries were deafening inside her head, but her throat refused to work.

The barking was muffled, but so close.

Laura tried to raise her head, but she couldn't move.

Help me.

A dog barked again.

Wait.

It was an entire *pack* of dogs.

Day One

Chapter One

Special Agent Tanya Stone shifted gears and took the offramp.

Black Rock, here we come.

Max, her police-trained German Shepherd, thumped his tail on the back seat, sensing the change in pace.

They'd had a pleasant drive from Seattle. The weather had been warm and sunny. A perfect day to put the Jeep's canvas top down.

Tanya glanced at her furry partner through the rearview mirror. "Ready for our first case, bud?"

Max barked in reply.

Tanya wanted to feel elated about her first FBI case. Instead, her excitement was tempered by a sliver of dread.

Black Rock was a prosperous seaside resort in Washington state with a population of ten thousand. It prided itself on attracting Hollywood celebrities, powerful politicians, and affluent retirees who sought anonymity in a charming locale.

The sea breeze felt fresher and the green flora lusher. But something strange and sinister was brewing underneath this idyllic, small-town charm. She felt it in her bones the minute she took the highway exit.

She instinctively touched her necklace, feeling the smooth ribbing of the gold locket on her chest.

The Ukrainian sunflower pendant had belonged to her mother. Tanya had removed it from her red-splattered neck the day she had died. The necklace had been dripping with blood, forming crimson spots on the hardwood floor of her childhood home, riddled with bullets.

When Tanya was a kid, her mother used to tell her the sunflower pendant warded off the evil eye. But that hadn't stopped those men from shooting her dead. Tanya didn't believe any of the old world mumbo jumbo, but she'd held on to the talisman. It was all she had of her mother.

Focus.

She forced those somber memories to the back of her head. This was the mission that would prove her worth to the bureau.

Susan Cross, Seattle's FBI director, had been cryptic. Black Rock would be Tanya's home for the next few months. Her job was to find the source of murders that had recently swept through the West Coast, confounding local law enforcement.

Who was behind the killings?

Organized crime?

A deranged serial killer?

Someone seeking vengeance?

No one had any idea.

Nothing connected the hapless victims who came from disparate backgrounds, genders, ages, vocations. They had been murdered in different ways, at different times, and in different towns along the coast.

There wasn't much on the local or national news that hinted at this mystery. It was like someone with the right connections and power was keeping a tight lid on the killings.

Susan Cross herself had been reserved. All she'd said was this was a dangerous undercover operation, where exposing Tanya's identity could mean life or death.

Cross had confiscated Tanya's FBI badge before giving her a new driver's license, a new birth certificate, a new gun license, and even new car insurance papers—none of which could be traced to the bureau. The Director had even ordered Max out of K9 training and seized his working collar.

Max pushed his wet nose through the front seats and turned his soulful brown eyes on Tanya's. She knew what he wanted. To stop the car so he could stretch his legs. And maybe chase a squirrel or two.

But she was on the job.

So was he.

It was Tanya's best friend, a private investigator, Asha Kade, who had rescued Max from a house of horrors in New Hampshire. Under Tanya's care, he had transformed from a scruffy pup to a search and rescue K9.

At three years old, he was still getting used to the rigors of a working dog's career. Tanya knew Max would protect her with his life, though there were days when he wouldn't pass up the chance to run after rabbits through the woods.

"No goofing, bud." Tanya reached behind to stroke his massive head. "We have to prove to Cross she made the right decision to pick us. If I don't get my paycheck, how do I pay for your kibbles? I can barely make rent as it is."

She slowed down as a large road sign caught her eye. It had one oversized letter on it.

H.

She squinted to read the smaller words beneath it.

Black Rock Psychiatric Institution.

The green arrow pointed at a narrow road that wound through a wooded area up a hill. Tanya couldn't help thinking it was the perfect setting for a slasher movie.

"A mental hospital in this tiny town?" she murmured to herself as she drove by the sign. "We'll have to check it out."

Her GPS said the local police station was five minutes from the town center. She turned into Marine Drive, Black Rock's main drag.

To Tanya's left was the Pacific Ocean, sparkling like diamonds under the early afternoon sun. A wooden pier cut through the shore toward a rocky crop a mile out on the water, where sailboats were docked.

Town center was a big term.

It was one long street that ran along the shoreline. She glanced around, looking for the sign to the precinct.

High-end boutique shops, gourmet ice cream stalls, and exclusive restaurants that offered a grand ocean view lined the drive. In the distance, she could see the top of the sprawling Pink Palace resort, rumored to have its own private waterfront.

A black limo was idling next to an upscale jewelry store. Its tinted windows were up, and a suited chauffeur was leaning against the passenger door, his eyes wrapped in Ray-Bans.

Tanya could smell the money here.

This was where the high rollers of the West Coast came to get away from it all. Especially to escape the paparazzi who flocked to more well-known celebrity destinations.

She scoped the street. There was hardly any traffic or pedestrians. It was early spring. Not the tourist season yet.

Such a pretty little town, thought Tanya.

Why do I feel so unsettled, then?

The PTSD symptoms from her combat days flared up at the most inopportune moments. Some days, her paranoia was worse than others.

She scanned the street again.

No, there's something off about this town.

The chauffeur by the limo looked up from his phone.

He frowned as he spotted Tanya's Jeep crawl down the street. He touched the side of his cheek and spoke to his earpiece. His other hand slipped into his pocket. The way his hand curled inside told Tanya he was grasping his sidearm.

Her heart beat a tick faster.

Does he know I'm FBI?

She reached for the glove compartment and pulled out her Glock.

Chapter Two

The door of the jewelry store banged open.

Out stepped a second man in a chauffeur's suit and wraparound shades. He was holding a girl by one arm.

She must have been seventeen at most. Her face was sullen, maybe angry. She looked like a schoolgirl in her green plaid skirt and white shirt and was trailing an expensive brown leather satchel on the ground.

She gave a half-hearted attempt to shake the man's hand off, but his grasp was strong.

Tanya came to a stop by the side of the street and pretended to check a window display while she watched them from the corner of her eyes.

The first man opened the back door of the limo and gestured for them to hurry. The man pulling the girl picked up his pace. The girl didn't speak, but her face clearly said she didn't want to get in.

Tanya realized this could just be a schoolgirl playing truant and being dragged back home or to school. She knew her PTSD triggered trust issues. Some days, everybody looked like the bad guy.

Susan Cross would kill her if she engaged in law enforcement while undercover. Still, she couldn't just sit and watch.

She opened the Jeep's door to step out when a bone-chilling scream came from the other end of the street.

Tanya whirled around, gun in hand.

"Help me!"

It was a woman's voice. Laced in terror.

Tanya dashed down the drive with Max at her heels. Undercover or not, she wasn't going to ignore a cry from someone in trouble.

"Get away from me!" came the piercing cry again. "Let me go!"

The terrified screeches were coming from a small alleyway at the end. The entire street should have heard, but no one else was rushing over. No one even stepped out of the shops.

Tanya swiveled her head back to see the limo drive away as if nothing out of the ordinary was going on. Turning back around, she raced into the narrow alley from where the cries had come.

Her eyes widened at the sight.

An elderly woman in a yellow jumpsuit and crystal-studded shades was hugging her handbag. With her free hand, she was doing her best to fend off two burly men.

With black bandannas across their foreheads and skull tattoos on their biceps, they looked like giants next to her. Gang members. If Tanya had to guess, they either had just got out of prison or would end up there before long.

What were they doing in a neighborhood like this?

The thugs circled the woman, smug grins on their faces, towering over her small frame. She looked about the same age as Tanya's mother would be now, had she lived.

Hot anger spiraled up Tanya's spine.

She gripped her gun and marched over, wishing she could use her firearm, but she knew better. If they were armed with automatic weapons, that would only put the woman's life at risk.

One man swooped down and plucked the handbag out of the woman's hands.

She flailed and shrieked. "Give that back! That's mine!"

To Tanya's surprise, she lunged forward and pulled at her purse straps. The goon jumped out of the way with a cackle.

The second man pulled a knife out of his pocket and pretended to jab her, guffawing. The poor woman screeched, covering her head with her arms.

The thugs were playing a sick game, but they were so engrossed in their victim, they hadn't noticed Tanya and Max stomp up to them from behind.

The old woman brazenly grabbed at her purse again. The thug's smile turned into a scowl. He raised his fist in the air.

"I'll show you, you little—"

"Stop that!" Tanya stepped up to them, her Glock behind her back.

The goons spun around, eyes widening as they caught sight of the tall woman in cargo pants and army boots. By her feet was a massive wolf -like canine bristling at them.

Tanya eyed the men testily, wishing she had her handcuffs and her badge. She was fit and trained, but these goons had several inches on her and biceps the size of tree trunks. The bulges in their back pant pockets told her they could be armed with more than just that blade.

"Give her purse back," she snarled.

"Who the heck are you?" snapped the bully with the handbag.

"Someone who's going to stop you from robbing a defenseless woman."

He laughed. "You think I'm scared of a chick?"

The man with the knife turned on Tanya, his mouth curling into a snarl. "You wanna join the party? Hand over your money, bitch!"

Max's growls grew louder.

The thug with the bag lunged at Tanya.

She ducked.

"Max, get him!"

Max pounced on the goon, his mighty jaws wrapping around his arm and pulling him to the ground.

That was when the man with the knife swiped at Tanya, the sharp edge slicing the air inches from her cheek. She spun around and raised her Glock.

But it was too late.

He came down on her like a concrete block. She crashed against the wall, her head hitting the hard brick with a sickening scrunch.

She tried to slam him back with her shoulders, but the thug had her pinned down with his body, his knife at her throat. Her hand that held the gun was pressed behind her. Out of reach.

She kicked and pushed, but it was like fighting an ox.

His blade dug into her neck, cutting her skin, drawing blood.

Chapter Three

Tanya raised her knee and rammed it between the thug's legs.

He let go with an agonized yell and buckled in pain.

Max whirled around and snapped at the man's heels. The goon kicked at the dog but missed.

Tanya grabbed his wrist and twisted it violently. The knife fell to the ground with a clatter. She punched his stomach and slammed him against the wall before ramming her Glock into his forehead.

"Call me bitch again!" she roared into his face.

The second man scrambled to his feet and backed down the alleyway, still clutching the woman's handbag.

"Get the bag, Max!" Tanya yelled.

Max whipped around. He jumped on the goon, sinking his fangs into his upper thigh and bringing him crashing down again. He was growling so loudly it sounded like a pack of wolves were fighting in that narrow alleyway.

He snapped the purse in his jaws and brought it back to the old woman, who was cowering in the corner.

Tanya pressed her gun into the forehead of the man in front of her.

"I have an excellent memory and can draw faster than anyone in this state. If I see you or your pal's face in this town again, I'll have your heads."

He glared back, his beady eyes boring into hers.

"Next time, I will make you feel pain, bitch." His tightened jaw and blazing eyes told Tanya he meant it.

She wished she could pistol whip him into a coma right there. "I suggest you take my words seriously. I don't make idle threats."

"Me too," growled the thug. "You just signed your death warrant."

Tanya grabbed him by the collar and peeled him off the wall.

"Get out!" she hollered as she kicked him away. "And don't come back!"

With an angry hiss, he whirled around and stomped toward his companion.

This time, Max didn't wait for a command. He lunged after them, barking. Without a glance back, the men picked up their pace and vanished around the corner, with Max at their heels.

Tanya turned to the victim, who was clutching her purse and staring at her like she was an alien.

She appraised the older woman.

The designer shoes, sunglasses, and the gold necklace around her dainty neck shouted her fashionista lifestyle. Now that she was close, Tanya realized there was something odd about this woman, something she couldn't pinpoint.

She sniffed the air.

Do I smell alcohol?

Though the woman's face was defiant, her hands were trembling.

"You were brave," said Tanya. "I hope there's never a next time, but if it happens again, I suggest you hand over your handbag. Your life's not worth it."

The woman pursed her bright maroon lips and hugged her purse closer.

"My dead husband's photos are in here. Larry at the drugstore is going to make them digital, so I can share them online."

"Nothing's worth getting stabbed," said Tanya. "Trust me. I know."

The woman shot her a stubborn look. "I wasn't going to lose them to those nitwit turkeys."

"Those nitwit turkeys could have killed you."

"Let them try. I work for the police chief."

Tanya did a double take.

The woman narrowed her eyes. "Haven't seen you around these parts. You from out of town?"

"Starting a new job with the precinct today."

The woman's eyes widened.

"*You're* the trainer the chief's been talking about? I was expecting a military type."

"I am ex-military."

It was Tanya's combat experience in Ukraine that had inspired Cross to hand select her for this solo mission.

At thirty-three, she had been a mature hire to the bureau. They had waived the age restriction as she had been a combat vet, but she had passed her training at Quantico with flying colors. That hadn't escaped Cross's sharp eyes. No other FBI rookie got this level of responsibility so early in their career.

Tanya bent down and offered a hand to the older woman. "Tanya Stone. Nice to meet you."

"I'm Wilma," said the woman, squeezing her hand. She pointed at Max, who was trotting over, a proud look on his face. "What's his name?"

"Max."

Wilma ruffled the dog's head. "You're a good boy. Got my purse back and chased away those turkeys, too."

"What do you do for the chief, Wilma?" asked Tanya.

"I'll have my shingle hanging over the dispatch desk as long as they keep paying me."

She's a dispatcher?

The way Wilma dressed, Tanya had expected her to be a wealthy retiree. Or a widow with a healthy trust fund. If she was still working, she'd expected her to have a job that paid a lot more than a junior municipal employee.

"I was just heading to the station to report for duty," said Tanya. "Let me give you a ride."

Without waiting for Wilma to answer, she whistled for Max and turned around to walk back to the main road.

"Tell me about the recent crime sprees," she said as Wilma shuffled alongside, trying to keep up with her long strides.

"Crimes?" said Wilma. "Black Rock's a peaceful town. I grew up here. We never have any trouble."

Tanya raised a brow. "That's not what I just saw."

"Oh, that." Wilma swept an errant hair from her forehead. "Pickpockets and petty thieves from Portland. Happens once in a blue moon. Black Rockers are good people."

"You nearly got mugged."

Wilma put a cold hand on Tanya's arm and pulled her back, stopping her in mid stride. Tanya spun around to face the woman.

"What is it?"

Wilma leaned closer and lowered her voice to a whisper. "Don't tell anyone what just happened, okay?"

Chapter Four

Tanya stopped when they reached the Jeep.

There was something about this older woman that reminded her of her mother. Bold. Stubborn. And too proud to ask for help or admit when things went wrong.

She turned to Wilma with a sigh. "It's our duty to report a crime."

Wilma's face scrunched up. "Nothing really bad happened in the end, did it?"

Because I came to help you.

"They pulled a knife on you, Wilma. They threatened you and me."

"You don't understand."

"Help me understand, then," said Tanya.

Wilma's lips quivered and her eyes filled with tears. "The new chief just started a week ago. If he knew I got into trouble, he could force me to retire. He could fire me. What do I do then?"

"Getting mugged isn't a plausible reason to fire anybody," said Tanya. "Not by any stretch of the imagination. Besides, I'll stand up for you."

"Please. I'm asking you to not tell anyone about this. I just can't...."

Tanya lowered her voice. "This wasn't an isolated incident. Bad things have been happening in and around Black Rock."

"Like what?" Wilma's gaze was cautious.

"Like serial murders."

"Maybe in the next town over, but not here. Not in my town."

The image of the girl getting pushed into the limo flashed across Tanya's mind.

"How about abductions?"

Wilma gave her a startled look. "How do you know?"

Bingo.

Wilma looked away and blinked. "That's just a wicked rumor."

"How many girls have gone missing so far?" asked Tanya.

"I don't know."

"What do the rumors say?"

"A handful of girls have run away from home. Here and there, over the years."

"Any idea what happened to them?"

"They took off to Seattle with boyfriends from out of town. If anyone says bad things happened to them, that's just vicious gossip. Like I said, they're all runaways."

"There could also be a trafficking ring at work. Or a serial sex offender."

"It could also just be the pirate from the high seas come back."

Tanya raised a brow.

She had battled Somali pirates while protecting merchant ships in the Gulf of Aden a few years earlier. Was this what Cross wanted her to do in Black Rock? Hunt down modern-day pirates?

She put her hands on her hips. "I didn't realize Washington state had a pirate problem."

Wilma pushed another errant hair back.

"When I was a little girl, my grandma told me the stories. The phantom pirate sailed in a ghost ship with a black sail. He stole girls from the villages. I used to have nightmares he'd snatch me one day. I never went to the beach alone after that."

Phantom pirates? Ghost ships?

Tanya tried to hide her annoyance.

If there had been no crime sprees, the FBI wouldn't have given Black Rock a second glance. Why was Wilma so protective of her hometown, especially after almost getting mugged herself?

"Chief Bold wouldn't have gone to the trouble to hire me if he didn't have a heavy workload," she said.

"He's from the big city," said Wilma. "Always expecting bad things to happen. He's a super worrier. This is a small town. A good town."

She glanced at Tanya from under her eyelids, like she was about to divulge a secret.

"Even the city council said no when the chief proposed to hire you."

Really?

"They said we didn't need you. They said they couldn't afford you. The chief had to fight to get you."

"Is that right?" said Tanya. Her fake contract didn't pay much. It would all go to the FBI coffers, anyway.

Wilma lowered her voice.

"You look like a nice girl, so I'll tell you this. Don't believe all the gossip. It's peaceful here. Not like the big city. You don't have to worry about crimes and such. You don't have to be so scared."

Tanya didn't reply.

There were few things in the world that frightened her. Small-town crime wasn't one of them.

Tanya had been baptized by gunfire at eighteen years old. It was the day the Russian militia gunned down her mother and took her younger brother to a torture camp. She never saw his body but rumors of his horrific death felt like stab wounds through her heart.

She taught herself to handle an assault rifle, shoot a sniper gun, blow up a bridge, track militia gangs, and hold up a train across enemy lines in her homeland of Ukraine. By her nineteenth birthday, the thugs who'd killed her family and ravaged her village had paid for their brutality.

Tanya's birth name was Tetyana Shevchenko.

But Tetyana didn't exist anymore.

This was one secret the residents of Black Rock would never find out.

The nightmares of her past still haunted her, the invisible wounds cutting deep into her psyche. Staying busy was what kept her sane. It was why she had joined the bureau. That, and her all consuming rage for justice.

Justice, her mother and brother never got to have.

But Wilma didn't know any of this.

It was time to change topics.

Tanya opened the passenger door of her Jeep for the older woman. "Who lives in Black Rock? Vacationing families? Retirees?"

Wilma seemed to perk up at the question.

"This is a resort town, so folks are always coming and going. We even have Hollywood celebrities. Did you know Angelina Jolie and Johnny Depp have beautiful houses up the hill? Sharon Stone too. Have you seen her? In real life, I mean? I have. Many times on Marine Drive. Drop-dead gorgeous, she is."

"Who else lives here?"

"Hot-shot politicians from Washington come when they lose an election and need to get away for a bit. I could drop some big names." Wilma babbled on, her tears forgotten. "Rich kids come for summer breaks too, if they're not partying it up in California. They're always cruising along Marine Drive in their fancy open cars, playing loud music. But no one says anything because they come from big families."

"Do they cause trouble?"

"Trouble?"

"Yeah, like illegal drugs. Abductions. Sexual assaults. Homicides. That sort of thing."

Wilma stared at Tanya.

"That's scandalous. How could you even think that?"

Wilma looked away and pushed her hair back from her forehead. Her face was flushed and her hands were shaking.

Tanya recognized those telltale signs.

Wilma wasn't telling the whole truth about Black Rock.

Chapter Five

Three uniformed men were conversing at the far side of the bullpen.

Their backs were to them.

Tanya turned to Wilma. "Which one's the chief?"

"The tall one." Wilma jabbed her in the waist and gave her a coy smile. "The girls around town have been saying he looks just like Jack Reacher on TV. What do you think?"

Tanya was surprised at how quickly Wilma had transformed from the frightened mugging victim into a friendly driving companion, eager to share her own gossip.

But Tanya wasn't looking for empty chatter. She wanted facts, facts the FBI had sent her to ferret out.

On their way over, Wilma had asked her to stop at Lulu's corner café. After getting her an iced cappuccino and Max a fresh bottle of water, Tanya had parked the Jeep next to a row of squad cars behind the precinct.

An ambulance had been idling in the far corner of the parking lot. Tanya had spotted two heads in front, talking animatedly.

"Justin and Stacey," Wilma had said. "They have an office inside, but they only come in to get supplies and pick up their paychecks."

"Are they that busy?"

"They just drive around most of the time. I can always reach them on radio, so it's not a big deal. To tell the truth, I don't blame them for not wanting to come inside this place."

Black Rock's police station was a shabby, one-story concrete bunker. Tanya could see the cracks on the walls and the heavy peeling on the roof. It looked like it would collapse into a heap of dust if even a low-level tremor hit the West Coast.

Tanya had followed Wilma through the waiting room to the secure area via the electronically locked door, with Max on a leash. A damp and musty odor had hit her nose as the inside door opened.

Inside the secure space was the bullpen, with desks and a row of computers. Two interview rooms lined one wall and a small boardroom was on the other.

The door to the chief's office stood wide open, but it was impossible to see if anyone was inside as the desk was piled high with manila folders.

Wilma pushed a jar of chocolate Oreo cookies to the side of her desk and put her coffee down. When she opened the bottom drawer Tanya noticed the golden liquid bottle in the corner.

Whiskey?

Wilma shoved her handbag in and slammed the drawer shut. She turned and looked up at Tanya, as if to make sure she hadn't spotted her hidden stash.

Tanya didn't say a word, but she could smell the strong liquor.

Wilma pulled up a rolling chair and plopped down. "It's nice to have a fresh female face around here. Lopez's the only other one, but she's got such a chip on her shoulders, I tell you."

"Have you worked here a long time?" said Tanya.

"My husband was chief, ages ago. He was a good man. Worked hard and did a lot for this town. I started at the station at seventeen, and never retired." Wilma grinned. "I'm seventy-one years young and I keep on ticking. I'll outlast all of them, I tell you."

"I'm sure you will."

Wilma's smile widened.

"You have such pretty features." She wagged a finger near Tanya's nose. "Take some advice from a wise old woman. Grow your hair. Put some makeup on to bring those pretty green eyes out, and for goodness' sake, get rid of these ugly pants and boots."

Tanya stared at the woman. "I'm on the job."

She spun on her heels and walked to the back of the station. Wilma was a puzzle she'd have to sort out later. It was time to meet the man who hired her.

The officer with the chief's badge looked up as she walked over. They made eye contact. Tanya blinked. Though she didn't want to admit it, her heart skipped a beat.

At five foot, eleven and a half inches, she towered over most men, but the chief was a few inches taller. Wilma was right. Chief Bold was as buff and brawny as they come. Those soft brown eyes probably made the women of this town swoon, she thought, but they won't work on me.

You could be the killer I'm supposed to be hunting in Black Rock.

The two officers flanking the chief couldn't have been any different.

One was in his late twenties or early thirties. He wore round rimless spectacles that made him look like a fit librarian and was the only one with a wedding band on his finger.

The second officer was older and looked like he spent more time giving out parking tickets than chasing criminals. His wide girth and graying sideburns told Tanya he was surfing till they gave him his pension. Or the boot out the door.

But in a small town like this, Tanya doubted the chief had many hiring options.

She offered her hand to him.

"Tanya Stone."

The chief jerked his head back like he hadn't expected her. He was quick to cover his surprise and shake her hand.

"Jack Bold. Glad you could make it."

The older officer standing next to him raised a brow. "*You* are our trainer?"

"I am."

"I thought it was going to be a man."

Tanya's face hardened.

He smirked. "I mean, I was expecting someone experienced."

"Combat war vet," Tanya snapped, swallowing the more colorful words she wished she could spit out.

Bold glared at his officer.

"Stone was trained by Israel's special forces. I'm surprised we could even afford someone with her skills. Show some respect."

The chief turned to Tanya with a semi-apologetic look on his face and gestured to his colleagues. "Meet my team. Officer Shawn Fox and Officer Ezra Jones."

Shawn Fox was the fit librarian. Ezra Jones was the man with the nasty attitude.

As Tanya held out her hand to the officers, she felt her gut signal to her.

If there was one thing she'd learned over the years, it was to trust her instincts. There was something about these two, but it was when she touched Officer Ezra Jones hand she felt her back stiffen.

Jones wasn't just a jaded cop with a surly mug.

He was a dangerous man.
The kind who'd stab you in the back without a hint of remorse.

Chapter Six

Chief Bold waved to someone by the entrance.

"Lopez. Over here."

Tanya turned to see a trim and toned female officer in uniform, her tawny hair tied back into a sensible ponytail.

Wilma was right. Lopez's uniform showed a rank slightly higher than her male colleagues and she looked more competent. But her shoulders were squared, and her face was set in an angry expression.

Tanya didn't like the look she gave her as she marched over.

You don't intimidate me, thought Tanya. She straightened to her full height and offered her hand. Lopez thrust her chin up as she shook it in a vise grip. She offered no smile.

"It was the FBI field office that recommended Stone," said the chief to his team.

All three officers raised their eyebrows. They were impressed, but their shoulders were taut and their faces remained unsmiling.

Bold turned to Tanya.

"Our crime rates have been steadily increasing. It's the same all across the country, but the incidents along the coast have been alarming. It's not what you'd expect to see in and around a resort town with such a small population. We have our work cut out for us."

Tanya shot a discreet glance at Wilma by the reception desk. She was placing a bowl of water on the floor for Max. He got up and lapped it while she petted his back.

On their way to the station, Wilma had begged her to not talk about the mugging. That went against everything Tanya believed in, but something told her to stay mum for now. There was more to this town and this team than met the eye.

"The mayor wants everything cleaned up yesterday," continued the chief, oblivious to the questions raging in Tanya's mind. "The problem is we have to work quietly, without giving a hint to the outside, as the tourists bring in hefty dollars. This makes our job much harder."

"What type of crimes are we talking about?" asked Tanya.

"Homicides, abductions, smuggling. I'm still catching up to the case files in Black Rock so I don't have the full picture yet."

"I saw two men push a teen into a limo on Marine Drive. It didn't give me a good feeling."

A chuckle made Tanya turn.

"That's not how we work," said Jones. "We don't go by our feels."

"She clearly didn't want to get inside," said Tanya.

"A truant," said Jones. "So many of these rich kids run around when they should be at school. She's probably at home now with her private tutor, cursing her parents."

A concerned expression came over Chief Bold's eyes. "Did she say anything?"

"Not a word, but she could have been too frightened to speak."

"Did she try to run away?"

"She sort of resisted but didn't—" Tanya stopped as she realized how paranoid she sounded.

"Could it have been a family member trying to get her home?" said Bold.

"Hard to say. I didn't have time to take the limo's license number. Got distracted...."

Jones shook his head and chuckled again. "You don't know the first thing about police business. Leave that to us."

"Who are you?"

Tanya turned to see Lopez scrutinizing her, animosity in her eyes.

"Private contractor," she said.

"I know that." Lopez squinted even more. "But who are you, really? Why are you in this business?"

Tanya stared at the officers who were watching her carefully, even the chief who had hired her.

I'm a woman who has killed more men than you can even imagine. They all deserved to die, but with every kill, I lost part of my soul.

But Tanya knew she could never divulge such a secret with these strangers.

"When I was a kid, I thought I was going to be a school teacher, but things changed."

Lopez opened her mouth as if to say something, then shut it. No one spoke for a few seconds.

"What are your qualifications for this job?" said Fox.

"I was the CIA's best sniper in the Middle East. Mossad hired me for their overseas security projects after that. I've hunted traffickers and terrorists from Monrovia to Somalia. Got a fifth-degree black belt in hand-to-hand combat." Tanya paused. "I've done contract work for the FBI, as well. I understand state-side police business."

"FBI, huh?" said Lopez, like she didn't believe her.

"Why would you come to a little town after running around the world?" said Jones, a condescending smirk on his face. "You're gonna be bored to tears."

"I was hired to do a job." Tanya gave him a steely look. "I'm here to give you training in Krav Maga martial arts and specialized weapons, so you're equipped to deal with this recent crime wave more effectively."

Fox frowned. "Who do you work for?"

"Myself."

"An independent contractor?" Jones' face turned dark. "What a windfall. I could do with a sweet private deal myself."

"Listen up, everyone." Bold turned to his team, hands in the air as if to say *stop it already*. "Stone's going to whip us into shape and give us the street skills we need. First session starts tomorrow morning at seven. I want to see all of you—"

"Chief!" a panicked voice called out from the other end of the station.

Everyone whirled toward the receptionist's desk. Wilma had one hand over her headphones and was waving to them urgently.

"Call just came in. Someone heard a girl scream for help. She was shouting about someone trying to kill her."

Bold jerked his head up. "Location?"

"Hiking trail behind Grimwood Estate. Three miles down."

"On our way."

He turned to his team. "Lopez and Jones, take a car. Fox, stand by for instructions."

"Will do, Boss," said Fox.

"I bet that's Laura Fredrickson," said Lopez, pulling her jacket on.

"Who's Laura Fredrickson?" said Tanya.

"Missing case," said Fox. "Fifteen-year-old female disappeared three days ago. Took a bus to a local restaurant for a job. Never came home."

"Cameras?" said Tanya.

"City's too cheap to install cameras in our public transportation," said Lopez as she pulled out her sidearm, checked it, and holstered it.

Fox made a face. "Or anywhere for that matter."

"For a town that makes good money off wealthy tourists," said Tanya, turning to the chief who was reaching for his hat and jacket, "your city council sure is frugal. Where does all that money go?"

"That's over my pay grade," said Bold as he marched toward the door. "We have a crime scene to attend to right now."

Tanya followed Bold out to the parking lot. She opened the Jeep's back door to let Max jump in.

Bold gave her a quizzical look. "Where are you heading?"

"Going to the crime scene."

Bold stared.

"I can help you in the field." Tanya pointed at her Jeep. "I've been told I'm faster than a rally racer."

The chief gave her a stern look. "Watch your speed. I don't want to give my contractor a ticket."

He stepped toward the nearest squad car, then stopped. "Stay at the station. You're not an officer on duty."

With that, he got in his car and slammed the door.

Lopez, with Jones in the passenger seat, took off first, sirens blaring. Bold was next to leave, his lights flashing.

Tanya jumped in her driver's seat and started the engine. She rolled the Jeep out of the parking lot and raced down the road to catch up to the crew.

You don't get to tell me what to do, Chief Bold.

Chapter Seven

"Looks like our missing girl," said Officer Jones to Chief Bold. "Dead as a doornail."

Tanya was right behind the chief. He had shot her an annoyed look when she had parked beside his squad car along the hiking trail, but he hadn't reprimanded her.

Yet.

I guess that's coming later, thought Tanya as she joined the two men on the path.

"Check for evidence," said Bold to Jones. "Take photos. Lots of them."

He spun around and walked over to Lopez, who was squatting next to the young girl's body in the ditch.

Tanya surveyed the surroundings.

They were on a narrow hiking path that snaked through a quiet, wooded area. This was the west end of town, where colossal mansions sat high on the ocean cliff, safely walled off from the rest of town.

There was no one in sight.

At first glance, it seemed like a peaceful location—one where birds sang, and trees bent over the high walls, offering generous shade to hikers on the trail. It was a place where you'd expect to see joggers after work and families with kids on weekends.

The ditch where the girl lay was next to a whitewashed brick wall that meandered along the pathway. On the other side of the trail loomed an imposing twelve-foot concrete barricade with barbed wire straddling the top.

A large sign painted in austere letters said, *PRIVATE. KEEP OUT. GRIMWOOD ESTATE.*

Max had jumped out of the Jeep and had taken a guarded position in front of that sign, his nose pointed toward the estate. Tanya thought she heard distant barking. Max's alert ears told her something inside that compound was bothering him more than the dead body in the ditch.

"Grimwood Estate," muttered Tanya, as she walked over to the dead girl.

Bold was by his squad car now, talking urgently to someone on his radio. Lopez was holding the victim's limp wrist in her hands. Making sure not to trample on evidence, Tanya stepped into the ditch and squatted next to her.

It was a teenage girl, her chestnut brown hair spread underneath her head like an angel's halo. Her face was pale and thin, and scrunched into an expression of terror.

The girl was lying on her side, in a plain white T-shirt several sizes too large that could have doubled as a nightshirt. It was so big the u-shaped neck cut low over her small breasts. The shirt had a rip at the bottom hem, like it had caught on something.

"Any idea what happened?" said Tanya as she scanned the frail body.

"No evidence of sexual assault," said Lopez. "Outwardly anyway. The medical examiner will confirm that. No major bruises, except for this…"

Tanya leaned over to see the girl's forearm. A trickle of blood was seeping from her right elbow, but the wound wasn't bigger than a pinprick.

"Injection mark?"

Lopez shrugged. "She got pricked by something. The ME will confirm."

Lopez got up to head back to her car. Tanya stayed with the girl, a sadness creeping into her heart.

Despite everything she had witnessed in the most dangerous hot spots in the world, it was heart-breaking to see a child like this. Tanya reached over and pulled the T-shirt up to cover the girl's chest.

"Wait a minute," she said to herself.

She put her hand under the girl's nose to feel her breath when the teen's pupils moved under her eyelids.

Tanya sprang back in shock.

"She's alive!"

Bold and Lopez whipped around.

"Call EMT!" yelled Bold.

Lopez grabbed her radio.

The girl's eyes flickered open. They were filled with fear, but she was breathing again. Hoarse, shallow, fast breaths.

Tanya leaned close. "Laura? You're safe, hun. We got you. Hang tight."

"EMT on its way," hollered Lopez.

The girl struggled to move her head.

"Stay still," said Tanya, placing a gentle hand on her shoulder. "We'll get you out of here soon."

Tanya looked up. "Water! She needs water!"

Lopez was hauling a first aid kit from the back of her squad car while Bold was barking down the radio to Fox. Everyone was on the move, except for Jones. He stood in front of the Grimwood Estate barricade, looking up, as if examining the sky.

Did he find something?

The girl gasped for air and Tanya turned her focus back to her.

"You're doing great," she said, squeezing the girl's arm gently. "We're going to take care of you now. Stay still."

Laura gargled like she was choking on her own spit. "The kid... the kid..."

Tanya put her ear closer to her mouth.

"The kid..." came Laura's trembling voice. She spoke so low Tanya wasn't sure she'd heard it right.

"Which kid, hun?"

"He chased me...."

"Who chased you? A kid?"

"No, the monster. He's... coming back... for more..."

Tanya blinked. *The monster?* Laura turned her pale blue eyes to her but could hardly keep them open.

"Who's this monster?" asked Tanya.

The girl clutched her hand but didn't speak.

"It's okay, hun," whispered Tanya, holding on to her. "You're going to be fine now. You're safe."

"He... he..." Laura's face scrunched up like it took all her energy to speak. "He was going to kill me...."

Lopez jumped down into the ditch with the emergency kit and a bottle of water.

Suddenly, the girl's head sank to the side, and her eyes rolled up into her sockets.

"Laura?" called out Tanya, panic shooting through her. "Laura? Wake up, hun. Keep your eyes open."

A powerful convulsion went through the girl's weakened body. Then, she fell still.

"CPR!" shouted Tanya.

Lopez pushed the first aid kit aside and took position.

Tanya pinched the girl's nose and bent down to give her artificial breath. Across from her, Lopez put her hands on the girl's chest to pump her heart back to life.

The two women worked side by side, while Bold watched from the path, yelling through his radio for the ambulance to hurry.

Lopez kept pumping. Tanya kept blowing. Tanya didn't know how long she worked, but all she wanted was for Laura to come to life again.

After what felt like an eternity, Lopez fell back on her haunches, wiping the sweat off her brow.

Tanya looked up sharply. "Keep pumping!"

Lopez shook her head. "She's gone."

Tanya double-checked the girl's pulse on her neck, then her wrists, but she knew Lopez was right.

Laura Fredrickson had taken her last breath.

Chapter Eight

C hief Bold stepped down and kneeled next to Tanya and
Lopez in the ditch.

The three crouched silently for a few seconds around the girl's
prone body, as if in vigil.

"Any ID?" said Bold.

Tanya shook her head. "All she had on is this oversized T-shirt
and her underwear."

"I can confirm this is Laura Fredrickson." Lopez pulled her
phone out and clicked through an image app. "Thinner and gaunt,
but it's her."

Tanya squinted at the girl's lifeless face. Laura's right cheek
seemed puffier than the left.

"Does she have something in her mouth?"

Bold and Lopez bent down to look.

"Anyone spare a glove?" asked Tanya.

Lopez whipped out a rubber glove from her pocket. Tanya put it
on before parting the dead girl's lips and pushing her index finger
inside her mouth.

"Something's stuck in the back."

"A lozenge?" said Lopez. "Candy?"

Tanya felt something rough. This was no candy. She pried it out of Laura's mouth, trailing saliva.

"What the heck is that?" said Lopez, wrinkling her nose.

"A note?" said Bold.

Tanya uncrumpled the wet paper and inspected the faint letters. "It's one word, but I can't make it out."

"She was hiding it," said Lopez. "This probably points to whoever took her."

"Let's give it a closer look at the station," said Bold.

Lopez thrust a plastic evidence bag under Tanya's hand. Tanya dropped the wet paper inside and turned to the officers.

"Just before she died she said something about a kid. I couldn't make it out, but then she mentioned a monster who'll come back for more."

Lopez raised her eyebrows.

"I could have misheard," said Tanya, "but she was trying to tell me what happened to her."

"I'll take anything right now to find out who did this to her." Bold turned to Lopez. "Add that to the report, would you?"

Tanya glanced up and down the lonely trail. "How did she end up here?"

A siren made them all turn to the trailhead where they had parked their vehicles.

The ambulance had arrived, but they no longer had a patient to attend to. The red and white van swayed along the uneven trail, its top skimming the oak branches that bent over the narrow pathway.

Bold sprang to his feet and turned to his other officer. "Jones?"

Ezra Jones turned around, hands in his pockets.

"Find anything? Shoe markings, tire tracks?"

"Nothing yet."

"With more traffic coming, the chances of us losing evidence increases."

"I know."

"Check under every stone, every blade of grass," snapped Bold, exasperation crossing his face.

"Sure."

The chief turned away from him, muttering under his breath.

Jones pulled his phone from his pocket and ambled along the trail, almost bumping into the paramedics rushing over with a stretcher.

Tanya frowned as Jones moved languidly, taking photos seemingly at random.

What's wrong with him?

A young girl had just died at their feet, and he was acting like he was at a Sunday barbecue, forced to watch over the grill.

Tanya turned to Lopez. "Who made the nine-one-one call?"

"A guard from Grimwood Estate," said Lopez, stepping away to give space to the medics. "He was walking the perimeter inside when his dogs started barking. That's when he heard a girl cry for help outside the wall."

"Didn't he come out to check?"

"That wall goes forever in both directions." Lopez pointed at the estate with her chin. "There's only one exit from this place. It would have taken him hours to walk out and about half an hour or more to drive here."

"So, he never actually saw her?"

"That's what he's saying."

"Is this the first time a missing girl was found here?"

Lopez nodded but her attention was on the medics, who were moving Laura Fredrickson onto the stretcher.

Everyone watched in silence as the paramedics covered the body with a plastic sheet, heaved the stretcher out, and carried the girl toward the waiting ambulance.

Tanya turned around and surveyed the concrete wall of the Grimwood Estate.

She checked the GPS on her phone but all the satellite imagery showed was an opaque green blob that seemed to go on for miles and miles.

This wasn't just another private property. This was a mini-Fort Knox that concealed thousands of acres of land.

What do they do in there?

Max seemed to have the same suspicions as he hadn't budged from his spot, his head cocked to the side. Listening.

"What do you hear, bud?" said Tanya.

He didn't move a muscle, his pointy nose aimed at the wall.

Tanya turned to Bold. "Could someone have dropped her from the other side of the estate?"

"Highly unlikely." The chief pointed to the top. "Those wires are electrified. They would have got electrocuted before the barbs ripped them to shreds."

Lopez walked over to them. "It's more likely that someone came along the trail and dumped her here. They could have come from anywhere."

Bold turned to Officer Jones. "You're familiar with the security guys at the Estate, correct?"

"Sort of."

"I'd like you to go to the Estate and ask the guard who called nine-one-one to come to the station."

"What for?"

"I need to know firsthand what he heard. Get the footage from the security cameras along this wall as well. Let's see if they'll be open to a friendly call. I don't want them to clam up and delay the investigation."

"They're super private and they don't like to—"

Bold spun around, a dark flush creeping up his neck. "We just found a dead girl. Tell them they can cooperate now or I'll get a warrant if I have to."

Officer Jones shrugged and turned around. Tanya watched him shuffle toward the squad car. Jones hated his job, and it showed.

She forced herself to keep her mouth zipped, but part of her wanted to ask why he hadn't quit already. Was it the steady paycheck and upcoming pension? Or was it something else?

The ambulance was leaving now.

It reversed at slow speed, beeping to let anyone know they were heading back along the path. In front of them, Jones did a three-point turn in his smaller vehicle and followed them.

Tanya was still coming to terms with Laura Fredrickson dying in her arms. She was thankful Bold and Lopez seemed to have dropped their guard, because all she wanted now was to find the criminal or criminals who left this girl to die in a ditch.

"What's going to happen to her body?" she asked.

Bold sighed. "They'll take her to the morgue. We should get more answers from the ME in two days."

"You have a medical examiner in your precinct?"

"Can't afford one full time. Until recently, this county didn't even have the need for one."

The chief rubbed his brow like he was getting a headache.

"Dr. Miller, the local physician, helps us out. He's trained on autopsies, thank goodness. He's a good man. I'd rather call him than transport bodies to another county or ask State Patrol for help. That means waiting for weeks, even months, for the paperwork to go through. I'd never get work done at that rate."

Max growled, making everyone turn around.

"What is it, bud?" said Tanya.

Distant barking was coming from inside the Grimwood Estate.

Max got on all fours and hunched his back, like he was ready to pounce.

Chapter Nine

“Security dogs on patrol,” said Bold.

Max growled louder.

"What's with all this security? What are they protecting in there?" asked Tanya.

"City records say there's fifty thousand acres of arable land inside."

Tanya squinted at the top of the Grimwood Estate's wall. "I don't see any cameras."

"I'm counting on them having a few on the other side. We'll go through the footage, whether they like it or not."

"Where's the entrance?"

"Twenty miles down." Lopez pointed in the direction where the ambulance and Jones had disappeared.

Tanya frowned. "How do they have only one entrance to a fifty-thousand-acre property?"

"When you can buy land the size of a county for cash," said Bold, "you can afford to close all exits to the property you bought."

Lopez smirked. "It keeps the riffraff away."

"Who owns the estate?" asked Tanya.

"A very rich dude," said Lopez. "City records show he bought it from a hog farmer who had no next of kin about four years ago. He made some major changes."

"Like what?"

"Secured the property to start. Electrified barbed wire, surveillance cameras, trained guard dogs, and a high-security team who look like a bunch of hired mercenaries."

Lopez pursed her lips and shot Tanya a pointed look.

"Mercenaries like me?" Tanya quipped before she could stop herself.

"The hogs got sold off, and they started construction on a massive mansion," continued Lopez quickly. "All for one old man."

"Who is it?"

"No one knows. No one's seen him about town. The only way he gets in and out is in a black Agusta chopper. We hear it fly over town almost once a week. It's super loud."

"That's a European brand," said Tanya. "Most Russian billionaires have them in their fleets."

Bold appraised her like he was seeing her differently after the day's events. "Sounds like you know a thing or two about them."

Tanya nodded. "Flew an Agusta once. A bullet-proofed bird."

Bold let out a low whistle.

Lopez's eyebrows shot up. "You're a helicopter pilot too?"

Tanya shifted uncomfortably as she realized the limits of her undercover role. "Any hints to the owner's identity at all?"

"The estate is registered to a numbered corporation," said Bold. "Some say the owner's a reclusive foreigner. Others say he's a celebrity or a high-level politician. Then, some think he's a Silicon Valley tech baron who's hiding from investors. All are unsubstantiated rumors."

"What about staff?"

"Other than the security team?" said Bold, thoughtfully. "He flew in a handful of help for the house. They're outsiders. That's what the mayor told me, anyway. He's the only person who has been invited into the estate and has met this man-with-no-name. No one else comes in or out of here."

"What do they do about food, water, and supplies?"

Lopez turned to her. "There's fifty thousand acres of land with a river running through it. Not to count a few deep wells he can tap into. Heck, there could be a cattle ranch and a wheat farm in there, and no one would be the wiser."

With a shake of her head, she walked over to the ditch to take pictures and document the remaining evidence.

The sun was setting, and a dusky twilight was settling on the pathway. Soon, they wouldn't be able to see much on this lonely trail with no lights.

The Estate's patrol dogs had stopped barking and Max was now sniffing something on the other side of the ditch. Tanya walked up to the whitewashed brick wall and knocked on it. "What's on this side?"

"The town's gated community," said Bold. "All the permanent folk live within these walls."

"Who would that be?"

"The mayor, city council, our judge, lawyers, a few retired politicians, and even our medical examiner. Old money."

"The bigwigs of town?"

Bold nodded. "They have an artificial lake in the middle. Kids' playgrounds, hiking trails, and even an eighteen-hole golf course.

Nifty place if you've got cash to burn. The highest bids go for the properties with one-hundred-eighty-degree ocean views."

"Can we get in?"

"I'll send my officers to check the common grounds, but I'll need a warrant to walk inside private property."

Tanya stepped away from the wall and squinted around the waning light. That was when she spotted it.

"Those are fresh tracks."

Bold followed Tanya's finger, which pointed at the ground near where Max had been sitting.

"The ambulance didn't come this far. Our vehicles didn't either," said Tanya, taking her phone out to snap a photo of the faint tire marks.

Bold shook his head. "We'll have to do another check."

Lopez's crabby voice came from inside the ditch. "I thought Jones took care of the trail, Boss."

"I have a feeling some things could have been missed." Bold squinted down the pathway. "We don't have much time before nightfall. Let's get to work."

The three of them combed the area for clues for the next fifteen minutes, when Max twirled around and started barking, facing the mouth of the hiking trail.

"A car," said Tanya, her ears perking up.

"Jones," said Lopez, shielding her eyes with her hand. "He's back quickly. Now, that's a surprise."

The police car was racing in their direction, spiraling dust behind it.

"He's not alone," said Bold, as an enormous black SUV behind the squad car came into view.

Jones braked abruptly next to Tanya's Jeep and poked his head out of the window. He nodded to Bold, but didn't get out of his car.

The SUV screeched to a halt behind him. The doors opened, and out jumped two men. They were muscular and had scars on their faces, ones you'd get in street fights or in prison.

They swaggered unsmilingly toward the chief. In their black combat pants, boots, and leather jackets, they looked like killers for hire. It was hard to see their expressions behind their shades, but Tanya could feel the tension in the air ratchet up.

She noticed Jones had remained in the car, like he was preparing for a fast getaway if things went south.

The men were covering the distance between them fast. That was when Tanya spotted the handguns flash from under their flapping jackets.

Her hand flew to her hip in an instant. She drew out her Glock. "Stop where you are!"

The men whipped out their weapons and aimed at her.

Chapter Ten

"Put your weapons down!" yelled Bold. "All of you!"

"I thought you wanted to talk to us, Chief," snarled the first man, not taking his eyes or gun off Tanya. "You lied to us."

Bold's face flushed a deep purple. He whipped around to Tanya. "Stone, put your weapon away!"

Tanya maintained her aim. "Them first."

"I said, now!"

She lowered her gun, but kept her finger close to the trigger. She was ready to shoot in an instant if the need arose.

Bold snapped around to the two men. "Stand down!"

To Tanya's surprise, they complied immediately. But Jones remained in the safe cocoon of his squad car.

"We have a dead girl in our hands," said the chief, his voice hardening. "Heard one of your people called it in."

"That was me," said the younger of the men. "My dogs heard her first. I was patrolling like usual. That's when I heard this girl crying outside. I swear I never saw her. Didn't know she died."

"What did you hear?"

"Wailing something about someone trying to kill her. Couldn't hear much because my dogs were going nuts around me. It was super weird."

"We don't want to get involved in the town's affairs," said the older guard, putting his hands up as if in defense. "Our boss doesn't allow us outside the gates. He'd blow a fit if he knew we're talking to you right now."

Chief Bold frowned. "I don't care what your boss thinks."

"This is a huge property, Chief. You were lucky Jay was walking this way. Our cameras record everything. No one came in or out of the estate today. I double-checked."

"Good. I'd like to see the security footage."

"No can do."

"Happy to call the judge for—"

"I swear, we had nothing to do with this. I tell my guys to never get involved because this is exactly the attention my boss doesn't want. He'd kill us if he knew."

Jay, the younger guard, gave a wistful look at his colleague. "Didn't know the rules, man. I'm the new guy. I swear I saw nothing. I just called nine-one-one."

Bold gave him a flinty look. "As you should, when you hear a crime underway."

Tanya stepped closer to the younger man.

"Where are you from, Jay?"

"Oregon," he mumbled.

His eyes shifted. That was a lie.

"How long have you been working at the estate?"

"Two weeks."

"That's enough," snapped the older guard, scowling at Tanya. "We didn't come here for an interrogation."

Bold stepped forward. "If you can share your footage, I won't bother your employer. When can I have it?"

"Can I get a guarantee of confidentiality?"

"I can't promise that, especially if we find incriminating evidence. If there isn't any, you have nothing to worry about."

The older guard let out an angry hiss. "The footage can't leave the station, and we can't have the press getting their noses into this."

"I'll do my best."

"I'll get one of my men to download the files when I get back."

Bold nodded. "I appreciate your cooperation."

The guard's shoulders relaxed. "Our boss is a little special. Likes his privacy to an extreme. I'm just following orders. You can understand that, can't you, Chief?"

"We're on your side, Chief," added the younger guard, flashing a smile his way.

Thou doth protest too much, thought Tanya.

If these two were so eager to put Bold's mind at ease, it only meant they were hiding something even bigger inside this wall. Something they didn't want Bold and his team to sniff out.

What would be bigger than one dead girl?

More dead girls?

"Thank you, gentlemen," said Bold. "I'm going to ask you to not leave town for now."

The younger guard grinned. "Our boss won't let us, anyway."

Tanya and Lopez watched as the two guards shook hands with Bold and got back in their SUV. With a salute to his boss, Jones followed them out, as if the men needed to be escorted.

"Never draw your weapon in front of me like that."

Tanya whirled around to face an angry chief stomping up to her.

"They didn't look like they were coming for tea," she said. "It was risk management."

Bold's face flushed deeper. "I know you work independently, but you're in my territory now. Respect the law, Stone."

"Those guys didn't look like the law-abiding type. Why didn't you probe them more?"

He let out an exasperated sigh.

"I'm new here too. I'm trying to build a rapport with the town folk, not antagonize them. The better I get to know them, the sooner I can figure out what's going on here. Drawing your weapon, cowboy style, won't help. I could have you arrested."

Tanya didn't reply. She and Bold stared each other down for a few seconds, as if each were waiting for the other to give in first.

The FBI office in Seattle received many requests from precincts around the state, both big and small. If Bold hadn't called Seattle asking for help, and if Cross had shuffled him to the bottom of the pile like she would have normally done, Tanya wouldn't be here.

Chief Bold gave Tanya an excellent cover for her mission.

With a resigned sigh, she nodded. "I'll be more careful."

Bold's face softened.

"You got a place to stay for the night? There's a motel near the station. It's not full at this time of year."

Tanya shook her head.

"I'm good. Booked a rental house before I came over." *Secured by the FBI.* "Thanks."

Bold gave her a friendly salute as if he was calling a truce. "I have a mountain of paperwork to fight through. We'll catch up tomorrow morning."

With a nod to the officers, Tanya walked over to her Jeep. One low whistle and Max came bounding into the vehicle. He circled a few times before settling in the back seat, tongue lolling out.

Tanya got in and watched Lopez and Bold walk over to the remaining squad car. Lopez kept glancing over her shoulder as she spoke, her hands gesturing with intensity.

Tanya knew what they were discussing.

Her.

Bold seemed to trust her, though she would have to follow his rules to maintain that trust. Lopez was cordial, but suspicious. Jones was openly belligerent. Fox seemed ambivalent, which meant he could go either way. And Wilma was just unreliable.

With a resigned sigh, Tanya put her keys in the ignition and turned the engine when her phone vibrated.

She carried two phones. One public phone, a number she had shared with the chief's team. The other was a burner phone issued by Susan Cross's office in Seattle.

Tanya grabbed both from her cargo pockets. It was her public phone that was buzzing. She clicked on the incoming text message, wondering why anyone would contact her this late.

FBI, eh? Heard you're in town.

Tanya sat frozen in her seat for five full seconds.

Someone in Black Rock knew her true identity.

Her phone pinged, making her jump. Max barked, startled. Tanya glanced at her screen to read the new message.

1000 Devil's Dyke Rd. Tomorrow. Noon. Come alone. NO COPS or I shoot.

Day Two

Chapter Eleven

Tanya called the FBI field office first thing the next morning.

They had to know of the anonymous message, but she hadn't been prepared for the director's gatekeeper.

His voice was curt and his words were blunt.

"Cross will get in touch with you if needed. Don't you realize this is a one-way communications channel?"

He hung up so abruptly, Tanya stared at her phone in shock.

With a feeling of disappointment, she realized though Susan Cross had chosen her for this mission, she was too low on the totem pole to talk to her directly.

After giving the local police crew their first training session, she sat down with them to go over the dead girl's case. High school yearbook photos confirmed the body of Laura Fredrickson, the missing girl.

Wilma sat quietly in a corner of the conference room during the discussion, looking great in her matching jacket and skirt suit, taking minutes. Or pretending to.

Tanya had smelled the alcohol as she had stepped past her to get to her seat. She tried to recall their first conversation. The receptionist had been scattered, talking about phantom pirates and ghost ships.

Tanya turned to her. "Hey, Wilma, didn't you say more girls have disappeared from town over the past few years?"

All eyes turned to the receptionist.

"Did I say that?" Wilma pulled out a tissue from her suit pocket, dabbed her mascaraed eyes, and sniffed. "I've such a terrible memory. Some days are better than others. I really don't remember."

Tanya summoned all her patience not to lunge across the table and shake her.

The dead girl's innocent face had kept her up all night, haunting her dreams. She was the last person she had spoken to. She wished she could put all her energy into finding who killed Laura Fredrickson, but she wasn't here to babysit the chief's team.

She was here for the FBI. And now, she had to ferret out who had discovered her undercover role.

Soon after the meeting ended, Lopez and Bold took off to share the news of Laura's death with her family. Fox started digging into online databases to find traces of the girl's activities before her disappearance.

Jones's task was to look into old files in the storage room for similar cases, since he was the only longstanding officer and knew the history of this town best. He had protested, saying that would be a giant waste of time, but had shuffled off to the back after Bold had glared at him.

Tanya was now bumping along a dirt road through what looked like abandoned farmland, away from the station. Away from Black Rock.

She swerved the Jeep to avoid a pothole. Max almost lost his balance in the back seat.

"Hang tight, bud," called out Tanya. "We're going to find out who blew my cover."

They bounced along the unpaved, uneven road for another forty minutes, with no evidence of life other than unwelcoming signs posted every few miles. The handmade wooden placards showed skulls and bones and warning messages to *turn back now*. She wasn't welcome in this area.

"Prepper turf," said Tanya to Max as they passed a crudely made sign that threatened to shoot trespassers on sight. "Preppers hate law enforcement. How did they know I was here? How on earth do they know I'm FBI?"

The Jeep wobbled in and out of a rut, making Tanya's head bang against the roller bar. She swung a hard right to take the corner and jumped on the brakes just in time.

A rusty iron fence set among the tall pampas grass crossed the path, only five yards from around the corner.

Tanya turned the Jeep sideways and drove alongside the fence, looking for a gate. When she found it, she stopped a few feet away and surveyed the area.

Max sat up alert in the back, staring at something beyond the fence.

"I guess even rural folk live in walled-off properties here," muttered Tanya as she double-checked her GPS. Her satellite map confirmed this was 1000 Devil's Dyke Road.

Her destination.

There was no address plate or sign anywhere. But she could hear strange grunts and groans from somewhere in the distance, where Max's attention was focused. None of it sounded human.

Tanya peered through the windshield. "What *is* this place?"

She unholstered her sidearm and straddled it in between her thighs, then clicked on the message app on her phone. She punched in the words and hit send.

I'm here.

Max barked.

Tanya looked up to see the gate being opened by unseen hands. She took her foot off the brake.

"Keep a sharp eye, bud."

Max whined in reply.

She rolled the Jeep onto the narrow wooden bridge.

"They built a gosh danged moat around their property," said Tanya, gesturing as if Max would understand. "Who does that?"

She glanced out of her window to look at the murky water running underneath the bridge. The trench was deep and would trap her vehicle if she fell in.

"This had better hold," she muttered as she tightened her grip on the steering wheel. She held her breath until the Jeep's wheels got off the bridge and she heard the crunch of the gravel path again.

A one-story structure and a large barn stood about eight hundred yards ahead in the middle of the unkempt field. They were the only buildings for miles around. There wasn't a soul in sight.

Something shiny and metallic glinted from the top of the house. It seemed like the entire roof was reflecting light.

What is that?

Glad she and Max both had their Kevlar vests on, she pressed on the gas and moved forward, her eyes darting back and forth. Suddenly, her shoulders tensed.

But it was too late.

She had been so busy scouting the buildings, she had missed the thin tripwire lying across the path.

The explosion rocked the Jeep.

Max barked like mad.

A hazy, foul-smelling smoke swirled through the vehicle, making Tanya gag.

A silhouette of a man with a straw hat popped next to her window like a freaky horror show puppet.

Tanya snapped her weapon up and fired. The man bounced back, then sprang forward like he was on a mechanical spring.

She stared at the apparition, her pulse pounding.

A scarecrow on springs.

Her bullet had gone right through its straw chest.

The smoke was receding, but Tanya crouched low, her heart thumping, her Glock ready for more surprise pop-ups. Max was barking nonstop, clawing at the door like he wanted to jump out and chase something.

The smell of sulfur spread through the air, irritating her eyes and throat. She pulled her jacket off and threw it over Max's head before covering her own nose with her hand.

He whined.

"Stay," said Tanya in a firm voice, as she peered through the gray fog swirling around the vehicle.

It took a few minutes for the smoke to clear and for her heart rate to slow down. There were still no signs of anyone. Whoever lived here wanted to frighten away intruders, not kill them.

Tanya shook her head. "A smoke bomb and a scarecrow? Seriously?"

What was their game?

Her eyes swept the path ahead, looking for more tripwires when an eerie cry came from the left field.

She whipped around.

Then came another high-pitched cry. And another.

The cries were getting louder and closer. They sounded like children in danger, children who couldn't articulate words, but were calling out for help.

Tanya swiveled her head around, her throat dry, her heart racing. *Did I find the missing girls?*

Chapter Twelve

"G*oats?*"

Half a dozen baby goats leaped through the grass toward her Jeep, their bleats sounding uncannily like a child's cries.

Max barked nonstop.

Tanya pushed through the road before the creatures ambushed her, but she couldn't move fast in case more unexpected traps lay hidden in her path. By the time she reached the main building, followed by the herd of goats, her back was drenched in sweat.

It was a farmhouse. A peculiar one at that. Now that she was close, the structure didn't look as dilapidated as she'd thought from afar.

The biggest satellite dish she'd seen at a private residence stood to the side of the building. The people who lived here were either seriously addicted to cable TV or were attempting to communicate with extraterrestrials.

A row of high-grade security cameras winked at her from underneath the gables. The roof was lined with solar panels, and all the windows were darkly tinted. If she had to guess from their thickness and reflective glare, they were bullet proofed too.

The front door was reinforced with black steel and secured with an electronic lock. She wouldn't have been surprised to discover concrete slabs behind the faded wooden slates that covered the entire house, and a weapon or two pointing in her direction.

This was no average prepper.

They were equipped for an army to attack.

Tanya twisted her head around, looking for signs of life.

A tractor stood by a pile of firewood. Next to it was a broken-down shed that housed an electric generator. Behind the tractor sat a black all-wheel-drive SUV with tinted windows—not the type of truck you'd expect a local farmer to have. She bet that vehicle was bullet proofed as well.

Hens and geese cackled and scratched the ground in front of the open barn. She thought she saw a horse's head poke out through the barn's door but couldn't say for sure. The faint smell of manure came from somewhere, like someone had recently fertilized a field.

What a strange place.

The baby goats had caught up and were now surrounding the Jeep, leaping up and down like whack-a-moles on steroids. Their little hairy heads and bulging eyes came into view over her window before disappearing and popping up again.

It would have been a comical sight, if not for the bizarre circumstances she found herself in.

Max was barking half-heartedly at the animals, but hadn't seemed to sense any other threat. Tanya trusted his instincts. He knew when danger was around the corner and had a nose for bad people. But this place was so outlandishly freaky, she couldn't let down her guard.

Clutching her gun, she slipped out of the Jeep, kicking her heels to keep the enthusiastic animals at bay. She kept the door open for Max to jump out, blocking the goats from getting inside.

"So, you came."

Tanya whirled around to face the most unexpected person. For a second, she thought she was seeing Morgan Freeman in person.

But it was his doppelgänger. He was watching her from the side of the house and didn't seem too concerned about the Glock in her hand.

"I trust you got here safely?" he said.

The rickety bridge over the moat, the smoke bomb, and the scarecrow she had just shot at sprang to mind. Tanya opened her mouth to hurl a good choice of furious words at him, then shut it again.

Who is this man?

He was around Wilma's age. Early seventies or thereabouts. His hair was gray and his forehead was crinkled, like he had had more than his fair share of sorrows in life. His demeanor wasn't friendly, but it wasn't hostile either.

Most importantly, he was unarmed. At least, outwardly.

Should I frisk him?

Max shimmied up to the man, sniffed his legs and sneezed. The man bent down and scratched the top of Max's head.

Tanya frowned.

"If I'd known you were bringing him along," said the man in a quiet voice, "I would have deactivated the smoke bomb."

To her surprise, he pulled out a red rubber ball from his pocket and offered it to Max.

Her dog took it and paraded around the yard like he'd just won a prize. The baby goats leaped around him in glee, happy he had joined in their play.

"Get back here, Max," called Tanya, annoyed to see her dog fraternizing with the enemy.

"Let him enjoy life a bit," said the man, leaning against the wall and crossing his arms. "He works hard for you."

"Who are you?" snapped Tanya.

He gave a small smile, deepening the wrinkles around his eyes.

"That's for me to know and you to find out."

Tanya almost growled back, but swallowed it in time. Just like the new police chief of Black Rock, she had to build rapport with the locals, even if this oddball was testing her patience.

"How did you find out my number?"

The man shrugged.

Tanya gave him a hard look. "It was you who messaged me last night, wasn't it?"

Another shrug. "Tough job you got in town."

Tanya narrowed her eyes. "What do you mean by that?"

"You're going after the big kahunas, I hear."

She scowled. "What the—"

He raised his hand to stop her, then pointed at the front door.

"She's waiting for you. You'd better not keep her, or she'll blow her top."

"Who?"

"If I were you, I would hurry."

Without another word, he ambled over to the vegetable patch next to the tractor. He kneeled in front of a tomato plant and picked up a pair of shears.

For a minute, Tanya wondered if she was still sleeping and having a bad dream. Either that, or she had fallen down the most fantastic Alice in Wonderland rabbit hole, if such things existed.

"Max, get back here," she said in a firm voice. "On guard."

He obeyed.

Sidestepping the goats, Tanya treaded carefully to the main entrance of the farmhouse, alert to movement from all directions. With her left hand, she briefly touched her mother's sunflower pendant. She needed her good luck charm now more than ever.

The front door was ajar, but she couldn't make out anything inside. Tanya climbed up the front stairs, one step at a time, with Max right next to her.

She took a slow and steady breath, keeping her Glock aimed at the opening.

Now!

Tanya lifted her boot high and kicked the door open.

Chapter Thirteen

Tanya and Max entered the empty living room.

The interior looked like a typical pensioner's old country house.

The inside was clean and well kept. But the rug on the floor was frayed, the yellow curtains were faded, and the green couches looked like they had time traveled from the seventies.

If she hadn't noticed the brand new solar panels, high-grade security cameras, and the massive satellite dish outside, Tanya would have expected this interior.

But this was no ordinary farmstead.

Max pattered around the living room with the red ball in his mouth, sniffing all the corners. He wasn't anywhere near as uneasy as she was.

Tanya stepped gingerly through the living room, searching for hiding spots, booby traps, weapons.

"Hello?" she called out. "Anyone here?"

Silence.

She stepped into the small corridor that seemed to open to the rest of the house. With her sidearm aimed in front, she swiveled her head from right to left, watching, listening, ready.

Outside, a goose cackled, and a rooster crowed.

What a peculiar place, she thought as she threaded silently through the house.

After inspecting the empty kitchen and bedroom, she stepped back into the corridor. Up ahead was a room with its door wide open.

She peeked in, her gun pointed forward.

The walls were lined with shelves from floor to ceiling. She stepped inside, passing rows of tomato tins, jars of pickled vegetables, bags of dried fruit, and cans of oil, feeling like she had entered the storage room of a small grocery store.

I was right. This man is a prepper.

But it was what hung on the back wall that had piqued her interest.

Her skilled eyes appraised the three Glock 17s, a shiny new M16s carbine, and an AR-57 semi-automatic rifle. Tucked in a corner at the back was a box of M18 smoke grenades, real ones that could induce serious damage, unlike the child's toy he had deployed by the moat.

The man had enough ammunition to fight an army regiment.

Did he have a license for any of these?

She flipped open a container full of 9mm cartridge boxes, a sudden realization dawning on her. He had let her into his house where he kept his arsenal unlocked and in the open, with no worry she'd use them against him.

Who is he?

Tanya turned back around. Max was waiting for her at the doorway, the ball still in his jaws. He wagged his tail and got up as she stepped out.

There was one more room down the corridor, in the back of the house.

After another scan to confirm no one had followed her inside and no traps were in her way, she inched toward the end of the corridor.

"Anyone here?" she hollered.

No answer.

She sidled up to the open door of the last room and jumped in, Glock aimed forward.

It took a few seconds for her to realize what she had walked into.

Tanya lowered her weapon and stepped up to the bank of computers. The FBI logo flashed on each screen. Two printers sat on a side table and an array of audiovisual equipment and radio communication devices hung on the wall above.

This was a mini mobile command center, one she had seen and trained on many times.

Does he work for the FBI?

She toured the room, checking everything while Max settled himself by the door.

"There's no one waiting for me here," she said out loud, as if her dog could comprehend. "What's he talking about?"

Max cocked his head.

Tanya turned to the largest computer and touched the keyboard. The screen sprang to life, but it was password protected. She tried the login credentials she used back at her office in Seattle.

Access Denied.

She tried variations, but the same pop-up kept flashing until the system locked her out for good.

Tanya wasn't a techie and couldn't unscramble a code if it was staring her in the face. That was why they had genius teams of PhD graduates from Caltech to do that type of work for the bureau.

She glanced around the room, feeling lost, like she was staring at a complex puzzle with no clue what the end picture even looked like.

"Where's Asha when I need her?" she mumbled under her breath.

But she wasn't on a private investigation with her friend anymore. She was alone to figure this out.

Tanya pushed the keyboard away and got up, ready to storm outside and shake that old man for information, when she noticed the red phone on the wall.

A large cross sign had been taped to the handle.

She grabbed the handset.

"Susan Cross's office."

Tanya jumped back in surprise, almost dropping the handset. It was Cross's assistant, the gatekeeper, the same rude man who had blown her off only hours ago.

"Tanya Stone," she replied, her voice hardening.

"You're late," came his annoyed voice down the line.

A red-hot flash of anger rolled up her spine. "Why didn't you tell me any of this when I called this morning? You sent me on a mad chase halfway across the state—"

"You were using a burner phone that could be intercepted. Now you're late. You've pissed her off."

"For frigging's sake, would you stop talking in riddles for once and give it to me straight? Geez, I swear to—"

The phone line crackled, and a female voice came on the line.

"Cross, here."

Chapter Fourteen

"**M**a'am," said Tanya, feeling like she was expected to salute the director.

"Ray will be your only comms channel from now on, understood?" came Susan Cross's crisp voice down the line.

"Ray?"

"Ray Jackson. I presume you have already met him? You haven't shot the man or anything, have you?"

Tanya bit her lip.

She had fired a shot on this property. Just not at Ray. As much as she wanted to, she couldn't tell Cross what she really thought of the crazy coot who used smoke bombs and scarecrows as intruder deterrents.

"No, ma'am."

"Tell me, what's the police chief focusing on at this moment?"

"A murdered schoolgirl. We found her in a ditch, dehydrated and starved, but with no visible injuries. The team's checking old case files for more missing girls. We might have a serial offender here."

Cross was silent, like she was contemplating something. "Perhaps."

Tanya spoke up. "Do I have permission to focus my efforts on this case? I was there when the victim died and I'd like to get to the bottom—"

The phone rustled as Cross moved on her end.

"Don't lose your view of the forest by getting lost among the blades of grass, Agent Stone."

Tanya bristled.

Laura Fredrickson wasn't a blade of grass. She was a schoolgirl whose life had been brutally cut short.

"The problem we're trying to ferret out is bigger than just one dead girl," said Cross. "Our first task is to identify who's who in that town. Their relationships and their animosities."

"Can I trust the chief? After all, he called the FBI for help."

"No."

Tanya drew back in surprise.

"Do we have any evidence that says he might be behind these crimes?" she asked, wondering if the director was hiding crucial information from her.

"Right now, we can't trust anyone. Consider the whole town as suspects."

An entire town of suspects?

"Are there other FBI agents undercover in Black Rock?" asked Tanya.

"I can't answer that question."

Why the heck not?

Tanya tried not to grit her teeth. Her colleagues at the bureau complained often of how some of their bosses, Special Agents in Charge, micromanaged them to death. But this was something else.

What's the opposite of micromanaging? Macro-managing?

Tanya didn't even know who her immediate superior was anymore, and she sure as heck wasn't presumptuous enough to believe she reported directly to Cross.

"If I knew exactly what you wanted, I'd dig it up for you," said Tanya, rustling up more gumption than she felt. "But right now, if I may speak frankly, I feel like I'm on a mad goose chase."

She knew speaking up like this was an enormous risk. Not just a professional one, but a personal one.

This case could make or break her, and let her keep the steady paycheck she desperately needed.

After rent, gas, and Max's kibbles, her pay went to the trafficking safe house for orphaned children in her village. But three years ago, a crooked CFO had emptied the orphanage's coffers and disappeared.

Something caught in Tanya's throat as she remembered her last visit. Five to ten-year-old girls and boys sitting in the cafeteria, eating soup, eyes down, fidgeting with the frayed hems of their hand-me-down shirts. The quiet had been heartbreaking.

There were only a few times in her life when Tanya had wanted to bawl her eyes out. This had been one.

Tanya knew what it was like to be a trafficked survivor. She didn't even want to think of the horrors these children might have experienced at such a young age.

All she could do was send them as much of her salary as possible so they could get back on their feet.

She needed this job.

"You've judged the situation wrong, Agent Stone," Cross was saying in her crisp, no-nonsense voice. "Something big is brewing in that town and has been for a few years. That new chief has no clue what he has on his hands."

"Exactly what does he have on his hands?"

"The increasing crime rates are a ruse for something bigger. That's why you're there. To watch. To listen. To learn and report back. Blend in and build trust. Those are your marching orders for now."

"May I speak frankly, ma'am?"

"Go ahead."

"I'm a fighter. I hunt and shoot terrorists. I'll take on anyone in combat, but I can't act. I can't play a role. And I don't have a diplomatic bone in my body."

"Then learn, Agent Stone."

Tanya's jaws clenched.

Why do I feel like I've been dumped into the middle of the Hunger Games?

When Susan Cross's voice came down the line again, it was a notch softer.

"I wouldn't have selected you if you couldn't handle the job. You're more than capable of working with the chief's team. All you have to do is keep your eyes and ears open."

She paused.

"Everything you have seen and heard counts. Keep close to the chief's files. Take note of who's connected to whom. That will help us build a case against whoever is unleashing this crime spree along the coast. Got it?"

"Yes, ma'am."

"You've faced worse in Ukraine. I understand you just graduated, but no one in my team has the combination of skills and field experience you do."

Cross stopped. A heavy pause weighed in the air. Tanya braced herself, feeling like she was waiting for the punchline.

"I have faith in you," said Cross, finally. "Do you?"

Tanya took a sharp breath in.

Cross was waiting for an answer patiently. Unusual for her.

"I do." Tanya let out her breath. "I always have."

"Good. Ray will contact you when we need to talk. You can trust him. We must keep these communications to a minimum. Your activities will be watched and I can't afford to have your position given away."

"Understood," said Tanya. "About Ray Jackson. Does he work for the bureau?"

"He's an old friend. He was my first supervisor. He's had an eccentric streak ever since I met him when I started at the FBI eons ago, but he's a good man. You can trust him. In fact, he's the only person in Black Rock you can trust."

"Do I report to him?"

"You report to *me*."

Tanya's eyebrows shot up.

"You're in uncharted waters. So, watch your back. I don't want to bring you back to HQ in a body bag."

Tanya made a face. *I don't plan on returning to Seattle in a body bag either, Boss.*

"I'm counting on you, Agent Stone."

The phone line went dead.

Chapter Fifteen

Ray Jackson scratched behind Max's ears.

"I prefer dogs to humans, to be honest," he said, addressing the pup. "I'm used to training Labradors, but you Shepherds are highly intelligent. More than most people I've met."

"Mostly German Shepherd," corrected Tanya. "Got a few Husky genes in him which technically makes him a mutt. But he's my mutt."

Ray looked up. "You must have twisted an arm or two to get him in the K9 program. In my time, they would have never let him in."

"So, you were a dog trainer, Ray?" said Tanya.

"That's not my name."

"What?"

"Cross calls me Ray Jackson these days, but it's not my name."

"What's your real name?"

"That's for you to find out, though I doubt you will."

Tanya gave a frustrated hiss.

"I oversaw the K9 team when I started with the bureau." He petted Max's back, pointedly ignoring her angry glare. "You need to brush him more often, Stone. I don't want to even know what the inside of your Jeep looks like."

"That's for me to know and for you to never find out," snapped Tanya, wondering how many more surprises were in store for her that day.

Ray shrugged. "I was a vet in my civilian life. I know these dogs as good as any."

"Why didn't you tell me you're retired FBI?" Tanya tried but failed to hide the irritation in her voice.

She still hadn't forgiven him for the game he'd played. If that scarecrow had been Ray, he'd be a dead man. And she'd have blood on her hands. The blood of an officer.

"I prefer to stay under the radar," replied Ray.

"Are there other undercover operatives in town?"

"I can't comment. I'm not involved with the bureau anymore."

"Like hell you're not involved." Any ounce of patience she'd had was gone. "What do you call the command center in the back of your house? And the direct line to Susan Cross's office?"

"She made me install that thing. I told her I'd message you when she needs to connect with you and she promised that won't be too frequent. I owed her a debt from a long time ago. This completes my part. That's all."

"What about the weapons and ammunition in your storage room?"

He shrugged. "I like to be prepared."

"For what? A wholesale attack from Canada?"

"I'm exercising my rights under the second amendment." He shot her an annoyed look. "This is a free country last time I checked."

Tanya cocked an eyebrow. "What are you doing here in the middle of nowhere?"

With a loud sigh which signaled he was done talking, Ray turned back to his tomato plants.

Tanya suppressed the urge to poke him in the back. "Most retirees go to Florida. Why come to Black Rock?"

"To be left alone."

"You're one oddball."

"So are you."

Tanya almost smiled. He was right about that. She never belonged anywhere, always the odd one out.

"What about your family?" she said. "Friends? Or have you become a monk?"

Ray turned around, an annoyed expression on his face.

"You won't leave me alone until I tell you, will you?"

"That's right."

"I have no family anymore. They were all shot to death."

His crumpled face suddenly looked more haggard.

Tanya dropped her hands in shock.

"They were executed by an unsub twelve years ago," said Ray in his soft voice. "My wife of twenty years and my only son were killed in an instant. Two years before I was supposed to retire. Like I said, I have no one left."

A pang of guilt crossed Tanya's heart. She wanted to say the right thing, but she had no words.

"The unsub knew I was the officer on his file and threatened to hound me till I broke. I moved my family to a safe place, but one weekend, I came home to see blood everywhere. I could have been more careful. I could have stopped him...." He paused. "But I didn't."

Tanya stood unsteadily on her feet, wondering if she should tell him her mother had died in a hail of bullets, too. Gunned down, not by a homegrown serial killer, but by a state-sanctioned militia gang.

"Did you arrest him?" she asked in a quiet voice.

"Rotting in jail for life."

Neither spoke for a minute. Ray stared at his tomato plants.

Sensing the somber mood, Max padded over to the house to sniff a barn cat.

Despite the tough exterior she carried around her, Tanya yearned for kinship. For the first time since she arrived in Black Rock, she didn't feel like an outsider. She and Ray had a connection.

Even though he wasn't the type to invite her for Sunday dinner, let alone coffee or even a chat, just to know he was here felt better than the cold welcome she got at the station.

Her phone interrupted their silence.

It was her regular cell. The chief was calling.

"Where are you, Stone?" boomed Bold's voice.

"Flood in my bathroom," replied Tanya, congratulating herself for the quick answer. "Pipe's almost fixed."

"A VIP is visiting the station in an hour. He wants to meet the new contractor."

"VIP?"

Wilma's voice called Bold in the background.

"Gotta go," said the chief. "Can you come in?"

"On my way."

Tanya hung up, slipped her phone into her pocket, and turned to Ray. "I have to get back to the station."

He didn't look back, his hands moving from plant to plant, as he checked the stems for aphids.

With a resigned sigh, Tanya whistled to Max.

It took her an hour to return to the station.

As she drove back, she made up a story in her head about old plumbing and a major leak in her rented house. It was a good excuse she could bring up again and again whenever she needed to get away without the team getting suspicious.

When she arrived at the precinct building, Wilma was standing outside, leaning against the front door with a coffee in one hand and her mobile phone in another.

With her heavy makeup and her perfectly coiffed gray hair, she looked like she belonged at a fashion magazine for boomer women rather than a small-town police station.

She looked up as Tanya and Max strode up to the front door.

"Hey, Wilma?" said Tanya, as her hand hovered on the handle. "Do you remember what you told me about the missing girls?"

Wilma stared at her, like she didn't understand the question. Then, she blinked and looked away. "I never said anything like that."

"You need to tell Bold anything that might relate to this case."

"I know nothing."

"I think you do."

Wilma looked up. "You want Jones. Talk to him."

"Did Jones work here when your husband was chief? Was he more professional, back then?"

Wilma shrugged. "Jones has always had an attitude problem. He comes from a hard family."

"Hard?"

Wilma remained silent for a few seconds, like she was trying to make up her mind how to reply.

"His parents were violent. Pathologically violent. All their kids ran away from home before they were twelve."

"That explains his anti-social behavior," said Tanya. "How did he ever become a sworn police officer?"

"My hubby tried to fire him. He gave him so many disciplinary actions I was sure he'd quit, but he hangs on. If you ask me, he's got backers in high places."

Tanya's eyes narrowed. "Backers?"

Wilma looked away again.

Tanya leaned closer. "Who are these backers?"

Wilma glanced at her from under her lashes, then looked away quickly.

"You wouldn't believe me if I told you."

Chapter Sixteen

"Try me," said Tanya.

But Wilma wasn't making eye contact anymore. She had turned back to her phone, her lips clinched shut. The message was clear.

Leave me alone.

Tanya entered the station with Max, with one more question troubling her.

What does a town's VIP want with a mere contractor?

Inside the secure area, Jones was hovering over Wilma's cookie jar. Lopez and Fox were nowhere to be seen. Jones scowled as she walked in.

Nice to see you too.

Ignoring him, Tanya strolled through the bullpen and peeked into the chief's office.

A short, balding middle-aged man in a pinstriped suit was inside, holding forth in a loud and monotonous voice. He carried an old-fashioned walking stick, though it seemed more like an aesthetic rather than a practical accessory.

Tanya caught snippets of his speech, something about a fund-raising event. This was a man who was used to people listening to him, showing him respect.

If she had to guess, this was the mayor of Black Rock.

Standing next to him was a lanky male wearing a crisp white shirt and dress pants. Tanya hadn't met him yet either. He looked sickly, almost anemic, and wore thick-rimmed glasses that made his eyes look bigger than they were.

"Ah, there you are," called Bold as Tanya came into view. Relief crossed his face, like he'd been looking for an excuse to stop his guest's monologue.

"I'd like you to meet Mayor Kenneth Bailey and Dr. Harold Miller, the town's physician and our medical examiner."

Tanya stepped in and tried not to wrinkle her nose at the potent smell of expensive cologne that seemed to have suddenly pervaded the chief's office.

Neither man smiled at her, and for a second time, she felt like her presence was unwelcome in Black Rock.

The mayor's handshake was firm and confident. He was a foot shorter than her, but he looked up, shoulders straight, his eyes boring into hers, as if he was challenging her.

The doctor shuffled awkwardly before he offered a limp and clammy hand. Tanya forced herself to not wipe her hand on her pants in front of him afterward.

Physician, heal thyself, she thought, wondering what was wrong with him.

Mayor Bailey turned to the chief. "Does she know the rules, Bold? Does she understand it's non-negotiable?"

Tanya scowled. *I'm right here. You can talk to me.*

"Discretion above all," said Bold, turning to Tanya. "All press briefings are done by the mayor's office. No speaking to journalists.

No social media while you're with us. All our cases are strictly confidential."

She nodded curtly. "I'm fully aware."

What did they think she was? A rookie?

The mayor pulled out a handkerchief from his suit pocket and wiped his sweaty brow.

"We can't have town folk disappearing and dying like this. This can't happen on my watch, Bold. I don't want to hear about this again."

"We're doing our best, sir," said the chief. "I'm understaffed and under resourced—"

"That's why we hired her!" Mayor Bailey whipped his cane toward Tanya, missing her arm by an inch. "You've got an extra hand on your team now, paid for by the city."

A frustrated expression came over Bold's face. "A contractor is a great start and I appreciate it, Mayor Bailey. But given our increasing workload, what would help me is a permanent officer position and an administrative clerk."

"This town isn't made of money. The only reason we're standing here at all is because of our visitors and the tourists. If they stop coming, we can all kiss our jobs goodbye."

"The team's stretched as it is." Bold spoke in a quiet but firm voice. "I can't push them any more than I do, especially given the extra work that's piling up."

Bailey took a threatening step toward the chief. Bold loomed over him, unafraid.

Our mayor's got a Napoleon complex, methinks, thought Tanya as she observed him.

"I know you're new to town, Bold, but remember who you work for." The mayor tapped his stick against the chief's chest. "Don't you ever forget it."

Bold remained silent, though a muscle twitched dangerously on his neck. If he wanted to, he could have picked the mayor up by one arm, but he seemed to be exercising extreme control.

The medical examiner gave a little cough.

"I er... can at... t... test to Ch... Chief B... Bold's commitment," he said, speaking for the first time since Tanya arrived.

All eyes turned to him. He blushed like he was embarrassed to have their attention.

"I... see how h... hard they work... every s... single day," the doctor stuttered.

The mayor beamed at the medical examiner. The doctor's face turned a slight pink.

"We're lucky you came back, Miller," said the mayor. "With your international recognition, accolades, and awards, you could have gone anywhere."

The doctor gave an awkward smile to the floor.

The mayor lowered his voice conspiratorially. "I tell everyone who comes to town that we have the best doctor in the state, right here in Black Rock. I swear most of the rich retirees buy property just because of you."

The physician's face turned a beetroot red. He pushed his spectacles up his nose and shuffled his feet like he wasn't sure how to respond.

Socially awkward genius, thought Tanya as she sized him up. *What's his story?*

"You're an honorable man." The mayor's beam widened. "Your generosity to my charity events is exemplary. You've done a lot for this town."

The doctor attempted an ungainly bow.

"Th... this... town was k... kind to my family when we n... needed help. It's my t... turn to p... pay it forward."

"Stop being bashful, Miller. You single-handedly replaced the roof at the psychiatric institution—"

The mayor stopped as if he had just remembered something important. He turned to the chief and leaned his cane against Bold's arm.

"That reminds me. My wife has a fundraiser for Zachary's charity tomorrow afternoon and I'll need your services."

The chief's face darkened.

"My rivals are out to get me," said the mayor. "You can't trust anyone these days. I need you and your team behind me."

Bold stepped back. "We're working on an important case and I can't afford to split our resources. I wish I could help—"

The mayor didn't seem to have even heard him. "Good man," he said, thumping the chief on the arm. "It's decided. I'll see you and your officers at two tomorrow."

Bold's jaws clenched, but before he could say anything, the mayor twirled around to leave, almost bumping into Tanya by the doorway.

He stopped and craned his neck up.

"Stone, is it?" he hissed.

"That's correct."

"This is my town, Stone. You work for me now, you hear? You better toe the line because my people are watching you. So, when I say jump, I want to see you jump."

Seriously?

Tanya stared at this small man, struggling not to lash back. If there was one thing she couldn't stand, it was a bully.

Bailey tapped his cane on her arm and leaned closer. She tried not to gag at the smell of his cologne.

"One wrong move," he said, narrowing his eyes dangerously, "I'll throw you out of Black Rock before you even know it."

Chapter Seventeen

Mayor Bailey strode out of Bold's office, swinging his cane dangerously.

Tanya shot the chief a look that said, *What was that all about?*

"That's our mayor for you." Bold shook his head. "He used that line on me too, if it makes you feel any better."

"He's under... a l... lot of pressure...," stammered the doctor. "He m... means well...."

"Easy for you to say." Bold walked behind the desk to his chair. "He's taken a liking to you, Doctor. Besides, you have history here. I'm still the new guy."

"Maybe you should give to more of his so-called fund-raisers." Wilma's voice wafted over from the other end of the bullpen.

That woman has ears of an elephant, thought Tanya.

"When I give to charity, I do it quietly," Bold muttered as he sat down. "I don't make headline news."

It was the doctor's reaction that caught Tanya's eye. His face flushed even more.

"The examination room is ready," said a disembodied female voice from nearby.

Everyone turned toward the open door. A middle-aged woman wearing white medical scrubs was standing just beyond the threshold.

Her formidable jowls, her hair cut close to the skull, military style, and that stern expression told Tanya you did not want to mess with her.

Is she another doctor?

Dr. Miller shuffled his feet. "Ah... N... Nurse Norma.... I was j... just c... coming...."

He shot the chief a nervous look.

Bold nodded. "Thank you for your help, Doctor. We're done here."

"Right, well... I'll h... have the au... autopsy r... report sh... shortly."

He turned around so abruptly, he elbowed an eagle statue off the chief's desk. It fell to the floor with a thud. Nurse Norma glowered at the doctor. Dr. Miller bent down to pick it up, fumbling, stuttering apologies, but kept dropping it.

"Butter fingers," scolded the nurse.

"Let me take care of that," said Tanya, picking up the statue and placing it back where it belonged.

"No harm done," said Bold with a wave. "Have a good day now."

Nurse Norma snapped her fingers and spun around. Mumbling under his breath, Dr. Miller followed her out like a lamb trailing its shepherd.

The chief's phone rang just then. With a nod, Tanya stepped out of his office. She followed the medical duo as they meandered through the station, thinking what a peculiar pair they made.

The nurse reminded her of the sharp-toothed hippos she'd seen when working in East Africa. Few knew that hippos were the world's deadliest land animal. They can outrun a human and crush them to death. Like this woman looked like she could.

Tanya scanned the bullpen. It seemed like all three officers were out on patrol.

She stepped up to the receptionist's desk.

Wilma had her nose inches from her screen, her monitor slanted down so anyone walking by couldn't see what she was browsing. But Tanya didn't miss the cruise ship logo on top of the website. Wilma was on the checkout page, her mouse hovering over the buy button, a credit card held discreetly in her left hand.

Cruises? Designer bags? Fancy shoes? She's living the good life.

Wilma minimized the webpage just as Tanya leaned over her desk.

"Wilma, do you know where they keep the evidence files?"

"In the storage room next to the medic's station, in the back." Wilma frowned. "What are you looking for?"

"The note we found in Laura Fredrickson's mouth."

"You're a detective now?"

"I'd like to examine it."

"It got mailed out already."

"Where to?"

"Chief told me to send it to the next county precinct. They have a forensics lab. The courier came in this morning."

Tanya raised a brow. Efficient was not how she'd describe Wilma. "That was fast."

"Just doing my job."

The receptionist's fingers drummed on the desk. She can't wait to get back to her cruise shopping, thought Tanya.

She leaned against the wall casually. "Hey, can you help me with something?"

Wilma's face fell as she realized Tanya wasn't leaving soon.

"If it's the Oreo cookies you're looking for, I hid a packet in the bottom drawer in the kitchen," said Wilma, a hopeful look on her face. "That way, Jones can't finish it all. It's yours if you want it."

"Maybe later." Tanya gave a dismissive wave. "What do you know about the doctor and the nurse?"

Wilma sat up, as if surprised by the question.

"Dr. Miller's a sweetheart."

"What about Nurse Norma?"

Wilma shrugged. "She's bossy."

"Are they a couple?"

The receptionist's eyes widened. She opened her mouth and closed it, then glanced at her monitor and back at Tanya like she didn't want to have this conversation.

Tanya leaned closer. "You can tell me or I can find out from someone else."

Wilma sighed.

"She sure acts like she owns him, but he's her boss."

"Is the nurse from around here?"

"She showed up one day looking for work, about five years ago. Said she's from Ohio. He hired her on the spot, and now she runs the clinic like a Nazi dictator."

Wilma paused.

"If you ask me, he should have done a background check, but it's too late now. She's got him in her clutches."

"What's the doctor's story? Is he sick?"

"That poor man had a dreadful time." Wilma tsked. "He started stuttering as a teen. I don't think he ever recovered from that horrible incident."

"What happened?"

"He's a good man. They were a good family—"

Tanya's phone buzzed in her pocket. She ignored it. "Go on."

Wilma lowered her voice.

"Dr. Miller is a super genius. Got best marks in all state in his senior year. Went to Harvard too. Don't be fooled by the stuttering. He got offers everywhere, but he came to his hometown. Who would want to work in a tiny town like this when they can make big bucks in the city? I don't know what we'd do without him."

"Sounds like he took his physician's oath to heart."

"But Nurse Norma. She's a whole other story." Wilma lowered her voice to a whisper. "When she took over the clinic, she hiked up the fees so only the west enders could afford him. She's all about the money, that woman."

"Is that right?"

"Dr. Miller told us we can talk to him anytime for free. He's always helping anybody who needs him. He doesn't even care if you have insurance or not. That man has a golden heart."

"How does Nurse Norma feel about that?"

Wilma made a face. "I'll say this. No one in town likes her."

Tanya's phone buzzed again. But Wilma was warming up, and she wasn't going to interrupt her flow.

"What about the mayor?" said Tanya.

"You mean, that short, mean man?" spat out Wilma.

"You're not a fan?"

"Him and that fancy trophy wife of his." Wilma screwed her mouth like she bit into a lemon. "He bought her from a Russian bridal catalog. Can you believe it?"

Tanya didn't reply.

"He thinks he's a hotshot, but he's just a low-grade, backwater politician." Wilma gave Tanya an icy stare as if she had something to do with the mayor's unpleasantness. "The way he struts around, you'd think he owns the entire town."

"Does he?"

Wilma poked a manicured finger on Tanya's arm. "It's all about the money. You should see him with the vacationers and celebrities, groveling, taking selfies, and always asking for funding. That man would sell his grandmother for a buck, if he could."

Wilma's face turned serious.

Tanya's back tingled.

Wilma knows a lot more than she's saying.

The receptionist leaned over and whispered. "You'd better watch your step. I don't think he likes you."

Chapter Eighteen

Tanya's eyes narrowed. "What do you mean by that?"

"He can be nasty."

Wilma swiveled her chair away from Tanya and pulled her mouse toward her, as if to signal the end of the discussion.

"Care to elaborate?" said Tanya.

Wilma clicked on something on her screen, deliberately ignoring her. She was done talking.

Tanya's phone buzzed again. With an irritated hiss, she pulled it out and checked the screen.

Asha Kade.

Her heart skipped a beat.

With a low whistle to Max to follow her out, she headed toward the main door.

She didn't dare take personal calls in front of Wilma. Tanya was sure she gossiped about her to others, just like she was sharing things about others with her.

Leaving Max to stretch his legs around the parking lot, Tanya jumped inside her Jeep.

She closed the door and made sure all the windows were up. If anyone saw her, she could always say she was taking a call about a family emergency.

Because it was.

That would be the only reason for her best friend to call her in Black Rock. With her heart in her mouth, Tanya accepted the call.

Asha's spirited voice came down the line.

"Heard you got stuck in a boring little town."

Tanya flopped back in her seat. "I thought someone had died or something."

"Sorry. How are things, hun?" said Asha.

A care call from her best friend was the only good thing that had happened to Tanya in the past twenty-four hours.

"As right as right can be," she replied in a crabby voice.

"Doesn't sound like it."

Tanya sighed. "I have a boss who won't tell me what my mission is, a crazy old prepper who's my sole connection to HQ, a bunch of local cops who don't want me, and the town mayor who just threatened me. Other than that, things are peachy in Black Rock."

"I can hear the strain in your voice."

"We found a missing teen lying in a ditch yesterday. She talked to me before she died, and now I can't get her face out of my head."

"My goodness. What did she say?"

"Something about a kid, and a monster chasing her."

"Was she delirious?"

"She was lucid. She was holding my hand and looking right at me. I've seen worse, but nothing breaks me more than to see a kid like that. Someone killed her and I want to find out who it is."

"That's why they sent you there. You're good at catching monsters."

"I'd rather face a bunch of Islamist terrorists with anti-aircraft missiles in the desert. But right now, what I have are small-town conspiracy theories, missing girls, a murder, and a boss whose only instruction is to keep my ears and eyes open."

Tanya shook her head, though Asha couldn't see.

"I always know who the bad guys are. All I have to do is point and shoot, but this is something else."

"More like cloaks and daggers," said Asha, sounding thoughtful.

"Like the work you do," said Tanya.

"Give me a cold case mystery any day. You can keep your Neanderthal terrorists and traffickers with their bazooka guns."

Tanya watched Max sniff the fire hydrant at the end of the parking lot. She was glad he had a fenced-in space to hang outside while she worked.

"Max is the only one who's keeping me sane," she said.

Silence on the other end.

Tanya pulled the phone from her ear and checked the screen. "Asha? You still there?"

Asha's voice came on the line again.

"I just wrapped up a case in Oregon. My next job's in Seattle in a few days, so I can stop by on my drive over."

Tanya frowned.

"No one will know who you are," said Asha, speaking fast, as if she could read Tanya's mind. "Besides, it will add to your story."

"What story?"

"An old girlfriend who's come to visit you in the pretty resort town where you started a new contract. You'll come across more normal."

Tanya sat up. "You can't come here. Not now. I'm on a job."

"I'll give your cover legitimacy."

"Are you nuts? I can't have friends and family over. Besides, if anything happens to—"

"I've chased Saudi and Indian traffickers with you, way before we were legal drinking age. You think I can't handle some small-town heat?"

If there was one common trait of her found family, it was a dogged stubbornness. And Asha was the most headstrong of the lot.

"No way. This is a bad idea."

"I'm just going to drop by and give you a hug. You sound like you need it."

Tanya raised her voice. "Didn't I just say no?"

"I'm already on my way, hun. ETA to Black Rock in forty minutes."

✦——■——✦

Tanya hung up and strode back into the station.

She walked through the empty waiting area, leaned across the front counter, and tapped on the glass. Wilma looked up from the romance novel she was reading.

Does this woman ever do any work?

"Where's Dr. Miller's office?" asked Tanya.

"Just around the block. You'll see the clinic's sign."

So, that's where Nurse Norma had come from.

Wilma gave her a confused look. "Are you feeling sick?"

"Dr. Miller's the ME for the Laura Fredrickson case, correct?"

"He's the medical examiner for all our cases. This isn't a town with hospitals on every block, in case you haven't noticed. What do you want with him, anyway?"

"I'd like to see the autopsy."

"Why do you want to see dead bodies get cut up?" Wilma called out as Tanya turned to leave. "I went to his surgery once. Oh, my gawd, the smell. I wouldn't go near if I were you."

"Thanks for the tip," said Tanya as she stepped through the main entrance.

With a shudder, Wilma turned back to her novel.

Max followed Tanya as she marched through the parking lot to the other end of the building, her head still whirring.

Did Asha really say she's less than an hour away?

She knew her friend could keep a secret, but she didn't know who to trust in this town. Her target could be any of them, even Chief Bold.

Shaking her head to clear the cobwebs of worry growing inside, Tanya walked toward the modular one-story structure next to the station. A blue BMW and a white Audi were the only vehicles in front of the building.

The shiny sign in front said, *Dr. H. Miller, M.D.*

The clinic was a modern, white-washed brick building with a bright red roof. Next to it, the ancient police station looked even more depressing.

She turned to Max as she reached the clinic's door.

"Stay, Max."

He took position in front of the door, his ears up, a guarded expression on his face.

Tanya pushed the handle down and stepped inside the clinic.

Chapter Nineteen

The fresh smell of lemon and lavender hit Tanya's nose the second she pushed the door open.

The clinic's waiting room had plush leather couches, fancy coffee tables, and a well-stocked beverage station. Next to this was a white dispensary for medication, and a long mahogany reception desk.

The place was spotless.

The clinic was empty except for Nurse Norma, who was on the phone behind the desk, her back to her.

Tanya stood by the door for a minute, wondering if she should clear her throat to announce her presence.

Nurse Norma was barking at a poor patient.

"It's *policy*. You must still pay for the full hour if you cancel within twenty-four hours. We've already gone through this, Mrs. Boone. I can't make exceptions."

Tanya took a few steps in and peeked to her left. The physician's room. She could see the examination table, a blood pressure monitor, and a table with swabs and gels and jars.

To her right was a large white door with a sign over it. *SURGERY.* Underneath were smaller letters that read *STAFF ONLY.*

Tanya turned toward that door, her pulse quickening.

That's where Laura Fredrickson is getting cut up.

With a quick glance to make sure the nurse was still occupied, she tiptoed toward the surgery. She opened the door and slipped into a brightly lit anteroom. The smell of antiseptic was strong here.

In front of her was a double swing door, like those you'd find in a hospital.

The sound of a mechanical whir propelled Tanya closer. She pushed one door open an inch and peeked inside. A foul stench wafted through the opening, making her want to retch.

Swallowing hard, she focused her eyes.

She felt like she was looking into a futuristic movie set. That, or she had time traveled to the twenty-fifth century. Everything in here was white, bright, sleek, and shiny, like a computer-generated surgical theater.

Intense operating lights illuminated the body on the steel gurney. Laura Fredrickson lay cut open, her skin pallid and gray, a paper tag on one toe.

High-tech computer monitors surrounded her. Two tall white machines stood on either side of the gurney, their robotic arms extending toward Laura like a chilling scene from a sci-fi horror movie.

Most medical facilities Tanya had seen during her work had been severely under-equipped, but Dr. Miller seemed to be doing well.

Nurse Norma must charge his patients a fortune, she thought as she watched him work on the girl. Black Rock teemed with a well-heeled clientele, and he was the only physician for miles.

Dr. Miller stood by the steel table, gloved, masked, and aproned, and was peering at something in the dead girl's open stomach. He reached in with a scalpel and moved something.

Unlike his awkward and jerky movements around people, he looked supremely confident examining the cadaver. *A super genius.* Wilma's words echoed through Tanya's head.

Dr. Miller reached toward a side console and pressed a button. A robot's mechanical arm jolted awake, startling Tanya. It turned ninety degrees, and crawled toward the girl's abdomen with a low, ominous hum.

Tanya's own stomach churned. She would take on a battalion of well-armed terrorists any day rather than watch these unfeeling robots probe the dissected flesh of a human body.

"What are you doing here?"

Tanya whirled around.

It was Nurse Norma, looking even more like an angry hippo than ever.

"Following up on Laura Fredrickson's case," said Tanya, keeping her voice firm.

The nurse's eyebrows shot up. "This is most unusual. No one comes in here during the autopsy."

"Where I come from, we work closely with the medical examiner's office. I'd like to find out what the doctor has discovered."

Nurse Norma stepped up to her, her hands clenched into fists, so for one second Tanya wondered if she was going to punch her.

Tanya could subdue her, but Norma's face told her she wouldn't go down without a fight. Besides, fighting the town's nurse was the last thing she wanted to do.

"What do you think you'll learn in there, anyway?" Norma pursed her lips in contempt. "You know nothing. You're just a street fighter for hire."

Tanya raised her eyebrows.

That's a cheap shot.

"I'll give the chief the autopsy report once it's finished," snarled Norma. "That will be after Dr. Miller has completed his operation. You can wait like everyone else."

Tanya wondered what made her this upset, but this wasn't a hill she wanted to die on. She stepped around the angry woman.

"Fine with me," said Tanya as she opened the door, feeling the nurse's glare like knife stabs on her shoulders.

She closed the door behind her and was about to step away when she heard Norma call out.

"Harold? That new girl from the station was snooping around."

Low, mumbling voices came from behind the doors. Tanya stopped in her tracks and strained her ears.

"Did she see it?" came Norma's voice, low and guarded.

She couldn't make out the doctor's response.

What didn't they want me to see?

Chapter Twenty

Tanya knew Asha had arrived before she even saw her.

Car tires crunched on the gravel path outside her rented home. Then came a volley of excited barks from Max, who had been stalking a squirrel in the front yard.

Tanya's temporary digs was a two-bedroom cabin at the end of a private street by the woods. Now rented to visitors, it had been the living quarters of housekeepers who had worked for the luxury mansions up the hill.

She was on the invisible border which demarcated Black Rock's West End from the East End. Set away from the town center, it was secluded and solitary.

Just the way she liked it.

"Max!" called out a familiar voice. "Nice to see you, big boy!"

Tanya popped the front door open, and almost got bowled over by her dog zooming, barking and whining in happiness. Max had never forgotten who had rescued him from that mad family in New Hampshire.

A petite woman in leggings, red boots, and a baseball cap that hid her long hair was by a rental car, hauling a red backpack out of the hatchback. She looked up.

"Tanya!"

Tanya stood on the threshold with her hands on her hips, but a warm glow spread into her heart.

It is good to see family.

Asha dropped the bag, ran over, and wrapped her arms around her.

"How are you keeping up, hun?"

"Good," said Tanya, only partly lying.

Asha brushed a clump of brown fur from Tanya's sleeve.

"When was the last time you brushed Max?"

"Last night."

"If your clothes are any evidence, you should have enough dog hair in your Jeep to stuff a mattress. You need to brush him every day."

Tanya threw her hands in the air.

"You come all the way here to complain about how I take care of Max? Really?"

"Just keeping an eye on both of you. That's all."

Tanya rolled her eyes, but she was glad Asha had come.

Asha wasn't just her best friend, she was her tribe. Their small group of fugitives and orphans had banded together to fight for survival in their youth. They were the only family she had left after her mother and brother had died.

Tanya never admitted to anyone the painful nights that plagued her, especially on those days when her PTSD blazed through her brain like wildfire.

"How's everyone doing?" said Tanya.

"David says hi," said Asha. "We still haven't got over how an independent badass like you could join the FBI. He told me to tell you that you can have your job back anytime you get sick of working for the suits."

Tanya smiled.

Asha's fiancé, David, was a former Mossad agent and her previous boss at the martial arts dojo in New York. Tanya's new FBI position paid a lot more than the dojo, but Asha and David had their own promises to meet and problems to manage.

And she had hers.

Her brow knotted as she thought how she could and would never renege on her oath to help the orphanage in Ukraine back to its feet.

Asha frowned like she could read Tanya's mind. "Are you keeping something from me? You know what your problem is? You don't know how to ask for help."

"What are you talking about? I'm fine."

Asha put a hand on Tanya's arm. "Hun, what happened to your mom and brother was really harsh. You need to talk about it. If not to me, talk to a therapist."

Tanya blew a raspberry. "Therapy? No frigging way."

"At least, let Katy and me organize a proper funeral for them, so they and you can rest in peace."

Tanya looked down at her feet. "They never found my brother's body."

"Let's do something for your mother, then."

Tanya shook her head. "It's too late for that."

"We miss you, hun," said Asha. "Katy, Win, Luc, Bibi, even little Chantal. Everybody's asking about you."

Tanya shot her a wonky grin. "I'll come home for Christmas."

Asha appraised the house and the yard. "Seems like you've got yourself a cool gig here. Maybe this will do you good. Keep your mind busy."

"I wouldn't call it a cool gig."

"You have a cute cottage to stay in and a town with ocean views to hang out in. You have nothing to complain about."

Tanya gave her a pained look, but Asha was too animated to notice.

"Did you know the Pink Palace has a haunted tour every Friday? There's also a creepy doll house near the pier. The inside looks like Willy Wonka's factory. Have you been on that promenade by the sea? Such a pretty little town."

"It's pretty little towns that hide the darkest secrets," said Tanya.

"Don't be such a drama queen."

"You haven't met the people who live here."

Asha looked at her more closely, concern crossing her face. "You haven't slept for days, have you?"

"I can't get that girl's face out of my head."

Asha squeezed her shoulder.

"Something happened to her," said Tanya, "and I can't hang around waiting for the chief and his clowns to figure things out. It's eating into me."

"You said this is a strange town."

"There are some bad things going on here."

"Speaking of bad things," said Asha, pointing at Tanya's Jeep, "I think you got a parking ticket. I thought it was free to park in your driveway."

Tanya looked at her vehicle to see the note tucked under the windshield wipers.

"Do I have to pay for parking here?" said Asha.

But Tanya was striding toward her Jeep, a frown on her face, and a hand on her gun. She yanked the paper from under the wipers and stared at the note.

It was written in squiggly capital letters like someone had tried hard to mask their handwriting.

"This isn't a ticket."

Asha rushed up to her.

"What is it?"

Tanya read the note out loud.

Get out of town or you'll end up in a ditch like that girl.

Chapter Twenty-one

"**S**omeone was here and Max didn't warn me."

Tanya surveyed the driveway and the cabin, her heart ticking faster. She scanned the tall pine trees behind the cottage, looking for a hint of shadows.

"Maybe it was someone he knows?" said Asha, taking the note to scrutinize it.

"He'd make some noise," said Tanya. "He wouldn't go all out like he did for you, but he would notice. That means they came when I took him into the woods half an hour ago."

"What were you doing in the woods?"

"Making sure the mayor's goons aren't there, watching me." Tanya bent down and checked the Jeep's undercarriage. *Nothing.*

Asha stared at her. "Are you looking for a *bomb*?"

Tanya jumped to her feet and stepped up to Asha's rental car. She kneeled to examine the tires, then inspected the ground.

"No tire marks other than yours and mine. No strange shoe prints either. That means they stayed on the grass." Tanya scoured the lawn for clues. "Whoever it was, they were careful not to leave a trace."

"Creepy," said Asha, hugging herself like it had gotten cold all of a sudden.

Tanya turned to Max, who was watching her expectantly, like he knew this was a serious situation. "Why didn't you warn me, bud?"

Max cocked his head and thumped his tail.

She put the note under his nose. "Go, search."

He got up and whined. Then he sat back down again, wagging his tail half-heartedly. She tried again, but no amount of cajoling worked.

"Did you forget your training already, big boy?" said Asha. "Your boss should have let him finish his training."

Tanya shook her head. "There's no scent to follow. That's the problem. Whoever left this wore gloves and made sure it was clean."

"Don't you have access to a lab—"

Tanya shushed her with a finger and walked inside the house, with Asha and Max in tow. She stepped up to the duffel bag open on the living-room floor and pulled out a walkie-talkie like device.

Asha's eyes widened.

Bug detector? she mouthed.

Without replying, Tanya crept around the living room with the counter surveillance tool in hand. Once she'd scanned the cabin, she patrolled the outside perimeter with Max, while Asha watched from the living-room window.

To Asha, the woods seemed darker now. That fun, seaside resort feeling had vanished and in its place, a sense of dread had settled in the air.

Tanya walked back into the house and slammed the front door shut. "Nothing," she said, throwing the scanner on the couch.

"I don't think the person who left this note realized they were threatening a federal agent," said Asha, reading the note again. "Tell me about the locals."

"The chief tolerates me, but he's desperate for help," said Tanya. "That's how he presents himself, anyway, but no one in his team wants me around."

"You're an outsider. The officers think you're encroaching on their turf. You've got to build connections with them to build trust."

"I saved the receptionist from a near-knife attack and what do I get for that?" said Tanya. "Not one thanks. She didn't want me to report it, then goes hot and cold on me. I don't even know if she's telling the truth half the time."

"If she's defensive, it means she's hiding something."

"If anyone's defensive, it's the mayor. He said something about his people watching me." Tanya spread her arms. "I can't figure any of them out."

"The dead girl in the ditch shares a mysterious message before she dies, then you find a threatening note on your car. Everyone's acting cagey, you can't trust anyone, and you're cut off from HQ." Asha stared at the note pensively. "I don't like this."

Tanya pointed at the note. "If anyone thinks they can run me out of town, they don't know a tenth of what I'm capable of."

"But you've always fought a known enemy," said Asha. "This is a riddle wrapped in an enigma locked in a puzzle box."

"You can say that again."

"You need to tell your boss about this."

"Her instructions are explicit. Don't call me. I'll call you." Tanya let out a sarcastic laugh. "Every time I contact HQ, the message I get is *Good luck, Agent, may the odds be in your favor.*"

"Do you think the locals know who you really are?"

"Negative." Tanya sat down heavily on the couch. "There are other agents who can play a cloak and dagger game better than me. I wish I knew why Cross chose me for this mission."

"What about your sniper skills?"

Tanya pointed at the sidearm in her belt holster. "This is all they allowed me to bring. You'd think they'd equip me better if that was the case."

"Hand-to-hand combat?"

"That's my cover. I'm supposed to train the local crew in Krav Maga and special weapons, but except for the chief, none of them seem interested."

"Languages?"

"Ukrainian and Russian?" said Tanya. "We're on continental America last time I checked."

Asha shrugged. "An organized Russian gang could be operating around here."

Tanya gave her friend a thoughtful look.

"The mayor's wife is supposedly a Russian catalog bride, but I can't believe everything Wilma says. She drinks on the job and is—"

Tanya's phone rang. It was her regular cell. She plucked it out of her pocket and put it to her ear.

"Bold?"

Asha could hear a man's voice on the other end.

With a curt, "I'll be right over," Tanya hung up.

"Urgent call. Gotta go." Tanya grabbed the anonymous note from Asha's hand and stuffed it into her pocket. "This will have to wait for now."

"Where are you going?"

"The mayor's wife is hosting a fundraiser at the town hall this afternoon. The entire team has been deployed for security and Bold wants all hands on deck. He didn't sound happy."

"That was an *urgent* call?"

"The mayor pulls his strings. The city pays his salary, so I guess he doesn't have a choice." Tanya made a face. "And I work for him too now."

"Let me come with you."

Tanya gave Asha a look that clearly said no.

"I'm good at analyzing behavior and figuring people out," said Asha.

"You're a civilian."

"Having a friend like me drop by will make you look more human."

"I don't look human?"

"I say this with a lot of love, hun, but you walk around like you'd enjoy putting the next guy who crosses you in a choke hold. That puts people's shoulders up. Having me around will bring their guard down. I can help you glean the information you need."

Tanya needed a second eye on this puzzle-riddle-enigma box, as her friend called it, and Asha was an experienced private eye who solved cold cases for a living.

At five feet with heels on, she came across nonthreatening. Strangers trusted her and people underestimated her. That was until someone pushed her into a corner.

But one thought rolled through Tanya's mind.

Am I going to regret this decision?

Asha got up and stepped toward the door.

"Let's go find Laura's killer."

Chapter Twenty-two

It took them ten minutes to reach Marine Drive.

"Fancy," said Asha, glancing at the town hall. "It's like a mini Hollywood soirée in there."

The hall's exterior was adorned with balloon bouquets, festive lights, and strings of flowers. A red carpet stretched from the driveway to the main entrance. An enormous banner hung across the building's front facade.

New Children's Hospital Charity Fundraiser.

A backdrop had been installed by the entrance so guests could pose for pictures taken by a lone photographer. There were no paparazzi in sight.

Two muscular bouncers in suits stood by the entrance, checking tickets and removing the velvet ropes for those who had proper invitations.

"They're keeping the riffraff out," said Tanya as they walked to the side door as instructed by Bold. Dogs weren't allowed, so Max had to wait in the Jeep.

Wilma ushered them in, asking no questions other than to praise Asha's red boots and ask where she'd got them. She was too busy gawking at the celebrity crowd to pay much attention to Tanya or her friend.

Tanya and Asha stood by the side door, observing the party.

Cheerful voices flitted through the hall, mixed with the clinking of glasses. The overpowering aroma of haute couture perfumes mingled in the air. People kissed each other's sculptured cheeks, California style, saying, *how lovely to see you,* and, *ooh, I love your dress.*

"There's more plastic in this room than in a Toys 'R' Us outlet," said Asha.

"Wilma said people from as far as London, Paris, and Dubai own property here," said Tanya. "Interesting, for a tiny town I'd never heard of."

"They don't advertise private havens."

A gaunt man with a sickly complexion was standing in a corner, looking like he wished he was elsewhere.

"Who's that lanky wallflower?" asked Asha, pointing discreetly.

"Dr. Miller," said Tanya in a low voice. "Supposedly a genius. He's the local physician and I bet this room is filled with his patients."

"Who's that woman next to him? She keeps bossing him around, pushing him to say hello to people."

"Nurse Norma," said Tanya, giving the nurse a piercing look from across the hall. "She runs his clinical practice and his life like a Gestapo."

"Are they a couple?"

"Would be a strange one if so, but I hear Dr. Miller's single." Tanya smirked. "For the record, the nurse doesn't like me one bit."

"Have you connected with *anybody* in this town?"

Tanya spread her arms. "Do I look like someone these people would invite for cake and tea?"

Before Asha could answer, a loud male voice called out.

"Stone, you got here on time."

Asha twirled around to face a tall man in a police chief's uniform marching up to them. She arched her eyebrows and smiled to herself. Tanya hadn't mentioned the new chief looked like Jack Reacher.

Please make him single, she thought. *And please don't make him a jerk.*

Bold stopped when he noticed the strange woman standing by Tanya's side.

"Chief Jack Bold, meet Asha Kade," said Tanya, gesturing to her friend. "She was driving up to Seattle and stopped by to say hello. Hope you don't mind me bringing her. She's family."

Bold offered his hand to Asha but didn't smile. "What do you do, Ms. Kade?"

"Asha is fine. I'm a high-school teacher. They just let us out for spring break, so I thought I'd visit Tanya and see this pretty town she's been raving about."

The chief turned to Tanya with his brows arched.

Tanya rustled up her best fake smile. "Ocean views and small-town charm. Can you ask for more?"

"I'm glad to hear you don't hate Black Rock."

"Never said I did."

Asha crossed her fingers behind her back. *Maybe there's hope for my hard-shelled workaholic pal after all.*

"I'm sure the mayor wouldn't object to a guest of my staff," said Bold. "If the bouncers give you ladies trouble, let me know."

"Thanks," said Tanya.

"I need you to stay by this entrance. I'm stuck playing personal bodyguard all afternoon."

"Doesn't the mayor have his own security detail?"

"As far as he's concerned, it's me and my team." Bold let out a resigned sigh. "Keep your eyes and ears open."

"Anything specific I should look for?"

"Anything suspicious."

Tanya suppressed an eye roll. It seemed like everyone just wanted her to keep her ears and eyes open. *Is this what I'd trained for all my life?*

Bold tipped his hat to Asha. "Enjoy your stay in Black Rock, ma'am."

Asha watched him leave with a quizzical expression on her face. "Why would a small-town mayor need a security detail?"

"My question exactly."

Tanya scanned the room.

Where's Jones?

She wondered if he was hovering over a buffet table.

She watched the chief say a few words to Lopez and Fox, standing on guard on either side of the podium. Then, he climbed up to the platform, where the mayor was standing with a blonde woman on his arm.

She was a head taller than Mayor Bailey and looked stunning in her shimmering gold lame dress. She swiveled her head around like a mechanical doll, flashing her bright smile at everyone.

"An Ivana Trump lookalike," whispered Asha. "The Botox lips, the bottle blonde hair, the chiseled cheekbones, the dress. She could be her twin."

Tanya shook her head and went back to scanning the crowd that was strolling in with sherry glasses in hand. A popular celebrity couple floated in with bodyguards in tow.

"Is that who I think it is?" Asha gaped. "If Katy knew where we were right now, she'd die of jealousy."

"You can't tell her."

Asha patted her friend's arm. "No one knows—"

The sound of a car screeching to a stop came from just outside the hall.

All the officers turned toward the entrance.

Then came the nerve-shredding, banshee-like scream that cut through the air.

"You killed her!"

Chapter Twenty-three

Tanya spun around and leaped through the side door.

A scuffle had broken out in the parking lot.

It was Officer Jones. He was struggling to hold a woman back.

Her hair was askew, and her plump face was splotched like she had been crying. Her jeans were stained and her T-shirt was crumpled like she had spent the night under a bridge.

Unlike the black limos and chauffeur driven luxury sedans parked in rows, she stood by a rusty Toyota that had seen better days.

"Lemme go!" She screeched and kicked, while Jones tried to wrangle her away from the hall.

Tanya raced over.

"Stupid woman!" shouted Jones. "Stay still, dammit!"

He was paying for not having kept up with his occupational fitness program. Plus, the woman's agony seemed to give her all the strength she needed to throw him off balance.

She broke free and scrambled toward the entrance, screaming, "You killed her!"

Gasps of horror rippled through the hall. The mayor's face turned white. His wife leaned against him and clutched his arm, as if she was about to faint.

The woman beat on the arms of the bouncers blocking the entrance. One of them seized her by the shoulders and shook her violently.

"Stop it!" called out Tanya. He was going to break her in two.

A shocked hush had fallen inside the hall, and everyone was staring through the open doorway. Bold dashed through the crowd just as Tanya grabbed the woman and pulled her away.

"I've got her," she said to the chief.

"She didn't run away! She never ran off!" wailed the woman. She dove to the ground with such force, Tanya had no choice but to let go or hurt her.

The woman sprang up and twirled around to face the crowd who were stepping away, revulsion on their faces. She shook an angry finger at the podium.

"You call yourself a mayor, but you do nothing for us! All you care about is their money!"

"Calm down, Miranda," said Bold, putting a hand on her arm. "Can we talk at the station? Please."

The woman buckled to the ground and broke into sobs, her body shaking uncontrollably.

"My girl is dead!"

Bold and Tanya picked her up and carried her away from the entrance as gently as they could.

Asha, who had been watching from the side door, followed them to the parking lot. They had just reached the woman's car when Lopez came running out.

"Sir!" she called out. "Mayor's asking for you. He wants to start the ceremony."

Bold let out an angry hiss.

"I've got this," said Tanya.

Relief crossed the chief's face.

"Lopez, at your station inside. Jones by the front door." Bold marched back toward the town hall, his face a dark shade of purple.

Lopez followed her boss inside, while Jones sneered at the woman before returning to his position by the entrance.

Asha pulled out a tissue from her purse and handed it to the crying woman.

The woman stood bent over, one hand on her car's hood and another on her heaving chest, wheezing like she was having trouble breathing.

"Breathe, hun," said Asha, rubbing her shoulders to soothe her. "You're going to be okay."

The woman looked up with tears pouring down her reddened cheeks.

"How can you tell me I'm going to be okay when my baby girl is dead?"

"I'm so sorry," said Asha.

"I don't want your sorries! I just want my girl back."

Tanya bent down to get her face to her level. "You're Laura Fredrickson's mother, aren't you? Can you tell us your name?"

"Miranda."

"I'm Tanya and this is my friend, Asha. I work in the chief's office."

Miranda stared at Tanya through tear-filled eyes, then turned to Asha, like she didn't trust either of them.

"I don't know what it's like to lose a child, but I'm so sorry you're going through this pain," said Asha. "A mother should never have to bury her daughter."

Miranda stared at her for a few seconds, then nodded. That seemed to calm her down, as if those were the words she had been yearning to hear all along.

"Everyone's saying she ran away, but my girl's a good girl. Someone took her!"

Tanya leaned in. "Do you know who took her?"

Miranda didn't answer.

"When you ran inside the hall just now, you said *you killed her*. Can you tell me who you were referring to?"

"All of them."

Tanya's eyebrows shot up. *"All of them?"*

"These people, this council, the mayor. They're all guilty. None of them care about us."

Miranda started crying again.

"All I know is they found my girl dead," she sobbed. "Jack... I mean Chief Bold told me they found her in a ditch on the hiking trail, but they don't know who did it."

"I was there," said Tanya in a quiet voice.

Miranda clutched Tanya's arm. "You saw my baby? You saw Laura?"

"I was there when she took her last breath." Tanya paused, searching for the right words. "She died peacefully."

Asha knew that was a lie, but Miranda kept her eyes on Tanya, like she was clinging to her dead child.

"Did she say anything?" whispered Miranda.

Tanya kept her eyes down, but didn't speak, Laura's last words swirling through her head.

The monster. He's... coming back... for more...

There was a time to share what happened with Laura's mother. Now wasn't that time. It would only break her into pieces.

"Why won't they let me see her?" asked Miranda, shaking Tanya's arm.

Tanya frowned. "I thought you came to the morgue to identify her body before the autopsy."

Miranda shook her head and took a trembling breath in.

"They told me until everything's done, I'm not allowed in Dr. Miller's surgery."

"You!" came an imposing voice from behind them. "Get out, all of you!"

Tanya whirled around, her hand on her weapon.

Chapter Twenty-four

A man in a black suit, with wires connected to his ears, was marching toward them.

Asha frowned. "Who's that?"

"I've seen him before," said Tanya, straightening up. "On the hiking trail. He works for the Grimwood Estate."

He was the older of the two men she'd seen. The head of their security team.

"What do you want?" snapped Tanya.

"You people need to leave. *She* needs to leave the premises now."

Tanya scowled. "Who do you think you are to tell me what to do?"

"Can't you see she's grieving?" said Asha. "Give her space to calm down."

The guard didn't even look at the crying mother. "The auction's about to start and we can hear her from inside. Get her off the grounds."

"I suggest you leave right now," snarled Tanya, stepping up to him. "I don't take orders from private security."

A small smile cracked on the guard's face. "Fine. But it's your boss who wants that crazy woman out of here."

Tanya's eyebrows shot up. "Chief Bold?"

"Mayor Bailey. If you don't want to, why don't you go inside and tell the mayor what you think of his instructions, yourself?"

He spun on his heels and swaggered back toward the hall, where Jones was watching with interest. He hadn't lifted a finger to stand up to them.

"Why aren't you all looking for the person who took my daughter?"

Asha and Tanya turned their attention back to Miranda, who was leaning against her car like it was the only thing keeping her upright.

"How can you all be partying it up when you should be out there looking for the monster who took my girl?"

Tanya dipped her head and checked inside Miranda's car. The keys were still in the ignition.

She turned to Asha. "Can you drive Miranda's car to her house? I'll follow with Max."

Asha took the mother by her arm. "Let's get you inside, hun."

She nudged Miranda to the side and opened the passenger door. "You can tell us more about Laura and what happened to her, okay?"

Tanya held the door open while Asha helped the mother in. Miranda seemed oblivious to what was happening around her, consumed by her grief.

"My first baby miscarried, so Laura was my miracle," she cried, collapsing in her seat. "Now she's gone too."

Asha and Tanya exchanged a glance, their hearts sinking to hear her story.

"They only care for the vacationers and tourists. What about the rest of us? We live here. We do all the dirty work."

Tanya frowned. "Dirty work?"

"Who do you think cleans, cooks, and serves at their fancy parties? Any time something happens to us, we get treated like mud." Miranda wiped the tears from her cheeks. "If one of their girls went missing, you'd have sent out amber alerts, called the FBI, and all that stuff, wouldn't you?"

Tanya felt the taste of bitter bile in her throat.

In her role, she had to remain professional and defend the town and the chief's team, but from everything she'd seen so far, that was getting hard to do.

Miranda swiveled around to Asha, who was getting into the driver's seat. "You see what's going on here, don't you? Whoever took my girl was the same one who stole all the other girls. Don't you see that?"

Asha's eyebrows shot up. "There are other girls missing?"

Tanya nodded somberly. "I need to have a chat with Bold when we get back. It was before his time, but I'm not sure he's been kept informed."

"Did these other girls show up d—" Asha stopped herself just in time. "Did they ever find them?"

Miranda shook her head. "They never came home. That's why I thought my baby was gone forever too."

"Did you know these other girls?"

"People said they ran away from troubled families, but that's a lie." Miranda scrunched her eyes. "I know their moms and dads. They never mistreated their kids."

She took a shaky breath in.

"Things were rough after Laura's father left us. I'm a single mom trying to do my best, but I loved my girl. She was doing so well, too. In the softball team and getting good grades. She wanted to be a vet...." She wiped her eyes. "We had such a nasty fight the day she disappeared."

"Fight?" said Tanya.

"She wanted to wear this skimpy skirt to school. It barely covered anything, so I said no. She told me I was being a dictator. I told her as long as she lives under my roof...." Miranda swallowed a sob. "Why did I yell at her? This is all my fault. It was just a skirt. A stupid, *stupid* skirt...."

She twisted around to Tanya, her face red with anguish. "You're going to find out what happened to my girl, aren't you?"

Miranda grabbed her arm through the window.

"Everyone's talking about the new gal who joined the chief's team. You chased away those thugs who tried to steal from Wilma. You didn't look away like the others do."

Tanya closed her eyes. News got around fast in this town.

"Please find my daughter's killer."

Tanya opened her eyes to meet Miranda's tear-stained, pleading face.

The day her mother got killed, Tanya had taken a silent oath to never look away when bad things happened to good people.

The chief could fire her. Cross could reprimand her. Demote her. Even let her go.

Screw Susan Cross.

Tanya knew what she had to do.

Chapter Twenty-five

Tanya and Asha sped through the streets of Black Rock, with Max in the back seat.

Asha grabbed the dashboard as Tanya took another sharp curve. "Why the rush?"

"Everyone's still at the fundraiser, but that will be over soon," said Tanya.

"I thought the party will go till late tonight."

"Bold will make any excuse to weasel out of his bodyguard duties. We don't have time."

They had just dropped Miranda off at her home.

Asha had made her a cup of tea, while Tanya had got her a blanket and settled her on her couch. They hadn't been able to get more information out of Laura's mother, as she had been too frazzled to think straight.

Asha had wanted to keep Miranda company, but Tanya had pushed her out of the door and into the Jeep.

"We've got to get back to the station," she'd said, slamming her door and turning the engine, before roaring onto the main street.

Max popped his head in between the front seats. Asha reached over to scratch his neck, her eyes sweeping over the landscape as they whizzed by.

"It's odd, isn't it?" she said. "Walled-off mega mansions on the ocean front and rundown trailer parks in the woods."

"What's so strange about that?" said Tanya, not taking her eyes off the road.

"Most US cities have a Latina 'hood, a Black 'hood, a Chinese 'hood, a Korean 'hood, but the neighborhoods here are a mixed bunch."

"Isn't that a good thing?" said Tanya. "That's like us. Like our family. I prefer it that way."

Asha stared out of the window, a contemplative look on her face. "The dividing line in Black Rock seems to be money. The rich in the West End and the poor in the East End."

"Better than racial divisions. Can't stand them. We all bleed red."

"Agreed, but the West Enders doth bleed a richer and thicker blood, methinks."

"Massacring Shakespeare now? What's got into you, Asha?"

"It's this town. It looks like an ocean front paradise at first glance, but there's a chill in the air, and it's not the weather."

Tanya didn't answer. They rode in silence, as if the chill had settled inside the car too.

Within ten minutes, Tanya was pulling into the precinct's parking lot.

"Who's that?" said Asha, pointing. "Pretty ballsy to stop illegally right in front of a police station."

Tanya slowed down and scanned the license plate of the tinted black SUV blocking the front entrance.

"Stay with Max." Tanya stopped the Jeep, unholstered her weapon, and jumped out.

The driver's door of the SUV clicked open and out stepped Jay, the younger guard from the Grimwood Estate.

Tanya marched toward him, her Glock in her hand.

What's he doing here? Doesn't he know everyone's at the town hall?

The man gave her a wary look and raised his arms hesitatingly.

"You're not gonna shoot me, are you?" He gave her a half smile, but his shifty eyes said he was nervous. The bulge under his shirt told her he was armed as well.

Asha watched Tanya stomp over, one hand on Max's collar to make sure he wouldn't jump out of the open window.

"What are you doing here?" Tanya demanded as she approached him.

"I got you the stick," said the man, his hands still up.

"What stick?"

"The chief wanted the camera footage from the estate. It's in one of those thingamajig sticks. Boss said to hand it over to you guys. He said email was too dangerous."

Tanya nodded. "Hand it over."

"I ain't giving you nothing until you put that away," said the man, eyeing her gun.

Tanya didn't move, but she suddenly realized the opportunity staring her in the face.

Information.

Intelligence that could be relayed back to Director Cross.

Tanya holstered her weapon and pointed at the front doors. "Get inside."

He shot a worried look at the building, then back at her. "You're not gonna throw me in jail, are you? Come on, man, I came because you asked me to. I've done nothing wrong."

As a contractor, Tanya didn't have the authority to detain anyone. And as an undercover FBI agent, she had no jurisdiction. But he didn't know that.

"I just have a few questions for you," she said, keeping her poker face.

"About what?"

"Won't take a few minutes. Step inside, please. You can lower your hands now."

He put his arms down and turned to the entrance with a dejected sigh.

Tanya gestured for Asha to join her.

Shouldering her day pack and putting Max on a leash, Asha followed Tanya and the man inside the station. Tanya opened the secure door to the bullpen, using the code Wilma had given her the day before.

Jay was watching Max warily from the corner of his eyes.

"Sit," commanded Tanya.

Both Jay and Max obeyed at once.

Tanya pulled up an office chair and sat down in front of the guard. Asha leaned against the nearest desk to listen in.

"What's your full name, Jay?" asked Tanya.

"Double-oh-eleven."

Tanya glared.

"Are you trying to be funny?" said Asha.

He gave them a stubborn look and pulled a card from his breast pocket. "It says so on my employee ID. That's what my boss told us to say if anyone outside asks."

Tanya scanned the card. It only showed his code name, a head shot, and the address of Grimwood Estate. She handed it back to him.

"Makes us feel good, you know, like we're James Bond," said Jay, pocketing his ID. "There's not much to do inside those walls than walk the perimeter, feed the dogs, and… er, watch movies."

Asha smirked. "With lots of bare naked ladies, I presume."

Jay looked away, his face slightly flushed.

Tanya leaned in. It was time to get on to more important matters.

"I need you to tell me exactly what happened yesterday when you discovered the girl."

"I told you people everything already, man."

"Try again."

Jay rubbed his forehead. "I was doing my rounds like I was supposed to. I got Randy, Butch, and Sarge out, our dogs, and went for a walk along the wall."

"What were you looking for?" said Asha.

He shrugged. "I'm supposed to call in if I hear or see anything suspicious, but no one comes near that place."

"How did you know there was a girl in danger?" asked Tanya.

"The dogs went nuts. Barking like crazy. I checked the top of the wall to see if anyone was trying to break in. That's when I heard the chick screaming on the other side of the wall."

"What did she say?"

"Something about someone trying to kill her. A monster or something weird like that. I got chills all over me. Never heard nothing like that before."

"Did you hear anyone else?"

"With the dogs going crazy? No, man. But I heard her scream. She said 'Help! Help!' I only called you people so nobody could say I did whatever was happening to her. It was a gut reaction, you know."

"Did you try to get to the other side to help her?" said Asha.

He gave her a pained look. "I wasn't getting involved in none of that, man. Hey, I was happy there was a big fat wall with barbed wire between us. If some freaky monster was running around outside, I didn't want to see any of that."

He turned to Tanya.

"It's your job to take care of freaks. Not mine. I'm just a security guard."

"For what it's worth," said Asha, "it's a good thing you called for help. She didn't die alone."

"I got into so much trouble for that, man. My boss shouted at me for half an hour straight. We mind our own danged business. Don't matter if the town is burning. We don't get involved in other people's crap."

"Harsh," said Tanya.

"Not my rules."

Jay straightened up and looked at her, like he had just realized who he was with.

"Why you asking me these questions?" He glowered. "You're not even in uniform. Who are you, anyway?"

Chapter Twenty-six

J ay pushed his chair back. "I'm done here, man."

Tanya stood up, her hand hovering over her gun. "The camera footage?"

An alarmed look crossed his face. "I'm just gonna reach into my side pocket and get that stick out, okay?"

"No funny moves."

"Geez Louise. Relax. You're strung up worse than Samuel L. Jackson on cocaine." He pulled out a flash drive from his jacket pocket and placed it on the desk like it was a ticking bomb.

He looked at Tanya. "Can I go now?"

She was glad he had stayed this long. He hadn't realized he could have refused and walked out of the door at any moment.

"Tell me one thing," she said. "Who do you work for?"

"My boss."

"Who owns Grimwood Estate?"

He shrugged. "Wish I knew that too, man."

Tanya arched an eyebrow. His voice and sincere facial expression told her he wasn't lying.

"Who hired you?"

"Double-oh-one. Head of Security. He called my temp agency. I do security work when I can find it." He turned to Tanya. "You saw him yesterday on the trail. But I never met the big, *big* boss, if that's what you're talking about."

"Don't you care to know who's paying your salary?" said Asha.

Jay spread his hands out. "I ain't asking no questions from anyone who's paying me seventy grand a year. All I gotta do is feed the dogs and walk the grounds every hour on the hour. I got myself a sweet gig, man. I got no questions for nobody."

"What's inside that wall?" said Tanya.

"A big ugly house. It's bigger than any of the other houses in this town. Sure there's no ocean view, but, man, it's like a concrete castle. It's so ugly, it's sick. Some folks have more money than eyes, I tell you."

"What's it like inside the house?"

"Never been."

Tanya frowned. "Where do you stay then?"

"Staff digs at the back. The cook and cleaner have their own place and the housekeeper has a house too. Us security boys have a bigger house with dorm rooms. Hey, I used to live in a slum in Detroit. I'm not complaining, man."

"I thought you said you were from Oregon."

Jay shrugged. "That's what the boss told all of us to say if anyone asks. They're super big on security in there."

Tanya leaned in. "What else is behind those walls?"

"There's a farm in the back. Got a corn field, fruit trees, and everything. They even have pigs and chickens and stuff. This foreign couple takes care of the animals but they don't talk to us. I never go down there, coz it smells like pig crap everywhere. Good thing it's not on my patrol route."

"What about the owner?" asked Tanya. "I presume he's a man? A businessman?"

"Never seen the old geezer. Everyone talks about him, but I don't think anyone has talked to him, except for maybe the housekeeper and the pilot."

The guard paused and his brow knotted.

"Sometimes, I don't think he even exists."

"Who's the pilot?"

"She looks just like a cop...."

The guard stopped and gave Tanya a sheepish grin.

"Not that there's anything wrong with that. Anyway, she got her digs next to us, and it's bigger and nicer. She don't talk to nobody. She thinks she's better than us."

He shook his head.

"But when the old man goes to Seattle or wherever the heck he flies every week, she starts up that bird and away they take off."

Tanya's eyes narrowed. Jay stepped back like he was afraid she'd punch him.

"Have you seen any girls?" said Tanya. "Young girls, teenagers, going into or coming out of your boss's house?"

"I told you already. I seen nobody. No one can go into that house except for the housekeeper, the cook, and the cleaning lady. That's the rules. That's what my boss told me."

"What can you tell us about the staff?"

"They don't even speak English. They come from Russia or somewhere weird like that. They look like those.... what do you call those old grandmas with scarfs on their heads?"

Tanya sat up. "Russian Babushkas."

He slapped his thigh. "That's what everyone calls them. The Babushka Mamas."

Tanya's back tingled.

There is a Russian connection.

Chapter Twenty-seven

"Play it again," said Tanya.

Asha clicked on the video.

They were huddled around Asha's laptop, watching the camera footage from the Grimwood Estate.

Max had settled by the door after Jay had left. Tanya had no reason to keep the guard longer. The last thing she needed was the chief and his team to come in and find out she was interrogating a witness without their consent.

"He was telling the truth." Asha rubbed her tired eyes as they looped the footage for the third time.

There was no sound, but the dogs' agitated reactions and the way Jay swiveled his head confirmed his story. He had heard something outside the walls but hadn't been able to pinpoint or investigate it.

They waded through the camera footage, checking the hour before and the hour after the incident at three times the speed, but there was nothing else to see.

Asha moved her mouse back and forth absentmindedly. "How do we know the Grimwood guards haven't doctored the footage? It's been over twenty-four hours since you found the girl. They had time."

Tanya stared at her friend. "Is there a way to find out?"

"With no special software, the best I can do is go frame by frame manually and look for anomalies."

"It would be great if you can do that." Tanya sighed. "I'd love to know what else is inside those estate walls. What are they hiding?"

"Remember that hog farmer in British Columbia?" said Asha. "He picked up prostitutes from the seedy part of Vancouver, killed them, and fed the remains to his pigs. No one knew what was going on because he owned an enormous property and controlled who came in and went. If you wanted to get away with murder, Grimwood Estate would be the perfect spot."

Tanya wrinkled her nose in disgust. "My gut says there are funny goings-on inside there too. Things maybe even the security guards don't know about."

"But the camera never lies," said Asha. "Whatever happened to Laura, it was something or someone outside these walls."

"Couldn't they have at least one camera pointing at the hiking trail?"

"Not our clowns, not our circus. That's the Grimwood Estate's mantra. They have literally walled themselves away from the world."

"Just like everyone else in this town."

Asha leaned back in her chair. "The killer could have driven up to the hiking trail from town and dumped Laura in the ditch."

"The guard didn't say he heard a car."

"He could have taken off before Jay and his dogs were near that section of the wall. Didn't you say you found tracks closer to the ditch?"

Tanya nodded. "That was Lopez and Jones. They drove by the girl in their squad car, did a U-turn when they spotted her. I made the match between the tracks and the tires."

She paused and looked at her friend.

"There's another possibility, no one seems to want to consider."

Asha nodded. "Someone dumped her from the other side. Who lives behind the white wall?"

"It's the West End gated community."

Asha raised an eyebrow.

"It's where the well-heeled lives," said Tanya. "The mayor, council members, the judge, the doctor, and the bunch of big shots in town who are all at the fundraiser right now."

Asha let out a low whistle. "That's why your crew hasn't honed in on that side yet. It's a lot of ground to cover."

"The residents are also going to resist anyone snooping around without justification," said Tanya.

"Can't the chief get a search warrant?" asked Asha.

"He asked. Did I tell you the judge lives there too?"

"A dead girl is enough, isn't it?"

Tanya sighed. "I thought the bureaucracy at the federal bureau was bad, but these small towns are worse."

"What about the other girls Wilma talked about?" said Asha, frowning. "Do you think there's any truth to that?"

Tanya sat up and looked at her phone. "We have one to two hours before the crew returns."

Asha narrowed her eyes. "What are you thinking?"

"Something Bold wouldn't want me to do." Tanya raked her chair back, got up, and turned to Max who was by the door.

"On guard, bud. Bark when you hear them."

Chapter Twenty-eight

"Four teenage girls missing so far," called Tanya from Bold's office.

Asha got up from her laptop and walked over. "So it is true."

"All within a twenty-four-month period. One every six months." Tanya paused. "Whoever it is, they're methodical."

Asha picked up a manila folder from Bold's desk and flipped it open. "What's this? There's not much detail in here. No interviews. No follow-through."

Tanya removed her feet from the chief's desk where she had spent the better part of an hour wading through case files. "They're all like that. A sloppy job all around."

Asha dropped the file on the desk and picked up another. "Officer Jones wrote these up. Why didn't Bold double-check them?"

"He started a week ago. Laura was the only girl who disappeared under his watch."

"What were Lopez and Fox doing?"

"Also brand spanking new. Been here less than a month. According to Wilma, who's an unreliable source, mind you, the mayor hired them a few weeks before the chief came on board."

"Sounds like the mayor loves total control. You'd think he'd leave the hiring details to the new boss." Asha shook her head. "What has the team done so far?"

"Zilch. They should have flagged these cases. They should have notified the FBI about the multiple victims."

"Chief Bold called the bureau for help." Asha leaned against the desk and crossed her arms. "He suspected things were bad. We can give him some credit."

"The mayor keeps distracting him with silly duties, so Bold's depending on Jones to bring him up to speed," said Tanya. "But I'd bet a year's worth of Max's organic kibbles Jones hasn't said a word. I doubt Bold has even had time to read these files. Some of them were stuck together with dried coffee stains from months back."

"Ew," said Asha. "Officer Jones stinks."

Tanya nodded. "If I were the chief, I'd fire him. Like yesterday."

"Why do you think Jones is keeping things from Bold? Pure laziness or deliberate deception?"

"He might have wanted the chief's job and is now trying to sabotage the new guy." Tanya paused. "He could also be our unsub."

"Unsub?"

"Unknown subject." Tanya stroked her chin thoughtfully. "Thing is, Jones doesn't look like he'd have the energy to lure four teenagers without getting caught. Our unsub is nimble, fast, and smart. That's not how I'd describe Jones."

"Could it be someone at the local school who knew these girls?" said Asha. "A teacher? An administrator? If one of them has a previous criminal record for flashing, harassing or assault, we might have our man. Or woman."

Tanya picked up her phone.

She browsed the local websites which outed registered sex offenders, but they were outdated or incomplete. None of the former felons listed online had any relations to the local school's staff.

Asha, who had been scanning media and newspaper websites on her phone, looked up with a frown.

"How come none of these cases are in the news? It's like they never happened. How is that possible?"

"You can blame Mayor Bailey for that." Tanya gave her friend a peeved look. "All press releases go through his office and he wants nothing negative to leak out."

"Even missing kids? Even after one of them turned up dying in a ditch?"

Tanya put her phone down with a frustrated sigh. "If I were in my Seattle office, I could have checked the databases in a nano-second..."

She stopped and pulled the case files toward her and lined them up.

"Let's check the victimology."

"Victimology?" Asha wrinkled her brow. "You're starting to speak like a true bureau agent, my friend."

Tanya didn't reply, her focus on deciphering the incomplete data. She scoured the documents again, one by one. Asha reached over the desk with her phone and snapped photos of the opened files.

Tanya looked up. "You just breached a bunch of privacy protocols."

"You mean like the security policies you broke by letting me in here?" Asha gave her a half smile. "I'm willing to risk it because, unlike your spirit squad, I plan to find out who's kidnapped these poor girls."

"Me too."

For the next half hour, Tanya perused the folders on the desk while Asha read the files on her phone.

"Jones couldn't have done a worse job if he tried." Asha dropped her phone on the desk with a frustrated hiss.

Tanya pushed the files away. "Let's take stock. What do we know so far?"

"They were around the same age," said Asha. "Janine's thirteen. Sara and Isabella are fifteen. Laura was sixteen this year."

Tanya nodded. "They also went to the same school down the road. The only school in town."

"Seems like Laura had a boyfriend," said Asha, checking her phone again. "Tim Patterson. Plays in the youth football league. Laura was dating the star player of her school."

"Stats say most women are killed by the men in their life."

Asha shook her head. "He's only fifteen. A kid. That's highly unlikely unless he comes from a seriously dysfunctional family."

"That's how serial killers get made." Tanya frowned. "But serial killers target in one demographic. These vics were in the same age group and gender, but there's one glaring issue."

"What is it?"

"Janine is African-American, Isabella is Latina, and Laura and Sara are Caucasian."

"So, heritage isn't a connection." Asha swiped through her screen. "Janine was in the school choir. Laura was in the softball team. Sara was into punk rock and goth stuff, and Isabella volunteered at the church."

Tanya spread her arms. "Again, no connection."

Asha looked up. "Remember Miranda's house?"

"What about it?"

"Until we went to her neighborhood, I thought everyone in Black Rock lived in ginormous houses in gated communities." Asha tapped Janine's file. "Look up her street address."

Tanya pulled up the online map on her phone. Within seconds they had triangulated the homes of the victims.

Tanya's brow cleared.

"Our connection."

Asha nodded.

"Someone's targeting girls from the East End."

Chapter Twenty-nine

"The unsub could be from their neighborhood," said Tanya.

"Could be someone they all knew," said Asha. "Easier to get away with it, without casting too much suspicion."

"We shouldn't rule out the West End, though," said Tanya. "Laura was dumped right in between the gated community and Grimwood Estate."

Tanya studied the online map on her phone and zoomed in on the hiking trail.

"Let's say she wasn't dumped but had been running from her captors. If that was the case, she didn't come from far."

Asha nodded.

"We need to talk to Miranda again. She was trying to tell us something about the West Enders."

Tanya frowned.

"What did the unsub want from these girls? The autopsy report isn't out yet, but Laura wasn't assaulted. At first glance, anyway. She just looked drained and dehydrated."

"Laura got away before the unsub did whatever they had been planning to do to her. I'd imagine the other girls never escaped and are now in a shallow grave somewhere." Asha gave Tanya a sad look. "Laura was the exception. Not the norm."

Tanya glanced through the office door to where Max was sitting by the bullpen's entrance. There was no sign of the crew but she knew they'd be returning soon.

She turned to Asha. "Find anything on the security footage?"

Asha shook her head. "To my untrained eye it wasn't doctored, but a good IT forensics lab could give a more accurate answer."

"Labs I don't have access to anymore." Tanya sighed. "We have a connection on our victims but we have no idea who the unsub is yet. What do we do next? Interview the ten thousand residents of Black Rock?"

Asha piled the case folders on the desk one by one, like she needed to put her hands to work while she thought things through.

"Didn't you say Jones called on the security guards from the Grimwood Estate after you found the girl?"

"Bold instructed him to," said Tanya.

"Would you say Jones knows the estate guards well?"

"He's from Black Rock. Been here the longest, so knows the residents better than the others."

"Don't you think it was strange one of the estate guards came to tell us to leave the town hall parking lot? Jones, the officer on duty, was standing in his spot, smirking at us. It was like they were a team."

"The guard said the mayor sent him," Tanya sat up, "but that could have been a lie."

Asha pushed the tower of files to the side and looked her friend in the eye. "Jones may look incompetent, but he knows a lot more than he's—"

Max sat up and barked.

Asha whirled around. "They're back!"

Tanya and Asha stepped into the bullpen just as Bold walked through the main door and took off his cap.

His face was red and his eyes were lined. Fox, Lopez, and Wilma trooped in after him, all in various degrees of frustration. None of them seemed to have enjoyed being pulled into the mayor's personal pet project. Even Wilma, and it showed.

"Where were you?" barked Bold as he spotted Tanya. "Could have done with an extra hand."

"Miranda wasn't feeling well," said Asha.

"She was in bad shape," said Tanya. "Ready to scratch everyone's eyes out, so I took her home and calmed her down. Trust me, you wouldn't want her at the station like that."

"I got the files you asked for," Tanya continued before Bold could respond. "Security cam footage from the Grimwood Estate. A guard dropped them off a few minutes ago."

"Great." Bold nodded. "That's what I like to hear."

Tanya pointed at Fox's cubicle just as he took his seat. "On your desk, Officer, for your leisurely perusal."

With a wave of thanks, Fox picked up the USB stick and slipped it into a port on his computer. Lopez and Bold pulled up chairs to watch over his shoulder.

As they were scanning the footage, Asha walked over to the reception desk.

"Did I tell you how much I love your Prada bag?" she said.

Wilma swiveled around in her chair, a surprised expression on her face.

"That's so nice of you to notice, my dear."

"Where did you find it? It's beautiful," Asha cooed.

Wilma's face lit up. "It was a birthday present I bought for myself."

"I'm so bad at choosing the right thing to wear. How do you do it?"

"You've got a lovely sense of fashion, yourself." Wilma's smiling eyes slid down to Asha's feet. "Those red boots are gorgeous."

"Thank you. But I could pick up a few pointers from you."

"Ask me, anytime."

Asha smiled. "Hey, where are the bathrooms in here?"

"Down the corridor, hun. Third door to your right."

"Thanks, Wilma."

Gesturing to Tanya to follow her, Asha slipped into the back of the building. They stepped into the women's washroom and shut the door behind them.

"What was that about?" demanded Tanya.

"Building trust," said Asha.

"I want to find a killer, not chitchat about purses."

"Have you ever thought about your guy?" asked Asha.

"I have no guy," said Tanya.

"The prepper man. The FBI retiree who's your connection to Seattle. He's your guy, isn't he?"

"If you put it that way."

"You said he was a loner who hoarded weapons. Could he be abducting the girls?"

Tanya's eyebrows shot up. "Ray Jackson is a seventy-something-year-old dude."

"A seventy-year-old could overpower a young girl if he held a gun to her head."

Tanya's cell vibrated before she could answer. It was her burner phone.

"Speaking of the devil," she said, clicking on the message app.

Asha peeked at the screen to read the text.

Your cover's blown. Be careful.

Tanya typed furiously. "You tell me now? Got a note on my Jeep today."

What did it say?

"To leave town or they'll come after me."

Tanya and Asha waited for Ray Jackson to reply, leaning against the bathroom counter, their eyes peeled on the screen.

Nothing.

After several seconds, Tanya typed again, her fingers moving so fast, Asha was sure the device would catch on fire.

"MUST TALK TO CROSS ASAP."

The answer came in an instant this time.

Not possible.

"Why not???"

She tells me when to call you.

A pause. Then came a second message. *I'm just a minion.*

Tanya typed back. "TRY HARDER, minion."

Asha gave her friend a warning look from under her brows. "You need to be more diplomatic."

All Tanya wanted was to drive over to Ray Jackson's property, trip wires and smoke bombs be darned, and shake him till his teeth fell out.

Instead, she typed.

"How did you know I've been compromised?"

I just know.

Tanya was about to throw the phone across the bathroom when the buzz came again.

You'll figure it out. I'd help if I can.

With a furious hiss, Tanya shut the app. "I don't trust anyone in this frigging town. Not Ray, not Jones, not Bold, not Lop—"

A grating noise made her whip around.

Someone was entering the bathroom.

Chapter Thirty

"You two found the toilet, eventually?" Lopez didn't even bother to conceal the sarcasm in her voice.

Tanya glared.

Asha smiled. "We were catching up. Been a while since we had a girl chat."

Lopez turned to enter a stall.

"What about you?" said Asha.

Lopez twisted her neck around, a guarded expression on her face. "What about me?"

"You're new to town too, aren't you?" said Asha. "Where are you from?"

For a moment, it looked like the officer was going to ignore them. Then, she let go of the stall door.

"San Diego."

"Why on earth did you come to Black Rock?" said Asha.

Lopez was silent for a few seconds, then, she let out a sigh. "It was the only way to get a promotion. I'm heading back as soon as I get two years under my belt."

Tanya's back prickled. Lopez had looked away when she spoke, like she didn't want them to see her eyes.

You're lying, thought Tanya. *Or you're telling us a half-truth.*

"You're not just another beat cop then?" said Asha.

Lopez shook her head. "Deputy Chief, second-in-command. I'll replace Bold if anything happens to him."

"Awesome. Good for you, girl," said Asha, nudging Tanya, whose icy glare on Lopez hadn't wavered.

Tanya nodded in acknowledgment. Lopez's uniform markings had already told her she had seniority, but her distrust for everyone in this town was getting stronger by the minute.

Lopez gave Asha a lopsided grin. "I get paid a bit more than the boys. Fox doesn't mind but Jones is another matter. He's made it clear he doesn't want a woman for a boss."

Asha rolled her eyes. "What ancient bat cave did he roll out of?"

Tanya frowned. "How well do you know Jones?"

"As much as you, to tell the truth," said Lopez. "He doesn't say much other than to make sarcastic jabs and empty the cookie jar every day. He hates his job. Not much of a team player."

"He's lived in this town all his life, right?" said Asha.

Lopez nodded. "Thinks he should have been chief, but he doesn't inspire confidence from anyone." She looked at Tanya. "Jones isn't happy us outsiders are here. If I were you, I'd watch your back."

With that, she twisted around and stepped inside the stall.

Tanya stared at the closed door.

Lopez didn't come to Black Rock just to get a leg up. She's running away from something. What would that be?

Asha pulled on her arm, distracting her from her thoughts. "Time to get back to work," she said in a chirpy voice.

Leaving Lopez behind, Asha and Tanya stepped out of the bathroom.

"That's the second time someone told you to watch your back today." Asha whispered as they walked up the corridor toward the bullpen.

Tanya turned to her friend. "You need to leave Black Rock tonight."

"What? *Why?*"

"My cover's blown. If they, whoever they are, know you're helping me out, they're going to target you too."

Asha shot her an indignant look. "You can't invite me to find out what happened to a dead girl and stop me halfway."

"I never invited you," whispered Tanya fiercely.

"I won't sleep if I don't finish this job."

"You don't have a job. This isn't even my darned case!"

Asha stopped and crossed her arms. "You need me."

"I can't watch your back too."

"*You* trained me. I've shot traffickers. I've blown up gangster lairs. You think I can't handle a few small-town crooks?"

"You think this is—"

Tanya stopped as the sound of footsteps came from the other end of the corridor.

Chief Bold stepped into the hallway. He was heading toward the kitchenette, but turned as he spotted them halfway down the corridor.

"You're still here?" he said.

"Hello, Chief." Asha rustled up a smile and a wave. "Maybe you can help. I'm craving pasta but Tanya wants Chow Mein for supper. We can't seem to agree. What do you think?"

Bold stared at them for a few seconds.

Asha stopped breathing and Tanya crossed her fingers, hoping he hadn't overheard their whispered conversation.

Bold glanced at the kitchenette, then back at them.

"Mind if I suggest something else altogether, ladies?"

Chapter Thirty-one

Tanya was secretly glad Asha had decided to stay.

Though she had been in town only for a few hours, everyone seemed to open up to her.

Bold had made the right decision when he'd wrangled up his staff into the station's boardroom for a pizza takeout.

To everyone's surprise, Officer Jones had volunteered to pick up drinks, humming to himself as he'd stepped out. The paramedics, Justin and Stacey, had joined the party. Wilma had called Dr. Miller from the clinic. Nurse Norma hadn't come, but no one seemed to miss her.

The shy doctor had joined in, stuttering and stammering as he told them about his favorite football team. While the others made small talk, Tanya observed every one of them.

Which one of you sickos left the threatening note on my Jeep?

If the culprit was among them, they were excellent actors.

Tanya didn't eat much, anger and exhaustion overcoming her. The night before, she had tossed and turned, an unending nightmare whirling through her mind.

The heat of the blistering desert sun, the furious shouts in Arabic, and the potent smell of gunpowder overwhelmed her senses. In her dream, she was crouching in the ditch with Laura Fredrickson, as bullets rained around them.

The monster. He's… coming back… for more…

Laura's dying words echoed in her head as she held on to the girl's hand, trying to keep their heads below the barrage of gunfire.

Tanya's past was colliding with her present. And through those fogged-up hazy images, one question swirled in her brain.

Who's the monster?

An hour later, after helping the crew clean up the pizza dinner, Asha and Tanya headed home with Max.

Tanya clutched the steering wheel, fighting to keep her eyes open, feeling every muscle in her ache. Next to her, Asha looked up from her phone.

"We just passed the town's school."

Tanya jerked up, alert. After a quick check in her rearview mirror, she squealed to a stop in the middle of the road.

Asha gave her an alarmed look. "What are you doing?"

Tanya did an illegal U-turn, turning her head to make sure she wouldn't hit traffic coming from either end. A family sedan sped past, honking angrily.

Tanya swung the Jeep onto the side road. "Let's check it out."

"At *this* time?" said Asha, clutching the dashboard.

"See these cars parked along the side?" said Tanya as they sped down the narrow lane. "I spotted them when we passed, but I didn't realize it was at the school."

"That means something's going on tonight," said Asha as she checked her phone. After a minute, she flashed the screen Tanya's way. "You're right. There's a football game."

The game was over when they arrived at the school, but people were still milling on the grounds. The parking lot was busy with parents and children straggling over to their vehicles.

Asha shook her head. "You'd think they'd hold a memorial for their dead student, not a tournament."

"That's Mayor Bailey for you," said Tanya. "He's decreed all events should go as planned and no one can talk about the victim."

Leaving Max in the Jeep, they got out and followed a group of teens making their way back to the school grounds, away from the parking lot. They were joking and jostling, like they were headed to a party.

Soon, the smell of marijuana and cheap beer hit Tanya and Asha's noses. That was when they noticed the large garden shed at the bottom of the school grounds.

The teens slipped inside, giggling, without even realizing they were being followed.

Tanya and Asha stayed back, debating whether to walk in, pretending to be teachers from the opposing team's school, when they heard the loud smooching nearby. They turned around and peered at the shadowy corner by the sports center.

Two teens were fumbling with each other's clothes, kissing with more noise than finesse. The shirtless young man stumbled over the sports bag at his feet. A pair of sneakers and a phone fell out but neither noticed nor cared.

"Tim Patterson," said Asha, recognizing the young man from the pictures in the case files.

"Laura's body's not even cold and he's already moved on to a new girl?" Tanya's mouth scrunched in distaste. "I'd love for him to be the unsub."

"He's just a kid—"

The girl's high-pitched screech made them both jump. Tanya pulled her Glock out and whipped around, looking for what had frightened her.

"Perverts!" screamed the girl.

With a wild look their way, she pulled her shirt down and darted across the lawn, her hair streaming behind her. Tanya and Asha stared as she dashed inside the party shed and banged the door shut.

"You sickos!"

They turned around to see the boy jumping up and down in fury. "You were spying on us!"

Tanya took a step forward. "Tim Patterson? We'd like to talk to you."

He replied with a rude gesture. "You chased away my girlfriend!"

Tanya holstered her weapon. "I thought your girlfriend was lying in the morgue."

Tim stopped and stared at her open mouthed. His eyes wandered to the gun on her belt like he'd just noticed it. He gulped.

Tanya sized him up. Tim was tall for his age and well built, but he was the kind who loved to bark but had no bite.

"What.... what do you want from me?" he stammered.

"We just want to talk to you, Tim," said Asha in the calm voice she reserved for the most sensitive of her private clients.

"Who... who are you people?"

"I'm from the chief's office," said Tanya. "We have a few questions about Laura."

"What do you wanna know?"

"When was the last time you saw her?"

Tim swayed unsteadily, gaping like a fish out of water. Tanya waited for an answer with her hands on her hips.

Asha stepped up to him, bent down, and picked up the phone that had spilled out with the jumble of smelly shoes from inside his duffel bag.

She glanced at the screensaver of him with another girl.

"You're one popular dude."

"That's mine!"

Tim lunged to grab his phone, but Asha pulled back and stepped away just in time.

"I love technology," she said as she stepped backward, clicking on the photo app. "Face recognition software works so fast."

"Gimme that!"

Tim took another step toward her, but Tanya's stern glare and her gun stopped him from snatching his phone.

Asha swiped through the images. "My goodness. You must be dating all the girls in this school."

Tanya stepped up to Tim. "Where were you two days ago?"

"How am I supposed to know?"

Tanya's voice hardened. "Think."

"Um... at football practice."

"You were playing ball twenty-four hours a day?"

He stared at her mutely for a few seconds, then rubbed his eyes. "We were playing in the next town. We were gone for three days. I just got back today."

"Which town?"

"Langley. On the peninsula, three hours from here. If you don't believe me, ask our coach. I swear I don't know what happened to Laura. She was gone weeks ago."

"That didn't worry you?"

"I thought she was mad at me. She's super jealous. Our teacher told us she ran away from home."

Tanya glared. "You never inquired after her?"

Tim gave her a strained look, but didn't answer.

"You could have at least called her family," said Asha.

"You mean that cleaner woman?" he spat out.

Tanya took another step forward, towering over the boy. "Yeah, the cleaner woman whose daughter you were dating. Didn't it cross your mind to—"

"Oi!" A loud yell came from behind them.

Tim glanced over Tanya's shoulders and started jumping up and down, panic in his voice. "Over here!"

Tanya and Asha turned around to see a bald man with large biceps march toward them.

"Coach!" Tim screeched, flailing his arms. "Help me! They're going to arrest me!"

"We were doing no such thing," said Tanya, giving him a stern look.

"Get away from my boy," shouted the coach as he approached them. "Stop harassing my players."

"We were just asking a few questions," said Tanya.

The coach came over and stuck an angry finger inches from her face.

"I know who you are. Just because you work for the chief doesn't mean you can come here and push my boys around."

"We're in the middle of a murder investigation."

"The mayor will hear of this. Just wait. You're fired!"

Day Three

Chapter Thirty-two

Tanya stared at the medical examiner in disbelief.

She was sure she had heard the doctor wrong.

It was way too early in the day and she'd had just one coffee. Asha and Max were still sleeping back at home. Leaving a note for her friend, she had raced over to the station to be on time for this staff meeting.

"The cause of Laura's death was a *stroke*?" she said.

Dr. Miller nodded, his face grave. "She... she d... died from n... natural causes." He looked away, like it was hard for him to share this news.

The boardroom lights highlighted his sickly pallor even more harshly. Next to the trim, toned, and tanned Lopez, the physician looked like a fading ghost.

"How does a teen who played high school softball die of a sudden stroke?" said Tanya. "Makes no sense to me."

Officer Jones took a loud slurp of his coffee and smirked. "You're a *doctor* now?"

"I have to agree," said Bold, flipping through the autopsy report on the conference table. "Laura was an active young teen. There must have been preexisting conditions."

The doctor nodded. "I'd... I'd hypothesize she was... an undiagnosed d... diabetic."

"What about that trickle of blood on her right arm?" said Lopez. "I swear I saw an injection mark on her elbow."

"She s... seemed to have p... pricked h... herself on a th... thorn."

"A *thorn*?" said Lopez. "Like a rosebush thorn?"

Dr. Miller shrugged. "It had f... fallen off.... s... so it's h... hard to say."

"Maybe she fought back against her assailant?" said Tanya, sitting up. "She could have drawn blood from her attacker or injured herself during the scuffle."

"There.... There is n... nothing under her n... nails. Her s... skin isn't b... bruised. N... no signs of f... fighting b... back. This is j... just a tiny prick.... Insignificant for n... now."

"What I want to know is how did Laura Fredrickson end up in that ditch?" Bold shot Dr. Miller an exasperated look. "Don't tell me she went for a hike along that trail in only an oversized T-shirt. Someone or something brought her to that place where she died."

The doctor gave him a despondent look through his thick-rimmed glasses. "I don't... know. My ex... expertise... lies purely in the m... medical r... realm."

"Did you find any other injuries?" said Bold.

"No evidence of s... s... sexual assault...."

"So, you're saying there's zero evidence of foul play?" said Fox, his brow knotted. "That's hard to believe."

The doctor looked even sadder than before.

The chief leaned back in his chair with a heavy sigh. The lines on his forehead and the circles around his eyes said he'd been up most of the night. "There has to be more to this story."

"What about poison?"

Everyone turned to Tanya.

"That injection mark could be the result of someone poisoning her," she said. "Or, she could have been forced to ingest something that brought on the stroke that killed her."

The doctor nodded.

The others waited expectantly as he struggled to get his words out.

"I... will... r... run t.... toxicology tests... and see if I... I f... find anything abnormal."

Tanya blew a raspberry. "This entire case stinks abnormally if you ask me."

"We sh... shouldn't j... jump to c... conclusions too quickly. There c... could be other ex... explanations."

Bold turned to the physician. "Okay, what's your hypothesis, Doctor?"

"It's n... not my p... place to do d... detective work."

"I'm asking for your expert opinion, Miller."

The doctor paused and glanced up at the ceiling as if he hoped to receive guidance from up above.

"She had b... been l... lost for a wh... while. She was w... weak and s... severely dehydrated. This... This could h... have led to her organs sh... shutting down which can r... result in... f... fainting and falling, and.... a high p... probability of a s... stroke."

The doctor whooshed his breath out, like those words had sapped all his energy.

"I... understand my r... report isn't... s... satisfactory to you..., but I can't, I can't... m... make things up. I.... rely on facts."

"Whatever happened to her, she didn't run away from home," said Fox, giving him a pointed look.

"She sure as heck didn't drop into that ditch either," said Lopez, shaking her head.

"You people gotta keep an open mind," said Jones, his smirk widening.

Tanya glared at him. "She's not the first girl to disappear from this town."

Wilma was at the reception desk taking a noise complaint, so she wasn't here to back her up. She doubted she would, anyway. Tanya couldn't admit to going through the case files on the chief's desk, but it was impossible to stay silent.

She leaned across the table. "I heard through the grapevine that other girls have vanished over the past two years. Girls in the same age group from the same school."

Lopez and Fox shot her startled looks, but Jones remained slouched in his seat, like he was contemplating what to have for lunch. The doctor stared in her direction, his face pale and expressionless as usual.

To Tanya's surprise, the chief nodded.

"I finally got through the files on my desk last night, after you all left." Bold turned to Jones. "You didn't mention these past incidents. What else are we missing?"

Jones looked up at his boss, like he just realized he was at a team meeting.

"I dug the files from the cave, didn't I?" He spread his arms wide. "You didn't tell me to write a book report. Besides, I didn't think they were connected."

Fox let out a surprised *sheesh*.

"Come on," said Lopez, thumping the table with her palm. "How come you didn't share this with us?"

Jones rolled his coffee cup. "My job is to catch bad guys, not wade through paperwork. Why can't we hire an intern for this work, anyway?"

Bold's face was slowly turning purple. He swallowed hard like he was trying to prevent his temper from exploding.

"We're operating on a shoestring budget. If it were up to me, I'd get you proper equipment, and I'd move us to a better building, not this rat-infested hole with asbestos in the walls. We all have to chip in if we're going to get the job done, people."

Bold spoke through clenched teeth. No one said a word. Tanya watched him with fresh eyes, wondering if she had judged him too harshly.

"I know I'm the new guy, but I gave an oath to protect the citizens of this town, and I meant it. That's why I'm here."

The chief scanned the room, his eyes steely and his face hard as concrete. "As your chief, I need to know what's going on. I'm not here to micromanage, but you must be upfront with me."

He turned to Tanya.

"That goes for you too, Stone."

Tanya's stomach flipped, but she kept her face straight. She held the biggest secret of them all. She wondered how he'd react if he discovered her true identity.

Does he know?

"I got a call this morning."

She sat up straight, prepared to face the consequences.

"Who called you?" she asked.

"The mayor."

Really?

"He said you and your friend harassed a high-school football player last night."

Bold glared.

"He asked me to terminate your contract."

Chapter Thirty-three

Tanya's phone buzzed.

Wilma had made a fresh pot of coffee which was percolating in the station's kitchenette. It was stale, bitter, and nothing like the superior Arabica brew at Lulu's Café. But after the day's events, Tanya was tired, angry, and desperate.

She had just reached for the coffee pot when her phone vibrated in her pocket.

She pulled out her regular cell to see the words *unknown number* scroll across the screen.

Is this another threat?

She peeked out of the door but the corridor was empty. Muffled office sounds were coming from the bullpen.

Bold was still upset with her.

He had accepted her apology at that morning's meeting, but not before reaming her out for going rogue. Jones had smirked through it all, like he'd enjoyed seeing her being cut down in front of everyone. Lopez and Fox had kept their eyes averted.

Her contract was still intact, but if she had gained any goodwill with the team at the pizza party the night before, it had evaporated that morning.

After another check along the hallway, Tanya stepped into the women's bathroom and locked herself in a stall. She clicked to take the call and put the phone to her ear.

"Hello?" came a shaky female voice from the other end.

"Who's this?" snapped Tanya.

"Miranda said to call you."

"Laura's mother?"

"I, er,... I, er,..."

Whoever it was, was fighting to get her words out. If Tanya had to guess, the caller had been crying. She softened her voice.

"Who's calling, please?"

"It's Hannah..." The woman on the other end spluttered. "Miranda gave me your number. She told me you took her home and... and... she said I can call you..." She trailed off.

"Call me about what?"

"My girl."

Tanya thought she heard a sob.

"I'm Janine's mom."

"Janine?" Tanya racked her memory banks. "She's the girl who disappeared six months ago, right?"

Another sob. This one was louder. "I just want my baby to come home. I know she's out there, somewhere. Please find her."

"Do you have new information on your missing daughter?"

"Miranda said you can help us. Can you come, please?"

Tanya clasped the phone to her ear. "The best thing you can do for your daughter right now is to come to the police station and share—"

"No! Please don't make me go there again."

"Why not?"

"They put us through hell. It was horrible. We can't go through that again."

"Hannah, listen to me. I don't know what the former team did when your child disappeared, but there's a new chief in town. He wants to help—"

A wail stopped Tanya.

"Miranda said you'd understand," cried the woman. "She told me you'd believe us!"

"Okay, why don't I come over with one of the new officers?"

"No!"

Hannah's screech was so loud Tanya had to move the phone from her ear.

"They're all working together, don't you realize that?" cried Hannah.

"Working together on *what*?"

Hannah sniffled on the other end. "Strange things happen here. Noah, my husband, keeps saying we need to move, but I'm going nowhere until I find my baby girl. I know she's alive. Find her!"

Hannah broke into sobs again.

Tanya shook her head. It seemed like everyone believed this town was enveloped in a conspiracy. If there was one, no one was sharing the details with her, and that included Ray Jackson and her cagey boss in Seattle.

Hannah blew her nose and spoke again.

"I thought I'd try you because Miranda said I could trust you." Her voice was low and crestfallen. "But I guess you're with them too."

Who's them?

The last thing Tanya wanted to do was alienate the chief's team even further. She needed them to complete her mission. Her mind whirred, as she tried to balance herself on this tightrope.

Hannah seemed willing to talk. She could have information that would give an insight into the bigger question Cross had thrust into her hands.

"All right, Hannah, give me your address. I'm coming over."

"Alone?" came the mother's feeble voice.

Tanya made a quick calculation. Asha was good with distressed clients. She also might hear or see something others would miss.

"I'll bring a friend. She doesn't work for the precinct."

Silence.

"She was with me at Miranda's. You can trust her."

Hannah replied a feeble okay before giving her home address.

Tanya ended the call and dialed her friend. Asha had taken Max for a walk on the pier by Marine Drive, but Tanya was sure that was an excuse to scope out the town and its residents a bit more.

When Tanya walked back to the bullpen, she felt self-conscious, like they all knew she was about to go rogue again. But the team was busy at their stations, buried in the case files Bold had divvied up among them.

An angry but muffled shout made her spin around. Someone was in the chief's office but the door was closed.

Tanya turned to Lopez. "Who's the visitor?"

Lopez shrugged but didn't answer.

Tanya tapped Fox's chair. "Do you know what's going on in there?"

"Who knows?" replied Fox, not looking up. He reached for another folder from the pile on his desk and settled back in his chair. "I leave the politicking to the boss. That's why he gets paid the big bucks."

"It's the mayor," Lopez muttered, not taking her eyes off her document.

Tanya stepped up to the office and peered through the window's half-closed slats.

They were right. It was the mayor, dressed in a blue suit that seemed a tad tight for his wide girth. He was shaking his cane at Bold. The chief stood behind his desk, hands on his hips, listening to his boss with a pained expression on his face.

She stepped back down to the bullpen. "Does he come here often?"

"The mayor likes to think everyone works for him and his wife." Lopez picked up her coffee cup and raised it in the air in mock salute. "All hail King Bailey."

"You gotta watch out for these pint-sized men." Fox grinned at Lopez, like they shared a secret. "They're always compensating."

The two officers buried their faces in their files again. Neither seemed to want to talk anymore.

Tanya turned to leave.

Just as she did, she locked eyes with Jones, who was staring at her from across the bullpen, an ugly expression on his mug. She had been feeling uneasy about him ever since they'd met. She couldn't figure out if he was contemptuous or angry with her.

Maybe both.

But there was something cold behind that lazy, bear-like physique.

She turned away, making a mental note to ask Susan Cross to check his history the next time she talked to her. Hopefully, there would be a next time soon, she thought as she stepped toward the door.

"Where are you off to?" said Wilma, looking up from her computer and giving her a school marm look.

"Asha's buying lunch. I promised to meet her early."

Tanya forced a smile through her lie, but Wilma didn't smile back. She had gone cold again.

When Tanya opened the door, she felt everyone's eyes on her back like steel daggers.

Chapter Thirty-four

"They treated us like criminals."

Janine's mother blew her nose into a tissue. "They said such evil things."

Asha and Tanya were sitting in Hannah's living room, while Max waited in the Jeep parked by the modest multi-family unit. This was a high-end abode compared to the trailer houses nearby.

Janine's parents clung to each other on their couch, deep lines of sorrow etched on their faces. Neither looked like they had slept in days. Asha wondered if they'd had even one good night's rest in the past six months.

"Who ran the investigation?" asked Tanya.

"Officer Jones," said Noah, Hannah's husband, his jaw tightening. "He talked to us only once. Can you believe that?"

She didn't reply.

"He came here the night our child went missing. Stood at the doorway like he couldn't wait to leave. He said he'd follow up, but never returned our calls."

"That's unusual," said Asha.

"In his defense, he was the only officer at the precinct at that time and was probably swamped. Still, he could've talked to us. Let us know how the search was going. This wasn't some lost pet. Our child was gone!"

"Did you go to the station to follow up?" asked Tanya.

"He was never there." Noah threw up his arms in frustration. "Every time I went, Wilma said he's not in. *Gone on a call. On patrol. An emergency.* It was a mess."

Tanya frowned. "What about the current chief? He has a new crew. Have they talked to you?"

Hannah turned to her, her face darkening. "I don't trust that man one bit."

"Why not?"

Janine's mother crossed two fingers and held her hand up. "This is how close the new chief and the mayor are. Thick as thieves."

Tanya had seen how upset Bold got every time Mayor Bailey pulled his strings. Bold wasn't a talented enough actor to pretend that kind of frustration.

Or was he?

She scooted to the edge of her seat. "Tell me about this mayor. Why do so many townsfolk not like him?"

Noah and Hannah exchanged a glance. Tanya's back tingled. Something told her the answer to that question was where her own mission lay.

"You've seen him, haven't you?" said Hannah, wiping her eyes. "Miranda said you were at the fundraiser gala."

"He's not the most pleasant fellow," said Tanya. "But I think your mistrust comes from something deeper."

"Darn right." Noah nodded. "He only cares about the out-of-towners and the Hollywood celebrities who buy summer properties. What about us? We're part of the community, but we get sidelined."

"How?"

"That road outside needs to be fixed, but do you think it ever gets done? We're missing streetlights and the city forgets to pick up the garbage most weeks. It lies out on the streets rotting. Half of east end boils their water because it's toxic. I can go on."

Next to him, Hannah shook her head and wiped her tear-stained cheek.

"Have you tried lobbying the city council to help you find your daughter?" said Asha. "Maybe becoming a squeaky wheel will force the mayor to do something."

Noah's eyes narrowed. "He's the one who accused me."

"Accused you of what?"

When Janine's father spoke again, his voice was so low, Tanya and Asha had to lean across the coffee table to hear him.

"He spread rumors around town that I abducted my girl."

"Kidnapped your own daughter?" said Asha in shock.

Noah's chin sunk to his chest. His eyes were now on the floor. "He said I did bad things to her."

Hannah let out a sob. "How can you even imagine such a thing? They want to destroy us."

Noah shook his head, still not looking up, like the shame was too much to bear.

"I told Jones he could take our house apart to find evidence of… All I wanted was for them to find my girl."

Tanya wrinkled her brow. "How do you know it was the mayor spreading these rumors?"

"Miranda overheard him talk," said Hannah.

"When?"

"She cleans one of the council member's house up on the hill. One day she heard her boss and the mayor talk on the driveway. He was complaining about how this bad press was going to keep the tourists away. That's when he said Noah had been abusing our girl. He said it was only a matter of time for them to find the evidence."

Hannah let out another sob.

"It took days for Miranda to tell me. She just couldn't.... I mean, it's not something you talk about. I told her Noah would never do such a thing. We love our girl. We gave her everything she asked for."

Tanya turned to Noah. "Did you get questioned or detained?"

He shook his head. "I live in fear they'll come to arrest me one day."

That explains their reluctance to come to the station.

"Word got around and neighbors stopped talking to us, except for Miranda," said Hannah. "By the grace of God, that woman believes us."

"Did you confront the mayor?" asked Tanya.

"He's got a bunch of gatekeepers at City Hall," said Noah. "They're always canceling my appointments. I tried to talk to him at one of his events but those black suits threw me out."

Tanya sat up. "The guards from the Grimwood Estate?"

"I don't know. Beefy, body-builder types. No one can get close to the mayor if you aren't invited. I can tell you, no one in the East end gets an invitation."

Next to her husband, Hannah was getting agitated.

Noah let out an angry hiss. "The new chief is part of his personal entourage now. I don't trust any of them."

Hannah was shivering like she had caught a fever. *She's having a nervous breakdown,* thought Asha as she observed her from the corner of her eye, wondering if they should pause the conversation.

"Bailey knows how to get everyone to work for him," said Noah. "He even rigs the elections—"

"This was all my fault!" Hannah burst out, pounding her fists on her thighs. "I'm the one who made Janine disappear!"

Chapter Thirty-five

Tanya sat up. "Why do you say you made Janine disappear?"

Hannah broke down into tears.

"We had such a horrible fight that day," she sobbed.

Tanya and Asha exchanged a quick glance.

"What did you fight about?" said Asha.

Hannah wiped the tears from her puffy cheeks.

"She wanted to wear this stupid skirt to school. I don't know where she got it from. Said all her friends were wearing nice things, why couldn't she. I told her it's what prostitutes wear. She yelled back at me. It was horrible. Why did we fight over such a silly thing...."

Noah put an arm around his wife's shoulders and pulled her in. "You can't keep beating yourself up like this. How did we know she wouldn't come home that night?"

Asha nodded. "She was just being a teenager, and you were being a caring mother."

"I pushed her away," said Hannah. "That's why she wanted that job. She said she was going to make her own money and find an apartment so she didn't have to follow my rules anymore."

Hannah looked up, tears trailing down her cheeks.

"She got on that bus to start a part-time job. That was six months ago. Please find her."

"I can't promise anything," said Tanya, feeling for the distressed mother. "I have to go through the chief, but I'll do everything I can."

"You'll talk to her friends, then?" said Noah, holding on to his wife. "We tried, but got nothing out of them. Maybe you'll learn something new."

"Of course," said Tanya. "Was there—"

Hannah jumped up from the couch and threw her hands down, like she'd had enough.

"Stop talking and go find my girl!"

She stomped out of the room, crying like her heart had been broken into a thousand pieces.

No one spoke for a minute.

"We've been on the edge ever since Janine disappeared." Noah spoke softly, his face turned down like he didn't want them to see him break down too. "They let go of Hannah from the hospital and I'm barely hanging on to my job. It's been hell."

"Hospital?" said Tanya.

"She's an orderly at the mental hospital. Used to be, anyway. Now she just cries and stares at the wall every single day for hours on end."

A door banged, and a muffled but anguished wail came from the back of the house, tearing at Tanya and Asha's hearts. Noah looked down at his feet, like he wished he could disappear into the ground.

Tanya stood up. "Mind if we look at Janine's room to start?"

Noah nodded, his hands gripping the sofa.

"Help us," he whispered hoarsely. "Make this nightmare stop."

Tanya and Asha stood at the threshold of Janine's bedroom door.

They took in the Hello Kitty pillowcases, books, figurines, and a host of Hello Kitty toys. Almost everything in the room, apart from a handful of clothes in the closet, was pink and adorned with Japanese anime cat art.

Asha stepped in but Tanya remained at the doorway. Asha turned and searched her friend's face.

"Something's bugging you, isn't it?" she whispered. "Is it Noah?"

Tanya shook her head. "He sounds legit. What I want to know is how girls keep disappearing in a small town where everyone knows what everyone is doing."

"This isn't your typical small town," said Asha. "The coffee shop on the main drag was empty almost all morning. The few people who came in got their drinks and rushed out. No smiles, no small talk. No one even said hello to Max."

"He always attracts a few fans."

"This town has no heart," said Asha. "Black Rock is where everyone drives in tinted SUVs with bodyguards."

"Except for the folk who live on the East End," said Tanya. "Remember, Laura and Janine took a bus to their interviews."

Asha frowned. "What about the bus driver?"

"Bold and Lopez talked to him. I heard the audio of the interview and read the full report from Lopez this morning. She's more thorough than Jones, thank goodness."

"What did they find out?"

"The local transit system runs on an honor system, so there are no records. The driver hardly noticed his passengers and couldn't say if she had been on the bus. Laura had most probably got in and left through the back door using her monthly pass. I'd bet Janine and the other girls did the same."

"The driver could be our unsub."

"He's way past retirement, takes medication for arthritis, and wears a hearing aid that obviously doesn't work. By the end of the interview, Bold was shouting his questions at him. But you're right. We can't rule anyone out. That goes for Jones, too."

Asha glanced around the room. "Where's Janine's computer? Laptop? Doesn't every kid have at least a cell phone these days?"

"She must have had it on her," said Tanya. "Jones should have pinged it, but from what I've heard so far, I doubt it."

"Can we still find it after six months?"

"If the unsub didn't take it apart and throw the SIM card in a garbage can. My money is on the phone lying in a ditch with no charge, which means it will be difficult to trace. We're tackling a cold-cold case."

Asha turned around, trying to see if there were any clues to what had happened to the girl. The pink coverlet on the bed overpowered everything. A dozen stuffed toys and dolls sat in a perfect row, leaning against the pink pillows.

"Hello Kitty's everywhere—" She stopped. "Wait. One of these things doesn't belong."

Asha reached across the bed and swung a fluffy bear by the ear. "A koala hiding among the kitties."

She spun around to show it to her friend when something slipped out of the bear's pouch and fell on the rug with a thud.

Tanya stepped in to look. Asha picked up the square object and read the inscription on the cover.

"Personal book of Janine Walters."
Tanya looked at her friend, her eyes gleaming.
"Janine's diary."

Chapter Thirty-six

"Typical teen stuff," muttered Asha as she flipped through the book.

"Favorite boy bands, latest manga comics, school drama...."

Tanya peered over her friend's shoulder. "Check the most recent stuff, closer to when she disappeared."

Asha flipped to the end and read the last entry out loud.

Can't wait to see T&D today!!

Asha frowned. "T&D? Is that a code name?"

"Does it show up anywhere else?" said Tanya.

Asha turned the pages from back to front, scrutinizing each page.

"There," said Tanya, poking at an entry made a week before Janine's disappearance.

OMG. OMG. T&D called me! I heart my white knight. I totally LOVE him.

Asha turned to the next page.

I've never felt soooo good. I want to tell the world but I have to keep it quiet or he'll kill me.

"Kill me, huh?" said Tanya.

"Check this out," said Asha, as she read the entry from the next day.

How could he do this to me??? He broke my heart! I hate him!

"A boyfriend who's playing hot and cold," said Tanya.

"Sounds to me like manipulation," said Asha.

Tanya nodded. "If I have to guess, T&D is older than her. Someone capable of pulling on a thirteen-year-old's strings to get what he wants."

Asha pointed at the bottom of the page. "What happened here?"

The ink marks had dug in, tearing the paper in places, like Janine had pressed her pen onto the page in anger. The lines were obscured by a crumpled patch and a water stain.

"Tears," said Tanya. "She was crying when she wrote this."

Asha held the page up to the light to make out the words.

I saw him at the asylum. With a huge bunch of red roses!! He never gave me any!

"The next part's hard to read..." Asha mumbled before continuing.

He has another GF! I totally HATE HER.

Asha brought the book down. "This asylum keeps popping up. Where is it?"

"Up the hill, just outside of town. There's a sign by the main highway exit." Tanya screwed her eyes. "Didn't Noah say Hannah used to work as an orderly there?"

"Janine must have spotted T&D when she and her father went to pick her mother up from work."

"I can't imagine a teen boy walking into a hospital with a bouquet of roses for their girlfriend," said Tanya. "Especially not Tim Peterson."

"Unless it was for a family member who's been institutionalized," said Asha. "For a mother, aunt, or cousin's birthday, maybe?"

Tanya lowered her voice. "This should eliminate the father."

Asha nodded. "This isn't the kind of thing an abused girl would write in her secret diary."

She glanced at the half-closed bedroom door. Noah and Hannah had been too distraught to speak, but that wouldn't stop them from listening in from the other side.

"Let's get out of here before they wonder what we're up to."

Tanya held her hand out. "We need to give this to Bold."

Asha slapped the diary on Tanya's open palm when a loose piece of paper flew out of the back of the book. She bent down to pick it up and gasped.

TOP SECRET.

Just below that line was a URL that simply read, *HotForMeFluffyBear.com*

"What the heck is that?" said Tanya, squinting at the paper in Asha's hand.

Asha had her phone out already and was typing the link into the browser's search bar. A password pop-up flashed across the white screen.

Asha typed "Janine" in the Username box and scanned the girl's room for clues.

"What do you think she would use for a password?"

"Koala bear?" said Tanya.

Asha punched in the words.

Access Denied. Check Your Password.

"Nope."

"Hello Kitty?"

Asha tried it and shook her head.

"What about T&D?"

After failing several combinations, Asha stopped, a disappointed expression crossing her face.

"The good news is the app hasn't locked me out yet. The bad news is if we add numbers, special characters, capital letters, this will take years. What we need is FBI's IT forensics lab."

"We're making this more complicated than it is," said Tanya. "She isn't a high-tech computer nerd or even a college student. She's just a kid."

Asha's fingers hovered over the password bar, her forehead scrunched.

"We have to think like Janine," said Tanya. "What secret word would you use if you were a thirteen-year-old kid in love with someone, a relationship you want to keep secret?"

Asha looked up, her eyes wide. Then, she started typing. "It's been staring us in the face all along."

"What's been staring at us all along?" said Tanya.

Asha showed her the screen.

MYWHITEKNIGHT

"I'll eat my hat, shoes, and Max's kibbles if this doesn't work," Asha muttered as she hit submit.

"Bingo," said Tanya as the password bar disappeared and a front page splashed across the small screen.

Their eyebrows shot up.

Asha's stomach turned. "What is this? Revenge porn? Sexting?"

Tanya shook her head, grimacing at the gallery of half-naked girls.

"It's a pedophile site."

Chapter Thirty-seven

Tanya pointed to the ditch by the hiking trail.

"That's where we found Laura."

"What a way to die," said Asha, glancing around her.

It was a serene scene if you ignored the barbed-wired wall along the pathway.

A sparrow chirped up on an oak branch and a dragon fly zoomed by the parked Jeep. A cherry blossom tree along the trail was blooming early, sending the faint smell of sweet spring their way.

When they had stepped out of Janine's room a half an hour ago, Noah had still been on the couch, a stiff drink in his hands. With his face cast downward and his chest rising and falling, he'd looked like he was meditating on his daughter's disappearance, every ounce of despair weighing on his shoulders.

Tanya knew Janine's parents needed to know what their girl had been subjected to, but now wasn't the time to share this troubling new information.

Noah hadn't looked up when they had walked back to the living room to say goodbye. He hadn't even objected to them taking his daughter's diary. Hannah had been nowhere to be found, and her door had remained closed.

Asha and Tanya had got back in the Jeep and driven over to the hiking trail by the Grimwood Estate. Re-examining the crime scene wasn't the main reason for taking the roundabout route to the police station.

Tanya knew that as soon as she handed Janine's diary to Bold, she'd lose any privileges she had gained so far. She had already got into trouble for going rogue once. Bold could deny her access and shut her out of this case.

Even fire her.

Driving the long way back gave Asha time to peruse the diary, entry by entry.

As soon as Tanya parked along the path, Max had jumped out and started sniffing around the ditch. Tanya and Asha watched him, leaning against the vehicle, trying to make sense of their discovery.

Asha pulled her phone out of her pocket and checked the screen again. It was still open to *HotForMeFluffyBear.com*.

She had found nothing new in the diary, but had felt the weight of her phone in her pocket. The thought of having to look through the pedophile site to identify the missing girls made her sick to her stomach.

Now, leaning against the Jeep under the shade of the oak tree, she swiped through the web pages, trying not to throw up at the pictures of the young girls in half-naked poses—photos someone had probably coerced them into taking.

None of the men's profiles showed their faces, depicting only a generic gray silhouette of a male head.

Asha scrolled through the chat forum. "They're following a script. There's nothing here that would identify them."

"I bet you they push the girls to their personal phones as soon as they can," said Tanya. "That minimizes comms and makes it difficult for us to track them down."

"Look at this." Asha pointed at a man's username at the bottom of the screen. "Tall & Dark. That has to be T&D."

"Janine's white knight."

"The girls used their first names," said Asha, trying to determine who was who. "We have Janine, Sara, Isabella, and Lara, whom I presume was Laura. On the other side, there's Tall&Dark, HotDaddy, YourDream, and Prince. Cheesy names a teen girl would fall for."

Tanya pointed to the timestamps on the chat page. "Look at the timeline. This app started two years ago, but there are only a dozen people on it and only a handful are girls."

Asha scanned the dates. "They're spaced out every six months, which matches the missing girls' case files." She looked up. "Could this be one pedo pretending to be all these men? Like a copycat of the lonely hearts killer."

"My suspicions exactly. This app is how our unsub lures his victims. Now we need to figure out his real identity."

"Anyone specific come to mind?"

Tanya went through the people she'd met in Black Rock so far. "Could be any of them."

"Could this be the town pimp?" said Asha. "He's luring girls for others. Maybe everyone knows about it, but no one talks about it. It's happened before."

"A pimp would be more prolific. They wouldn't go after one girl every six months."

"Good point."

"Pimps would also be more careful. Organized crime gangs bring in groups of victims from out of town or out of the country.

Girls are a commodity and trafficking is a serious money-making business for them. This app is an amateur product."

"True. I'm still surprised we got in."

"This isn't an organized effort." Tanya paused. "Serial offenders are a different beast altogether."

"How different?"

"They operate alone and they operate locally. This unsub was picking these girls off methodically."

"Makes me sick to my stomach. What makes anyone do such a thing?"

"Every serial killer's underlying raison d'être stems from horrific child abuse," said Tanya. "They do what they do to take back the power they lost when they were tortured as kids."

"So, we're looking for a male with serious childhood trauma who may be covering it well. Someone with enough knowhow to set up this app." Asha looked up, her face clearing. "The mayor's a nasty little fellow on a power trip, isn't he? Maybe he's compensating for a rough childhood, trying to get validation through these sick deeds."

"You could be right," said Tanya thoughtfully, "though I don't think—"

A sudden buzz made Asha jump.

"It's my phone," said Tanya, plucking her cell from her pocket. "It's Bold. He's going to kill me if he finds out where I am."

She clicked on her message app and stared.

"What is it?" said Asha, seeing her friend's face change.

"Another schoolgirl's vanished."

"What?"

"Her parents made a missing person's report today."

Tanya closed the app and slipped the phone into her pocket, a troubled expression coming over her face.

"We have to hand the diary to Bold ASAP."

"Hang on," said Asha. "It's not six months yet. It's not even a week. How did another girl disappear today?"

"The unsub's getting desperate. Either that, or something has triggered him to adjust his timing. Typically, serial offenders like routine—"

Tanya straightened up and frowned. She stared at the back of her Jeep. "What the hell?"

Asha looked around the vehicle, her heart racing. "Do you see someone? Who is it?"

Tanya marched to the back of the vehicle and pulled out a small card that had been stuck to the rear wipers.

Asha stared at the piece of paper, her mouth open.

"Another note? When did that happen?"

"Could have been at the station or when we left the car by Hannah's house. I should have noticed it sooner. I'm losing my touch."

Tanya flipped the card over, and her face darkened.

Asha walked over. "What does it say?"

Tanya looked at her friend. "I think I know why the unsub changed his timing."

Chapter Thirty-eight

It was a blurry black-and-white photo.

Asha and Tanya stared at the grainy picture of three girls sitting in straight metal chairs.

Their hands and legs had been bound, and their mouths had been gagged. Their foreheads were held back by a rope and their eyes were closed. Though the image was fuzzy, the girls looked drained, just like Laura Fredrickson had been.

"Looks like an experiment they used on prisoners during World War Two," said Tanya.

Asha scrutinized the picture. "This is old. I don't think these are our missing girls. Maybe he did this before somewhere else, and now he's in Black Rock targeting more victims."

"It could also be a recent picture, photoshopped to look aged."

Tanya flipped the photo over and goose bumps sprang up on her arms. Asha's eyes widened as she read the message on the back.

Got a death wish? You & your pal will be in the electric chair next.

"Electric chair?" Asha whispered, horrified. "Is that what he's doing to these poor girls?"

"The unsub's feeling cornered," said Tanya. "He knows we're onto him. That's why he took the girl today."

"Like a warning?"

"The only reason I can think of."

Tanya hollered as she reached for the driver's side door. "Max! Get back here."

A muffled whine came in the distance.

"Hey, Max! We're heading out, bud."

The dog bounded through the long grass.

"What's that in his mouth?" said Asha, squinting.

"Drop," Tanya commanded as Max trotted up to her.

He lowered his massive jaw to the ground and let go.

"A ripped piece of cloth," said Asha, bending over and peering at the item. "Look, it's got a dried bloodstain on it. That's why he picked it up."

"Could be part of Laura's shirt." Tanya looked up at Max. "Where did you find it, bud?"

Max wagged his tail and gave her an expectant look.

Tanya ruffled his head and fished a rubber ball from her pocket as a reward. "Good boy. Wish you could talk, my friend."

As Max scampered around the vehicle with his toy, Tanya opened the trunk to fish out a plastic bag to gather the evidence.

Asha glanced up and down the hiking path.

The trail was empty. An eerie quietness had settled around them. The sparrow had flown away, and the dragonfly had disappeared. Even the leaves in the oak branches had stopped rustling.

Asha was glad Max was with them, but she couldn't help but feel troubled.

Something about this place made her feel cold. Like unseen eyes were observing them from somewhere along the trail.

She turned to Tanya, who was bagging the piece of cloth. "Can we get out of here? I feel like someone's watching us."

Wilma looked up as Tanya and Asha walked through the secure door of the station.

On her computer screen was a half-done Wordle puzzle. The faint smell of alcohol wafted around the receptionist.

"Where's Max?" said Wilma.

"In the parking lot," said Tanya. "He prefers open spaces."

"Smart dog. Some days I'm sure I'll end up with asbestos cancer, from being cooped up here all day long."

Tanya scanned the empty bullpen. The chief's office was closed. It was dim in there, and hard to see if anyone was inside. "Where's everybody?"

"Conference room," said Wilma, giving her a knowing look.

"I need to talk to Bold urgently."

"He's in there with the big boys and girls. Special meeting. Told me to tell you to join them when you get in."

Wilma pointed at Tanya. "Just you."

"I'll go get coffee and donuts for everybody," said Asha. "I gather you haven't treated your new workmates yet?"

Tanya raised an eyebrow. "I'm supposed to get coffee now?"

Wilma turned to Asha and made a face. "I'm glad you're here to remind her of her manners."

Tanya spread her hands. "I'm an ex-military contractor. I don't—"

Asha gave her a friendly punch to the arm. "You go to your meeting and I'll get coffee from Lulu's. It'll be waiting for you when you guys are done."

Tanya nodded.

You sly girl, she thought. She knew Asha was only trying to endear herself to the crew, so she could be part of this investigation.

Asha twirled around and stepped out of the door with a wave.

"Now that's a good friend," said Wilma, wagging a finger at Tanya. "You've got to listen to her more often."

Trying not to roll her eyes, Tanya stepped over to the conference room, clutching Janine's diary in her hand.

She stopped as she reached for the handle, Wilma's words echoing in her head. "He's in there with the big boys and girls."

Is the White Knight in this room?

Chapter Thirty-nine

The chief's team had gathered around the oval conference table.

Even Dr. Miller and Nurse Norma.

Fox had his laptop open and was typing, while next to him Lopez was reading a file.

"I hear we have another missing case," Tanya said as she took her seat.

Jones, who had been sitting with his chair casually tilted back in the corner, smirked. "Another day, another girl."

Bold spun around. "Some respect for our victims, Officer?"

"Our latest disappearance is Nancy Stewart, a fourteen-year-old from the East End." The chief tapped the folder in front of him with his pen. "I'm planning on this being the last case of missing girls this town will ever see. We're going to put a stop to this."

Tanya placed Janine's diary on the table and glanced around.

The chief's team may show their dislike of her in subtle ways, but it was Nurse Norma who was watching her with a hostile scowl.

Is she still mad because I walked into the autopsy room without permission?

Next to the nurse, the medical examiner was fidgeting as usual. Though he was the most senior person here, at the same level as the chief, if not more in the mayor's eyes, he acted like he didn't belong.

Tanya corrected herself. *No, he doesn't want to be here.*

He saw her watching and gave her a forlorn look.

Tanya couldn't get the sickening image of the girls in the electric chairs out of her head. The person who'd left that photo and the anonymous notes on her Jeep could be anyone.

Even someone in this room.

She knew it was her responsibility to share her discovery, but her gut had tightened and her shoulders were tensed. *Not now,* screamed her instincts. She covered the diary with her hand and pulled it back toward her.

No one seemed to notice.

Tanya cleared her throat. "How did this vic disappear?"

"She told her parents she had a job interview at a local gift shop," said the chief. "She got on the same bus, driven by the same driver. I'd specifically asked him to keep an eye out, but he saw nothing. It's like there's a magic vacuum in that danged bus."

"Sir." Fox looked up from his laptop. "Just got a reply from the mayor's assistant. He said the council will vote on our request tomorrow. The only thing holding them back is the town's privacy policy."

Bold tsked angrily. "Another girl's vanished and they're going to debate policy? This should be a slam-dunk *yes.*"

Tanya turned to Fox. "What was the request for?"

"Surveillance camera at the back of the bus. Mayor doesn't like the idea due to invasion of privacy..."

Lopez puffed her cheeks and blew.

"There's one more thread we need to follow through," said Bold, drumming his fingers on the table. "The girl who went missing today had a fight with her parents about clothing, just like Laura did."

Tanya raised a brow. *Just like Janine did too.*

"This can't be a coincidence," said Lopez.

Tanya almost spoke up.

She was now sure how the unsub lured his prey.

The White Knight persuades the girls into wearing inappropriate clothes, which inevitably leads to arguments with their parents. That's when he promises to rescue them. That's his carrot.

If the girls had already shared revealing photos online, he threatens to expose them if they don't comply with whatever he wants them to do, even run away from home and into his arms. That's his stick.

The unsub is a master manipulator.

She bit her lip. There would be a time to share that. Not now.

But Bold's focus was elsewhere. He was holding up a document, his face turned to Dr. Miller.

"I appreciate you doing the lab work for us, but this is still thin."

Nurse Norma turned to the chief, her lips curling into a contemptuous sneer. Something about that reassured Tanya.

Nurse Norma thinks she's better than everybody. It's not just me.

Dr. Miller blushed as all heads turned his way. He pushed his spectacles higher on his nose.

"I... t... tested the b... blood samples... for t... toxins and..."

The physician swallowed hard. The chief clutched his sheets of papers so tightly his knuckles turned white, like he wished he could speed the doctor up.

"Negative," finished Dr. Miller. "They c... came... negative."

Bold raised a brow. "Have you tested all potential toxins?"

Dr. Miller looked like he was in distress. "I h… haven't had the t… time…."

"I'm trying to get to the bottom of this before we have more victims on our hands," said Bold, his voice laden with exasperation.

Miller shook his head sadly. "I w… want to h…. help, but… you m… must… un… understand."

He shuffled his feet and glanced around like he was searching for the correct words. Nurse Norma puffed her chest and put her elbows on the table. She leaned toward the chief and glowered, like he was an unruly child.

"You're not our only client," she said. "We have many important patients to attend to."

"Another girl went missing today," said Bold. "We don't have the luxury of time."

"Do you realize how complex lab work is?" Norma snapped. "You cops don't understand what we do. You people can't begin to imagine lab work even if you tried."

In his corner, Jones's mouth twisted into a crooked smile like he enjoyed watching the new chief sweat.

"I'm simply asking you to prioritize this work," said Bold, ignoring the spiteful sting.

"You need to learn to be patient, Chief Bold," said Norma, her condescending tone deepening. "When I say we need time, we need time. We're the experts. We're educated professionals following process as it should be followed. We're not cooking noodles in a microwave here."

Jones chuckled.

Norma leaned back, a smug look on her face, like she had just stuck it to Bold and his crew, calling them fools without actually using the word.

Tanya stared at her, the long and dreary lessons on behavioral science she'd been forced to take at Quantico flickering to life in the back of her head. She realized why the nurse acted the way she did.

Norma's overbearing behavior hid a sense of inferiority. People with deep self-esteem issues were driven to do whatever they could to feel powerful.

Would she kidnap and kill too?

That was the question.

As if she could read her mind, Nurse Norma turned to Tanya, her eyes glowing.

Tanya felt a chill go up her spine.

It's like she can read my mind.

Chapter Forty

B old scraped his chair back and got up.

"I have only one request for you, Doctor." His voice was curt, and he was no longer addressing the nurse. "Expedite your tests. Lives are on the line."

Without waiting for a reply, he snapped his notebook shut and turned to his team.

"Lopez and Jones, I need you to interview the girl's classmates, teachers, the bus driver, and anyone who got on that bus around the same time as her."

"Will do, Boss," said Lopez.

"Fox, see if you can persuade the store owners along the bus route to share their security footage as far back as they have. Go through them to see if you can spot any of these girls getting on or off the bus."

"On it, sir," said Fox, bringing his laptop closer.

"The sooner we figure out what's going on, the sooner we can get these children home."

"Do you seriously think these girls are still alive?"

Everyone turned to Jones.

Bold's jaw stiffened. "Our priority is to find them, regardless. Understood?"

Jones turned to Nurse Norma and winked. "Better keep your autopsy room open for more work soon."

He either severely resented the new boss, or enjoyed making crass jokes. Jones was a wild card. Tanya knew she did the right thing.

She turned to the chief who was about to march out of the door. "Have a minute?"

The two officers and Lopez turned their heads.

"In private." Tanya kept her gaze on Bold, though she felt the eyes of the rest of the team on her back.

Bold raised an eyebrow and nodded.

"My office."

Thank you, said Tanya under her breath.

A minute later, she walked in through the chief's office door. She had Janine's diary in her hand and her heart in her mouth.

She hadn't received permission to talk to the girl's family, plus she'd taken Asha, a civilian, with her to discuss a criminal case. She wondered if she'd get fired this time. It wasn't Bold she was worried about. It was the talk with Susan Cross that she dreaded.

On the other hand, if Bold was guilty of these crimes or knew who was, this mission was about to get interesting.

Tanya closed the door behind her and turned to face the chief.

"I owe you an apology," he said before she could speak.

"Excuse me?"

Bold took his seat behind the desk. "I shouldn't have called you out in front of everyone this morning."

Tanya searched the chief's face.

"This isn't an excuse," he said, seeing her expression, "but I haven't slept for a week and I'm forgetting how to treat my colleagues right."

"Apology accepted," said Tanya.

I've got bigger issues on my mind.

Bold gave her an earnest look. "All I ask is for you to keep me in the loop at all times and be honest with your dealings. Can you promise me that?"

The next words almost refused to come out.

"I guess I owe you an apology too," said Tanya finally.

Bold smiled a small smile.

He won't be smiling when he hears the next part.

Tanya dropped Janine's diary on his desk, then placed the grainy photo of the three girls in the electric chairs next to it.

Bold jumped in his chair.

It took her ten minutes to explain what she'd found, leaving out Asha being with her and anything that would give away her undercover role.

The chief listened without interrupting, his face expressionless. But the light pink flush that was creeping up Bold's neck didn't escape her.

When she finished, he leaned back, frowning. "Why didn't you share this at the meeting just now?"

Tanya stood quietly, wishing Asha was here because she would know the most diplomatic way to explain—

"You don't trust Jones, do you?"

She looked at him in surprise.

"I've seen how he snipes at you," said Bold. "He does that to all of us."

Tanya tried her best to hide her relief for the rescue line he'd handed to her.

"Hannah and Noah were scared to talk to your team because Jones sidelined them when he was acting chief," she said. "Seems like he'd rather undermine the investigation than find the girls."

"You're confusing him with our town mayor." Bold gave her a weary look. "I need to work on my criminal cases, not play bodyguard to local politicians. Sometimes I feel like my boss is sabotaging my job."

Welcome to my world, thought Tanya.

"I wouldn't worry about Jones too much. He's a long-timer who has turned into a bureaucrat," said Bold, shaking his head. "Met a few in Chicago like that. Give me time and I'll straighten him up into the law enforcement officer he signed up to be."

"What about the medical staff?" said Tanya.

"You mean, Dr. Miller and Nurse Norma? They're not staff. They don't work for me or the city. They have their own private practice."

"Do you trust them?"

"If they weren't here, I'd have to ask other counties or the state for support, and that's an even bigger headache." Bold sighed. "I'm not as high on Miller's priority list as his paying clients are. His pro bono work doesn't happen fast, but it's better than the alternative and it's free."

Bold looked her in the eye.

"Like you, all I want is to find the missing girls alive. I appreciate your enthusiasm and I have to admit your discovery takes us further ahead than we were before."

He paused, his glower deepening.

"One more rogue incident like this and I'll have to let you go. No discussion. No debate. You can pack your things and leave town."

Tanya nodded. "Understood."

He gave her a piercing glare like he didn't believe her. He got up, strode across the office, and flung his door open. Calling his team in, he gave them fresh instructions to investigate the diary and the photo.

As soon as they left to carry out their tasks, Bold turned to Tanya.

"There's something you need to know."

He lowered his voice.

"The house where you found that book was my childhood home."

Chapter Forty-one

"I thought you were from Chicago," said Tanya.

"I'm a Black Rock boy," said Bold. "Grew up in the East End."

"How did Janine's family end up living in your house?"

"We sold it to them. I left town soon after. That house and this town held too many bad memories."

Tanya's heart skipped a beat.

"How long ago was that?" she said.

"Decades ago. I was just a kid."

"Why did you leave town?"

Bold narrowed his eyes, as if he was gauging whether to trust her.

Tanya relaxed her shoulders, leaned against the wall, and crossed her ankles. She tried her best to look casual and friendly, but her heart was ticking faster.

This could be related to what Cross wanted her to uncover in Black Rock. Tanya had felt all along there was more to the police chief accepting a position in a small town and tolerating a bullheaded mayor and a micromanaging council.

"Chicago PD took a chance on me," said Bold as if he had decided to trust her. "I rose through the ranks to Deputy Chief. Oversaw the criminal networks group just before I left. We did good work."

He took a voluntary demotion?

"A big city has tons of opportunities for someone like you," said Tanya. "Why give it up?"

"I have unfinished business here."

Tanya's eyebrows shot up.

"My father worked as a hand for the old farmer at the Grimwood Estate," said the chief.

Grimwood Estate? Tanya always got a bad feeling whenever that name cropped up.

Bold turned toward the window, like he was talking with himself rather than with her.

"That was before the new guy bought it out." His forehead wrinkled at the memories. "I remember how my father would come home every night, smelling of blood."

Tanya jerked up.

"Blood?"

"My dad worked at the slaughterhouse in the farm. They bred pigs, cows, and chickens. Whatever he did in the abattoir during the day turned him into a monster at night."

The chief went silent for a minute.

Tanya struggled to not demand he finish his story.

Bold rubbed his temples like he was in pain.

"When I was a kid, I watched my father beat my mother every single night."

He turned back to the window like it hurt too much to look at her while sharing his innermost secrets.

"I hated coming home from school because I knew what would happen. He took the belt to me too, but I didn't care about me. The hardest thing was to watch him attack my sweet mother, day in and day out. I just couldn't watch."

His lips trembled. He bit them as if that would force them to stop.

"He'd yell at us for hours. He'd threaten to twist our necks like he killed his chickens. He used to say he'd slice our heads off like he did to those poor cows before he skinned them and cut them up for meat."

Tanya watched the brawny man crumble in front of her, questions whirling in the back of her mind.

Is he making this up? Is this an act? What's his game?

Bold twisted around to make eye contact with her again.

"You're a no-nonsense straight-shooter, Stone. I don't agree with your methods, and you're annoying as heck, but I feel like I can trust you, unlike most in this gawdforsaken town."

Tanya rearranged her face into a stoic expression. He didn't know how much she was pretending under his very nose.

Or did he?

Either way, she didn't trust him back. Not until he proved to be on her side.

"Then one day," continued the chief, "I decided I would kill my father. I was twelve."

"Did you?"

"He kept a set of butcher knives in the kitchen. I'd already picked the sharpest one and hid it under my pillow. That night when he would be passed out, drunk on the couch, I was going to slice his throat, just like he threatened to do to us."

Bold's face was lined with a mixture of sorrow and rage. She could almost see him as a frightened twelve-year-old.

"I felt like a coward for years, watching him beat my mother and hearing her cry for him to stop. I was going to be a man that night and do the right thing."

"What did you do?" Tanya whispered, pulled into the story despite her suspicions.

"I came down the stairs, ready to stop the nightmare for good."

Bold put his hands to his face and rubbed hard, like he wanted to rip those awful memories from his head. Tanya observed him guardedly as the words she'd shared with Asha only hours ago flashed across her mind.

Every serial killer's underlying raison d'être stems from horrific child abuse.

"Before I could get to him," continued Bold, unaware of the tsunami waves crashing through Tanya's head, "he killed my mother."

Tanya gave an involuntary shudder.

"When I came down, his paws were wrapped around her small neck. She was gurgling on the floor."

Bold was breathing hard now.

"I did the only thing I could think of. I ran over and stabbed him. Again, and again and again."

Chapter Forty-two

"Did you kill him?" whispered Tanya.

"He sprang back and stared at me like a demented demon, covered in blood." Bold spoke in a voice so low he was barely audible. "He was still alive. I didn't know what to do. That was when he lunged at me."

Tanya's shoulder's stiffened.

"I was sure he was going to kill me. But he turned around and ran out through the front door."

The wrinkles around Bold's eyes made him look much older than his age. Tanya wondered if she was wrong. This wasn't a made-up tale. This was real.

"My mother's dying cries stopped me from running after him to finish the job. When I turned to her, she was already taking her last breaths."

Something bitter came to Tanya's throat.

"I spent the rest of my life in foster homes. It was only by the grace of God, a police couple from Chicago adopted me. They became my perfect family, where I learned what it felt like to right the wrongs of this world."

He looked at Tanya. "Do you know what I mean?"

Tanya swallowed. "Where's your father now?"

"Where he belongs. Locked up for good."

The chief's desk phone rang, rattling them.

"It's the mayor's office," said Bold with a heavy sigh. "I have to get this."

Tanya headed toward the door.

"Stone?"

She turned around. Bold was looking at her.

"Your visit to Janine's home brought back a lot of memories. Thank you for letting me share."

Tanya tried to think of an intelligent response. If his story was true, she knew exactly how he felt. Both their mothers had died at the hands of brutal violence, and no amount of justice would bring them back.

She yanked the door open, stepped out, and closed it behind her. She stood still for a few seconds by the door, trying to breathe again and collect her thoughts.

Is Bold the unsub? Is he trying to tell me he is, in a roundabout way?

Her gut didn't send alarm bells, but from the cases she'd read, he fit the profile to a T.

Then again, so did she. And Asha, and all her found family members.

No. Not every abused child turns into a psychopath.

Plus, Bold had only been in town for a week, and these cases went back two years. It had to be someone else, unless he had been traveling back and forth from Seattle to kidnap the girls. It was a potential hypothesis but a stretch.

Tanya surveyed the bullpen, thinking what a strange day it had been.

Wilma was scanning Janine's diary to create a digital record, Lopez was squinting at a map of the town on her computer, while Fox was examining the macabre photo of the girls in the electric chairs. Jones wasn't in.

Tanya frowned as she realized someone else was missing.

Asha.

And the coffee she'd promised.

That was a long time to walk over and back from the café around the corner. She checked her phone. There were no new calls.

"How do you do that, Stone?"

Tanya turned around to face an unsmiling Lopez.

"You come storming in here, get involved in our work, do things your own way, and get away with it." Lopez was trying hard not to grit her teeth, but it showed. "Seems like you're gunning for a job here."

"I have no plans to work here permanently."

Fox glared over his laptop. "This is a small town. Word gets around. You're interviewing our witnesses. Our victims' families. You're not doing this for the fun of it. What do you want, Stone?"

Tanya gave her best nonchalant shrug. "I thought you'd appreciate some help."

"I don't know what it was like where you worked before," said Lopez, her dark eyes flashing. "But around here, we like to work together, you know, like a team. And we respect the hierarchy."

Before Tanya could reply, her phone buzzed. She turned to it, thankful to be saved by the ring, if only temporarily.

Asha's number scrolled across the screen. Tanya clicked to take the call.

"What happened to the coffee—"

"Help!" came Asha's voice, high pitched and feverish.

"Asha?"

"Help me!"

"Where are you?" yelled Tanya into the phone. "What's going on?"

She didn't notice the chief's office door open and Bold step out. The three officers had all turned their attention on her.

"Stay back!" screamed Asha on the other end. Tanya didn't have to put her phone on speaker mode for everyone to hear her cries.

"What's going on?" said Bold.

"It's Asha," said Tanya, in a shaky voice. "She went to get coffee, but something happened."

"Tell me where you are!" she hollered into her phone.

"Lulu's!" screamed Asha. "Stop! Get away from me!"

"She's fighting someone off," said Lopez, momentarily forgetting their spat. She grabbed her sidearm from her desk. Fox did the same.

Keeping her phone to her ear, Tanya spun around and bolted toward the door.

"Hang on!" she shouted.

Asha was panting hard, like she was running as well. Then came the sound of a car engine.

"Get your hands off me!" screamed Asha.

"I'm coming!" Tanya struggled to pull on the door.

Bold sprinted over and yanked it open. Pushing him aside, Tanya ran through the waiting area toward the station's main entrance.

Outside, she could hear Max's barks, echoing through the parking lot. He came barreling over as he spotted her dash out of the front doors. Bold, Lopez, and Fox scrambled after her, while Wilma stared at her crew, her work forgotten.

Tanya raced down the street toward Lulu's Café. She didn't even notice Max running next to her heels and the three officers behind her.

"Asha!" screamed Tanya. "Hang on. I'm coming!"

Chapter Forty-three

A SHA

I feel eyes on me.

Asha whirled around.

The coffee shop was empty and there was no one outside.

She had walked a few blocks to scope the neighborhood before coming in and had instantly regretted not bringing Max with her. Throughout her walk, she hadn't been able to shake the feeling someone was watching her.

Lulu's Café was a quaint bistro tucked into a street corner, a couple of blocks from the police station. With a forest green awning over its patio, stylish rattan chairs, and tables, and a glass display filled with homemade cakes and croissants, it felt warm and welcoming.

The heavenly aroma of fresh-baked buns should have been comforting. Except, something felt distinctly odd.

"How about the black forest with a cherry on top?"

Asha turned to face the gray-haired owner of the café across the counter. Lulu was holding a chocolate cupcake in her hand, her plump face brightened by twinkling eyes and a friendly smile.

"That looks delicious." Asha rustled up a smile, though her spine tingled with uneasiness. "I've been craving chocolate all morning."

Lulu brought out a box to package the cake. "And a cup of Ceylon tea for yourself, sweetie?"

"Yes, please."

Lulu placed the cake box on the counter and lined up the drinks.

"Two Arabica dark roasts for the chief and your friend Tanya. A café latte for Fox, an espresso for Lopez, Wilma's fancy caramel chocolate coffee, and a Pup Punch, my special treat for good dogs."

Asha placed the cups in the cardboard drink carrier.

"Is that all?" said Lulu.

"You know the station's crew better than me. What do they order with their drinks?"

"Wilma keeps a stash of Oreo cookies at her desk, so they only come for sweet stuff when that jar gets empty." Lulu shook her head. "What kind of witchcraft is that? Wilma's got a sweet tooth, but she's always bragging about her girlish figure. I want to know her magic."

"You and me both," said Asha with a smile.

Lulu punched in the prices for the drinks. "If only I had her genes and her money."

"Does Wilma come from a wealthy family?"

"She gets her husband's pension. Other than that, I don't know, but she's always got nice things. No kids. No pets. No problems. Just her, her fancy bags and gorgeous shoes."

"What about Officer Jones? You're sure I don't need to get a cup for him?"

Lulu looked up from the register. "He goes to a different coffee shop near Marine Drive. Good thing he stays away too."

Asha pulled out her wallet. "He can be a bit brash, can he?"

"Brash?" said Lulu, taking the money. "He's been power tripping ever since I remember. It was worse when he was acting chief. He got away with a lot. Now, Chief Bold? That man's gone through hell, but he's a real gentleman."

Bold's gone through hell? Asha made a mental note to share this with Tanya.

"Jones is from Black Rock, then?" said Asha.

"Born and raised," said Lulu, handing her the change. "The mayor wanted to promote him to chief, but some of the council members outvoted him. First time that ever happened."

"Jones must have been upset?"

Lulu leaned across the counter and lowered her voice. "Jones comes from a troubled family, and he never turned out right. Drunk father, cheating mother, a juvenile delinquent for a brother. They fought tooth and nail every night, over what, only heaven knows. We all stayed away from that house. But you never heard it from me."

"My lips are sealed."

Asha wondered how much more information she could glean from Lulu without arousing her suspicions.

"I've been all over the country," she said, "And this is the prettiest town on the West Coast. I can see why it's a magnet for celebrities. You're so lucky to live here."

Lulu sighed. "I'm only saying this because you're a nice girl." She dropped her voice though there was no one else in the café. "I wish these hot shots didn't come here every summer."

"Aren't they good for business?"

"Oh, sweetie, do you think they come in here? They live by the sea on the West End. They go to the fancy, highfalutin French coffee shops on Marine Drive for their low-fat oat milk lattes."

She shook her head.

"I get the construction workers, the medical staff from the hospital, the schoolteachers. Regular folk, you know? My neighbors."

"Why is there such a divide between the locals and the vacationers?" said Asha. She was sounding more like an anthropologist than someone who'd just dropped in for coffee now.

"It's the mayor's fault," said Lulu, a scowl breaking across her face. "He favors the West End. Caters to their every need and has fancy functions for them. The events are tightly controlled too. No one from the East End is even allowed."

"He sounds terrible."

"I blame his wife."

"What about her?"

"You should see how she treats the help in her house. They can't talk to her unless she talks first. They can't even look her in the eye. Treats everyone like dirt. She fired a girl once because she forgot to dust her vanity mirror one morning. She thinks she's some kind of royalty."

Asha sighed. "I've seen this servant-master culture overseas. The way rich families in the Middle East and South Asia treat their domestic help is inhuman."

I was one of those domestic servants, thought Asha. But she wasn't about to divulge her childhood trauma to Lulu, however nice she came across.

"Maybe the mayor's wife is a snooty Arab princess," Lulu was saying. "I thought she was Russian. She's a nasty piece of work, either way."

Lulu put her hands to her temple and rubbed the sides of her forehead.

"Lordy, my headache's getting worse."

Asha picked up the drink tray with a guilty look. "Sorry. Didn't mean to—"

"Not your fault, sweetie. I've been battling a migraine all morning." Lulu gave her a friendly wave. "Come back. We don't get too many friendly visitors from out of town. The ones who come drive in limos, are surrounded by men with guns, and send their assistants to get coffee."

Asha smiled. "I drive a rental, have no bodyguards, and fetch my own tea."

Lulu winced. "I'm going to find myself an extra-strength pill before this headache kills me. You go say hello to everyone, sweetie."

She turned around and shuffled to the back of the store, massaging her temples.

Carrying her drink tray, Asha walked through the empty café, toward the glass doors in front. She stopped when she got to the entrance and peeked out.

She'd been so engrossed in the conversation, she had forgotten the sensation that someone was watching her.

That feeling was back.

She peered through the glass doors.

The street was empty.

Asha pushed the door open. The coffee was hot, and the cups didn't sit well in the wobbly carrier. She descended the front steps and stepped onto the pavement, balancing the tray carefully.

Footsteps.

She looked up, but she was alone. It was a wide open, public street, not a place where you'd feel unsafe.

Asha moved away from the entrance and turned in the station's direction. Just as she passed the café's patio, she heard the footsteps again.

She turned around.

She'd just spotted the masked figure creeping alongside the café wall, when someone clamped a black cloth around her face.

The drink tray fell to the ground, the scalding liquid splashing on her legs. She screamed, but her voice was muffled by the cloth. She rocked her head back and forth to loosen the blindfold, but whoever was behind her had a tight grip.

Asha couldn't see. She could barely breathe.

She kicked and punched wildly. She thought she heard a gasp from one of them, but the attackers were as silent as ghosts.

She swung back and forth, trying to destabilize them, her heart pounding in fright. But the two assailants were strong.

Or were there more?

That was when she felt a stinging prick on her shoulder. She pulled back in shock.

What was that?

She dug her heels in and jabbed the person behind her with the sharp end of her elbow. There was a foot by hers. She raised her heel and stomped on it, grinding hard.

The person behind her lost their grip.

Asha didn't waste one second. She scrambled off, ripping the black cloth from her face and fumbling for her phone in her pocket.

"Hey, Siri," she screamed into the phone, "call Tanya!"

She was in the back alley of the café now.

A noise made her turn.

She spun around to see two figures approaching her from the side of the building. Their outlines were hazy and shimmery, like they were walking on hot tarmac.

"Stay back!" she shouted. "Tanya! Help me!"

She heard a warbled voice through her phone, but couldn't make the words out.

"I'm at Lulu's!"

She blinked to see better, but her vision was getting blurry and the figures were getting fuzzier.

What's wrong with me?

"Stop! Get away from me!" screeched Asha.

She tried to move her legs, but her limbs felt as heavy as lead.

What's happening to me?

She didn't notice her phone fall to the ground.

Hands grabbed her.

Asha punched and kicked wildly.

Something soft and wet wrapped around her nose. She gagged at the smell. She pulled one hand free and yanked it off, knocking her baseball cap from her head.

She doubled over gasping, wanting to retch, but every ounce of energy was fleeing from her body. Everything was blurry, like she was looking through a thick white smoke. Her head felt like it was on fire.

She thought she heard a car door open.

Then, the world went black.

Chapter Forty-four

Tanya's brain swirled like a tornado, fueled by fear and guilt.

I told her to leave town. I told her this would be dangerous.

She scanned the road in front of Lulu's Café, her heart pounding. Running footsteps came from behind. She whirled around, almost bumping into Bold.

The chief gestured to Fox. "Search the café."

Fox jumped up the steps, toward the front door.

"She's not in there," shouted Tanya. "I heard a car. Someone took her away from here!"

But Fox had already disappeared inside the coffee shop.

Fury broiled inside of Tanya. "We need to get on the road *now*."

"We don't know what the vehicle looks like or where it went," said Bold. "I don't have the luxury of a chopper or drones to fly over town. We'll be chasing our tails."

He signaled to Lopez. "Start by looking for evidence here. When we're done, we'll reconvene in the boardroom."

Tanya shot him an angry look. "We don't have time for meetings."

"Hold your horses. Before we go in guns blazing, we need to gather the facts systematically. Otherwise, we could easily get off the trail."

Lopez gave a side-eye to Tanya. "That's what they taught us at the police academy."

Tanya ignored the jab, too furious to react. She clenched her hands into fists, badly wanting to smash something, preferably the unsub, maybe the officers themselves. Instead, she released her hands, knowing they were right.

It was time to think logically.

She turned around and around, her eyes gleaning for clues. *A ripped cloth caught in a crack of the wall. Flattened grass to show a struggle. A dropped coffee cup. Anything.*

A doggy sneeze made her spin around. Max was sniffing the café wall, his eyes focused intently on something.

She rushed over. "What is it, Max?"

He didn't look up. He trotted alongside the wall, his furry rear swinging from side to side, his snout stuck to the ground.

If Tanya could trust one thing, it was her dog's sense of smell. She scrambled after him until he disappeared around the building. As soon as she turned the corner, she saw the carnage.

A paperboard coffee carrier lay upside down on the ground, next to a smashed cupcake. Six cups were on their sides, shattered, their contents spilled all over.

"She was here!" she hollered.

Max was heading to the rear of the building now. Tanya dashed after him. Bold came rushing over.

They stopped and scanned the asphalt tarmac behind the café. *Empty.*

"What was she doing in the back?" said Lopez, running over.

"She was trying to get away from the unsub." Tanya's heart hammered faster. "But a car was waiting for her here."

Her stomach tightened.

Asha was a petite woman, but Tanya had seen her operate an assault rifle against marauding traffickers in Nairobi. She had even taken on a gang of rapists on the streets of Mumbai. Tanya and the rest of their family had been there to back her up, but Asha Kade was no scared teenage girl.

Still, Tanya couldn't stop the horrifying possibilities swarming her head.

She surveyed the area.

A small alleyway ran behind the café's parking lot, wide enough for one car to pass at a time. The lot was large enough for eight vehicles, but only one spot was occupied. A yellow Mini was parked at the end, the café logo splashed on its side.

"That's Lulu's car," called out Lopez as Tanya dashed toward it.

She peered inside. It was empty. She punched the top of the car and cursed loudly.

"Easy there," said Bold, coming over.

"There were two or more people or she wouldn't have vanished like this." Tanya turned her furious eyes on him. "I was wrong. This isn't a one-man show. It's a group. A gang!"

Bold tapped the radio on his shoulder. "Wilma? I need you to download the footage from the camera in front of the station. Have it readied for us."

He turned to Lopez and pointed at the cedar hedge growing along the lot. "Search the perimeter."

"Nothing to report," came a voice from behind them.

Fox was jogging over.

"Lulu didn't see or hear anything after Asha left," he said, stopping by them.

"Where was she all this time?" said Bold.

"She had a headache, so she went to the bathroom to look for her pill bottles. She said she sat down on the toilet seat with the door closed and waited for the pain to pass."

Tanya frowned. "No one came in or out of the café during that time?"

"She would have heard the front door bell ring, but she said she didn't hear anything."

Tanya suddenly realized Max wasn't by her heels anymore. *Where did he go?*

He was sitting patiently by the far end, near the alleyway. Something small and flashy glinted by his feet. He barked as he saw her look his way.

Tanya raced over, snatched the device from the ground and held it up.

"Asha's phone!"

Bold and Fox dashed over.

"Can you find out what calls came or went just before you talked to her?" said Bold.

Tanya tapped the phone, but the password screen stopped her. She scrunched the device in her hands like she wanted to crush it.

Damn you, Susan Cross. I need resources from Seattle.

Bold took the phone from her before she could damage it. "Fox, give it a try."

Fox took it with a frown. "An IT lab would give us faster results."

"We don't have fancy forensics. Give it your best shot."

Fox stepped to the side, his brow knitted in concentration as he clicked on the screen.

Bold squinted at the bottom of the alleyway. "You were right. Someone had a car here waiting and pulled her into it."

"All clear," called out Lopez, emerging from behind the hedges.

"Let's check the alleyway," said Bold. "Tire tracks, paint marks from a car, anything to identify the vehicle. That will be our best bet."

Bold and Lopez treaded up and down the alleyway, heads down, scouring the area. Tanya watched them, trying to unscramble her racing mind.

We're wasting time.

The asphalt was crumbling along the sides. Tire marks wouldn't appear unless they burned serious rubber. But she knew Bold was only doing due diligence.

"Where does this alleyway go to?" she called out.

"Turn right and it goes by the station," Bold replied, without looking up. "Turn left, and it heads downtown to Marine Drive."

"Are there any cameras along this road?"

"Only the one outside the station which Wilma is checking."

Tanya called to Max and stomped over to the front.

I know where they took her.

Chapter Forty-five

Tanya reversed the Jeep.

The gears ground loudly, grating her already frayed nerves.

She swung sharply out of the station's parking lot, almost bumping the chief's squad car. In the back seat, Max dug his claws into the upholstery to not fall over.

Only moments ago, Tanya had frightened Wilma by storming into the station to demand if she'd seen anything in the security footage. The receptionist had blinked a few times before stammering that the file was still downloading.

It took Tanya ten minutes to arrive at the mouth of the trail where they had found Laura Fredrickson. Keeping a sharp eye out, she drove along the lonely path toward the cliff at the end.

She parked at the edge of the path and let Max out. He strolled around, sniffing and exploring, but within seconds Tanya knew he hadn't caught a scent. Asha was nowhere near here.

She felt her blood pressure rise.

Where did they take her? What do they want with her? Who—?

Her eyes fell on the high wall with the barbed wire next to the trail.

Grimwood Estate!

Tanya jumped back in her car with Max. She gunned down the trail, following the wall, searching for the entrance. Sweat streamed down her back, but her eyes were alert.

Several miles down, a long black steel gate greeted her eyes. Cameras lined the wall but there was no intercom to be seen. The place looked as forbidding as a high-security military installation.

She got out of the car and banged on the gate, but no one answered. She hollered and yelled, and banged again. She knew they were watching her through the security system. They could see her and maybe even hear her, but this was a futile exercise.

With a loud curse, Tanya jumped back in the Jeep. She zipped through the traffic, barely registering the shocked looks on other drivers' faces. Good thing it was a quiet morning. She was traveling at four times the speed limit.

Soon, she hit Marine Drive.

Tanya scoured the area, her adrenaline pumping and her hands clamping the wheel.

Where are you, Asha?

She stopped the Jeep along the road and jumped out with Max. She stormed into the first store on the drive, startling a young girl behind the jewelry counter.

"Did you see a small Asian woman, yoga pants, red boots, long black hair?"

The girl stared at her blankly. Tanya demanded again. The girl shook her head, mutely. After a search around the shop, she stepped out and barged into the next store.

When she assisted the military in her past life, she had learned to sweep through spaces rapidly. And now, Max's superpower nose amplified her ability by an order of magnitude.

But one thing was becoming obvious. Asha wasn't on Marine Drive either.

Tanya jumped back in the Jeep with Max and took a sharp U-turn, ignoring a Porsche honking angrily behind her. She pushed the gas pedal and sped back toward the station.

Her mind swirled like a hurricane as she scanned the road.

What kind of vehicle was the abductor driving? Was it an SUV? A truck? Or was it a limo, like the one that girl got pushed into?

Though the roads were clear, she felt like she was trawling through a mud field. She soon realized racing around Black Rock's roads would get her nowhere fast.

Her thoughts turned to the chief's team. Everyone, except for Jones, had jumped in to look for Asha, but something hadn't felt right.

It was Bold who had kept her in his office, stringing her along with a tale about his dysfunctional childhood.

Had that been a distraction while someone took Asha? Did he press a secret button on his desk that called on a third party to take action? Why would Bold want Asha to be kidnapped?

Janine's diary!

It held important clues. And she had handed it over to him. Tanya slapped her forehead.

Was this a warning for her to stop investigating?

If Bold was the unsub, why did he hire her? Why did he welcome Asha and even invite her to the team's pizza night? Was that to disarm them, so they would let their guards down?

Bold had been standing by the window the whole time she was in his office. He'd only sat down at the end. There had been no way for him to send a secret signal without her noticing.

Tanya frowned.

What she needed was clarity, not confusion, but right now, her imagination was racing in all directions.

Think, girl, think.

Tanya drove along the back alley toward Lulu's Café.

Bold, Lopez, and Fox were still in the parking lot, taking photos and examining the grounds. Jones was still missing. He had been at the station when Bold had passed the diary to his team.

If she should suspect anyone, it was that man.

Tanya parked the Jeep on the side of the street and marched up to the chief.

"Where's Jones?"

"On patrol," said Bold, not looking up from his phone on which he was scrutinizing a photo.

"I presume you didn't find her," said Lopez, giving her an almost sympathetic look.

Tanya turned away. She hated to admit it, but she needed their help. She just wished she could trust them.

Bold looked up, his expression softening as he spotted her face. "We'll find her soon. You have my word."

Tanya remained silent. She didn't trust herself to speak, and the last thing she wanted was to alert these people to her suspicions.

"Our man is getting daring," said Bold, the lines between his eyebrows deepening.

"You think it's the same guy who kidnapped the other girls?" said Fox.

Bold shot him a worried look. "If more than one unsub is snatching women from this town, we have a bigger problem on our hands than I thought."

"Asha's a small woman. She could easily pass as a teen from the back," said Lopez. "Maybe our man changed his modus operandi and was stalking his next victim? She just happened to be in the wrong place at the wrong time."

"He would have dropped her as soon as he realized she was an adult," pointed out Fox. "Abductors normally don't bother with anyone who fights back. Too much trouble."

Lopez narrowed her eyes. "That means he targeted her. Did he know she was Stone's friend? Taking her would only attract our attention. Unless—"

"The unsub is trying to provoke us," said Bold, finishing her sentence.

Chapter Forty-six

The chief's radio cackled to life. Wilma's voice came down the line mixed in with static.

"Mayor Bailey wants to talk to you."

"Now?" said Bold.

"There's a fundraiser this weekend. Something about protection services."

"I'm dealing with an emergency."

"He called twice this morning already."

"He can call again if he wants to," barked Bold. "I'm on a job."

"Okey dokey," said Wilma. "Over and out."

Lopez spat to the side. "Why does Bailey always call when we're in the middle of a job?"

Fox massaged his forehead. "We need more help. What about the FBI, sir? Don't they get involved when kids disappear like this? Do you think they can give us a hand?"

"I called the Seattle office two days in," said Bold, wiping his brow. "That was when I realized our cases are unusually high. Got some administrator who said I wasn't high on their priority list. He said to contract out till they can free up resources."

He turned to Tanya, who had been listening closely.

"He's the one who gave me your name and number."

That must have been Susan Cross's assistant, the short-tempered man who monitored everything that came in and went out of her office.

It was time to call Ray Jackson and demand to be connected to Cross, whether he liked it or not.

She turned around when she saw Max was sniffing a blackberry bush, halfway down the alleyway. She trudged over, her feet heavy and her brain blurred with apprehension.

Max had a determined look on his face, but there was nothing at his feet this time. Tanya bent down and surveyed the shrubbery he had been sniffing.

Caught in a branch and hidden out of sight was a square piece of white cloth next to a blue baseball cap.

Tanya snatched the hat and waved it in the air. "Found her cap!"

The others rushed over.

Tanya bent down to grab the white square cloth as well, when Lopez pushed her aside.

"I got this."

Lopez swooped down and plucked it out using a rubber-gloved hand.

"I thought you checked the bushes," said Tanya, struggling to contain her anger. "How could you miss this?"

"It's dark in there," said Lopez, a hint of annoyance in her voice. She crumpled her nose as she slipped the cloth into a zip-lock bag. "Smells like nail polish."

Tanya's eyes widened.

"Chloroform."

Lopez held up the plastic bag for all to see.

"She must have pulled it off, or it fell during the scuffle. It's an important clue."

"This is even better," said Tanya as she thrust Asha's baseball cap under Max's nose. "Go, search, bud!"

Max sniffed it before trotting up and down the back alley. He then circled the parking lot, went around the café building, waddled inside the coffee shop, then climbed back down the steps, with the entire crew following him.

"He's lost the scent," said Bold as they traced the route for a third time. "This confirms they took her in a vehicle."

Tanya slammed the cap against her thighs.

She stepped away from the group, feeling her stomach churn. *Get it together,* she scolded herself. She needed her cool head to prevail now more than ever.

She clutched her mother's pendant, wishing it could tell her who took Asha and where.

Tanya was her found family's big sister. She'd watched over them, protected them in the harshest situations. She'd already lost her mother and only brother. She couldn't lose members of her found family too.

Lopez's phone rang.

She said a curt hello, listened for a few seconds, and hung up abruptly.

"That was Jones," she said, turning to the chief. "He's on his way."

"Where was he all this time?" asked Bold, his voice hard.

Lopez swallowed like she didn't want to answer.

"Well?"

"At Timmies donut shop, sir."

Just then, a squad car with lights flashing came racing down the back alley.

The chief turned his head. "Jones!"

The officer stepped out of the car. "I was on patrol."

"We have work to do." Bold's voice was sharp. "Another girl was reported missing this morning, and now, Asha Kade's gone."

Jones turned to Tanya, surprise on his face. "The little chick who was visiting you? She got snatched too?"

Tanya struggled to not pummel him, when a familiar black SUV pulled up behind the squad car. Out stepped the older guard from the Grimwood Estate.

What's he doing here?

"Hey, Chief," called the guard as he swaggered over, cocky like he knew he'd get what he came for.

He stopped a few feet from the team.

"Mayor wants me and my boys to pull your people in. There's a big function this weekend. He's been trying to call you all morning."

The chief's face darkened.

"I'm not some private company you can call on whenever you need help."

"But Mayor Bailey—"

"This conversation isn't going to happen."

"Maybe you didn't hear—"

"I heard very well. I don't care what you do as long as it's legal. But I'm a public servant who works for this town and I have a job to do."

The guard glared. "Seems like you've forgotten who's paying your salary, Chief."

Bold glowered.

A sneer crossed the guard's face. "Are you itching to get fired, Chief Bold?"

Everyone froze.

Bold stepped up to the guard.

The two men were eye to eye now. While the rest of the team had backed away, Tanya stepped closer, her hands curled into fists.

She hadn't trusted either man until now. But the chief was putting his career on the line to do the right thing. She wasn't going to stand by and see him lose. Not now. If Bold got hit, the Grimwood guard would have to deal with her.

Max let out a low growl by her feet. He had come to the party too.

Good boy.

The guard's eyes flickered as he shot Max a nervous look, but he held his position.

The chief jabbed a finger at the guard's chest.

"You can tell the mayor to stop sending his lackeys. He can't round up public servants for private protection. That's a misuse of public funds. I suggest you turn around and head back."

"The old chief never—"

"I'm the new chief. I don't care whose boots the former chief licked or didn't lick. You won't push me around like you did with him."

They glared at each other.

"I'm going to ask you to leave now," snarled Bold. "This is a crime scene and my officers are on duty."

The guard took a step back, his face a mixture of disdain and disbelief.

He glanced over at Jones standing on the sidelines as if asking him for help, but the officer merely shrugged. Bold spun around and aimed a stern look at Jones.

"Everything I said goes for you too."

"I did nothing wrong," said Jones.

"Here's what you need to know." Bold shot him a withering glance. "We do things the right way from now on. We follow the law that we're supposed to enforce. I don't want to see or hear anything otherwise."

"Are you accusing me?" said Jones.

"You're an officer of the law. You've sworn to protect and serve. Remember that."

Jones stepped forward, his right hand clenched into a fist.

Chapter Forty-seven

Chief Bold paced the boardroom as he waited for Fox to get in contact with the state police.

The standoff between him and Jones in the parking lot had lasted seconds, but had felt like an eternity.

If Jones had wanted to show up his boss, he'd done a good job, but Bold hadn't backed down. He'd asked Jones to stand down and get back to work. To everyone's surprise, Jones had complied.

Tanya knew that was a ruse. The more she thought of it, the more she distrusted Jones.

She was now observing the chief discreetly from across the conference table. She was unsure of what to think of him anymore. He had shown himself to be a man of integrity, and to Tanya, integrity was everything.

But she knew better than to trust blindingly.

Bold could be the best actor north of Hollywood. She hadn't forgotten Susan Cross's words. No one in this town was free of suspicion.

If there was one thing she learned from her combat days, it was that the people who were trying their hardest to be allies were the ones to watch out for.

Keep your friends close and your enemies closer.

It was a battle mantra, she'd never forget.

After the team had documented all the evidence from around Lulu's Café, they had reconvened inside the police station. Even Wilma was there, her notebook and pen in hand.

Tanya had shared all of her findings so far, making sure nothing she said revealed her true identity.

Her loyalty was to the FBI, and there were certain lines she couldn't traverse. She prayed they had enough to find her friend and the missing girls.

Tanya clutched the baseball cap in her hand. All they needed was to pinpoint the correct area of town, and Max would do the rest.

Hang tight, Asha. I'm coming.

Fox looked up from his laptop.

"The amber alert was issued for Nancy Stewart two minutes ago, according to your instructions, sir. There are no applicable alerts for able adults under the age of sixty, so they have nothing for Asha Kade."

"Good enough." Bold nodded. "When we find one, we'll find the other."

He turned to his team.

"This was an aggressive attack in broad day light. If Lulu had been at her usual spot, she'd have called us in a heartbeat. He's getting brazen. That means those girls may be in even more danger if they're alive. We're going to stay up as long as we have to in order to find them, understood?"

Fox and Lopez nodded.

"Track your overtime and call your families. We won't be sleeping for a while. Wilma, that includes you."

"Sure thing, Jack," said Wilma.

"Asha logged on to the pedo site from her phone," said Tanya. "I think that's how he tracked her down. This would mean the unsub has tech skills, right?"

Fox nodded. "That could help us narrow him down, but if this unsub has no prior convictions and isn't in any of our databases, we'd never know."

"What about her phone?" said Bold. "Did you get in?"

"Not yet." Fox gave his boss an uneasy look. "I'm not a trained computer engineer, sir. I just mess around on weekends. I'm not sure I can do this."

"Keep trying. Any calls she got today could lead us to the unsub."

"Or unsubs," said Tanya. "We don't want to rule out a duo, trio, or more. Maybe even a local gang." *Or the entire darned town.* The words almost slipped out.

"Do we know where that app is located?" said Bold.

"Apps and websites can be hosted on any server in the world, so that won't help us," said Fox. "If I can get to the back end I might find out where most of the traffic is going, which could pinpoint a location, but I need time for that."

Lopez sat up. "Do we have any search warrants from the judge yet, Boss?"

Bold turned to her.

"I'm still waiting, but nothing stops us from knocking on the doors inside the gated community. Another teen's missing and we have an amber alert out. It's a good excuse to ask if anyone saw or heard anything unusual. I'd like you and Jones to take on that task."

"Roger that," said Lopez.

"They'll never talk to us," said Jones. "You're asking for trouble."

Bold whipped around. "I don't care what trouble we have to wade through, we're going to find them."

"All I'm saying is—"

"I want you to bring me solutions, not objections."

"Yes, Boss."

"There are people in this town who are more concerned with saving face than bringing justice to victims. That can't impede our jobs. Is that clear?"

"Sir!" chorused the team.

Tanya nodded. At last, she was hearing all the right things from the chief's office.

"Stone," said Bold. "We need to search the other missing girls' rooms, like you did with Janine. There might be clues to where they were taken. That's your task."

Without waiting for her to answer, Bold clapped his hands. "All right, everyone, it's all hands on deck."

"Wait," said Tanya. "What about the psychiatric hospital?"

"The loony bin?" said Jones.

"Janine's diary said she saw T&D there with a bouquet of red roses," said Tanya, ignoring the man.

"I've known Janine since she was a wee girl," said Wilma. "She made up imaginary boyfriends because her parents won't let her date. Used to tell crazy stories."

"She comes across like a drama queen, to be honest," said Lopez.

Tanya frowned. "What if T&D stands for Tall & Dark on the app?"

"We'll search the girls' houses first," said Bold. "That's our priority. The hospital's next."

"Jack?" Wilma put her hand up like a schoolgirl. "What do you want me to do?"

Bold turned to his receptionist.

"I need you to contact the missing girls' families to let them know we'd like to search their homes again. Warm them up. You know them well. They'll take it better coming from you."

Wilma nodded and gave a thumbs up.

"I forgot to tell you, the mayor called just before we started. I told him you're only taking official police business calls from now on."

She cracked a sly smile.

A surprised smile flickered on Bold's face. "Thank you, Wilma."

Lopez and Fox nodded, but Jones sat in stony silence.

Chapter Forty-eight

"Ray Jackson?"

No answer.

"Pick up, Ray Jackson."

Tanya was in the precinct's parking lot, calling him on her secret burner phone. She had been trying to get a hold of him for the past ten minutes.

Inside the station, Fox was making another attempt to hack into Asha's phone. Wilma was making calls to the victim's families, and Bold was on the phone with the state police patrol trying to rustle up search teams. Lopez and Jones were out, knocking on the doors of the gated community residences.

Tanya paced back and forth by her Jeep, while Max watched her like a hawk, as if he was waiting for a command.

"Pick up the phone, dammit."

Ray Jackson picked up on the tenth ring.

His voice came garbled but his tone was clear. "What do you want?"

"This is an emergency," said Tanya. "They kidnapped another kid and took my friend."

"Asha Kade's been abducted?" said Ray.

Tanya took a sharp breath in. "I don't recall telling you her name."

"I know you have family in New York. I did a background check on you. Did you expect me to not look you up?"

Tanya wanted to lash out, but she closed her eyes and let out a breath before opening them again.

Now wasn't the time for that conversation.

From what Cross had said, Ray was the only person she could trust in Black Rock, however irritating his methods were.

"Do you have any idea who took her and where?"

"How would I know that?" said Ray.

"You seem to know more than most people around here."

"That's because they're all lying to you. I'm the only one telling you the truth. I had nothing to do with it, and I don't know what happened."

"You have enough surveillance equipment for a local branch of the CIA. You can't tell me you're not using it on this town just like you're spying on me. You know more than you're letting on."

Silence.

"One of the missing persons is a fourteen-year-old schoolgirl," snarled Tanya, losing the last ounce of patience she had. "Doesn't that bother you at all? Have a heart, for heaven's sake."

"My heart was ripped out a long time ago. The day my family was massacred. But you already knew that."

Ray Jackson's voice was deadpan, like he was giving her the weather report. Tanya cursed under her breath. Why did she always have to meet the most insane people on earth?

"I need to talk to Cross."

"You know my answer."

"The chief and his team are scrambling. They don't have the equipment, the resources, or even the training. I can't say a word about my actual role, and I have to pretend I'm some dimwit contractor."

"Perfect."

"How's that perfect?" snapped Tanya.

"That's what Cross wants. You can report back when she's ready to hear from you. You've got to follow the rules and stop messing around."

He paused, like he was contemplating something important.

Tanya waited.

"Cross has her sights on Washington, DC," said Ray. "HQ is her next step up. You don't want to be the one jeopardizing that shot for her."

Tanya willed herself to calm down. "I don't give a damn about her career aspi—"

"You need to. She's your boss."

Tanya swore.

"You've never spoken to Susan Cross face to face, have you?" said Ray.

"I've talked to her on the phone twice. Her office lackey is the one who set me up here and sends instructions." She paused. "Why?"

"Most agents do whatever they can to stay off her radar. If you met her, you wouldn't be itching to see her."

"My best friend was just kidnapped. Probably by the same person who abducted the other girls—"

"Why in good lord's name did you invite her over? You're on the job. Not on a family vacation."

Tanya gripped her cell tightly, feeling her fingers dig into the metal.

"You were trained for this," said Ray. "You can take the heat. Help the team and you'll find your pal."

Tanya summoned all her energy and softened her voice.

"I need your help, Ray."

"Look, Stone, I want to help you. I do." Ray let out a sigh. "But I can't."

"You've got ammunition and more computer power than all the local precincts combined. Can you at least open your door for us to use them to track this unsub?"

"If anyone finds out I'm here, you'll be toast. Literally. Heads will roll and you'll have more blood on your hands than just a few missing women."

"Stop talking in riddles, Ray."

"Here's what you need to know," came Ray's voice, more conciliatory. "There's more to this town than just girls gone missing. What happened today is a red herring."

"Asha isn't a red herring!"

"Settle down. I'm trying to help you. Here's what you need to do. Start with the person you least suspect. Who is it?"

"At this moment, it's Chief Bold." She spoke in a low voice, after glancing over her shoulder to see if anyone was near the parking lot. "He's turned around and is doing the right things."

"Don't take everything he says as gospel is all I can say. Watch for cracks in his behavior. Ask yourself why he uses certain tactics. Yes, you work for him undercover so play your role, but be prepared for anything."

"What about the others?" whispered Tanya. "I trust Jones the least."

"Like I said, keep your eyes open."

"How about Lopez and Fox? What about the mayor and the council? Doctor Miller and his nurse? Is there anyone I can trust in this town?"

Ray remained silent.

"Hello? Are you there?"

Tanya pulled the phone away from her ear to check if she had lost the connection. She hadn't.

"Talk to me!"

Ray's voice came back online, muffled and crackly. "I've kept this line open for too long."

"Wait a sec." Tanya's voice turned hard. "You know the town, and you know the people. Why did Cross choose me when she had a more qualified candidate right here by Black Rock?"

"You're a rookie but you have the experience of a veteran," said Ray. "Being new to the bureau means you're not a jaded old geezer like me. You want to prove yourself and she knows you will and can do anything she asks. She's one smart woman."

"I'm not asking why she picked me. I'm asking why she didn't pick *you*."

"I'm retired."

"Horse manure. And I have a bridge to sell you."

Tanya heard him take a deep breath in.

"If anyone in this town learns of my true identity, I'd be as good as dead."

"Who's got it in for you?" asked Tanya.

"You know the rules, Stone. The Need-to-Know policy applies."

"If anyone needs to know, it's me. Give me a break—"

"If you think you're in need of a break now, brace yourself, because the games are just beginning."

Chapter Forty-nine

A SHA

Asha rubbed her fatigued eyes.

It was dark.

A thick, pungent smell permeated the air. It took a while for her to place it. It was the tangy odor of cleaning chemicals.

Her head was woozy and her muscles were strained like she had run a marathon. Her stomach roiled, and for a moment, she wondered if she was going to vomit.

She was sitting on something semi-soft.

She put her hand down and felt underneath her thighs. Her hand pushed into the material. It was a cushion. No, a mattress. She could feel something soft by her toes, but she didn't dare reach over to touch it.

Behind her shoulders was something hard and cold to the touch. *A headboard? A concrete wall?*

The feeling of being watched, the same feeling she had gotten when she walked out of Lulu's Café, washed over her.

She froze, holding her breath.

Is anyone else in here?

She wanted to look around, but she was immobile with fear, wondering what horrific nightmare she had woken up to.

It took a minute for the feeling to pass. Asha started breathing again, short, shallow breaths.

She assessed her surroundings.

An eerie blue light was emanating from a corner, the only illumination in this nebulous space. She squinted to see better, but her eyelids felt heavy, like something strong was pulling them shut again. The more she focused on the light, the blurrier it got.

What's wrong with me?

Asha waited, hugging her knees until her eyes grew accustomed to the darkness.

She could now see the four walls surrounding her. She was in a small windowless room. The only items in here were the cot she was on and whatever created that strange blue light in the corner.

Other than her breathing, she could hear nothing. The room was enveloped in a quiet and uncanny silence, like the walls and the door were soundproofed.

She turned her head around.

I'm alone.

For a moment, she wasn't sure whether to feel relieved or terrified that she was by herself. That was when she saw the outline of a door to her left, several feet from her cot.

What's on the other side?

Asha willed her feet to swing over the bed, but her limbs seemed to have a mind of their own. She felt her calves and feet, wondering for one horrifying moment if she'd lost them.

No, her body was still intact.

She was wearing the same yoga tights and shirt she had put on that morning, if it was still the same day. She felt around the cot to see if her phone was buried somewhere, but she found nothing but sheets and a blanket.

Asha turned her attention back to the blue light.

A computer!

A small beige desktop that looked like it had time traveled from the nineties was sitting on a steel stand in the corner. That was when she noticed the round black object protruding from the wall several feet above the stand.

Asha wracked her muddled brain.

I've seen that thing before...

A quiver of fear shot through her as she realized what it was. It was a surveillance camera. She was right. Someone was watching her.

Her mind raged.

Who are you?

What do you want with me?

The questions came in fast and furiously. That was the jolt of energy she needed. Asha's brain cleared, and she felt her limbs again.

Using all her stamina, she pushed her feet to the edge of the cot and swung them over. She recoiled as her naked feet touched the bare floor.

Where are my boots?

Taking another deep breath in, she pushed herself into a standing position. Her legs wobbled. She reached out to the wall to stabilize herself. Placing one foot in front of the other, and feeling like she was moving through a thick fog, she advanced toward the door.

She reached for the knob and grasped the cold metal. She twisted it to the left and pulled hard. Neither the knob nor the door budged. She turned it to the right and pulled. Nothing. It didn't even make a sound. The door was airtight. And locked.

She jiggled the knob desperately, but she was only wasting precious energy.

Asha let go and stepped back as another idea flashed through her brain. There had to be a light switch somewhere. She touched the wall by the door, but all she could feel was the smooth concrete surface.

She was in a prison.

There was no denying it.

Her breath was getting shallow again. Her chest constricted with claustrophobia. The walls were closing in and the room felt smaller.

Asha closed her eyes to settle her nerves.

I'll figure this out, like I did all those other times.

She opened her eyes and rotated in the direction of the computer terminal. She hadn't heard a hum or ping from it. She plodded toward it, her feet more solid on the ground as her legs felt stronger.

The flickering screen was filled with graphs and charts. The titles and labels all read like scientific gobbledygook to her. The computer itself was a lone piece of equipment which wasn't attached to any wires. There was no keyboard or mouse to access it either.

Is it a touchscreen?

She reached toward the monitor and put a finger on a chart. It didn't move. She pressed her fingers on the images, numbers, and letters, but they remained static.

She pulled her hand back, disappointed.

Is someone operating this computer remotely?

She lifted her chin and stared at the camera above her, wishing she could rip it off the wall, but it was too high.

With a resigned sigh, she turned back toward the bed. Her heart leaped to her mouth as she spotted another, smaller door.

An exit!

She stepped toward it and grabbed the handle. She jumped back in surprise as the door flew back in her hands. As soon as her heart soared at the thought her escape was near, she realized what she was looking at.

A toilet.

A bathroom with a ceramic sink, commode, and nothing else. There were no windows or exits from this closet-sized room. There was no light switch either, and if she closed the door, it was as dark as midnight inside.

She stepped back into the main room, her mind spinning.

A cot, a toilet, a computer, and a security camera. And that smell of disinfectant.

With a horrifying shudder, she realized where she was. Someone had kidnapped her and brought her to the town's mental asylum.

Asha whirled around and stomped over to the main door. This time, she pummeled on it.

"Let me out!" she screamed.

Chapter Fifty

B old deployed the entire team.

Tanya got Max to sniff each of the missing girl's clothes and follow their scents, but only the most recent trails led anywhere.

Max kept trotting from Laura Fredrickson and Nancy Stewart's homes to the main bus stop in the East End, only to turn around and give Tanya a doleful look. All traces of the girls who'd disappeared prior to them had vanished a long time ago.

"This confirms the last two got on the bus," said Bold as he watched Tanya offer her dog a treat as a reward. "The question is where did they get off."

Asha's baseball cap didn't take Max anywhere in the East End, which meant she hadn't been brought to this part of the town.

Time was running out.

Whenever someone went missing, the probability of finding them alive diminished with every passing hour.

Tanya usually held her wits about her, but having someone so close taken so suddenly while on her watch wreaked havoc in her head. A chill went through her as an image of Asha being strapped to an electric chair, gagged and bound, flashed through her mind.

That's not helping, she scolded herself silently.

After two hours of exhaustive searching, the crew returned to the station empty handed.

They had found no more diaries, hidden messages, photos, or clues that would tell them where the teens or Asha had been taken. All the girls' cell phones were still missing.

Max sat by Tanya's feet in the bullpen, as the team brainstormed their next steps.

"Dead ends." Fox rubbed his tired eyes. "At least, the families cooperated today."

Bold gave his receptionist a nod. "Thanks to Wilma who paved the way for us."

"Just doing my bit," said Wilma with a small smile.

Bold's face turned grim. "The sad thing is they believe their daughters are alive. I'm afraid the news we're going to give them might not be good."

"We found one interesting thing," said Lopez as she flipped through her notes. "Every one of the girls fought with a parent about a skimpy skirt before they disappeared, even the girls who vanished last year."

"That could mean the unsub knew them well," said Bold. "They got close enough to the girls to convince them what to wear and fueled the teenage rebellious fire in them."

"So, it's someone from the East End then?" said Fox.

Bold scrunched his forehead. "I don't want us to make that assumption too quickly."

Tanya turned to Lopez. "Find anything inside the gated compound?"

Lopez shook her head. "No one heard or saw a thing. We got a few housekeepers but most of the owners were home. Everyone opened their doors to talk for a few minutes, but without a warrant, there wasn't much we could search."

Tanya sat up. "If a thorn pricked Laura's elbow as the doctor says, she was running through thorny bushes while trying to escape. That's one reason for that trickle of blood on her arm."

"The front yards in that neighborhood are all flat lawns, cedar hedges, and swimming pools," said Lopez. "If anyone's growing thorny flowerbeds or bushes, it would be in their backyards."

"Which we don't have access to," said Bold, shaking his head.

"Did you try the mayor's house?" asked Fox.

"We got his butler," said Lopez. "Bailey wasn't in."

"I've called the judge several times now about the warrants." Bold rubbed the back of his neck in frustration. "I have his direct line, but it always reverts to his danged assistant who tells me he's not available."

Jones snickered. "He's out golfing."

Tanya caught looks of contempt on Lopez and Fox's faces. That angry flush crept up Bold's neck again. But Jones might have a point.

"The judge could be evading you." Tanya gave Bold a pointed look. "He could be part of this."

Even Mayor Bailey.

"We're gonna talk conspiracy theories now?" said Jones, raising an eyebrow.

The chief shook his head. "Things move slowly in small towns, Stone. It's been a culture shock for me too, after Chicago."

He turned to Fox. "Did you dig up anything on that photo with the electric chairs?"

"No fingerprints," said Fox. "Other than Stone's and Kade's, it was clean."

"What about the girls in the picture?"

"Too grainy to make out their faces. Someone made that photo to look like it had been taken from a nineteenth-century camera, but I'm betting all my money it's recent. Whoever did this is good."

"I feel like we're pulling on a bunch of strings but none of them are connected," said Lopez, rubbing her tired face.

"What about the mental hospital?" said Tanya.

Wilma shook her head. "I know these girls. They have such wild imaginations. To be honest, you'll be wasting your time going there."

Tanya remembered her drive into Black Rock that first day. The lonely road that curved its way up the wooded hill and that solitary "H" sign on the road had felt out of place.

Ominous, even.

Tanya turned to the team. "How many people are getting sick for this tiny town to build an entire hospital here?"

"It's not a proper hospital, and it's not *that* big," said Wilma. "Not many folk stay there for long, anyway."

"I know one person who got stuck in the asylum for years," piped up Jones.

All eyes turned to him.

"Someone you all know, too."

Chapter Fifty-one

Tanya's spider senses tingled.

Jones rarely opened up.

Fox leaned back in his chair and looked at his colleague with interest. "Care to share?"

Jones shifted in his seat, as if he regretted the impromptu revelation, but the look in his eyes told Tanya he knew exactly what he was doing.

"Forget it," said Jones with a nonchalant shrug. "I don't know anything."

"You just said you knew," snapped Lopez.

Tanya could feel a strange electric current in the air, like everyone was on edge.

Her mind raced.

She recalled Bold's disturbing childhood story. When she'd asked him where his father was, he'd said, "*Where he belongs. Locked up for good.*"

She had assumed he was doing life in a state or federal prison, but he could have been sent to Black Rock's psychiatric institution, if deemed mentally unstable enough.

Is Bold's father T&D?

Tanya's eyes moved to Officer Jones sitting in the corner, a superior sneer on his face as usual.

Didn't Wilma say Jones grew up in a violent family too? 'Pathologically violent' had been her exact words.

Is Jones T&D?

Lopez leaned over to Jones, curiosity burning in her eyes. "Who is it? Tell us."

Before Jones could say anything, Wilma reached over and patted his arm. "It's not very nice to talk about neighbors behind their backs. Gossiping is so mean."

Bold sat up, a strange expression on his face. "Seems like you know who it is, Wilma."

The receptionist's mouth turned upside down.

"Well?" said Lopez. "Aren't you going to tell us?"

Wilma screwed her face. "Well, there's Joseph."

"Who's Joseph?" said Fox.

"My neighbor's son," said Wilma. "We're not supposed to say retarded anymore, but that's what everyone called him those days. His parents couldn't do much. They had three other children to take care of and he was such a handful. That boy had so many problems—"

"Who else?" Tanya spoke in a sharper tone than she'd intended.

Wilma is always all over the place.

"There's poor little Sally. She's deaf, blind, and can't talk. Her mom and pop couldn't afford to send her to a specialist, so they stuck her in there and forgot about her. So sad. But what can you do? It's not like they were terrible parents. They did their best, you know?"

Tanya leaned in. "Who's in that hospital right now that's connected to this team?"

Wilma pursed her lips, like she wasn't about to disclose any secrets.

"It's Liz," came Jones's voice.

Wilma shot him an angry glance, like he'd divulged a town secret no one was supposed to talk about.

"Who's Liz?" said Fox, exasperation showing on his face.

"Elizabeth Miller," said Jones.

Wilma shook her head sadly. "That poor girl. Such a hard life—"

Tanya put a hand up to stop her and turned to Officer Jones.

"Did you say *Miller*? As in related to our Dr. Miller?"

"That's what I said, didn't I?" said Jones. "Do I have to spell out the name for you, too?"

"I thought Dr. Miller had no family alive," said Fox.

"She's Miller's sister," said Jones.

"He never mentioned this to me," said Bold.

"Dr. Miller is a very private man," said Wilma.

"I'd guess Miller wouldn't want anyone to know he has a connection with the asylum," said Lopez, a thoughtful expression coming over her. "That would be the end of his lucrative practice with the West Enders."

Wilma gave her a stern look.

"Do you think that poor man wants to be reminded of what happened so long ago?"

"What happened?" said Fox and Lopez at the same time.

Wilma glanced down at her hands on her lap, her lips moving silently, like she was praying.

"Why was his sister institutionalized?" said Tanya, exasperation in her voice.

It was Jones who answered.

"Liz tried to kill herself. That's why."

Tanya was sure she caught a glint in his eyes.

He's mocking us.

Chapter Fifty-two

Wilma's face scrunched like she was about to cry.

"That poor girl got locked up ages ago. Lots of wicked gossip those days. I'd never spread rumors like that."

"What rumors?" said Lopez.

"Liz got pregnant at fifteen," said Jones, his smirk widening.

Tanya glared at him. He was enjoying how this awkward conversation was unraveling and he especially seemed to revel in Wilma's discomfort.

You're one creepy man.

Wilma sighed heavily.

"It was a boy from her school. Everyone tried to hush it up, but the poor baby died. Then, their father had a fatal heart attack. So, Dr. Miller was left alone to look after his sister. He wasn't even eighteen."

"How did Liz's baby die?" asked Fox.

"Sudden infant death syndrome," said Jones. "Or so they said."

"Oh, little Zachary." Wilma wiped a tear from her eye. "He never got to see life past his fifth day on earth. Burying a baby is a heart-wrenching thing."

Tanya frowned.

Zachary.

Where did I hear that name before?

She remembered the first day she'd met Dr. Miller.

He had been with Mayor Bailey in Bold's office. The mayor had gushed over how much the doctor had donated to the town's charities. The doctor had said he was only paying it forward, helping a town that had supported his family during a difficult period.

She was sure it was during that conversation Zachary's name had popped up. But for the life of her, she couldn't remember how or why.

"What about Miller's mother?" said Fox. "Where was she all this time?"

"Passed away, giving birth to Liz years ago," said Wilma with another sigh.

"All that trauma must have left a mark on him," said Lopez with a tsk.

"That would explain his chronic stutter," said Fox.

Tanya's brow furrowed. "Does Miller moonlight at the psychiatric hospital?"

Wilma gave her a shocked look. "Heavens, no. Why on earth would he do that? He's got a very good clinic in town. He doesn't need the extra money."

"Miller's not a loony doc, Stone." Jones sneered. "He fixes broken legs and gives flu shots. There's a difference, you know."

Tanya ignored the jab. "Why didn't he open his clinic on the West End, where he and his clients live? Wouldn't that have been more convenient?"

"Because this is where his father started his practice. His father was a doctor too, didn't you know?"

A leer crossed Jones' face. It was the face of a man who knew something that no one else did and was watching them fumble in glee.

"Does he visit his sister at the hospital often?" said Tanya, trying to wrestle the conversation back on track.

Wilma shook her head.

"Last time he went to see Liz, it was five years ago. They say she stabbed him with a crochet needle. It was news all over town. You can't blame her. She's really gone in the head. He doesn't go there anymore."

Tanya's spine tingled. She was missing something important, something staring in her face, but she couldn't pinpoint it.

"He's a fine doctor," said Wilma. "He gives free checkups to our neighborhood, and he never takes our money. Ask Miranda and Hannah. Ask anyone in the East End. We shouldn't talk about his private affairs like this. This is so wrong."

"This could apply to our case," said Tanya.

"He's a good man!" Wilma blurted, her voice quavering in anger.

Bold got up and raised his hands.

"This conversation is over. Dr. Miller is a colleague. If we have questions, we can ask him to his face."

Tanya rubbed her eyes, wondering if she was letting the paranoia from her combat days overcome her. What she needed was a sober second voice, like Asha's.

Her stomach fell as she realized they were no where nearer to finding her than when she had vanished.

"Let's show some professionalism, people," Bold was saying. "We need to give Dr. Miller the same respect as we would want. If the tables were turned, you'd want that too, wouldn't you?"

Before anyone could reply, the phone in his office rang. Bold spun on his heels and marched inside.

Tanya got up and walked over to the exit. "Come, Max."

"Where are you heading off to?" called Lopez.

"I don't have time to sit around and chitchat," said Tanya.

"We have protocol and policy to follow, Stone."

"You do. I don't."

"Do you even have a plan?" said Fox.

Tanya turned to face the officers in the bullpen.

"My plan? Catch the unsub before anything happens to Asha."

"How are you going to do that?" asked Jones.

"Find T&D and make him talk."

Chapter Fifty-three

Tanya stepped out of the station, her mind in a flurry.

She was glad Max was with her. Asha's disappearance had hit her like a sickening punch to the stomach, but having her furry companion softened the blow somewhat.

She strode through the station's parking lot, heading toward Dr. Miller's clinic. She remembered how he'd stuttered and stammered as they discussed the autopsy results. He knew something, but didn't or couldn't articulate it.

There was also an elephant in the room no one was talking about.

Mayor Bailey.

He pulled the strings of everybody in this town. The doctor, like everyone else, was just a pawn.

She had distrusted the mayor ever since she met him. Her gut had sent alarm bells as she'd reached to shake his hand. She was now sure he was behind Laura's death and the girls' disappearances.

Is he running a kidnapping ring? A trafficking racket? Or is this an underground cult?

She still didn't know why the girls had gone missing or why they would take her friend, but the bigger puzzle was getting clearer.

This was why Susan Cross and Ray Jackson had been so cautious.

The corruption that rained down on Black Rock came from the highest echelons, but the FBI didn't have sufficient evidence to stop the culprits. A premature or false accusation would only make the unsubs scurry underground. She had to tread cautiously.

Tanya stopped in her tracks as a more troubling thought flashed across her mind.

Did the corruption go all the way to the FBI? Is this why Cross is so cagey? Is someone from the bureau engaged in criminal activity right under her nose?

This could explain why Ray Jackson refused to share information, claiming Need to Know.

She glanced down at Max who was standing by her feet, his head cocked to the side.

"First, we'll find Asha and the girls. Then, we'll figure out what disease is eating this town, okay, bud?"

She continued on the path. Max moved assuredly, like he knew where they were supposed to be heading.

Tanya stepped up to the front entrance. The blue BMW was no longer in front of the clinic but the white Audi was.

This time, she didn't ask Max to stay in the parking lot. She let him sniff Asha's cap again and gave the search command before opening the door.

Nurse Norma was bustling behind the counter, but had her jacket on, like she was about to leave. The waiting area was empty.

Max started sniffing around the room, his nose to the ground, working fast. After giving him a head start, Tanya strode up to the front desk and knocked on the counter.

"Where's Miller?"

Norma whipped around.

Tanya took a step back in shock.

The nurse looked like she had been in a bar fight. She had a cut on her nose, a bruise on her forehead, and a white gauze that partly covered what looked like a fresh burn scar on her left cheek.

"I don't believe you have an appointment," said the nurse with a scowl.

"I don't need one," said Tanya. "I'd like to speak with him immediately."

"He's not here. We're closing."

Though she was projecting a confident voice, Norma didn't have her usual self-assured poise.

What happened to her?

Tanya glanced down at Max who had returned to sit by her heels, and was waiting for his next command. Her heart fell as she realized Asha wasn't in this clinic either.

What about the other girls?

She spun around and popped her head into the physician's examination room.

"Hey," called out Norma. "Who do you think you are, coming in here like this?"

The exam room was empty. Tanya whirled around and marched toward the surgery.

"You can't go in there!" shouted Norma.

Stop me, thought Tanya as she flung the door open and stepped inside the anteroom with Max. From behind her, she heard Nurse Norma grab the phone on her desk.

Go right ahead, thought Tanya. *Call the chief. But you won't stop me from finding Asha and the girls.*

She pushed the surgery doors open.

The bright lights had been shut off. The room was empty and had been scrubbed clean, but in the darkness, the surgical robotics and the empty steel gurneys looked even more nightmarish.

She wrinkled her nose as she spotted the fridge with the glass doors again. The rows of plastic bags containing blood sat next to a jar with a human heart. Or, at least, what looked like one.

Is that Laura's heart?

No one could take a cadaver's organs without permission from their family. The thought of anyone ripping a heart from a dead body made her want to retch. She was glad for the overpowering, pungent smell of Lysol.

Tanya stepped up to the nearest cabinet and yanked on the handle. *Medical equipment.* She moved to the next cabinet and the next. She scoured the room, searching for hiding places, secret compartments, or invisible exits.

She pulled open a large steel drawer on the far wall and almost jumped out of her skin. It was Laura Fredrickson, lying on a steel slab. Cold air rose from her stitched-up body.

Why isn't she covered?

The surgery door banged open, and Norma barged in. She rushed toward Tanya and slammed the cadaver fridge drawer shut.

"How dare you? I'm going to tell the whole town how you came in here, harassing us!" She pointed a furious finger at Tanya. "This is a private medical facility! When the mayor hears about this, he'll fire you!"

I've heard that before.

Tanya had noticed the limp in the nurse's gait as she had come in. She looked Norma up and down, wondering if she'd had a hand in Asha's disappearance.

"Go right ahead," said Tanya. "You might stop me, but you'll be on the line to answer a few questions too."

Norma's eyes widened.

"Where's the doctor?"

The nurse glared. Her legs were set apart and her hands were clenched into fists, like she was ready to throw a punch. Tanya wasn't worried. She would be making a big mistake if she attacked her. A deep, throaty growl came from Max, as if he concurred too.

Norma's eyes narrowed. "The doctor's whereabouts is none of your business."

"It is when my friend gets kidnapped."

The nurse's face flushed red. "What are you insinuating?"

"Who approved the autopsy report on Laura? It said she died a natural death with no identifiable causes. Curious, don't you think?" Tanya's voice cut like steel.

The nurse opened her mouth to speak, then clamped it shut again.

Tanya pointed at the cadaver drawer. "What are you hiding in there?"

"How dare you accuse us like this!"

"You're withholding evidence. Asha found out and now she's gone too."

Norma's neck throbbed like she was about to blow a vessel. "You know nothing!"

"I know more than you think I know. Is Mayor Bailey pulling on your strings too, Norma?"

The nurse spluttered like she was choking on her saliva.

"We're all doing everything we can to stop this madness," she said. "This is why the mayor hired Chief Bold. To find the girls, not harass and accuse the good citizens of this town."

"Then you should have no problem with me asking about the autopsy report."

Norma's face fell.

Tanya waited, feeling a shift in her stance.

When the nurse looked up, her eyes were no longer filled with fury. She let out a resigned sigh and shifted her feet, as if she had decided to tell the truth for a change.

"Dr. Miller never came in today."

Chapter Fifty-four

"**M**ayor Bailey called this morning," said Norma.

Tanya raised a brow. "Why am I not surprised to hear that?"

"The mayor's been feeling under the weather lately."

"He looked pretty healthy the last time I saw him."

"We don't judge. When our patients call, we tend to them."

"Where's the doctor right now?"

"Still at the Bailey residence."

"A whole day for a house call?"

"He's a demanding patient." The nurse looked unsettled all of a sudden. "Since the doctor's there, he probably asked him to check on the rest of the family and the domestics."

"Is your good doctor one of his puppets too?"

Norma glared. "How can you speak of him like that? You don't know him. You don't know any of us. You're just an outsider."

So are you, thought Tanya, but she kept that to herself.

"If you're so keen to find out where the doctor is, why don't you go to the mayor's house and see for yourself?"

"I mean to," said Tanya.

Norma pointed a finger toward the door.

"Then leave right now and stop harassing me. Get out!"

Tanya gave a low whistle to Max. She wouldn't get anything from her, not in this state.

"Time to go, bud," she said, brushing past the fuming nurse.

Tanya and Max stepped out of the clinic doors and walked back to the station's parking lot.

When she got to her Jeep, she checked the front and back windshields for notes and bent down to check the undercarriage, while Max trotted around the car, sniffing.

"Stone!"

Tanya whipped around.

It was Lopez.

What does she want?

The officer jogged over. "Do you always check your car for detonators?"

Tanya shrugged, trying to look casual. "Habit from combat days."

"You can't go off like this, Stone. We have a process to follow."

Tanya opened the back door for Max to jump in. "One girl has already turned up in a ditch. What are the chances the others are dead or are getting close to?"

"Bold's going to be mad as heck when he finds you've gone AWOL."

"Where's he now?"

"On the phone with the mayor."

Maybe Ray Jackson was right. Maybe the chief was in this too. He could be stalling her, stopping her from finding out what was really going on.

"What are they talking about?" said Tanya.

"All I know is they're having an argument again." Lopez paused, a worried expression coming over her face. "I don't think the new boss will last long."

"What are you talking about?"

"If this keeps up, Bailey will get rid of Bold."

"He can't just fire the chief. He'll have to justify it."

"Bailey has more clout than you think."

"Well, you're next in line," said Tanya, her voice dry. "Congratulations, Chief Lopez."

Lopez shook her head. "The mayor won't be looking to me. Jones will get the job and that won't be good."

We agree on one thing, thought Tanya.

When Lopez spoke again, her voice was heavy. "We need to find those girls. They're not just victims. They're somebody's kids, sisters. These cases have been ignored for far too long."

She paused.

"You going off on your own isn't helping. If you know something, you need to share it with us so we can tackle this case together."

Tanya stared at her for a second. Lopez had sounded sincere about the girls, but she would only slow her down.

She stepped over to the driver's side door. "I can't sit around waiting for you guys to get your act together. I need to find my friend. Alive."

She jumped in the Jeep and turned the engine.

The last image she saw of Lopez was through her rearview mirror. She was standing next to her squad car, hands on her hips, staring at the back of her disappearing Jeep.

Tanya wished she could trust her. She wanted to depend on Fox and Bold too. Even the flighty Wilma.

She raced down the narrow streets of Black Rock, bearing down on the accelerator. The Jeep's engine roared.

In the back, Max barked like he understood the urgency of the situation.

Tanya glanced at him through the rearview mirror.

"It's time to meet the man behind the curtain, bud."

Chapter Fifty-five

I t took Tanya fifteen minutes to drive up the hill toward the gated community.

She sped up the steep incline. Unlike Miranda and Hannah's neighborhood set among the backwoods, this suburban West End had spectacular ocean views.

She slowed down as she came across a white double gate on top of the hill. The road ended here.

On one side was the sheer cliff that dropped to the shore about fifty feet below. On the other side was the twelve-foot whitewashed wall that meandered around the compound and seemed to go on forever.

Several miles farther along this wall, they had found Laura Fredrickson taking her last breaths.

Tanya stared at the barrier, knowing she could climb over it. But she needed solid evidence to justify breaking into this upscale private community. There were limits to how many rules she could bend, without getting yanked back to Seattle, or worse, losing her actual job.

She gazed out at the view, trying to clear her head.

She could smell an oncoming storm. The sun, which had been shining all morning, was disappearing behind a gray cloud. The wind was picking up, and the waves looked bigger. Soon those rain clouds would spread over town.

Fitting, thought Tanya as she drummed her fingers on the steering wheel.

Think, girl, think.

She sat up.

When things were muddled and the path wasn't clear, the best course of action was *action.*

She jumped out of the vehicle and stepped up to the intercom on the side of the gate. Just above the numbered pad was a small security camera. Ignoring it, she scanned the list of residents until she found what she was looking for.

"Bailey."

She pushed the buzzer next to number twenty-three.

She leaned against the wall, waiting for the crackle of the intercom. It would probably be the butler, she thought.

What can I say to convince him to let me in?

That was when a metallic clang came from behind her. Inside the Jeep, Max barked in warning.

Tanya whipped around.

The gates were opening.

Is someone coming out?

She peered through the gap to the driveway, but there were no vehicles waiting on the other side.

Tanya stared at the camera. Someone had seen her.

That was easy. Too easy.

The entrance was wide open now. Tanya jumped into the Jeep and put it in gear before whoever opened the gates changed their mind.

She rolled through the opening into what seemed like a magical land.

Palm trees lined the cobblestoned driveway. The lush lawns on either side of the path were manicured to perfection. Set back and nestled among the verdant gardens were the mega mansions.

Some were modern with floor-to-ceiling glass walls. Others were styled like Spanish villas with red-tiled roofs and stucco walls. Every one of them had tiered garden terraces and kidney-shaped pools in front.

A few of the houses were barricaded behind high fences, so only their top floors were visible from the driveway.

Walls within walls.

Despite the beautiful surroundings, Tanya's shoulders and back were up, like she was expecting an ambush at any moment.

"This isn't an ISIS hotbed in a Middle Eastern desert," she told herself as she drove in low gear. "This is a wealthy suburb on the West Coast of the USA."

She kept her eyes peeled, but no one jumped on her Jeep, threw a hand grenade, or took a shot at her.

She kept driving, scanning the house plates for number twenty-three.

Max thumped his tail and gave an excited bark. A strange, garbled sound made her swing around. A trio of the biggest birds she'd ever seen strutted across the lawn to her left. Two were brown, but the last one had a magnificent tail of shimmery blue.

"These people keep *peacocks* for pets. Can you imagine that, bud?"

She stopped as she realized she'd gone too far, distracted by the flashy birds. She reversed to one house down and scanned the name plate.

Bailey. Number twenty-three.

There was no intercom or phone by this gate, which meant the household only took planned appointments.

What now?

Tanya plucked her phone from her pocket, wondering if the mayor's home number was listed with his office number on the city hall website. She doubted it, but there was no harm in trying.

That was when Max barked.

She looked up to see the gate open, operated remotely just like those in front.

Her gut tightened as she watched the steel barrier glide back, exposing a three-story manor set several yards away on the top of a cliff. She could hear the ocean waves crashing below.

Other than that, it was eerily quiet in the walled-off grounds.

Tanya pulled out her Glock.

Someone wants to see me as badly as I want to see them.

Chapter Fifty-six

Tanya rolled through the opening.

The grounds were expansive but empty.

A loud metallic clang told her the gates had shut behind her. A jagged silver rod flashed from the heavens, followed by a clap of thunder from above. The storm was getting closer.

Her shoulders tensed even more.

"We're in the lion's den now," she whispered as she drove along the driveway.

A light rain had begun to fall. The cobblestones were getting slippery, but her tires had good traction. Keeping her eyes on the path but staying alert to her periphery, she kept driving toward the manor.

They passed two modest buildings and an Olympic sized swimming pool along the way. Soon, she rolled into the widened driveway in front of the sprawling three-story mansion.

Parked in a neat row were a black SUV with tinted windows, a black limo, a white Range Rover, and a Mercedes sedan with a vanity plate that read *Mayor*.

Tanya swiveled her head.

Where's Dr. Miller's blue Beemer? Has he left already?

She searched for the best spot to park in case she needed to leave in a hurry. She scanned the other vehicles before stopping at the very end, next to the limo.

"Do you think this is the same limo we saw on our first day, bud?" she said. "Too bad I didn't get the plate, but Wilma was screaming like a banshee at the other end."

Max growled.

She turned to him. "You don't like it here, do you?"

He stood up on all fours, bumped his snout on the back window, then sat back down again.

Tanya picked up her Glock and racked the slide. "Sometimes, I think you have better instincts than me, bud. My head gets clouded with too many ideas. You, on the other hand, are pure intuition."

She stopped as she realized something.

"You've tolerated Bold so far. Come to think of it, you haven't growled at anyone in the team other than Jones. Does this mean I can trust them? What about Ray Jackson? You seem to actually like him."

Max thumped his tail on the seat and whined.

Tanya placed Asha's cap under his nose again.

"Go search, bud." She opened his door to let him out. "If you feel like taking a bite from the mayor's butt, go right ahead. That goes for those goons from the Grimwood Estate too."

As soon as she got out of her Jeep, Tanya felt eyes on her.

She was under surveillance, but that was to be expected. Whoever it was, they had been watching her ever since she pressed the buzzer at the front gates of the compound.

Max was strolling around, sniffing the car tires and tree trunks, but didn't have his snout glued to the ground and that focused expression on his face like he did when he caught a scent. Tanya's stomach sank as she realized Asha might not be here either.

She scanned the driveway, then the house. There wasn't a soul to be seen.

She examined the large bay windows. Most of them had heavy curtains drawn across, but one window on the second floor caught her eye.

An Ivana Trump lookalike was staring down at her, one hand holding the embroidered curtains back.

The mayor's infamous wife.

Tanya stepped away from her Jeep. "Let's go see what they want from us, bud."

She and Max walked past the vehicles on the driveway and stepped up the marble staircase that led to the massive double doors.

Tanya was sure Mrs. Bailey wasn't the only person watching her approach. Her eyes darted to the corners of the house, the roof, then back to the windows, searching for shadows.

Her holstered Glock was loaded and her dominant hand remained on her belt, ready to draw in a split second.

The front door opened before she even got to the top step. A young woman dressed in a black and white maid's uniform stood on the threshold, expressionless.

All the alarm bells in her gut rang, but Tanya maintained her poker face and confident posture. The last thing she would do was give away even a hint of nervousness.

So far, they had let her in with no questions asked. She jumped up the remaining steps, wondering how she was going to explain her unconventional visit, out of the blue.

"Ms. Stone?" said the maid, preempting her from figuring out what to say first.

Tanya nodded.

The maid opened the door wider. Tanya took a step closer, thinking this was an invitation to enter, when she spotted the immense shadow lurking behind the woman.

A burly man, who looked like a WWF wrestler in a gray suit, stepped around the maid and blocked the entrance. He moved his jacket ever so slightly to show his sidearm.

"Your weapon, please," he said in a soft voice, holding his hand out.

"I don't lend my gun to anyone," said Tanya.

"Then you can't come in," replied the maid, speaking in a monotone like she was more robot than human.

Tanya looked her over. The maid's posture and tone were self-assured and her body was trim and fit. This was no housemaid. This was a security personnel in disguise.

The sound of heels clicking on the marble floor came from inside the house. Tanya glanced over the maid's shoulder.

It was the mayor's wife. She stopped and stared at Tanya for three full seconds before spinning around on her heels and disappearing from view.

"She won't see you if you bring that in," said the maid, pointing at Tanya's belt.

"I came to see Mayor Bailey."

"He's occupied at the moment."

"I heard he's with Dr. Miller," said Tanya. "I'm here to talk to both of them."

The maid frowned. "Dr. Miller isn't here."

"Didn't he come in this morning to see the mayor?"

"Dr. Miller hasn't been here for weeks."

Tanya frowned. Who was the liar? Nurse Norma or the mayor's security guard dressed as a maid?

"I can wait for the mayor until he's free, then." Tanya gestured toward the lawn. "Happy to wait out here all night if I have to."

The maid glared. Tanya held her gaze. Neither spoke. For a moment Tanya felt like she was in a fight club, facing her opponent, waiting for the bell to ring.

The WWF lookalike leaned closer as if he was about to tell her a secret. Tanya didn't move a muscle, her hand still on her holster.

"It's Mrs. Bailey who invited you in," he whispered.

"Why?"

"She wants to talk to you. Privately."

Chapter Fifty-seven

T anya leaned back in surprise.

"Why does she want to see me?"

"You'll have to ask her that," said the maid.

Tanya's mind raced.

This could be a trap. Then again, walking through those doors meant she was putting herself and Max in potential danger, regardless of who lured her in.

Does the mayor's wife know where Asha is? Does she know what happened to those girls? Is Asha here, hidden somewhere?

Tanya pointed at Max. "You can have my weapon but he's coming with me."

The maid's face didn't change. "Mrs. Bailey will see you in the drawing room."

Tanya pulled out her weapon and slapped it on the WWF wrestler's fat palm.

"I want this in my line of sight at all times."

The man opened his mouth to answer, but a butler's bell rang from deep down in the corridor, stopping him.

He gestured to Tanya. "This way."

She stepped into the hallway with Max, her boots sinking into the plush Persian runner. Flanked by the maid and the guard, she started walking along the corridor.

The engraved ceiling, and the gold framed paintings that lined the red-paneled walls made her feel like she had entered an oligarch's home in Moscow.

On the outside, the house had looked like a modern mansion. But the inside was decorated in opulent antique Russian decor that belonged to a century ago.

Though the hallway was spacious, Tanya couldn't help but feel claustrophobic. It was like the wood-paneled walls were closing in on her, sucking the air out of her lungs. Dark clouds were gathering in her brain, paranoia threatening to overcome her senses.

Focus, girl, focus.

Max followed her obediently, giving no signals he had picked up a scent. Tanya's brain raced as she tried to figure out how to get him to search this massive house without having the guards draw their weapons on them.

Asha and the girls could be in a sealed basement or in the attic, and no one would know. Not even Max.

Think, girl, think.

Her escorts stopped at a large door made of carved wood. After a light knock, the male guard clicked it open.

Tanya gawked.

A massive crystal chandelier hung from the high ceiling, its golden light bouncing off the ornate walls. The expansive windows overlooking the ocean made the space seem even larger than it was. Even with the stormy clouds above and the light rain coming down, the view was magnificent from up here.

But it was the sole occupant of this room who had captured Tanya's attention.

A heavily made-up, middle-aged blonde woman in a fur-trimmed suit sat in an Empress chair by the fireplace. In her hand was a tumbler filled with a translucent liquid.

Vodka?

The mayor's wife didn't get up as Tanya and the ushers entered the room. A semblance of a smile crossed her blood-red lips as Max trotted in after them.

More than ever, Tanya felt like she had fallen down a rabbit hole into the extraordinary world of Alice in Wonderland. And now she was about to meet the Queen of Hearts.

Tanya automatically reached for her sunflower pendant. Something about the woman gave her an urge to call for her mother's protection.

The male guard gestured toward the second Empress chair next to the fireplace.

I don't even know her name, thought Tanya as she crossed the room toward her hostess.

"*Zdravstvuyte*," said the woman as Tanya sat down.

"*Zdravstvuyte*," repeated Tanya, stunned at the formal greeting. "You're Russian."

The woman bowed her head slightly. "My family descends from the House of Romanov."

The mayor's wife spoke in an accented but flawless English.

Tanya's eyebrows shot up. "Russian *royalty*?"

"Not today, obviously. My lineage goes far back to those days when the world was a much better place than it is now."

Right. When you had peasants for slaves.

Tanya opened her mouth to reply but shut it again. What do you say to someone who just mentioned their royal pedigree?

She's a fraud. She has to be.

But the woman's bright blue eyes pierced through her, like they cut right into her soul.

She may not have royal blood, but she's a witch, all right.

Mrs. Bailey let out a sigh as if she could see the storm raging in Tanya's head.

"You're still new to town, my dear. You have much to learn. I, on the other hand, know more about you than you know about me."

It took every ounce of patience for Tanya to sit still.

"How do you know about me?"

"This is a small town," replied Mrs. Bailey.

"Why did you want to see me?"

"I wanted to get a good look at you."

"Do you always invite newcomers in to get a good look at them?"

"Only the special ones."

Tanya bit her tongue, restraining herself from shouting at her. This woman didn't fight with fire. She fought with words and emotions, and that made her even more dangerous.

"You're worried, I see." Mrs. Bailey nodded to the maid who was standing by the door with the guard. "A drink for this young lady, please."

Tanya put a hand up to say no. She gave the mayor's wife a steely look.

"My friend was just kidnapped in broad daylight."

"I heard. I hope you find her soon."

"Can you tell me where she is?"

The woman raised a perfectly shaped eyebrow but didn't respond. A grandfather clock chimed in a corner of the room. As if on cue, a flash of lightning came through the bay windows.

This place gave Tanya the creeps.

For a semi-second, she wondered if the missing girls' screams were being stifled underneath the floorboards of the drawing room. Mrs. Bailey seemed just like the type of person who would do something horrific like that.

Tanya took a deep breath in to settle her nerves. It was time to talk straight.

"The least you can do is tell me if my friend is still alive."

"If I knew, I would tell you."

The expression on the woman's face seemed genuine. She was searching Tanya's face, sizing her up.

Tanya's brain whirled.

Something wasn't right. Why go to all this trouble just to see a contractor?

That was when the realization hit her.

This is a show.

A diversion.

Chapter Fifty-eight

Tanya was about to get up when Mrs. Bailey leaned closer.

"They were right," she whispered.

Tanya leaned away from the woman. "About what?"

"You have Slavic features."

"Who are *they*?"

"You're from the Motherland."

"I'm Ukrainian. Not Russian."

"Your tone is judgmental, my dear."

"I only judge by the content of your character."

Mrs. Bailey fluttered her prettily painted eyelids. "What good does rekindling fights from our home countries do here? Don't you think it's time to put our differences aside?"

Tanya scowled. "I didn't come here for a fight. I came to find the missing girls and my friend."

"We're both immigrants in America." Mrs. Bailey shot a discreet glance at the guards by the door. "To them, we're foreigners with no home to go back to."

Tanya stared at her.

Didn't she hear a word I said?

The mayor's wife reached over with a red-tipped fingernail as if to brush Tanya's arm. Tanya pulled back in distaste. She hated being touched by strangers, least of all by a modern-day Cruella de Vil.

Mrs. Bailey smiled. "We're more alike than not, my dear."

Tanya pushed her chair back and stood up. This conversation wasn't making any sense, and she was no closer to finding her friend.

"I didn't come here to entertain you," she snarled.

She whipped around to the guard standing by the door, her gun still in his palm.

"I'd like to see Mayor Bailey and Dr. Miller. Take me to them now."

The guard cleared his throat and turned to the mayor's wife with the deferential bow.

"I already explained to Ms. Stone that Mayor Bailey is occupied, and Dr. Miller isn't here."

Tanya had interrogated enough terrorists to notice the micro facial adjustments of people who harbored secrets. The glance Mrs. Bailey and the guard exchanged told her they weren't telling the whole truth.

The image of the skittish Dr. Miller sprang to mind. It was easy to imagine him being held in the basement of this house, shackled to an electric chair like those girls.

"The chief's office is investigating a slate of serious crimes," said Tanya. "Lives are on the line. I must speak to the mayor."

"What an unfortunate state of affairs." Mrs. Bailey tsked as if someone told her the weather was about to get worse. "Casts a pall over our pretty little town."

I've had enough.

Without a glance at the woman in the Empress chair, Tanya stormed out of the drawing room.

She stopped as the guards closed the door behind her.

What she wanted more than anything was to dive into the belly of this mansion and see what was hiding behind those red-paneled walls. But the guard still had her handgun.

As if she read her mind, the maid lifted her apron a few inches to show her she had a sidearm too.

Max growled.

Tanya was out gunned and outnumbered. The guards glared, as if challenging her to make one wrong move.

Tanya's brain buzzed. She was in their territory. They could easily justify their actions by saying they were defending their home. Getting killed wasn't going to help Asha or the missing girls.

She spun around and marched down the corridor toward the front of the house with Max trotting next to her. The guards followed, their footsteps echoing through the hallway.

"You wasted my time," Tanya growled as she reached for the front door.

She snatched her weapon from the guard and stomped down the steps. Her stomach roiled as she realized she'd been played. The mayor's wife and Nurse Norma had tricked her. Delayed her.

Asha and the girls were still missing.

Please, please be alive.

Chapter Fifty-nine

Tanya got off the freeway and pressed on the gas.

Instead of the medical facility she expected to find sheltered behind the highway, she was on a lonely stretch of road which seemed to wind up the quiet wooded hill for miles.

She followed the signs to the psychiatric institution.

The thunderstorm had teased Black Rock, but the gentle drizzle had never stopped, giving the air a melancholy and brooding feel.

As she drove up the hill, Tanya wondered how deep in the rain forest this hospital was located.

It felt like she had entered another world. This area couldn't be more different from the ocean promenade of Marine Drive or the luxury gated community on the West End. A weight of sadness hung in the air, like the gray clouds above her.

Tanya took yet another curve on the hill and spotted her destination. A handful of red brick bungalows were set in a circle, tucked among the tall evergreens.

A sign in front confirmed this was the establishment she was looking for. It also said smoking, alcohol, and animals were forbidden.

As soon as she parked the Jeep, Max got on all fours, ready to leap out and explore. *I'll have to figure out how to get him inside,* thought Tanya.

She frowned as her eyes swept over the almost empty parking lot.

If Bold was keen to find Asha and the girls, he would have sent his team to the hospital as soon as he had got off the call with the mayor. Lopez or Fox should have been here, but there were no squad cars in the vicinity.

Tanya shook her worries off. Asha's life was on the line and she had already wasted precious time.

She rolled up her window, leaving a gap, enough for Max to get fresh air but too narrow for him to jump through.

"I'll come back for you soon, bud," she called out as she turned to leave. "You can do your magic then."

Pulling her jacket collar up and hunching her shoulders to keep the rain from trickling onto her back, Tanya sprinted to the building in the center. The door opened after just one knock.

A lanky young man, about eighteen years old, in a surfer T-shirt and faded blue jeans stood in the doorway with a bright smile on his face.

"Hi! I'm Joseph!"

"Hello," said Tanya guardedly. "I'm, er, here to speak with someone."

"I can help you!"

Tanya arched a brow. He seemed too young, too enthusiastic, and too casually dressed to be an employee of a psychiatric institution.

He squinted through the open doorway. "Is that your dog?"

"It is."

"I love pups!" He turned to her, eyes wide. "What's his name?"

"Max."

"My uncle had a puppy called Max, too. He was all black, and he became super huge, like yours." He spread his arms as wide as he could to show the size of the dog.

The chronic twitch by his eyes was the only sign something was amiss. That, and this childlike conversation she was having with him.

Tanya glanced over his shoulder, looking for adults. Nurses, doctors, orderlies.

Her eyes widened. This was no ordinary medical facility. There were no unending, white-washed corridors here. There were no industrial fluorescent lights that flickered and drove even the sane insane.

Instead, wooden beams crisscrossed the vaulted ceiling, giving the space an airy feel, and the calming smell of lavender wafted in the air. Pine bookcases lined the walls and comfy armchairs were scattered throughout the lush living room.

A large painting of an eagle hung on one end and a wrought-iron fireplace was on the other. At the center of this room was a high desk with two computers.

The reception desk was empty.

Tanya had expected to see patients ambling aimlessly in hospital gowns and overworked staff in scrubs running around with harried expressions on their faces. Instead, the handful of people here were sitting, reading, knitting, or drinking tea or coffee.

She felt like she had walked into a luxury West Coast chalet on a Sunday afternoon.

She turned back to the young man who was waving at Max and making *woofing* noises. This was the opening she had been looking for.

Tanya put on her best smile. "Would you like to say hello to Max?"

His eyes lit up. "Can I pet him? Really?"

"Really."

"That would be super awesome. I want that! Please!"

"Stay right here." Tanya lowered her voice. "I'll go get him."

She spun on her heels when a deep male voice called out to her from behind.

Chapter Sixty

"**M**ay I help you?"

Tanya whirled around.

A short man with rimless spectacles was walking toward the entrance. He was dressed in casual street clothes, so that she couldn't be sure if he was a patient too.

"And you are?" she said.

"I'm in charge here."

He looked just like the other folk in the room. Tanya frowned. *How am I supposed to distinguish between employees and the patients?*

"Is there someone in an official capacity I can speak to?" she said.

The man puffed his chest as if he was offended she hadn't considered him.

"I'm a registered social worker and I'm in charge of patient care today."

She glanced over his shoulder. "Where are the other staff?"

"Everyone else is off today."

"What about the doctors?"

"They only come when they have appointments with the patients."

"Are these doctors from Black Rock?"

"Some of them drive from Seattle and others come from the counties around here. This is a private insti—"

He stopped and narrowed his eyes.

"You must be looking for a proper hospital," he said. "There's a doctor at the other end of town. Dr. Miller. His clinic is next door to the police station."

"Hey, Max!" hollered the boy by the door, startling the man.

Inside the Jeep, Max had scrambled over to the front seat. He was staring through the windshield, tail wagging, curious of what was going on.

The man in charge reached over and tapped the young man's shoulder. "There's a movie playing in the theater, Joseph. I think you'll like it."

They have a movie theater in here too?

This institution must have a very generous donor, thought Tanya. Something told her she knew who that would be.

The boy didn't budge from his spot, his voice rising in excitement as he called out. "Come over here, boy!"

Tanya turned to the social worker. "Seems like he'd like to play with my dog. Happy to bring him inside."

"Animals aren't allowed."

"Wouldn't hurt to let him pet a dog, would it? I don't mind."

The man put his hands on the young man's shoulders and turned him around forcibly. "There's a cool film playing right now. I think it's about dogs."

"Does it have a big puppy like that?"

"Why don't you watch it and tell me?" The man gave him a gentle push in the back. "You'll get an extra snack tonight, if you do."

The boy's face lit up.

The man snapped his fingers and raised his voice. "Jamie, could you escort Joseph to the movie theater for me, please?"

A woman who'd been reading on a nearby sofa got up, took the young man by the arm, and ushered him away.

Tanya stepped inside the foyer, her attention on the man in charge now.

"I came to see Elizabeth Miller."

"That's not possible."

"Why not?"

"Visiting hours are over. Plus, she doesn't see anyone other than her brother."

Tanya stared at him. *Didn't Wilma say he hadn't visited his sister in over five years?*

"Does he come here often?"

"Every week."

Tanya took another step closer.

"I need to see Elizabeth Miller urgently. It's a matter of life and death."

He blinked rapidly as if in confusion. "Who did you say you were again?"

She hadn't. "I'm with Chief Bold's team."

His eyebrows shot up, then he took a step back, one hand on the door like he was about to shut it on her. "I, er, I don't think I should be talking to you."

"I can come back with a warrant and the officers to look at your records, if you'd prefer."

Tanya had no jurisdiction to order a search or a warrant, but that seemed to do the trick. After gulping for a few seconds, the man turned around and walked over to the reception desk.

He pulled a chair in front of a terminal and pulled the mouse toward him. Tanya stepped up to the desk and leaned over to peek, but a screen protector prohibited her from seeing anything.

The man looked up, his face lined with concern. "Is everything alright with Dr. Miller? I'm supposed to see him for my prescription tomorrow."

"He's fine," said Tanya. "Now, where may I find his sister, please?"

He glanced around the living room, his brow furrowed. Tanya followed his eyes.

"She's outside," he said.

"In the rain?"

He frowned as if that thought had only crossed his mind then too.

He pointed at an armchair in a corner with a bright green shawl draped over the back. "That's where she sits every afternoon, reading."

Tanya tried but failed to not show her impatience. "She could have gone to the bathroom. She could be in her bedroom or visiting a friend in their room. She has to be here somewhere inside."

The man looked at the monitor and shook his head. "I know for sure she's not in the building."

"How do you know?"

"Her ankle monitor."

Tanya raised a brow. "Where exactly is she right now?"

"In the woods."

Chapter Sixty-one

"Do you track all of your patients like this?" said Tanya.

"Only if the family wants it," replied the man.

"So, Dr. Miller asked for it?"

"I don't think I'm supposed to be sharing—"

Tanya leaned across the counter. "When exactly did Dr. Miller visit his sister last?"

"I... er..."

Tanya tapped the top of the computer. "Check the visiting dates, please."

He shook his head. "Sometimes he just stops by with gifts. If he doesn't come inside, we don't record it as a visit."

She searched the man's face, looking for a twitch, a blink, or a change in breathing that would tell her he was lying.

"Did he come with a dozen red roses recently?" she asked.

"I believe she had a birthday."

"Can you give me the date?"

"Look here, we just got our privacy training, and I don't want to lose my job." He gave her an anxious look. "Maybe you should come back with a letter from a judge or something."

Tanya stepped away from his desk and rustled up a casual smile. "Thank you. I appreciate your time. I'll see myself out then."

With a curt nod, he turned back to the monitor.

Tanya strolled toward the entrance, but halfway across the room, she twisted her neck around. The man was hunched over, engrossed in his screen, the top of his head barely visible over the computer terminal.

She spun to the left, marched over to the corner armchair, and scooped up the green shawl. Balling it in her hands, she scurried toward the door, keeping the scarf away from the reception desk's line of sight.

"The exit is that way," came the man's voice from behind her.

Tanya lifted a hand up as if to say thanks and kept walking toward the main entrance.

It was a relief to be out in the open. Seeing her, Max barked. Tanya scooted into the Jeep and shut the door.

"I need your help, bud."

She unraveled the scarf on the back seat. While Max sniffed the garment, Tanya put the Jeep in reverse and pulled out of the parking spot.

That was when the skin on her neck prickled, like someone was watching her. She glanced at the rearview mirror.

A pale face was peering through a window in the corner of the main building.

It was the kid who had hankered to meet Max. His hands were planted on the glass and his nose was scrunched against the window. His eyes were on her. He looked like a frightened boy, pining to escape, calling for help.

That face troubled her. She wondered if this institution wasn't as cozy and welcoming as it presented itself to be.

She turned her attention back to the road and stepped on the accelerator.

After taking a few curves on the driveway, Tanya stopped in the middle of the road. She glanced back to check if the hospital compound was no longer visible. If she couldn't see the buildings, that meant anyone in or around the institution couldn't see her either.

Perfect.

After another check in both directions to make sure the coast was clear, she shifted gears and did a three-point turn. The Jeep careened over the uneven ground. She maneuvered the vehicle over the side of the road and rolled into the woods.

She had chosen a spot where the trees were sufficiently far apart, but twenty feet in, the woods thickened with shrubs. She eased the car behind a grove of dense bramble.

Tanya was glad she owned an all-terrain all-wheel drive, but she now wished she'd chosen one in military green rather than the standard black. She crossed her fingers, hoping no one driving along the road would turn their heads and notice the metallic glint coming from in between the trees.

The rain will help, she thought, thankful for the turn in weather. After inching back and forth to get as much camouflage as possible, she put the car in park and turned to Max.

"Ready to get to work?"

He wagged his tail.

Tanya picked up the scarf from his seat.

"Go, search," she commanded.

She leaned across him and clicked the back door open.

Max didn't wait to be told twice. He jumped out and buried his nose in the leaves on the ground, that intense focused expression coming onto his face again. Soon, he was scampering into the woods, heading up the hill.

Tanya locked the Jeep and hurried after her dog, Elizabeth Miller's shawl in one hand and her Glock in the other. A shiver ran through her. It was chilly in the woods. Cold and wet.

She'd soon find out if the man in charge had been lying to her.

Chapter Sixty-two

Tanya's phone buzzed, startling her.

She slithered on a pile of wet leaves as she stopped to check. It was her regular cell. She pulled it out of her pocket and glanced at the screen.

Bold.

Is he checking up on me?

Tanya declined the call and looked up to see where Max had gotten to. He was so focused on his task, he hadn't even stopped to see if she was following.

Her cell buzzed again. This time, she ignored it.

Max's tail was disappearing around a cluster of birch trees. He was heading back in the institution's direction. Tanya's heart sank.

Please don't tell me you've gone back inside, Elizabeth.

She jogged toward her dog.

The woods were thinning and she could see the side of one of the brick buildings through the wet foliage. Max was running along the primary structure toward the rear of the compound, dodging fallen tree trunks. But he was too close. If that boy was still staring out of the window, he would spot them in an instant.

"Max!" she whispered hoarsely. "Halt!"

He stopped and turned around, cocking his head.

"Hey, bud," she said, as she nudged him away from the building. "This way."

Max didn't move.

"I said this way."

He whined, a confused look on his face.

Tanya cursed Susan Cross for yanking him out of the K9 program prematurely. He was a great dog, but he needed more training.

The rain was coming down insistently now. Soon, the woods would be drenched and the scent trail would disappear. She kneeled and wiped the water droplets from Max's head.

"We're doing this my way, okay, bud?" she whispered.

Her phone buzzed.

Dammit Bold. I'm busy doing the job you should be doing.

Max let out a low growl, staring in the direction of the parking lot. The sound of a car engine came her way. Tanya blinked away the water from her eyelashes and peeked through the leaves to catch a familiar sight.

I'm the one who needs more training, she realized, swallowing hard.

The chief's squad car was in the institution's driveway, in the same spot she had parked her Jeep, only moments ago. She could make out the outline of Bold's head in the driver's seat, his phone to his ear.

Her cell buzzed again.

She reached into her pocket and reached for it with a sigh. If he fired her, Cross had the power to pull her from this town before she found Asha.

She accepted the call.

"Yes?"

"Stone?" came the chief's voice, just as curt. "Nurse Norma has lodged a formal complaint—"

"I'm tracking the missing girls," snapped Tanya.

"I thought we decided—"

That was when Max barked, making Tanya jump.

"What the heck, Max?" she hissed.

He whined in reply.

"Where are you?" Bold turned off the engine and stepped out of the car. Tanya watched as he slammed the door shut and trudged to the edge of the woods to peer through the tree line.

She let out a heavy sigh.

Bold squinted through the trees. "Are you only a few feet away, looking for victims?"

"Are you trying to give away my position to the entire hospital?" Tanya whispered angrily into the phone.

Bold jumped the ditch and strode through the wet leaves in her direction. Max wagged his tail to see him approach.

Tanya looked down at her dog. "What's with you, bud? You need to choose your friends more carefully."

"What the heck's going on?" said Bold as he marched up.

He stopped when he saw the sidearm in her hand.

Tanya waved the green shawl in the air. "This belongs to Elizabeth Miller."

"You stole it."

"I borrowed it. I'm trying to find her, so I can return it."

"I don't have time for games, Stone."

Tanya scowled. "Asha's been abducted, and you think I'm playing?"

"What's your grand plan? They told me you left several minutes ago, but I didn't see you on the drive up here."

"They won't let me talk to Miller's sister without a warrant."

Bold sighed. "That's what they told me as well."

"But I've got something better than a court order."

He groaned. "You've gone rogue again."

"Elizabeth is somewhere out here, and I think she might know what happened to the girls and Asha."

Bold's eyes darted back and forth. "Where is she then?"

"You interrupted us while we were on the hunt."

The chief turned to Max. "Okay, smart pup, show us what you've got."

Tanya bent down and thrust the scarf under Max's nose again. "Go, search," she commanded.

Max took off, following his nose. He ran around the building and meandered through the trees, moving deeper into the forest.

Tanya and Bold scrambled after him.

"Why is he taking us to the back?" said Bold as he jumped over a log, almost slipping on a moss-covered, rotting branch. "You know what's at the other end of these grounds, don't you?"

"What?" said Tanya, shooting him a curious look.

"The cemetery."

Chapter Sixty-three

"The asylum's cemetery?" said Tanya.

"It's where they bury patients with no next of kin," said Bold. "Sometimes families just don't claim the bodies."

"What's Elizabeth doing here in the rain?"

Bold didn't reply, his focus on not slipping on the wet leaves. Max kept thrusting forward in between the trees. Tanya dodged an overhanging branch, trying not to lose sight of her dog.

With every step deeper into the woods, her shoulders tensed and her back tingled like someone else was in the woods with them. She glanced around but there was no one.

"Hey," she said, stopping to catch her breath. "Do you feel like someone's watching us?"

Bold halted, panting. He scanned the surroundings. Other than the sound of Max scurrying through the foliage ahead, the woods were quiet.

Suddenly a branch snapped nearby.

Tanya whipped around, her heart racing.

"This way!" Bold sprang in between two pine trees to his immediate right. Tanya crashed after him, her weapon at the ready.

They jumped into a small clearing littered with rotten leaves and fallen branches. They rotated slowly, backs to each other, fingers on their triggers, but it was empty and there were no signs of anyone having been here.

Max barked in the distance.

"He's found something," whispered Tanya.

"We need to be cautious," Bold whispered back. "He could have met the unsub."

"If Max is in trouble, he'd be yapping his tail off. I know that bark. He's found Elizabeth."

"Be prepared for anything."

They stepped stealthily through the woods in the direction of Max's bark. They were circling a thicket when they spotted him.

Max was sitting at the edge of the forest where the tree line ended and a large clearing began. He was staring out at the crumbling headstones jutting out of the high grass.

The asylum's graveyard.

The smell of wet earth mingled with that of decaying wood. Under the light rain, the unkempt cemetery looked even more bleak, like a desolate place where ancient tribes left their sick to die among the vultures.

"Someone was digging," Bold whispered, pointing to an open pit five feet from the edge of the woods. A muddied shovel still lay in the hole.

"Max must have scared them away," whispered Tanya. She glanced around the dreary landscape. "Where's Elizabeth Miller?"

Max hadn't moved from his spot or come over to greet her like he usually did, which meant he was protecting what he'd found.

Slipping in between the trees, Tanya got closer. Max stood up and shook himself, spraying rain droplets on her.

"Hey, bud," said Tanya. "What—"

Her heart jumped to her throat as she spotted his discovery. A prone woman was concealed among the grass next to him.

"Bold! Over here!"

She kneeled to examine the body.

It was a thin, middle-aged woman with short hair and deep creases on her ashen face. She was wearing slacks and a green jumper, the same color as the shawl in Tanya's hand. Her clothes and hair were soaking wet, which meant she had been out in the open for a while.

Bold came up and squatted next to her.

He put his fingers on the side of the woman's neck to check for a pulse, then turned her over to look for open wounds. That was when they noticed the stream of red trickling across her forehead.

Her hair, matted with rain and blood, covered most of her face. Tanya pulled on the metallic medical bracelet on her wrist and read the name.

"Elizabeth Miller."

"The unsub lured her out and struck her," said Bold.

Tanya moved the hair strands to get a better look at the laceration. "Whoever it was, they were facing her when they hit her. It was someone she knew."

Bold cleared the rainwater from his forehead. "That open grave was for her. They were ready to bury her."

Tanya nodded. "She must have known where Asha and the girls were taken."

Bold got up and scanned the graveyard and the misty woods beyond, searching for shadows he might have missed.

"They could still be here," he said in a low voice.

Tanya didn't answer. Her hand had been on the dead woman's arm. She had felt it move. She sprang back startled as Elizabeth's eyes snapped open.

"She's alive!" cried Tanya.

The chief whirled around. With a shocked gasp, he kneeled next to the woman again.

"Ms. Miller?" he said, touching her shoulder.

Elizabeth opened her mouth to speak but shut it again.

"You're going to be okay, Ms. Miller. I'm going to get you out of here."

He leaped to his feet. "Stay with her." He turned to the side and pulled out his phone to dial the medics.

Tanya stayed next to the woman, a hand on her arm, a strange sense of déjà vu coming over her.

The last time she'd been next to a dead person who'd come alive was in a ditch by the hiking trail near Grimwood Estate. Laura Fredrickson hadn't been so lucky and had expired five minutes after they had discovered her.

Elizabeth's eyes flickered.

"Help... me," she whispered, her voice hoarse.

"Don't move," said Tanya. "You're going to be fine. We'll get you to safety...."

She scrunched her forehead as she tried to remember what Wilma had called Dr. Miller's sister.

Liz.

She leaned in closer.

"Stay awake for me, Liz," she said. "Hang in there, hun."

Elizabeth blinked. Her face was so pale, it was surprising to see her move. Tanya clasped the woman's hands in hers and prayed under her breath.

Please don't die on me. I need you alive to help me find Asha.

Chapter Sixty-four

Bold pulled his jacket off, folded it, and placed it underneath Elizabeth's head.

"Ambulance is on the way. They were close by, thank goodness. We need to get her to Miller's clinic right away."

"I don't think that's a good idea," said Tanya. "Unless you want the unsub to finish the job."

Bold looked at her, the lines on his forehead more pronounced than usual. "Are you still after Harold Miller?"

"He's a suspect as far as I'm concerned."

"You think *he's* going around kidnapping these girls?"

"Looks can deceive, but you know that." Tanya stopped, as she wondered if she should voice her suspicions.

Miranda and Hannah could be right. The mayor and the chief worked closely together, speaking almost every day. Bold's displeasure at the mayor could be a ruse.

A superb act.

Bold narrowed his eyes. "Why would the doctor try to kill his own sister?"

"To keep her silent about his crimes. Why else would she be here, bloodied, and lying next to a freshly dug grave?"

Bold stared at her.

"I don't think he's working alone," added Tanya. "I'd bet he's taking orders from somebody who has a tight grip on him."

The chief's face cleared. "Nurse Norma. She practically runs his life."

Tanya observed him as she said the next words. "I was thinking more like the mayor."

"You're kidding me."

Before Tanya could respond, the sound of an emergency vehicle's siren cut through the air. It was coming from beyond the woods, in the direction of the hospital's driveway.

Bold snapped his head around. "We can't move her. Not without potentially causing more damage. We have to guide the medics here."

"Max and I'll stay."

"I don't like leaving you here by yourself."

Tanya shot him an incredulous look. "I've hunted ISIS terrorists in the Arab deserts and you're—"

Bold put his hands up in defense. "Sorry. Didn't mean to... I'm not used to..."

Tanya didn't answer, though her brain whirred.

If he's trying to get me away from Elizabeth so the unsub can finish the job, that won't happen. Not on my watch, mister.

Bold turned away from her, his phone to his ear. Soon, he disappeared into the woods.

Elizabeth whimpered.

Tanya turned her focus back to the injured woman, wishing she had brought a bottle of water from the Jeep.

Elizabeth opened her eyes.

"Who did this to you?" said Tanya softly.

"Help... Zachary...."

Zachary?

Tanya frowned. That name kept popping up.

Mayor Bailey's voice flittered into her head. He'd mentioned that name when he talked about the fundraiser she and Asha had attended briefly, the one Miranda had gate crashed, crying about her dead daughter.

Wilma had talked about Zachary too. It was the name of Elizabeth's baby. But he was dead. The boy had succumbed to sudden infant death syndrome at only five days old when Liz was just a teenager.

"Zachary's going to die," whispered Elizabeth.

Tanya's frown deepened. She must be hallucinating from the severe pain.

"Help him...." croaked Elizabeth.

"Are you talking about your son, Liz?"

She nodded. "Harold's got him...." Her chest convulsed.

Tanya placed a hand on her shoulder to stop her from moving. "You need to stay completely still."

"He's sick... He... he can't live... save him... please save him...."

"How old is Zachary?" said Tanya.

When Elizabeth spoke, it was in a low and hesitating voice, but her eyes were lucid.

"Fifteen.... Fifteen years, eight months, four days," she whispered, not taking her eyes off Tanya. "I've been... keeping count."

Tanya wondered if she was lost in a psychotic world, induced by whatever medication they had administered to her. There had to be a good reason for the institution to have kept her for years.

Elizabeth tried to shift her head and squeezed her eyes shut like that simple movement hurt. She won't live for long, thought Tanya. The least she could do was humor her.

"Don't worry, Liz. I'll save Zachary for you."

Elizabeth's eyelids fluttered.

"Tha... thank you..."

Tanya stared back. Elizabeth had clear, hazel eyes. They were the intelligent eyes of a sane woman.

It was the first time she had taken a good look at her face, preoccupied with stopping the bleeding from her open wound.

"Harold...," whispered Elizabeth, her eyes locked with Tanya's. "He's had him.... ever since.... he put me in here."

"Why did your brother institutionalize you, Liz?"

Elizabeth's chest heaved, and she closed her eyes as if she wanted to conserve her energy.

A million and one questions swarmed Tanya's mind. *Why would Miller keep his nephew and put his sister away? If he was the unsub, why did he kidnap the girls? And what did he want with Asha?*

Tanya surveyed the woods.

Max was on guard nearby, ready to alert her to an intruder at a moment's notice. The paramedics and Bold were nowhere to be seen, though the emergency sirens had shut off several minutes ago.

What's taking them so long?

She turned back to the injured woman.

"Liz? Do you know where the missing girls are?"

Elizabeth nodded, but her breath was getting raspy and her body was growing cold. She was slipping into shock.

"Is Asha Kade with them?" asked Tanya.

Another nod.

"Where are they now?"

"At Harold's.... house..."

Miller's house?

Tanya suppressed the urge to dash through the woods, jump into her Jeep, and race toward the doctor's home. But she couldn't leave this dying woman alone in a cemetery next to her own burial spot, with the unsub potentially lurking in the woods.

She tried to piece the puzzle together.

Somehow those missing girls and Asha were connected to the Miller affair, whatever it was. Maybe Asha had figured out what was going on and the doctor snatched her to silence her. Maybe the doctor was working alone, after all.

"He said.... I was mad." Elizabeth was talking again, haltingly, like she was measuring each word against the little energy she had left.

Her hands were now deathly cold. Her body was fighting to keep her alive by pumping essential blood supplies away from her limbs to her organs. Tanya knew she would be gone if those paramedics didn't get here soon.

"I want to... see Zachary... before I die," gasped Elizabeth. "He's very sick.... blood..."

Blood?

Tanya wiped the rainwater from Elizabeth's face. "Why did your brother incarcerate you?"

"He hates me..."

"Why?"

"Because.... I killed our.... father."

Chapter Sixty-five

"You *killed* your father?" said Tanya.

"He was a monster," whispered Elizabeth. "I... poisoned him..."

Laura's dying words swirled through Tanya's head.

The monster. He's... coming back... for more...

"What did he do to you?" said Tanya.

Elizabeth's eyes filled with tears. "He punished me every night."

"What do you mean? Why did you kill your father, Liz?"

"Because Zachary is his son."

Tanya stared at her in shock, unsure if she had heard her correctly.

Loud hollering came from the woods. It sounded like an army platoon was rumbling in their direction. Tanya turned back to Elizabeth.

"Why did your brother take the girls and Asha? What does he want from them?"

Elizabeth turned her head, but before she could reply, the paramedics burst through the tree line. They threw the stretcher down and shoved Tanya aside.

She leaped to her feet.

"Max! Let's go!"

Tanya sprinted through the woods, with Max leading the way. He seemed to sense the urgency of the situation and was heading straight toward where she had parked the Jeep. The rain had stopped, but everything was still slippery.

Running footsteps crashed through the trees from behind Tanya, and soon, Bold caught up to her.

"What's going on, Stone?"

Tanya didn't answer, her focus on avoiding the branches jutting from under the slimy leaves, ready to trip her up.

Bold grabbed her arm, stopping her in mid-stride. She shook him off and kept running, a tsunami of emotions whipping through her brain.

If Elizabeth's story was true, she had gotten pregnant by her own father.

Such horrific violence would have never happened overnight. He had probably groomed his daughter after his wife's death and tortured her throughout her childhood. Then, when she'd birthed a child, she had killed the man responsible for her nightmares in revenge.

It was too wild of a story, too crazy to even contemplate. The chief, the mayor, and the entire town revered their distinguished physician. They would never believe such a tall tale about his family without evidence.

But if that had truly happened, the father deserved whatever Elizabeth did to him. If it had been up to Tanya, she would have put a bullet through the child abuser's head without an ounce of remorse.

Some evil should never be tolerated on earth.

Tanya shook her head to clear it.

But is it true? Is Elizabeth psychotic? Did Miller take Asha and the girls? Why?

Tanya was running past the hospital's parking lot when she lost her footing on a moss-covered branch. She slammed headfirst onto the forest floor. She doubled over, out of breath, wincing at the searing pain in her left ankle.

She looked up. Max had disappeared from view, and was probably already by the Jeep.

Bold ran up. "You all right, Stone?"

He squatted by her foot, but Tanya pushed him away, panting hard.

He offered a hand.

Her ankle hurt badly, but she knew she could overcome it. She had to, if she was going to find Asha and the girls alive. She turned to see Bold was still holding his hand out toward her.

"Sometimes I feel like you're on a mission all by yourself, Stone," he said. "I want to help you find your friend. I'm on your side."

His eyes seemed sincere. Tanya took a deep breath in and let it out. In that second, she made a decision—one she wasn't sure she wouldn't regret later. She was going to do the thing Ray Jackson and Susan Cross advised her not to.

She grabbed Bold's hand and wobbled to her feet, wincing in pain.

"We need to get the medics to check you," said Bold, concern in his voice.

She shifted her foot and flinched, but held on to his arm.

"Get me some compression bandages from the ambulance," she said.

"Are you joking?"

"I've tracked a terrorist with a broken foot for miles in the desert. I can walk to my Jeep at the other end of the woods."

Bold shook his head like he couldn't believe what she was saying.

"There's no time," said Tanya. "We have to get to Miller's house *now*."

"Miller? Why?"

"Elizabeth said that's where he took the girls. That's where Asha is."

"You were accusing the mayor only minutes ago."

"I don't trust him or his wife, but the girls are our priority."

"Why would Miller kidnap them?"

"Something to do with Elizabeth and Zachary."

"The baby boy? Didn't he die more than a decade ago?"

"Elizabeth said Zachary is alive. He's in Miller's house."

"She's probably got a concussion—"

"I believe her!"

"She could be on heavy medication, hallucinogens, and who knows what else they give patients in this place."

Even if Tanya wanted to, it wasn't easy to explain Elizabeth's revelation to the chief, when she was still struggling to come to terms with it herself.

She looked Bold in the eye.

"Zachary was the product of rape. Elizabeth just told me her father abused her as a child. Her brother kept the son when he was born and put her in the asylum. Maybe it was to keep her quiet about the situation."

Bold's jaw dropped.

"She couldn't have made up a story like that in that condition," said Tanya. "She spoke clearly. She was telling the truth."

Bold's face hardened. "And the missing girls? Is Miller abusing them right under my nose?"

"He could be recreating what his father did. We have to search Miller's house from top to bottom."

"We can't go in without a warrant."

"Are you ready to have another girl die under your watch, Chief?" Tanya glowered. "If he's holding Asha and the girls, I'll shoot that man myself."

Bold gave her a warning look. "You can't—"

"I'm a free agent," snapped Tanya. "I'm going to save them, whatever it takes."

Chapter Sixty-six

B old revved as he sped down the asylum's driveway.

Neither he nor Tanya spoke. The tension was so strong, Tanya felt the muscles in her back tighten up like the key on a wind-up doll.

As soon as Bold got close to the spot where her Jeep was, she rapped on the dashboard for him to stop. She opened the door and jumped out, ignoring the throbbing in her ankle.

"Where's the doctor's house?" she called out as she hobbled across the ditch toward Max, who was waiting by the shrubs.

"Next to the mayor's," called out Bold.

Tanya stopped in her tracks.

Did I drive by Asha when I visited the mayor's wife only moments ago?

The chief put his lights and sirens on and roared toward the highway.

Tanya scrambled over to the Jeep and hustled Max inside. It took her several minutes to catch up to the chief.

Her heart hammered as she weaved in and out of traffic, keeping the Jeep's nose inches from Bold's bumper, wishing she had flashing lights and a siren too.

She didn't know if Elizabeth had been hallucinating and if they were on a wild goose chase. All she wanted was to find Asha and get her far away from this crazy, crazy town.

Tanya dashed up the hill toward the gated community on the West End, her injury forgotten as her mind shifted focus.

Lopez and Fox were already waiting by the main gates. Bold must have called them in. She screeched to a halt behind the squad cars.

Bold was now by the number pad next to the entrance. She waited in the Jeep with Max, her heart thudding inside of her.

The more she thought of it, the more she was sure Miller was their man, and that she was dealing with a manic mind. She didn't even want to imagine what horrors Asha and those girls were facing.

The gates slid open.

All three officers jumped into their squad cars and rushed inside, one after the other. She gave a silent prayer of thanks the chief had access to the community.

She raced in after the team, passing the mansions she'd gazed at in awe only hours ago. They sped by the garden with the peacocks and the mayor's residence and came to a stop in front of a gated property at the far end of the common grounds.

Bold jumped out of his vehicle, ran over, and banged on the gate. Fox remained in his car, giving instructions to someone on his shoulder radio. Lopez was on her phone, calling the doctor's number.

Bold kept pushing on the intercom button and banging on the gate. "Open up, Harold! We need to talk."

Tanya turned to Max. "We don't have time for this."

She pushed her seat back to get a better look at her sprained ankle. It was swathed by the bandages Bold had rifled from the ambulance at the hospital parking lot. She tightened them to the point she could hardly feel the ache.

"That should do it," she murmured to herself. In the seat behind her, Max whined and twirled around in his seat.

Tanya opened the back door to let him out and scrambled out of the Jeep after him. She stepped a few feet back from her car and took a runner's position.

"To your right!" she hollered.

As soon as Bold turned, Tanya sprinted toward the gate, zooming past him. Using the momentum, she leaped high in the air and grabbed on to the top of the steel bar.

"What the heck are you doing?" the chief shouted from below.

Using every ounce of strength she had, Tanya pulled herself up, ignoring the fire that blazed through her biceps.

She swung a leg over and straddled the gate. Without a glance at the hollering officers, she jumped down to the other side before they could stop her.

A flash of fire shot through her injured ankle as she hit the ground. She scrambled to her feet, wincing in pain, and took a few deep breaths to recover.

On the other side of the fence, Max was barking his head off.

Tanya scanned the grounds.

Dr. Miller's house was modest compared to the opulent mansions in this community. It was a square concrete block, cold and clinical, almost like a utilitarian medical facility.

A shudder went through her.

Is Asha inside?

Bold banged on the gate. "Open up, Stone!"

She whirled around and pulled at the heavy frame. It didn't budge. The gate was supposed to be operated electronically and she could see no manual release anywhere.

But with the crew pushing on the other side and Tanya hauling it from this side, they cracked it open a few inches. A furry nose pressed through the narrow gap, and soon, Max squeezed in, his tail wagging.

"Good boy," said Tanya.

Bold and his team kept pushing, but the gate got stuck on a rut on the ground.

I don't have time for this.

Tanya pulled out her weapon. She could now search the doctor's house without having to worry about policy or protocol.

Calling to Max, she darted up the driveway. Just as she reached the front of the house, the door banged open, and a large shadow loomed on the threshold.

Nurse Norma.

The nurse stepped out into the open, scowling. That was when Tanya saw the cleaver.

She aimed her Glock at the nurse. "Drop the knife!"

Max growled.

Norma didn't blink.

The nurse was no longer wearing her jacket. The scratches and bruises on her arms, previously concealed, were now visible. She had also removed the bandage on her cheek and had applied a sickly yellow gel all over her raw blisters.

Did Asha do this to you?

Tanya wondered how this woman could be so fearless in the face of a Glock and a growling German Shepherd. She wondered if Bold was right.

Maybe *she* was the crazed psychopath behind all this.

"What are you doing here?" said Norma, her voice venomous.

Tanya climbed up the front steps slowly, her sidearm aimed at the nurse's head. "I'd like to ask you the same question."

"I live here," snapped Norma. "I saw you on the security camera. You jumped that gate. I swear to everything under the sun you'll rot in jail. You're a common criminal!"

"Me breaking the law is the least of your concerns right now."

The nurse glowered. "First you trespass our private clinic and now you break into our house? How dare you harass me like this?"

"I'm here to rescue the girls," snarled Tanya as she stepped up, without wavering in her gaze or her aim. At her heels, Max let out another growl.

Tanya knew that if the nurse was insane enough, she could do serious damage with that knife before she could subdue her.

"Get away from me!" screamed Nurse Norma. "I'll shred you to pieces!"

"Is Asha in here?" said Tanya, stepping closer. "And the girls?"

Norma lifted her cleaver high and slammed it down.

Chapter Sixty-seven

Tanya ducked.

"Watch out, Max!"

The cleaver fell with a clang on the marble step, inches from his paws. Tanya kicked the knife into the hedges at the bottom of the steps and pressed the gun into the woman's temple.

With her free hand, she grabbed Norma's wrists and twisted her around. The nurse let out a painful shriek.

"Let me go!"

"Take me to the girls!"

Tanya shoved her through the doorway. Norma stumbled inside the house, her face red in fury.

Max followed them in, his hackles up.

The front foyer opened to a starkly furnished living room, the size of a New York apartment. There was another exit that seemed to connect to a corridor on the other end.

The only furniture in the middle of this space were two leather sofas and a glass coffee table. Lining one wall, about thirty feet from the couches, was a floor-to-ceiling mahogany bookcase. A series of framed modern art hung against the adjacent wall. Tanya could almost hear the echoes in this empty room.

She let go of the nurse's wrists, pulled Asha's ball cap from her back pocket, and threw it on the floor.

"Search, Max!"

Max sniffed the cap and twirled around. Tanya watched her dog trot around the immense living room, then walk into the corridor at the far end, his nose to the ground.

Tanya's heart beat a tick faster.

She's here!

Grabbing the nurse by the collar, Tanya pulled her toward the end of the hallway. A large foyer with a spiral staircase greeted Tanya's eyes. All the rooms were closed. Other than Max's toenails clicking on the marble floor, there was an eerie quietness in the stale air.

Max sniffed each closed door, glanced up at the staircase for a moment, then returned to the living room. He meandered in between the couches and the coffee table, then sniffed around the bookshelf.

To Tanya's surprise, he did another tour of the living-room's perimeter, then another, his snout glued to the floor.

She frowned. *What's he doing?* There was no one in this room. She turned to the nurse. "Where are the girls?"

"I don't know what you're talking about."

Tanya had met enough con artists to know that was a bald-faced lie.

"Do you know who I am?" spat Norma. "I work for Dr. Miller. I know the mayor. You're harassing an upstanding citizen of this town. The mayor will never let you get away with this." Norma's eyes scorched into Tanya's. "If I were you, I'd leave town before you get into any more trouble than you already are."

"Upstanding citizen? Tell me another one." Tanya's eyes bored into the woman's. "I hear the boy, Zachary, is alive. Are you going to deny that too?"

Norma stiffened.

Bingo.

"I hear he's a very sick young man," continued Tanya. "Can you tell me why Dr. Miller has kept him a secret?"

The nurse didn't move but Tanya could feel a change in her energy. She was getting close to the truth and Norma was getting uncomfortable.

"Elizabeth Miller told me everything," said Tanya.

The nurse's face remained guarded, but she didn't speak.

Tanya shook her by the collar. "What's your stake in this sick game? Are you an employee? Are you a partner to the doctor's crimes? Or do you run this sick show?"

An angry flush crept up the nurse's cheeks.

"You'll be implicated in whatever's going on," said Tanya. "Laura Fredrickson's death is on your hands. If any of the other girls or my friend have been harmed, their blood is on your hands too. Do you know what that means?"

The angry sneer never left the nurse's face, but Tanya could see she was struggling to keep still.

Tanya shook her head in mock sympathy. "Too bad they don't hang killers in this state. If I had my way, I'd bring the penalty back for psychos like yourself and your precious doctor."

"You have no idea what you're talking about." The nurse's voice was low and guttural, like the sound of a cornered animal.

"I think I've hit the nail on the head," said Tanya. "You two are twisted wackos—"

"You know nothing!" screamed Norma, agitated.

Max whirled around and barked at her.

"Even he can see you're lying," said Tanya.

A muffled bang came from inside the house, making both women jump. The nurse's face turned pale.

Max growled. He put his nose down on the marble floor and sniffed suspiciously.

"What is it, Max?" said Tanya.

"Put your weapon down!" shouted a familiar voice behind her. It was the chief.

Nurse Norma threw her hands up and flailed like a wet fish. "Help me! She's going to kill me!"

Bold swung around to face Tanya. "Let Norma go."

Tanya glanced behind him. Lopez and Fox were at the foot of the steps, their weapons drawn and aimed her way. Her heart pounded.

Are they all in on this?

"Please help me," cried Norma, her voice quivering. "Get her off of me. Save me!"

Tanya turned to Bold. "Elizabeth Miller was telling the truth."

"Step away from her, Stone," he said. "I'm going to have to answer to you holding a weapon against an unarmed civilian."

"She had a knife!" Tanya glared at the woman who only moments ago had threatened to shred her to bits with a cleaver.

"Where is it?" said Bold.

"I kicked it into the rosebushes."

"Let her go," said Bold. "I'll take over from here."

After taking a long breath in, Tanya withdrew her weapon and stepped back.

In that millisecond, the nurse plucked out a scalpel from her pocket and lurched toward her. Tanya jumped out of the way.

"Put that down!" roared Bold, as he lunged toward Norma.

"Watch out, Boss!" hollered Fox.

Bold ducked as the blade slashed inches from his head. Fox stormed up the front steps, his sidearm aimed at the nurse.

"Put the knife down!" he hollered.

She lunged at him.

With an agonizing yell, Fox staggered back, clutching his arm. Lopez leaped up the steps to catch him before he stumbled down.

Bold jumped on the nurse and twisted the knife out of her hands. Within seconds, Nurse Norma was in handcuffs.

Tanya snapped her fingers at Max and stepped inside the hallway, her heart racing. She would deal with the team later.

Where did that banging come from?

She turned to Max, her eyes narrowed. "Did you hear that too, bud?"

Max barked in reply.

That was when she heard the faint voice. It was muffled and far away, like it was coming from the belly of the house.

It was a woman.

Tanya staggered back, reeling.

She recognized the voice.

Chapter Sixty-eight

"Asha?" shouted Tanya, whirling around, her heart racing.

But the cry had stopped as abruptly as it began.

Did I imagine that?

She turned to her dog. "Go search, Max!"

Max gave her a confused look, then trotted back into the living room. She followed, calling out to him, wondering if he had forgotten his training, like Asha had said.

In the living room, Bold was talking to someone over his shoulder radio.

Lopez was leading Fox down the front steps, presumably to her car where she kept her first aid kit. Tanya noticed the growing red stain on Fox's left arm. On the floor by the foyer was a trail of blood and the stained scalpel that had slashed him.

Norma sat slouched on the ground by the threshold, handcuffed and restrained, but her sweat-drenched face was a picture of rage. She looked like a caged tiger, ready to lash out if you got too close.

Bold turned to Tanya as she walked in. There were raw scratches on his face and neck. Norma had put up a good fight.

"She's not talking," he said. "I called in for extra hands from the neighboring county. They should be here soon."

Tanya didn't answer, her mind elsewhere. That cry had been faint, and it had sounded like it had come from down below.

Is there a basement under this house?

Tanya kneeled to examine the floor, but it was solid. She scraped the couches back. More marble slabs.

"What are you doing?" said Bold.

Tanya stomped over to the nurse. "Where's the entrance to the basement?"

The nurse pursed her lips and her fiery eyes challenged her.

That was when the muffled bang came again.

Max barked.

Bold spun around. "What was that?"

"Asha!" shouted Tanya. "Where *are* you?"

Bold's eyes darted around the room, then back to Norma. "For the hundredth time, Norma, where are the girls?"

A faint smile cracked across the nurse's face like she enjoyed watching them flounder.

Tanya turned to the chief. "Have you been in this house before?"

He shook his head. "The mayor and his wife were invited for a Christmas dinner a while back, but the doctor's pretty private. No one else I know has been here. I know why now."

"The girls are in this house. I just know it."

"If we have to take this building apart," said Bold, "we'll do it."

His radio crackled. He turned to speak into the mic on his shoulder. An unrecognizable male voice came down the wire, talking about a backup crew.

Tanya spun around and stepped back into the corridor.

I don't have time for a search party.

Whistling for Max to follow her, she treaded back into the hallway.

The morbid story Elizabeth Miller had shared with her was ringing in her head. *What does that have to do with the missing girls?* she wondered as she opened the door to the kitchen.

It was empty.

She tried the dining room, then the laundry room, a guest bedroom, and two bathrooms. She checked every closet, door, and cabinet on the first floor, however large or small.

After scouring the rooms, she climbed up the marble staircase to the second floor. She walked through sparsely furnished bedrooms and their ensuite bathrooms, but there was no one, and no secret entrances to the basement anywhere.

She would have sworn the house had been unoccupied, if she hadn't heard the strange cry earlier.

Where are you, Asha?

There was a closed double door at the end of the second-floor hallway. The master bedroom, thought Tanya as she treaded toward it, her Glock at the ready.

But the room was empty, and nothing seemed amiss.

Except for one thing.

Taking a sharp breath in, Tanya stepped up to the wall of framed photos behind the king-sized bed. These weren't the kind of pictures you'd put in the living room.

In one photo, Dr. Miller, in a striking red leather thong and chains, was towering over a naked Norma with a whip in his hand. The nurse was handcuffed to the bed and clearly seemed to be enjoying it.

Her eyes widened as she took in the leather whips, chains, handcuffs, and gags. In the photos where Miller looked directly at the camera, she could see the hunger for power in his eyes. This was a complete transformation from the shuffling, stuttering physician she knew.

One thing was obvious. Dr. Miller was the dominant and Norma was the submissive in this peculiar relationship.

Tanya turned away from the photo wall feeling like she needed a dozen showers to get rid of the fetish images from her head. But there were some things you could never unsee, however much you wished to.

She walked over to the dresser which had an inordinate number of Hallmark cards set in a row.

Someone's birthday?

Tanya picked the first and read the inside. It was a long and sappy love note from Norma to Miller. All the cards were from her to him, but there were none from him to her.

She's obsessed with the doctor. And he's using her.

A criminology lecture at Quantico flashed through Tanya's mind. A French couple dubbed the Virgin Hunters abducted and killed almost a dozen girls in the eighties. They terrorized families in France and Belgium until they were caught and jailed for life.

Were Norma and Miller Virgin Hunter copycats?

Tanya put the cards down, her stomach churning. She now knew why Nurse Norma was so protective about the physician. Also, she wasn't the one in charge.

It was Dr. Miller they were after.

She turned around to leave when she spotted the small, framed photo, turned upside down on the vanity table by the bed. She flipped it over.

It was a photo of a sickly boy, looking barely in his teens. It only showed his pale face. His mournful expression gave Tanya goose bumps.

Was this the boy who was supposed to have died, but had somehow lived?

Is this Zachary?

Chapter Sixty-nine

Who is this mysterious boy?

Tanya pulled the photo out of the frame and checked the back. There were no markings or writing anywhere to indicate who he was.

She put the photo back on the table. It was time to see what Bold was up to.

Tanya was coming down the marble staircase when she realized Max hadn't joined her in her search.

"Max?" she called from the corridor.

"He's in here," came Bold's voice from the living room.

Tanya walked in to see the chief scrutinizing the bookshelf on the far end. Max was sitting next to him. He whined as she stepped inside the room, as if calling her over.

Bold didn't turn around. "Find anything?"

"We need to get Miller," Tanya replied in a grim voice. "Norma's just the sidekick."

Bold pulled a stack of books from the top shelf. "She's no innocent bystander though. I'd bet my pension on it."

Tanya turned to her dog. "What are you doing, bud?"

Max barked.

"He's been sniffing this wall," muttered Bold, as he examined the wood panel in the back of the top shelf.

"Are you seriously looking for a secret entrance?"

"Did you find a door to the basement anywhere else?"

"What makes you think there's a way through here?"

He straightened up and turned to her. "When someone's hiding something in plain sight, they look in its direction. Makes them feel superior. It's a matter of—"

"Ego," completed Tanya as she turned to see Nurse Norma scowling their way.

"A psychological tic," said Bold, nodding. "I know you like to go off guns blazing, but it helps to slow down a smidgen and reflect. Plus, your dog is keen about this area. There's something here."

Tanya stepped up to the shelves. She pushed a row of books to the floor and felt the back panel.

Nothing.

No knots, handles, or knobs. Just smooth polished wood.

She was about to push off another stack, when she realized Max was earnestly sniffing an enormous hardback that lay to the side on the floor.

She grabbed it and flipped it open.

"What's this?" she gasped.

Bold spun around. The inside of the book had been neatly carved out. Nestled in between the cut pages was an electronic fob.

Tanya snatched the fob and clicked on the button.

She and Bold turned around, expecting a mechanical whir from somewhere. But nothing happened.

Max remained in his spot by the bookshelf, a curious expression on his face, and didn't rush off to investigate any corner of the room.

Bold frowned. "Dead battery?"

Tanya pressed the button again.

Nothing.

"Let me try," he said, plucking the device from her hand.

Typical man.

Tanya turned her attention to the hollowed-out book. The title read, *Nine Pints: A Journey Through the Money, Medicine, and Mysteries of Blood.*

Blood again.

She tapped her finger on the book cover. "The doctor has a row of blood bags in his surgery. Elizabeth said something about blood but didn't explain."

Bold was trying the fob, pointing it in all directions. "Don't tell me you think the doctor is a vampire now."

Tanya surveyed the room, her finger still tapping on the book cover. Her gut told her she was close, so close to finding Asha and the girls.

Nurse Norma was evading eye contact now.

Bold dropped the fob on the coffee table and turned back to the bookshelf, hands on his hips. "We have to find the receiver."

"Receiver?"

"The box that catches the signal. Like how a garage door opener works." He pulled out more paperbacks from the shelves and placed them on the floor. "It has to be hidden behind here."

He pushed the last of the books down, letting them crash to the floor. Max jumped to the side before one hit his head.

"There's nothing here," said Bold as he knocked on the back of the wooden shelf.

"You almost hit Max—" Tanya stopped.

She stared at the most recent books that had fallen on the floor. *Hematology. Pathology of Blood Disorders. Blood Collection. Blood Chemistry.*

"Elizabeth wasn't hallucinating when she said blood." She picked a book at random and opened it, expecting a hollowed-out inside, but it was intact.

Bold realized what she was doing and got on his knees to join the search. Together, they flipped through the books with *Blood* on the title, looking for hollow insides, loose notes, hidden messages, anything.

After several minutes, Bold wiped the sweat gathered on his brow. "There's nothing here."

Tanya picked up the original book with the hollowed inside and ran her finger along the cover. Blood had a deep meaning to Dr. Miller.

She scanned the room.

Nurse Norma's face had turned pink. They were getting close. She knew it.

The hair on Tanya's arms stood as she realized they had been staring at it all along.

"Look at that!"

Bold glanced around him. "What?"

She strode over to the modern paintings on the adjacent wall. If someone had handed a can of paint to a kid and asked them to splash it haphazardly on the canvas, these would be the results.

Each painting had one unique color. One was blue, another was yellow, and the last one was red.

Tanya pointed at the corner painting. "What does this look like to you?"

Bold stared at it.

"A blood splatter."

Chapter Seventy

Tanya lifted the painting off the wall.

She held it by the frame to scrutinize it when Bold jumped toward her.

"The receiver!" he shouted, pointing.

Installed on the wall, previously hidden behind the canvas, was a small, shiny box.

Tanya dropped the painting and grabbed the fob from the coffee table. With her heart racing, she aimed it at the box and pressed the button.

A loud click made her step back in surprise. A rumble was coming in the direction of the bookshelf. It was parting in the middle, folding backward, creating an opening the length of the wall.

Max barked, like he was saying, *I've been trying to tell you about this all along.*

A secret room!

Tanya and Bold drew their weapons.

Tucked behind the wall, where the bookshelf once had been, was a study. It looked like a vintage library in a colonial mansion—one you'd see in old movies where aristocratic men retired for after-dinner cigars and whiskey.

"What in heaven's name is this?" muttered Bold as they stood shoulder to shoulder, their sidearms aimed forward.

Tanya stepped toward the opening, dumbfounded. Before she could stop him, Max bounded inside. They followed him in, tensed, eyes and ears on alert.

An antique mahogany desk on a Persian rug took most of the space. Behind it was a plush leather chair. In the other corner were large sofas set around ornate coffee tables. The walls were made of dark wood panels. The floor was hardwood, not marble like elsewhere in the home.

The room was empty.

Bold and Tanya treaded around the secret study.

That was when Tanya spotted it behind the desk. She picked up the red backpack which Max had been sitting next to and waved it in the air.

"It's Asha's day pack."

She ripped the bag open.

"Laptop, bottle of water, wallet. It's all in here. She has to be in this house somewhere."

"Where exactly did you hear that banging?" asked Bold.

"From below, like from a basement."

"I'd say the entrance is in here." He gestured to the other end of the room. "You take the right side. I'll search the left."

Max remained by Asha's bag, watching them work intently through every inch of the room for the next few minutes. But it was in vain.

Tanya stomped on the wooden floor, exasperated. "Does this sound hollow to you?"

But Bold seemed preoccupied with something on the mahogany desk. The computer.

Tanya felt the floorboards, trying to identify loose panels or hidden latches. Finding nothing, she laid her head down and cupped her ear to listen.

Silence.

Her stomach sank as she worried if Asha was being punished for alerting them.

Who knows what that crackpot doctor is doing?

She thumped her fist on the floor and hollered. "Asha!"

Bold jumped, startled.

That was when the banging came again. This time it was clear.

It was an SOS.

Tanya's heart leaped.

"It's Asha!"

Max threw his head back and howled. The banging came in rapid succession in reply.

Tanya jumped to her feet and faced the chief. "We have to rip the floor open."

Bold gestured toward the computer screen. "You have to see this."

"We don't have time—"

He jabbed at the monitor. "Look at this!"

She stepped behind the desk.

An architectural blueprint was rotating on the screen. It was moving too fast to catch the details, but she knew what it was. A schema of a square-shaped building.

Bold tapped the bottom part of the diagram.

"See here? This is what's below us."

Tanya stared open mouthed, as she realized what it was. "That's no basement. That's an underground labyrinth."

Chapter Seventy-one

"The lower floors are reinforced on all sides."

Bold shook his head as the blueprint on the screen rotated faster and faster.

"This is way too sophisticated. We'll need more than an excavator to rip this place open."

Tanya pushed him aside and sat down in front of the computer.

"The key to the basement entrance must be electronic, just like the bookshelf. We just have to find it."

A white bar popped up as soon as she touched the mouse.

She swore. "Password-protected."

Bold reached for the radio on his shoulder. "Lopez? How's Fox doing?"

"Alive," came Lopez's voice. "Lost a bit of blood, but Justin and Stacey are here. They're putting a tourniquet on him."

"Can he talk? We have a computer puzzle for him."

More crackling came over the radio as Lopez conferred with someone in the background.

Bold waited.

"Stacey wants to take him away, Boss," came Lopez's voice. "But Fox wants to come in. I'll bring him over as soon as they wrap him up."

Tanya wasn't listening. The conversation she'd had with Asha in Janine's room was still fresh in her mind. She pulled the keyboard closer and tried all the password combinations she could think of, her fingers tapping furiously.

White Knight

White$Knight

WK

Tall&Dark

"That's going to take forever." Bold leaned over her shoulder. "We need one of those password cracking thingamajigs and someone who knows how to use it."

Tanya looked up as if she just realized something. "What we need is someone who knows what the password is."

She jumped out of the chair and grabbed her gun. She marched through the opening and stepped into the living room.

Nurse Norma bared her teeth as she approached her.

Tanya squatted on the floor and pressed her Glock against the nurse's neck.

"What's the password to the doctor's computer?"

Norma glared.

"Give it to me, unless you want to get splattered on the wall like one of those paintings."

"I told you to leave town," growled Norma, her face crunched into a hateful sneer. "Now you'll die just like Laura."

"I asked a question."

The veins on Norma's neck throbbed, either out of fear or anger. Maybe both.

"I'll never betray Harold."

Tanya pushed the gun further into the woman's neck. "This isn't my first rodeo, Norma. I'm not worried about one more kill."

The nurse's eyes widened momentarily, but her mouth remained clamped shut.

"Stone!" Bold's angry voice came from behind her.

Tanya ignored him, her eyes on the nurse. "Give me the password."

"I'll never share it with anyone."

"Is it numbers? Words? A name? His sister's name? The kid's?"

The nurse's face flushed at those last words. Tanya sprang to her feet, spun on her heels, and marched back into the study.

Bold was glowering at her.

"You can't threaten to kill people under my watch," he hissed as she stomped by him and grabbed the chair.

Tanya hunched over the computer and started typing again.

Zachary

She hit enter.

A red bar popped up. *Access denied.*

She tried again.

SaveZachary

Denied.

Behind her, Bold was talking to Lopez over the radio about a construction crew.

Zachary&Elizabeth

Denied.

MyNephewZachary

Denied.

MyNephewZachary199%$$&^%##!!!

Denied.

Tanya pounded her fist on the desk. Bold was right. Even if she had part of the password, the possibilities were endless.

She took a deep breath and put her fingers on the keyboard again. One more time.

ZacharysBlood

The password bar disappeared, and the desktop flickered to life. Tanya jumped in her chair in surprise.

"I'm in! I'm in!"

Bold spun around. "Geez, you should buy a lottery ticket before the day is over."

Tanya stared at the screen.

Where do I even start?

She clicked on the Documents folder, but all the files were titled with numbers and what seemed like medical terms. None of the applications on the desktop looked familiar or told her anything.

Tanya scrunched her forehead. Normally, this was when she'd call on Asha for help, but that wasn't going to happen now.

Max barked, startling her.

"Sir?" came a halting voice from the living room.

Tanya looked up from the computer to see Fox dragging himself toward the opening, one arm bandaged.

"In here." Bold stepped across the threshold to help him. "You sure you're up to this?"

"I'm good." Fox shuffled over, taking in the secret room with a shocked expression on his face.

Tanya got up and helped ease Fox into the chair behind the desk. Fox placed his injured arm on the table and stared at the computer.

"What are we looking for?"

"We need to find the entrance to the basement," said Tanya. "It could be an application, a program, an electronic key, if that makes any sense."

Fox stared at the screen, immobile for a few seconds so that for a moment, Tanya wondered if he'd suffered a head injury too.

Then, Fox pulled the mouse toward him using his good hand. He clicked on a series of files, his nose inches from the screen. He selected an application named D&HGB.

Tanya squinted at it. "What's that do?"

Fox winced as he shifted his wounded arm to a more comfortable position. "Never seen this app before. Looks out of the ordinary."

"They all look out of the ordinary to me," muttered Bold.

Fox clicked on a tab in the application and pulled back, as if in surprise.

Tanya leaned over to look. "What is it?"

Fox didn't answer. The same 3D image of the screensaver Bold and Tanya had seen earlier appeared. It was more precise and took up the entire screen.

Tanya's heart beat a tick faster. "That's the blueprint for this house."

Fox frowned. "Maybe, but this is a gaming app."

Tanya and Bold exchanged a puzzled glance.

Fox moved the mouse to an icon on the schema and clicked. A pop-up box appeared with a bunch of gobbledygook letters and a bar that simply said *Submit*.

Fox closed it and clicked on another icon. Then another. He worked intently, clicking methodically, opening and closing pop-ups, reading the information at lightning speed, while Tanya and Bold watched, neither making head nor tail of what they were seeing.

Fox clicked on a link at the bottom of the screen and gasped.

"What is it?" said Tanya and Bold at the same time.

Without answering, Fox lifted his index finger and clicked *Enter*. A rumbling noise came from behind the mahogany desk.

Tanya and Bold looked up in alarm. It sounded like a low-level earthquake was about to hit the house.

Tanya bent over the desk to look.
Her jaw dropped.
Bold leaned over next to her.
"Holy mother of...."
The earth was opening below them.

Chapter Seventy-two

The deep motorized rumble sounded like something out of a horror movie.

Max's back was hunched and his hackles were up, like he was ready for a fight. He paced up and down the edge of the room, growling.

When the wood panels on the floor fully parted, it formed a square opening of six feet by six feet in the middle of the room. It was so dark inside, it was hard to say how deep it was, or if anyone was down there looking up at them.

"Son of a gun," said Bold.

"A trap door," whispered Tanya.

She dropped to her knees by the crevasse and turned her phone light on.

"Steps." She bent down and hollered. "Asha?"

No answer.

"Boss?"

It was Lopez, rushing into the study.

"Watch out!" shouted Bold and Tanya, holding their hands out.

Lopez teetered on the edge of the yawning hole, swinging her arms, until she jumped back. She stared at the opening. "What in good gracious is this?"

"The entrance to Miller's hideout," said Tanya. "Asha and the girls should be down there."

"Still alive, hopefully," said Fox.

Tanya's heart skipped a beat. She didn't want to consider the worst-case scenario. Not now.

Lopez turned to Bold. "Chief James has wrangled his team and will be here in half an hour."

Bold nodded. "I'm going down. Stay here and watch my back. We don't know where Miller is yet."

"But, Boss," said Lopez. "We'll have backup soon. Shouldn't we wait?"

"I'm not waiting for—" Tanya growled, but Bold put a hand up.

"Not when the lives of these young women are in danger. Every minute that passes increases the odds of their deaths."

Lopez stared at her boss for a second. "Understood. And I agree, sir."

Tanya breathed a sigh of relief. She would have gone down on her own anyway, even if they had held a gun to her head. It was good to know they were prepared to risk their safety for the girls and Asha.

Maybe, she thought, I judged this crew too quickly.

"Should I take Norma to my car?" said Lopez. "She's threatening to sue us for police brutality."

Bold glared. "If she thinks she can slash my team and get away with it, she doesn't know what she's got coming. Let her wait."

"Roger that. I'll be on standby."

Fox, who had been squinting at the computer, looked up. "All is quiet on the front below, sir. Can't see anyone yet."

Bold whipped around to him. "You can see what's going on down there?"

"Cameras in the tunnels. It's quite the setup."

Tanya stepped behind him and peered at the screen. "Any sign of the victims?"

"None yet, but I can't see inside these rooms."

The others joined them behind the desk. Fox traced the maze on the screen with his fingers.

"This will be your starting point when you get to the bottom of the steps. You'll see a tunnel that curves around and ends up in a fork. Beyond that, there are more tunnels that crisscross each other. Most of these corridors seem to have rooms on either side. There are two more floors below this one, so they could be anywhere."

"That's a good start." Bold tapped the mic on his shoulder. "Will radio work down there?"

"The walls look like they're made of thick concrete slabs. I doubt radio comms would come through."

"What about cellular?" said Tanya.

Fox scrunched his forehead. "We'll find out after you've gone down. I can get more details once I study this schema properly, but that'll take a day or more."

Tanya shook her head. "We have hours, maybe minutes."

"Whoa!" Fox jerked back in his seat.

He pointed at a long hallway in the underground structure. While they watched, a door at the end of a tunnel closed automatically.

"Who did that?" said Bold. "Was it you?"

Fox looked up, a nervous twitch on his neck. "There has to be another control room. Miller's manipulating the maze from there."

Tanya stared at the screen, a chill coming over her.

"He knows we're here," said Lopez, swiveling her head around for cameras. "He's watching us right now."

Fox pointed at the screen. "He just closed another door."

Tanya checked her weapon and stepped up to the yawning hole. "He's trying to stop us. Let's go!"

Chapter Seventy-three

Tanya clambered into the abyss, using her phone light to guide her.

"We need a better light than my phone," she said out loud.

The second she spoke, the staircase to the basement lit up. She spun around, startled.

"You're welcome," came Fox's voice from behind the desk.

Tanya stepped further into the hole with Bold by her side, their weapons at the ready. Max followed them down, warily sniffing the corners.

The steel stairway was deeper and steeper than they had first thought, but there was enough space for two adults to walk side by side.

The adrenaline spikes in Tanya's veins had masked the ache in her ankle as efficiently as a potent dose of morphine. Knowing she was so close to finding Asha made it easier to ignore the knife-like stabs in her lower leg.

"Well insulated," she whispered, as they reached the last step. "Doesn't smell of earth or decay."

"Smells like a hospital to me," whispered Bold as he stepped down to the main corridor.

Except for their breathing, they could hear no sound inside this subterranean maze. The tunnel's walls were made of heavy steel. The bright fluorescent lights above them gave a stark and lonely air, which made Tanya feel like they were entering the bowels of the earth itself.

The chief glanced around him and shivered. "This is what nightmares are made of."

Tanya checked her phone. "We have reception. One green bar."

"We're still in the proximity of the entrance." Bold clicked his radio and spoke in a low voice to the mouthpiece on his shoulder. "Lopez, can you hear me?"

"Loud and clear."

"Stay alert. Will contact you as soon as we find the girls."

"Roger that."

Tanya let Max go in front as he seemed eager to explore. "Stay close, bud," she commanded as he trotted in front of them.

Tanya and Bold followed silently, watching out for Dr. Miller or whoever else was working with him in this bizarre underground maze.

"When did he build this?" whispered Bold. "The construction must have been visible and loud enough. How come no one heard about it?"

"This house is inside a walled property within a gated community," whispered Tanya. "He could have pretended to be digging a deep foundation or a well and no one would have known."

"Must have cost a fortune."

"Affluent clients and high fees. Wealthy patients are known to leave inheritances to their physician, and he had a good pool of candidates."

"I remember Harold when we were kids," said Bold. "Nerdy and quiet, but smart. Nothing in his personality said he could be capable of doing any of this."

"I'm no expert, but I'd say it's Jekyll and Hyde syndrome," said Tanya, the BDSM photos in the master bedroom swirling through her head. "The meeker they are as Jekyll, the more vicious they become once they turn to Hyde."

Max was sniffing something on the wall a few feet ahead of them. Tanya stooped to examine it.

Her heart sank. "Fresh blood."

They kept walking along the tunnel, their weapons aimed forward. Tanya's arms were covered in goose bumps.

This is just the type of place the doctor could set up a death trap.

They got to the fork just as Fox had shown them on the app. There was no one in the vicinity, but something told Tanya they weren't alone.

They peered into the two corridors on either side. They seemed to go for several yards before they crisscrossed with more tunnels. A row of closed steel doors greeted their eyes on both sides.

"Right or left?" said Bold.

"It's a fifty-fifty chance either way."

Just as Tanya spoke, Max squeezed in between her legs and stepped into the tunnel on the left. He trotted through it confidently, not looking back.

"Did he catch a scent?" said Bold.

"Hard to say, but I trust his instincts."

They followed Max in.

Tanya walked up to the first door and reached for the handle.

"I'll cover you," said Bold, taking position behind her.

To Tanya's surprise, the handle moved. Keeping her weapon aimed forward, she pulled the door open.

That was when she realized the handle locked in position from the inside. Holding on to the door so it wouldn't shut behind her, she surveyed the room.

Two unoccupied gurneys lay side by side in the middle. The leather straps that hung from the beds made Tanya's blood freeze. You don't strap a corpse to a steel table. This meant, he was tying live humans to these.

For what purpose?

Did he torture those girls like lab rats?

Bold peered over Tanya's shoulder.

He had walked into Dr. Miller's private surgery once. Nurse Norma had shooed him off, but not before he saw the robotic machines and fridges with strange organic items floating in glass jars.

That place had looked like a torture chamber from a science fiction novel. It had creeped him out, but this was worse.

"What does he do here?" he whispered from the doorway.

Tanya had no answer, but she couldn't erase the terrifying thoughts swirling in her head.

A dull thud came from farther down the corridor.

They whipped around.

It was coming from the fourth door to the right. Max was sitting by it, an expectant look on his face.

They scurried over.

While Bold monitored the corridor, Tanya put an ear against the door. The sound had stopped, but her gut told her someone was inside.

She pushed the handle down, her heart in her mouth. She knew Dr. Miller could be waiting for them just behind the door.

Suddenly, someone on the other side yanked the door open.

Tanya let go and sprang back in shock.

A blood-curdling scream echoed through the tunnel.

Chapter Seventy-four

Asha pounced on Tanya, brandishing a long steel bar.

"Back off!" she screamed. "Or I'll kill you!"

Bold staggered back as the bar slammed on his arm.

"Asha!" shouted Tanya, her hands in the air to protect her face. "It's us!"

Asha stopped swinging her makeshift weapon and stared at them.

Max barked, his voice echoing through the tunnel. Tanya lowered her Glock and stared at the bloodied apparition of her friend.

Asha's cheek had a cut and a black eye was forming on her right side. Her pants were shredded at the calf, and her hair looked like it'd been spun in a hurricane.

Max started jumping around Asha, wagging and licking her anywhere he could.

"It *was* you," said Asha through swollen lips as she bent down to ruffle his head. "I thought I heard barking upstairs."

"What happened to you?" said Tanya.

Asha put her hand up. "I look worse than I feel."

"Ladies?"

They turned to Bold who was scanning the tunnel, a worried expression on his face. He gestured to Asha.

"You need to get back up *now*. My team is waiting. They'll take care of you."

Asha kicked the door behind her open. "I'm not alone."

That was when Tanya and Bold noticed the strange eyes watching them.

Three teen girls in oversized white shirts, just like Laura Fredrickson had worn, were cowering in the back of the tiny room. One of them was in a wheelchair.

The missing girls!

Tanya scrunched her forehead, trying to recollect the photos in the case files.

Aren't there supposed to be four of them?

The room was a storage closet filled with medical supplies. One shelf had been pushed to its side, its contents spilling on the ground. She noticed a steel bar on the shelf had been removed.

Good thinking, Asha.

The girls huddled in the corner, watching them with suspicious eyes. They were rake thin and pale, like they had been starved and dehydrated, just like Laura Fredrickson had looked lying in that ditch.

Tanya turned to Asha. "How did you find them?"

"I pretended I was drugged."

Tanya's eyes bulged. She knew her friend was resourceful, but this was something else.

"Norma and Miller attacked me at the café parking lot," said Asha. "They tried to chloroform me, but I pulled it away before they stuck me in the car. I fought back, but Norma was vicious. She even had a whip."

"What did they want?" said Tanya.

"They wanted to know how much we knew. That's the only reason they didn't kill me, I think."

Asha paused and licked her swollen lips before swallowing hard.

"They brought me here and locked me in a small room. They were watching me through a camera, so I pretended to be sleeping and waited. When Norma came in with a bowl of soup an hour later, I jumped out of the cot and slammed it in her face."

A crooked smirk broke on Asha's face, like it hurt to smile.

That explains the nurse's burned cheek, thought Tanya.

Atta girl.

"I locked her in and ran out. The doors open from the outside, so I just kept trying each room to see if I could find the girls."

"Who banged and called out when we were upstairs?" said Tanya. "Was that you?"

Asha nodded. "After I moved the girls in here, I peeked out just as Norma ran up the tunnel like there was an emergency. That was about half an hour ago."

"Around the time I jumped the gate. She said she saw me on their surveillance cameras."

"I followed her and saw her go through the trap door to the floor above," said Asha. "I tried it after she left, but it was locked. That's when I heard the barking. I knew Max had to be nearby. At least, I hoped it was him and you weren't far behind."

Tanya suddenly remembered the fourth girl. "Where's Janine?"

"I didn't find her."

Tanya's heart dropped. *Did Miller already kill her?*

"Ladies! We don't have time," said Bold, his voice urgent. "We have to get everyone out of here right away. I'll take the wheelchair—"

That was when a gunshot rang through the tunnel.

Everyone dove to the floor.

The bullet ricocheted off the wall and slammed into the half open storage room door.

Tanya stared at the slug embedded into the steel.

Missed by two inches.

Chapter Seventy-five

Bold whipped around and pulled the trigger.

The echo of the shot almost deafened them.

Tanya shoved Asha and Max inside the storage room. She crouched behind the steel door, her weapon aimed at the other end of the tunnel from where the initial shot had been fired.

Who was that? Miller?

Her eyes darted back and forth. That was when she caught the shadow hovering where the hallway ended and crossed another corridor.

"Bold!" she shouted as she fired her weapon. "He's got a direct line to you!"

The chief yanked the nearest door open to use it as a shield, like she had. They waited, watching, listening, but the shooting had stopped as quickly as it had started.

The only sounds came from their own heavy breathing and the vibrations of their phones. Fox and Lopez had heard the gunshots or had seen the action on the app.

Bold pulled his cell out.

"No, stand by, Lopez," he whispered furiously. "You'll be walking into a gunfight if you come down now."

In the room behind Tanya, she could hear the sobs of the girls and Asha's whispered reassurances.

Bold turned to her from across the corridor. "He's gone for now. I've got you covered."

Tanya stepped into the room, holding the door open with one hand.

Max was by the teens, as if he knew they needed protection. The girl in the wheelchair held on to his back with a trembling hand. Tanya was glad he hadn't moved away.

She turned to Asha. "I'll take the one in the wheelchair. You bring the other two."

Before Asha could answer, another shot rang out. They ducked instinctively. A weapon fired close by. Bold was firing back.

Tanya took her position behind the door again.

After a minute of silence, the chief and Tanya stepped back inside the storage room, sweat streaming down their faces.

"He's gone for now," said Bold. "But he'll be ba—"

A banshee-like wail came from deep within the maze, cutting him off.

The hair on the back of Tanya's neck stood up. The girls cowered behind Max, clutching his back.

"What the frigging heck was that?" whispered Bold hoarsely.

Asha picked up her steel bar and stepped toward the door.

Bold grabbed her by the shoulder and pulled her back. "Didn't you just hear that ungodly scream?"

Asha shrugged him off and shot him a grim look. "That was a sick boy."

Tanya's brows shot up.

Zachary?

The otherworldly shriek came again. It didn't even sound human.

Asha yanked the door open.

"There's a psycho out there trying to kill us!" said Bold.

"You two take the girls up," said Asha, stepping out. "I made a promise, and I'm the only one who knows where he is."

"Are you crazy?" Tanya reached over to grab her friend, but Asha whirled around and dashed into the corridor.

"Get back in here!" shouted Bold.

"I'll get her," said Tanya. She turned to her dog. "Max, stay with the girls."

Tanya ran out, her heart in her mouth, sure her friend would die in a hail of bullets at any moment.

You'll get us both killed!

She saw Asha nip into a side corridor she hadn't even noticed before.

Tanya sprinted over.

But Asha had already vanished into the depths of the labyrinth.

Chapter Seventy-six

Tanya caught up to Asha at the end of the second corridor.

She seized her by the arm.

"What do you think you're doing?" Tanya whispered sharply. "Trying to get us killed?"

"You shouldn't have followed me," said Asha. "Go, help those girls. Let me help the boy. I promised him. I can't leave him here."

She turned around and clambered down a flight of stairs Tanya hadn't even noticed.

"Get back!" Tanya called out.

But Asha had disappeared into the floor below.

Cursing under her breath, Tanya followed her down. All her friend had was a steel bar. That wouldn't serve her well in a gun fight.

But Tanya was no longer sure where they were anymore.

All the corridors looked the same. How her friend figured out where to go in this maze was a mystery. They had crossed several tunnels now, and she wasn't sure how they would retrace their steps.

Several yards ahead of her, Asha slowed down as if she was looking for the right entrance. Tanya followed, keeping her friend's silhouette in her line of vision, and her eyes alert for shadows.

It was darker on this floor, the only illumination coming from the security lights along the walls.

In the darkness, Tanya caught sight of a large red door. Next to it, was an imposing metal door with a sign that said *incinerator*. It smelled like she was walking by a slaughterhouse.

Suddenly the tunnel flooded with light.

Tanya whirled around, her finger on the trigger, expecting to face an armed Miller. But there was no one behind her. Or in front of her.

Fox? Did you do that?

Her phone had remained silent. She pulled it out of her pocket. With a chill, she realized the last green bar had turned red. They were completely isolated now.

Tanya spun around.

Her stomach sank.

Asha was gone.

Where did that girl go to? What in goodness' name is going on down here?

She strained to listen, but all she could hear was her pounding heart. There were no sounds of doors opening or closing, or footsteps running.

She scoped the space. There were three doors in this corridor.

Did she walk into one of these rooms?

A faint cry came from somewhere.

Tanya whirled around, her heart thumping faster.

Asha?

The cry came again.

Wait. That was someone else.

It was a girl's cry. Faint and muffled.

Tanya turned around slowly. Each of the rooms had thick, steel doors and could be hiding anything. Or anyone.

She bit her lower lip, wondering if this creepy maze was making her imagination go wild.

Where's Max when I need him?

The cry came again.

This time, she made out the words. Someone was calling for help. It sounded like they were in pain. And it was coming from the room with the red door.

Tanya stepped toward it, her Glock aimed forward. The closer she got, the stronger the metallic copper smell was, and the more she felt like retching.

She touched her mother's sunflower pendant with a prayer before she reached for the door handle.

Tanya scolded herself for being such a chicken. She was a combat war vet who had been in much more challenging situations than this, but this maze made her flesh crawl.

She pulled on the handle.

The door clicked open, but it was heavy. She squinted through the narrow opening. It was pitch black inside. Dark and cold. Tanya shivered under her jacket.

The pungent copper smell overpowered the air, like someone had dropped a gallon of blood down the sink. Her stomach lurched. She wanted to cover her nose, but she had the door propped open with one hand and was holding her weapon in the other.

She pulled the door open another inch, the muzzle of her gun pointing inside. The corridor light shone into the room but only went so far. It was a big room.

A surgery.

No, it was a laboratory.

At first glance, the room seemed empty, but Tanya could feel a presence inside.

Then came the slow and shallow breathing from the dim corner in the back.

Chapter Seventy-seven

"Who's in here?" Tanya called out into the darkness.

Silence.

She pulled the door an inch further and scanned the nearby walls for a light switch. To her immediate right was a garbage bin and to her left was a long steel counter that seemed to go on forever.

Using the door to shield her body, she thrust her arm in and cocked her gun.

"Come out or I shoot!"

"Don't hurt me!"

Tanya froze.

It was the frightened voice of a young girl. It had been throaty, like she was having difficulty breathing.

Tanya pulled the door open a few more inches and waited for her eyes to adjust to the darkness. Soon, she made out the outlines of more shelving, stainless steel fridges, and what looked like lab equipment.

She checked her phone, but the bars were still red. If someone was in trouble inside this room, she had to save her. As much as she wanted, she couldn't be in two places at once.

She gritted her teeth.

Where did you run off to, Asha?

The breathing coming from the far corner had become shallower and faster.

"Who are you?" called out Tanya.

"Help me!"

"What are you doing in here?"

"I want to go home."

Tanya stepped inside the room, holding it ajar with her foot, and pointed her flashlight in the direction of the voice.

Her heart leaped to her mouth.

Janine!

She was sitting upright in what looked like a small cot and was struggling to get out.

"Hang on, hun," said Tanya. "I'm coming."

This door locked from the inside, just like the other rooms. Tanya pulled the garbage bin and wedged it between the door and the frame before stepping inside. It wasn't the safest option, but it would have to do.

She was about to head over to the girl when her eyes caught sight of the glass case on the wall to her right. Behind it was an electrical panel of some sort.

The light switches!

She reached over to pull the case open, but it was locked.

Damn you, Miller.

Using her phone for illumination, she turned around and crept through the maze of counters and shelves toward Janine, her gun at the ready.

Her eyes scanned the room, her senses on full alert, half expecting Miller to jump out from behind a counter at any moment.

Janine raised her head.

"Please get me out of here. Please!"

She looked pale and dehydrated, and was wearing a plain white T-shirt, just like Laura had.

"It's okay, sweetie," said Tanya. "I'll take you home."

She stepped closer.

That was when she realized why Janine was struggling to climb out. The girl's hands were handcuffed to the steel bars of the bed. Her forearms had needles in them, the long tubing connecting to plastic bags sitting on steel trays beside the cot.

Tanya stared at the contraptions in horror.

Janine turned her tear-stained face to her. "He's draining my blood."

Her eyes were so glazed that Tanya wondered if Miller had drugged her. She took stock, taking in the girl's frail body, the needles, and the strange machines surrounding the bed.

"You're going to be fine, hun," she said, holstering her weapon. "Stay completely still, okay?"

Janine started to cry, her chest heaving with every sob.

As Tanya reached for the needle inserted into Janine's right arm, her mouth went dry. She swallowed hard.

Can I just pull these out? Will she go into shock? Am I going to kill her?

Janine whimpered.

That was when the door scraped open.

Someone's coming in!

Chapter Seventy-eight

Tanya stared at the ghostly figure by the doorway.

Wilma?

Wilma kicked the garbage bin aside and stepped inside. The steel door shut with a clang. A loud click told Tanya the lock had engaged.

"Hey!" she yelled. "You just locked us in."

"You're not going to get out." Wilma's voice was strangely guttural.

Tanya jerked back in surprise.

Wilma glided toward them without even a glance around her. With a chill, Tanya realized she was so familiar with this lab she could make her way through the maze of counters and shelves in the dark.

Even in the dim light, Tanya caught the maniacal glint in her eyes. It was like the receptionist had changed her personality overnight.

"What are you doing in Miller's dungeon?" said Tanya.

Wilma didn't reply.

That was when Tanya spotted the serrated knife in her left hand and the pistol in her right, hidden by her long, flared sleeves. The sidearm was pointed to the ground, but she knew that could change in a second.

Janine wailed and pulled at the handcuffs, rattling them against the steel poles. Tanya stepped in front of the cot to shield the girl and raised her Glock.

Wilma didn't flinch.

Tanya cocked her weapon.

"Stay back! I'll shoot!"

Wilma stopped.

A voice inside Tanya's head was screaming. Wilma was old enough to be her mother. She couldn't shoot her, could she?

Wilma smiled to see her hesitate.

"I wouldn't do that if I were you, my dear. Dr. Miller's watching."

Tanya's eyes darted to the dark recesses of the lab, her heart racing.

Is Miller here? Hiding in this room all along? Or is she lying?

The older woman chortled. "You thought you had me figured out, didn't you?"

Tanya felt a warm flush rush up her neck.

Behind her, Janine rumbled in her cot, whimpering in desperation. The girl had already looked weak when Tanya had found her. She didn't know how long she would last in these conditions.

She kept her gaze in front. "I should have known you were part of this racket."

"What racket?" Wilma cocked her head demurely. "It's all for a good cause."

"Kidnapping girls and bleeding them dry isn't what I call a good cause."

Wilma didn't reply, but stood with her back straight and her chin up, as if challenging her.

"Why did Miller want these girls?" asked Tanya. "Is this a perverted game, part of his BDSM routine?"

Wilma made a face. "Don't be so sick."

"The sicko is Miller's father," snapped Tanya. "Elizabeth told me everything."

Wilma raised an eyebrow. "You think *Senior Dr. Miller* is Zachary's father?"

Tanya did a double take. She sounded genuinely surprised. "Isn't he?"

Wilma didn't answer but her face had contorted into something strange.

"Put your weapons down," growled Tanya. "We'll go upstairs together and you can tell Chief Bold and me what the heck is going on in this gawd forsaken vault."

"Bold?" Wilma cackled. "You won't be seeing him again, my dear."

Chapter Seventy-nine

Tanya's heart skipped a beat.

"Does Bold know what you're up to? Is he part of this scheme too?"

"Bold's a goody two-shoes." Wilma sniffed. "My husband was the smart one. We lived the high life. Now he's gone, I get nothing but a stupid pension."

"The high life on a small-town police chief's salary? Was your husband getting kickbacks?"

Wilma didn't answer, but her face told her she had hit close.

"Who from? The mayor? Council members? Someone else on the West End?"

Wilma's face turned dark.

Tanya's head cleared as more puzzle pieces came together.

"The kickbacks stopped after your hubby died. That's when you turned to Miller. You're blackmailing him, aren't you?"

"I'm helping him!"

Gotcha.

"You knew his family secret, and you took advantage of it. You and your husband were con artists."

"You make us sound like we were criminals. We were only helping everyone out."

"You *are* a criminal." Tanya's voice was sharp.

"How dare you?" shrieked Wilma.

She's delusional.

"Now I know how you can afford the expensive shoes and cruises," said Tanya.

"A girl needs gifts." Wilma's lips curled in contempt. "You'll find out when you get to my age, honey. Your pretty face won't get compliments anymore. You'll get wrinkles and sunspots, and everything will sag. You'll end up becoming a minimum-wage paper-pusher in an asbestos-filled office, working for a bunch of dumb cops."

"Those thugs who were mugging you on my first day," said Tanya. "They weren't trying to steal your purse, were they? You didn't want me to report that crime because—"

"It was a minor disagreement," snapped Wilma. "They wanted more money for their work and I told them no."

"What did they do for you? Lure the girls so you can get your cut?"

"Sometimes you need to use a bit of force."

Tanya's stomach churned. She took a step closer to Wilma.

"You seem to have a death wish."

That sly smile cracked on Wilma's face again. "If you shoot me, Dr. Miller's going to fill this room with toxic gas. You and Janine will die in five minutes. You're the one with a death wish."

"If you wanted to gas us, you wouldn't have come in here for a chat."

"I thought it would be more fun to see you die in front of my eyes."

She paused, her cold eyes boring into Tanya's.

"You thought it was Jones all along, didn't you? You misjudged me. Like everyone else in this town. I hate it when people underestimate me."

Her voice rose to a fever pitch.

"You think I'm just a little old woman, too stupid for anything? That's what everyone thinks. All the while I know everyone's secrets and you all know nothing. Who's the smart one now?"

Tanya grimaced. *Cold and calculating is what you are.*

Wilma stepped forward and raised her arm, her gun aimed at Tanya's head.

Janine rattled her handcuffs.

"No!" she screeched. "Lemme go! I wanna go home!"

Wilma cocked her weapon.

Tanya fired.

Janine shrieked.

Wilma collapsed to the ground in a crumpled heap.

Chapter Eighty

A loud hissing came from somewhere in the room.

Janine started sobbing.

It sounded like air was escaping from a pressurized chamber. Tanya swiveled around, her heart racing.

She scanned for signs of smoke, but there was nothing to see or smell. But she knew there were enough noxious gases that were both odorless and colorless.

Was Wilma telling the truth?

She raced to the front of the room, pointing her flashlight in all directions.

Where's that coming from?

She whirled around, her heart pounding.

We have five minutes!

She grabbed the door handle, but it didn't budge.

Damn you, Wilma.

That was when she realized there might be another way to get out alive. Tanya stepped up to the glass-covered electronic panel and raised her arm.

"Janine!" She brought the muzzle of her gun level with the side of the case. "Close your ears!"

"What are you doing?" cried the girl. "I wanna get out of here!"

Tanya tilted her head to the side and lifted one arm to shield her face.

"Get down!"

She fired.

The glass splintered in all directions, jagged pieces slamming onto her shoulders and chest.

Ignoring the stings on her arms, Tanya stepped up to the panel, her boots scrunching on the broken glass. The small print was now visible under the switches.

Door.

She flipped the switch.

A loud click came from the door.

It's unlocked!

She slammed it open and kicked the garbage bin back in position to keep it ajar.

"Don't leave me!" screamed Janine.

Tanya whirled around to see the girl was pulling the needles from her arms.

She dashed over and yanked the remaining syringes out, not knowing how much damage she was inflicting. But the noxious fumes were filling the room fast and Miller could be on his way to finish them.

Tanya pulled the last needle from Janine's arm and grabbed her hand. Blood droplets dripped onto the girl's T-shirt.

"Stop moving!"

Tanya snatched the handcuffs and stuck the needle into the keyhole. Janine froze as she realized what she was trying to do.

When the cuffs fell off, the girl pulled her hands toward her and stared at them as if she couldn't believe she was free.

Janine was too weak to walk, but Tanya couldn't carry her and be prepared for an attack as well. She surveyed the room for a wheelchair.

Wilma lay lifeless on the ground, a trail of blood flowing from the gaping hole in her head, but she didn't have time to think about what she'd just done.

The hissing sound was getting louder, and she already felt light-headed.

"Hold tight."

Tanya pushed her arms under Janine's legs and scooped her up.

Carrying the girl, she stumbled toward the door, hoping against hope Miller wasn't waiting for them. Janine wrapped her arms around her neck and buried her face on her shoulder, like she didn't want to see what was outside.

Tanya kicked the door open and stepped out.

Chapter Eighty-one

The corridor was empty.

An eerie silence had fallen in the labyrinth. All Tanya could hear were Janine's whimpers and her own heart thudding against her chest.

Where's Asha?

She's still down here somewhere.

As if in reply, the unearthly screech she'd heard before cut through the maze.

Janine jumped with a shriek. Tanya almost dropped the girl.

It's that boy.

She laid the girl on the floor and pulled out her phone.

Still red.

Tanya was about to pick Janine up when she noticed movement down the corridor.

She spun around.

"Who's there?"

A strange rustling came from beyond the tunnel. Then, a silhouette darted across the opening and ran into the corridor on the left.

"Miller!" she hollered. "Give yourself up! You have nowhere to go!"

Tanya ran into the tunnel where the shadow had disappeared to. It crossed the corridor before it vanished into the bowels of the maze. She followed, her Glock aimed in front.

She was halfway down the next tunnel where she thought the shadow had gone to, when she realized her surroundings had changed.

She stopped and gaped.

This was a new section of the labyrinth.

The corridors were wider and better lit. A red rug ran the length of the floor and the smell of blood and disinfectant was replaced by something more pleasant.

Lemon and lavender.

Tanya stepped forward cautiously, her eyes scanning the area.

There were two rooms on either side, but unlike the ones she'd seen before, the doors here were made of dark wood—like those you'd find in an upscale suburban house.

One door was ajar.

She stepped up to it and reached for the handle with one hand, while holding her gun with the other.

There was someone inside. She could hear them move about.

Miller?

Chapter Eighty-two

Tanya peeked inside.

The windowless room was twenty times the size of the closet where they had found the girls. And it couldn't have been more different.

Superman posters adorned one wall. Comic books were piled high on the carpeted floor and an electric guitar leaned against a desk strewn with gaming consoles. A small fridge had been placed next to the bed.

The acrid smell of medicine was unmistakable. Various screens surrounded the bed—machines Tanya would have expected to see in an intensive care ward.

Tanya pushed the door open.

Asha turned around, startled.

"It's *you!* You almost gave me a heart attack."

She was by the bed, holding up a pallid looking boy, struggling to get him into a wheelchair. With his scrawny limbs and emaciated body, the boy looked like a refugee from a famine.

Zachary?

Tanya turned to her friend. "I found Janine. She's in critical condition."

"He needs immediate medical attention too, but he can't be rushed."

Tanya checked the door. This also only unlocked from the outside. Despite the well-stocked and comfortable setting, the boy was a prisoner in this underground labyrinth as well.

Keeping a firm hold on the door, she reached over for a book and rammed it in between the door and the frame.

"We have to hurry," said Tanya, walking over to help Asha. "Miller's on the prowl."

Asha turned to the boy. "Zachary, this is my friend, Tanya, who I was talking about."

Zachary squinted at Tanya.

So, Elizabeth was right. Her son had been kept alive all these years.

The boy struggled to lift a lanky hand and opened his mouth. Tanya braced herself for another screech.

"H... h... hi...." He turned away shyly and swayed from side to side.

"Hi Zachary," said Tanya, a sting of sorrow crossing her heart. *What a life he must have had.*

Asha plucked a blanket from the bed and placed it on his lap. "I told you she'd come and rescue us, didn't I?"

Tanya grabbed Asha by the arm and whispered in her ear. "We don't have time."

"He's seriously sick," whispered Asha hoarsely. "He's been bedridden most of his life and hooked to all these machines. Took me ages to free him. We can't pull him out just like that."

"Why not? What's wrong with him?"

Asha pointed to a medical chart lying on the bedside table.

"That says he's a chronic hemophiliac. My guess is Miller stole the girls' blood for transfusions, to keep him alive. Why didn't he take him to a hospital for proper treatment? Why would he do such a crazy thing?"

Tanya took a sharp breath in.

Miller's his uncle and brother.

That's why.

Tanya stared at the boy who was reaching for a bottle of water on the table with his limp arm, but grasping air instead. Asha picked up the bottle and placed it in his lap.

"I'll open it for you outside, okay? Now, we have to hurry."

The boy gave her a small smile.

"Tha... thank you."

"Genetic disorder," said Tanya to herself, not realizing she was speaking out aloud. "It's common in..."

Asha looked up. "What are you talking about?"

Tanya shook her head.

"Nothing. Let's go. I've left Janine alone for too long."

Asha grabbed the wheelchair's handles and spun it around.

"There's an elevator on the other end of the corridor, near the incinerator. I think that goes to the first floor."

"I'll go get Janine."

Tanya turned to the entrance, but her gut signaled danger.

"Let me check first," she whispered. "Stay back till I give the all clear."

She stepped up to the door, her Glock at the ready. It banged open as she got within three feet of it.

It was Miller.

And he wasn't alone.

Chapter Eighty-three

Miller had Janine by the throat.

He was dragging her, holding her in a vise grip. He had a syringe at her neck and the girl was shaking uncontrollably.

Tanya's heart dropped.

I should have never left her.

She whipped her gun at his head. "Let her go."

The doctor made a motion as if to dig the needle into Janine's neck.

"Stop!"

Miller turned his wild eyes toward her.

A raging monster had replaced the introverted physician. His face was blotchy, and his hair stood on end. The enormous eyes behind those thick spectacles emanated an unfathomable darkness.

Tanya had no idea what was in that syringe. He could be bluffing, but she had already gambled with Janine's life once.

"She gave you her blood. Isn't that enough?" said Tanya. "Let her go and we can talk."

Though her voice was composed, her heart was hammering inside of her.

"And hand all the cards to you?" said Miller. "What do you take me for? A fool?"

Tanya jerked her head back in surprise.

What happened to his stuttering and stammering? Was that an act?

She took a deep breath in, willing herself to remain calm. She needed to distract him enough for him to turn that syringe away from the girl.

"I talked to Elizabeth," she said. "She told me everything. I know you incarcerated her in the mental hospital."

"She killed our father," snarled Miller, his eyes blazing. But his grip on Janine was still strong.

"She's your sister," said Tanya. "The mother of your nephew. Your brother."

"*What?*" Asha's incredulous voice came from behind her. "What are you saying?"

"She's a whore," said Miller, ignoring Asha. "She didn't deserve to be a mother. She was sinful!"

Zachary let out an ear-splitting screech.

Tanya's heart sank.

Poor kid. He shouldn't be hearing any of this.

"She was just a child," said Tanya. "Your father harmed her. Did you hurt her too?"

Miller's face flushed but his hand holding the syringe never wavered.

"How dare you!" His voice cracked. "I just wanted it all to stop. That's the only reason I did what he told me to do."

"What do you mean?" said Tanya.

"He said he was going to make a man out of me. Elizabeth was drugged. She never knew. So I just…" He stopped and swallowed hard. His face flushed a deep red.

"I was ashamed!" Miller screeched.

Tanya suddenly realized what had happened long ago, and why Wilma had looked surprised when she'd mentioned her conversation with Elizabeth.

Her voice hardened. "What were you ashamed of, Miller?"

Tears streamed down the doctor's face.

"Zachary is my son!"

Chapter Eighty-four

The only sound in the room was Zachary's sobs.

Tanya stared into the physician's soulless eyes.

The last pieces of the puzzle were coming together.

It was easy to forget Miller had also been a kid when his sister had been abused. Older, but still, an impressionable child who had been under his father's influence, just like his sister had been.

"Why put Elizabeth away?" said Tanya, any tinge of pity she'd felt evaporating just as she'd felt them.

The doctor didn't answer.

Miller had fooled everyone. This had been a foul family affair all along. One that Norma and Wilma had willingly supported for their own twisted personal reasons.

"Were you scared she'd tell the truth?"

Miller straightened up and his eyes hardened. "I have a reputation to protect."

"Are you kidding me?"

"I have credentials, awards, a pedigree. It's why my patients come to see me. They pay me well. If any of this got out to the town, I'd be ruined. My life would be over!"

He hissed so loudly, Tanya was almost sure she spotted a forked tongue in his mouth.

"I should have killed the witch," he snarled.

Tanya shot him an icy stare, a sudden urge coming over her to pistol whip him till he bled.

"Hold on a minute, people," came Asha's voice from behind her. "Are you telling me you're Zachary's father? And that his mother is still alive?"

The doctor turned and gave her a startled look. His eyes flitted down to Zachary, like he just realized the boy and she had been in the room all along.

With a silent thanks to her friend, Tanya took a discreet step closer to Miller. She made eye-contact with Janine. The girl was still shaking, but she seemed to understand what she was about to do.

Good.

"This is crazy," said Asha from behind her.

"Y... you... lied!" screamed Zachary. "You... s... said y... you're my un... uncle."

"Where is Zachary's mother?" demanded Asha.

A loud sob came from the boy. "I w... want to see my m... mother!"

Tanya inched closer.

"Shut up!" shrieked Miller, his fury on Asha now.

More sobs came from the boy behind her.

Tanya felt a pang of guilt.

Every word spoken would be like knife stabs to Zachary, but every second the doctor was focused on the boy, it gave her the opportunity she was seeking.

"I did this to protect you," cried Miller. "Your mother never deserved you. Our father punished her because she was bad. Can't you understand?"

Zachary let out another hair-raising scream.

That was all the distraction Tanya needed.

She sprang forward and slammed Miller against the wall with such force, he let go of Janine.

"Watch out!" she yelled as the syringe fell to the ground, like a dagger honing in on its target. Janine rolled away just in time.

Tanya snapped her attention back to the doctor, but it was too late. He had pulled a handgun from his pocket. It was pointing at her forehead.

Tanya froze.

Miller's eyes were cruel.

He smirked. "You think I didn't come prepared?"

It was like time had stopped. No one spoke. Miller and Tanya stood two feet apart, the barrels of their guns touching each other's temples.

A dull thundering sound came from somewhere in the labyrinth, like an army was marching over them.

The backup.

Tanya grimaced as she realized they would be dead by the time Bold and the backup crew tried all the tunnels and all the closed doors.

"Please," cried the boy. "I want to see my m... mother."

"Your mother's dead!" screeched Miller. "They're lying to you!"

"It was you who lied to him!" Asha's furious voice cut through the room. "You're a sick man!"

The doctor spluttered. His face flushed. With no warning, Miller spun around and aimed his gun at Asha.

"Down!" shouted Tanya.

Asha yanked the wheelchair and dove to the floor. The wheelchair crashed, pinning Zachary and Asha underneath it.

Miller fired.

The bullet ripped through the top of the chair and blasted into the guitar, smashing it into a thousand pieces.

Tanya pulled the trigger.

Her gunshot reverberated like thunder.

Zachary's ear-splitting screams echoed through the room.

Tanya watched the doctor's lifeless body slide to the floor, spreading a splatter of blood on the concrete surface.

It looked just like the painting on his living-room wall.

Day Four

Chapter Eighty-five

Lopez flipped through the photos of Miller's underground labyrinth, her face scrunched in revulsion.

"So, this wasn't a sextortion scheme or a pedophile ring?"

"That was Miller's cover," said Fox, adjusting his arm sling. "His aliases, White Knight, Tall & Dark, and the rest, had one job. To convince the girls to share half-naked pictures. Shame is a powerful tool."

Bold grimaced. "He had no interest in the girls other than to bleed them dry."

The team had gathered in the station's bullpen, evidence boxes, paperwork, and coffee cups from Lulu's Café scattered on their desks.

Max was sitting at Tanya's feet, unleashed, as the others now seemed comfortable with his presence. He nuzzled against her crutches, while she scratched his neck.

Tanya was paying for ignoring her sprained ankle.

Stacey and Justin, the paramedics, had sat her down at Miller's house and iced her swollen foot before wrapping it with a brace and handing her a set of crutches. They had glowered when she had protested. For the sake of peace, she had accepted and was glad she did.

The team had been working nonstop, collecting and recording evidence. No one had mentioned Wilma's name, still too shocked at the depth of her deception and that she had worked among them.

"The man's creative. I'll give him that," said Lopez. "Used innocent kids to keep his own secret child alive, and set up a sex site to lure girls to their deaths."

"Only Laura died," pointed out Fox.

"He was rotating through them, but as soon as they got too weak, he was going to discard them." Lopez waved a photo in the air. "What do you think this incinerator in the last tunnel was for?"

Tanya shuddered at the thought. That was where she and Janine would have ended up if Wilma and Miller had gotten their way.

"Miller didn't return to Black Rock out of the goodness of his heart." Bold picked up a file that bore the emblem of a prominent hospital in a nearby state. The stenciled lettering in front read, SENSITIVE. "He was looking for fresh blood."

He flipped the folder open.

"The Hoffman University Hospital, among others, fired him for malpractice. Says here he caused grievous harm in several cases for years, but the details are sketchy. The hospital is hiding behind patient privacy laws."

"Caught him too late, then covered their butts. They deserve a class action lawsuit," said Lopez. "Too bad it's not our jurisdiction."

Bold shook his head. "Those poor girls never knew what was coming to them."

"Zachary was O positive," said Fox, picking up a paper from a file. "It's the most common blood type. All Miller had to do was cherry pick the healthiest girls from low-income families and get Wilma to push the right buttons. Voila, he had his supply in this town."

"Everyone sang his praises, saying he gave free health care to the East End," said Lopez. "All the time he was prowling for victims."

"Miller, Norma, and Wilma fooled everyone," said Bold. "Even me."

Fox swiveled around in his chair. "It was Norma who messaged you and left notes on your Jeep, Stone. I found the doctored image of the electric chairs on her laptop. I'd guess Wilma gave her your number. They wanted to scare you off."

Tanya gave him a steely look through her shades.

Good thing I don't scare easily.

"What about the paper I took from Laura's mouth?" she asked.

"Wilma lied to you," said Fox. "I found it in the shredder bin. It's with the forensics lab in the next county over. They'll recreate it for us."

"We have enough evidence on our hands without that note," said Bold. "Norma's talking. She's bargaining hard for a reduced sentence."

Lopez shot her boss a solemn look. "I wouldn't have shed a tear if Stone had shot her too."

Tanya sat quietly, her downcast eyes fixated on her empty coffee cup. But her mind was elsewhere. She hadn't been able to get rid of the image of the subterranean boy's room from her head.

Justice at all cost, had been her battle cry after her mother's murder. But as she sat with her muddled thoughts in the cold light of day, she wondered how true that was.

"I've scarred Zachary for life," she said, speaking to her cup more than to the crew.

The officers looked up.

"What do you mean?" said Lopez, frowning.

"I killed his father in front of his eyes," said Tanya in a quiet voice, "just after he learned who he really was and how he was conceived."

"You had no choice," said Bold.

Tanya didn't look up. "I shot Wilma in front of Janine. What's her life going to be like after that?"

"These kids were already damaged," said Fox, shaking his head, "by Miller. Not you."

Bold leaned over. "If the ethics board or city council come asking about the gunfire in the dungeon, I have your back, Stone. That's a promise."

He paused.

"Mother and son have been reunited, and the remaining girls are back home. That's what matters. That's what we need to focus on."

Tanya sat up and shook herself to clear her mind, though there was one more troubling thought she couldn't shake off.

"Where's Jones? How come he's never at the station these days?"

Lopez flashed her a smug grin. "Drew the shortest straw. On traffic duty."

Bold gave her a warning look. "If he didn't volunteer to be out there, you wouldn't be in here working on the case, Lopez."

Lopez put her hands up in mock defense. "Just glad it's not me."

"Me too," quipped Fox. "If he wants it, he can have it."

Tanya wondered if Jones was truly on patrol. Or elsewhere.

While she now knew he had played no part in the kidnapping horror story, she hadn't forgotten how he had misled and delayed them from the beginning. He was also tight with the shifty guards from the Grimwood Estate.

Was Jones incompetent, or was he hiding something?

Mayor Bailey and his wife didn't inspire much confidence in her either. There were deep secrets in this town, secrets she had yet to dig up.

Bold slapped Tanya on her shoulder. "Chin up, Stone. You did a darn good job. Over and beyond what I hired you for."

Lopez gave her a thumbs up.

Fox gave Tanya a wry smile. "Don't know how I would have reacted if Wilma had come at me like that. Or Miller for that matter. You did real good."

Tanya glanced around her, glad her eyes were cloaked by her wraparound shades.

So, this is what trust feels like.

Something in her shifted. Max had sidled up to the chief for a head scratch that morning and had even accepted a treat from Fox.

Maybe I need to stop being so paranoid.

A buzz came from Tanya's pocket. It was her regular cell.

She pulled out the phone and clicked on the message app. She stared, not hearing the joke Fox shared or the laughter that rippled through the office.

Black Rock's not done with you, Agent. Your death wish will be granted.

A chill went down Tanya's spine.

Agent?

This wasn't Ray. This wasn't even Norma. Then, who was it?

Norma's threats had always been directly related to this case, and she had never even hinted at knowing Tanya's true identity. Besides, the nurse was in police custody with no access to a phone.

Tanya glanced around the bullpen.

Whoever sent this wasn't here. None of them had their phones out, unless they had scheduled this text in advance.

Can you even do that?

She made a mental note to check with Asha. She would know.

Maybe it's Jones. How did he find out about my undercover role?

Her finger hovered over the delete button.

No, this is going to Susan Cross and Ray Jackson. It's time they took these threats seriously.

"Everything all right?"

Tanya looked up to see Bold watching her, concern in his eyes. She snapped the app shut and pocketed her phone.

"Family stuff."

Someone rapped on the glass barricade at the empty reception desk.

It was Asha.

"Came to say goodbye," she hollered, waving through the window.

Lopez walked over and opened the secure door. Asha stepped inside with a bright smile, despite the black eye she had been sporting for days.

"All packed up. I'm heading to Seattle tomorrow." She came behind Tanya's chair and squeezed her shoulders. "Take care of my good friend while I'm gone, guys. Be nice to her, now."

Lopez rolled her eyes.

"Like she needs taking care of," scoffed Fox.

Bold dropped the file he had been holding and picked up his hat. He looked around his team.

"What do you all say to the Dog House pub tonight? We can say goodbye to Asha and take a break from shop talk. Drinks are on me."

"I'd love that," said Asha.

Lopez jumped to her feet. "If you're buying, I'm in, Boss."

Fox grinned and got up.

One by one, the crew stumbled out of the office.

Asha and Tanya followed them to the station's parking lot. Tanya opened the back door of the Jeep for Max to jump in and threw in her crutches next to him.

Asha smiled at her from the passenger seat in front. "I feel lighter already. With Miller, Norma, and Wilma gone, Black Rock feels like the quaint little town again. I think you'll like it here."

Tanya nodded for her friend's sake. But her mind was on the warning text message.

She hopped over to the driver's door and got in. She pulled the Jeep out of the parking lot and followed Bold's car toward Marine Drive, only half listening to Asha chattering next to her.

Dark clouds were gathering inside her head. Tanya reached for her mother's sunflower pendant and squeezed it for luck.

While the others were relaxing as this case drew to a close, she still had her bigger mission. But now, she had more questions than answers.

Who knows I'm undercover in Black Rock?

What do they want with me?

※ ※ ※

Thank you for reading HER COLD BLOOD! I hope you enjoyed the story.

Would you like to read the epilogue story? Learn more about the town of Black Rock and its locals. See how Chief Bold reacts to Asha admitting to be a private detective, and what he proposes to Tanya that gets her worried....

<u>Download the epilogue chapter of this book here!</u>
www.books.tikiriherath.com/ts-1-doghousepub

✦—■—✦

Want more spine-tingling mystery thrillers with Tanya and Max?

HER LAST LIE is the next book in this series. Turn the page to start reading the next book right here.

Tanya stumbles across a stomach-churning sight one morning by the stormy beach—a young female corpse with no head. A devious serial killer with morbid intentions is haunting this small seaside town. Tanya will have to fight her past nightmares to unmask the "beach butcher," as the town folk have dubbed him....

Turn the page to start reading the next book right here!

Continue the adventure with
Her Last Lie!

Chapter One – BLOOD WINE KILL

❖───❖───❖

"You will kill tonight."

I heard her sharp voice and stared at the dagger.

Its ivory handle was carved with mysterious Egyptian symbols. It lay innocently in her white gloved hand, but I had seen that slick blade pierce through skin and bone.

The Star of Death.

My stomach lurched.

Can I do it?

She moved across the ballroom's marble floor, toward me.

Even from twenty feet away, I felt her arctic-blue eyes boring into mine. They were like luminous lasers that could incinerate me in one hot second.

But I couldn't look away.

The Queen, as she called herself, didn't walk. She floated with sinewy grace, her pose regal, her face stern.

She was clad in a stunning red Victorian ball-gown of silk and satin. Her diamond studded tiara glittered under the crystal chandeliers that dropped from the cathedral-like ceiling.

She was one of the most mesmerizing women I'd met, but her sylphlike movements reminded me of a cobra stalking its pray.

My shoulders tightened. A bead of sweat trickled down my back. Only one wild thought swirled through my troubled mind.

Can I kill tonight?

The blood pounded so loudly in my ears, I barely heard the murmur of voices around me.

They were the voices of beautiful people in luxurious Rocco gowns and fancy tuxedos. Hollywood stars and starlets. Venture capitalists and hedge fund managers. Celebrities and influencers. All drinking vintage red wine from crystal glasses, waiting for the ceremony to begin.

The Queen was so close, I could smell her fragrance now.

She got it from an exclusive boutique on Manhattan's Billionaire's Row. I know because she took me there last summer in her private jet, and told me I could have anything I wanted for my twentieth birthday. She hadn't batted an eyelid when I pointed at the sapphire studded eau de parfum from Switzerland that cost seven thousand dollars.

She bought me that day.

There was no turning back, after that.

The Queen thrust the precious dagger toward my chest. I stepped back in alarm.

Her lips quivered with anticipation and her eyes blazed like wild fire.

"Take it," she said, her beautifully painted lips curving into a coaxing smile.

My throat went dry. I could feel the others' eyes on me from all corners of the hall, staring, judging, mocking.

From the corner of my eye, I spotted the man in the black tuxedo and top hat standing by the fireplace, a condescending sneer pasted on his face. It was like he couldn't wait to see me fail.

I was sure his snooty girlfriend was hovering nearby, swishing around in her golden evening gown, boring everyone with the last yachting trip she made to the Bahamas. Or wherever.

An angry flush crept up my neck.

I hate them.

With trembling fingers, I reached over and touched the carved hilt. The handle felt cold against my skin, like death itself.

I pulled back.

"I chose you because I know you can do it. Because you're worth it." The Queen's face was inches from mine, her perfume intoxicating my senses.

My head started to spin.

I want to, but I'm not ready.

The knife's tip touched the French lace ruffle of my bodice. One twist of her wrist, and she could slash my chest in half.

Every fiber in my body screamed at me to walk away.

But I couldn't.

"This will be yours tonight."

The Queen had unveiled her other hand. On her gloved palm was a dazzling diamond bracelet. The red vial pendent glowed under the light, beckoning me to pick it up.

That wasn't a ruby.

"Do you really want *them* to win?" she hissed in my ear.

I glanced behind her. The top hatted man's arrogant smirk had widened. He had seen me hesitate.

Something dark stirred inside of me. I could feel the slow boil of my hot blood surge through my veins. My heart quickened and my face flushed.

No. I can't let these losers have the last say.

I snatched the dagger from the Queen's hand and gripped it, feeling it's power shoot up my arm like it was alive.

"Good girl."

I stared at the ominous red stains on the blade, but I knew that wasn't rust.

"I never wash after my kills."

With those words, the Queen swirled around, and stepped away from me. Sweeping the marble floor in her majestic ball gown, she headed toward the man in the top hat to tell him the news. His smirk had vanished.

This time, I smiled.

Today is the day I take my power.

"Wine?"

I turned to see a female server in a crisp black shirt and pants next to my elbow, a silver tray in her hand. That used to be my job, once. Not anymore.

I picked up a glass.

This should help.

I brought the crystal close to my lips, smelling the human blood mixed in with the Château Margot. A shiver ran down my spine. Each glass got only a few drops as per tradition, but the scent lingered.

Maybe it was just my imagination, but I grasped the glass and savored every drop.

My confidence was back.

The Queen is right. I'm going to show them who I really am.

The resounding trumpet call from the corner of the hall startled everyone. The room hushed to an expected silence, and all eyes turned on me.

The Queen had taken a seat in her plush crimson throne. Next to her, a golden-haired harpist played a heart-wrenching song that would have made me cry any other day.

Not today.

My heart pounded inside my chest. My hands were wet with sweat but I clutched the dagger even tighter.

I straightened my shoulders and lifted my head high.

I rotated around and gazed at the stage that had been set across from the Queen's dais. It was decorated with elaborate mini lights and exotic flowers, fit for a lavish wedding. A large shrouded object took center stage, draped in a white cloth.

The air suddenly felt heavy, like a thick fog had rolled in from the ocean and had settled over us. My throat constricted.

A young man dressed in a crisp footman's uniform hastened up to the platform and pulled away the cloth with a flourish.

A few shocked gasps escaped from the onlookers at the sight of the naked girl tied to the cross. Even if you had seen this scene a hundred times, it was always unexpected.

The air in the room was getting warmer, and the tension, thicker.

The girl on the cross raised her head. Her eyes widened and her face scrunched in horror as she realized the ceremony was about to begin.

I walked toward the podium, putting one foot in front of the other, the dagger in my hand steeling my heart.

I could feel the eyes of the man in the top hat and his nasty girlfriend on my back. I could almost hear them snicker as they wondered if I was strong enough. I clenched my jaw.

I'll show them.

The girl on the cross struggled as I got closer, but she looked broken and defeated, like life had already been drained out of her. The bloodletting rite had begun at noon. It was her blood we were all drinking.

Behind me, a low chant came from the crowd, melding harmoniously with the haunting melody from the harpist.

I was ten feet from the cross now.

The voices got louder, echoing through the hall.

I pulled up the skirts of my gown and climbed the steps on to the stage where the cross was. Where the girl was. I couldn't trip and fall. Not now. Not in front of them.

The girl on the cross let out a cry. They hadn't drugged her enough, but that was inconsequential now.

I walked over to the cross, my head spinning.

Must be the wine.

I stood for a moment and observed the terrified young woman. She was about my age. Her skin looked baby soft and white as snow under the sparkling chandeliers. She almost looked like me. We could have been twins.

I raised the dagger high in the air.

My hand trembled.

Stop shaking. You can do it!

The chanting got louder.

I brought down the knife.

A bone-chilling scream cut through the hall, shredding my nerves.

The dagger fell from my hand and I crumpled to the floor.

Then, darkness fell around me.

To be continued...

Continue reading HER LAST LIE.
www.tikiriherath.com/thrillers
And find out how to get early access to all the books in the
Tanya Stone FBI K9 series.

HER LAST LIE is the next book in the Tanya Stone FBI K9
Mystery Thriller series.

Find out what happens when Tanya Stone stumbles across a stomach-churning sight one morning by the stormy beach—a young female corpse with no head.

A devious serial killer with morbid intentions is haunting this small seaside town. Agent Stone will have to fight her past nightmares to unmask the "beach butcher," as the town folk have dubbed him.

Get HER LAST LIE now so you won't miss out on another fast-paced and spine-tingling murder mystery thriller with Chief Bold, Special Agent Stone, Max, and the eccentric characters of this small seaside town, each of whom hold a secret.

Get your thriller fix here!
www.tikiriherath.com/thrillers

Available globally in e-book, paperback, and hardback editions on all good bookstores everywhere. Also available for free in libraries everywhere. Just ask your friendly local librarian to order a copy via Ingram Spark.

Author's Note

D ear friend,

Did you enjoy this novel?

My promise is to give you an exciting escape with every book I write, and I sure hope I have done so.

If you have a minute, would you leave an honest review of this book on Goodreads, Bookbub, or any of the online bookstores? Just one sentence would do.

Honest reader reviews help get my books selected for international promotions and I get to reach more readers around the world. Thank you from the bottom of my heart!

Have you heard of The Rebel Reader Club?

My reader club is a super fan community where you can get early access to my new books before anyone else in the world.

You will also have access to bonus true crime and K9 stories, fun swag like postcards, reader stickers, and bookmarks, bookish merchandise like signed paperbacks, and VIP tickets to *Tea with Tikiri,* and more.

And you get to decide what you want to be. A Detective, a Special Agent, or an FBI Director.

Click the link below to check out my reader club. You can read *Her Deadly End* for free too.

Come, join the fun and get your thriller fix!
https://reamstories.com/tikiri

See you on the inside.
My very best wishes,
Tikiri
Vancouver, Canada

PS/ Have you downloaded the epilogue of this book yet? Read about the Black Rock town and its locals. See how Chief Bold reacts to Asha admitting to be a private detective, and what he proposes to Tanya that gets her worried....
Get your bonus epilogue chapter to Her Cold Blood here:
www.books.tikiriherath.com/ts-1-doghousepub

PPS/ If you didn't enjoy the story or spotted typos, would you drop me a line and let me know? Or just write to say hello. I would love to hear from you and personally reply to every email I receive.
My email address is: Tikiri@TikiriHerath.com

PPPS/ Last one, I promise.

I have a secret to share with you.

In this series, Black Rock is set in the state of Washington, USA. But did you know it's based on my seaside hometown in British Columbia, Canada?

Yes, the town exists.

The long pier, the Dog House brewery & pub, Lulu's coffee shop, Marine Drive with its gourmet ice cream shops, and even the Pink Palace resort are based on real places.

This town is located ten minutes from the US border, so from my patio, I can see the San Juan islands, the Olympic Mountain range, and the beautiful blue bay that separates Canada from the USA. This is an idyllic paradise where sailing, paddle boating, and beach picnics are far more common than serial killing, unlike in my books....

The Reading List

The Red Heeled Rebels universe of mystery thrillers, featuring your favorite kick-ass female characters:

Tanya Stone FBI K9 Mystery Thrillers
www.TikiriHerath.com/Thrillers
NEW FBI thriller series starring Tetyana from the Red Heeled Rebels as Special Agent Tanya Stone, and Max, as her loyal German Shepherd. These are serial killer thrillers set in Black Rock, a small upscale resort town on the coast of Washington state.
Her Deadly End
Her Cold Blood
Her Last Lie
Her Secret Crime
Her Perfect Murder
Her Grisly Grave

Asha Kade Private Detective Murder Mysteries
www.TikiriHerath.com/Mysteries
Each book is a standalone murder mystery thriller, featuring the Red Heeled Rebels, Asha Kade and Katy McCafferty. Asha and Katy receive one million dollars for their favorite children's charity from a secret benefactor's estate every time they solve a cold case.
Merciless Legacy
Merciless Games
Merciless Crimes
Merciless Lies
Merciless Past
Merciless Deaths

Red Heeled Rebels International Mystery & Crime - The Origin Story
www.TikiriHerath.com/RedHeeledRebels
The award-winning origin story of the Red Heeled Rebels characters. Learn how a rag-tag group of trafficked orphans from different places united to fight for their freedom and their lives, and became a found family.
The Girl Who Crossed the Line
The Girl Who Ran Away
The Girl Who Made Them Pay
The Girl Who Fought to Kill
The Girl Who Broke Free

The Girl Who Knew Their Names
The Girl Who Never Forgot

✦———■———✦

The Accidental Traveler

www.TikiriHerath.com

An anthology of personal short stories based on the author's sojourns around the world.

✦———■———✦

The Rebel Diva Nonfiction Series

www.TikiriHerath.com/Nonfiction

Your Rebel Dreams: 6 simple steps to take back control of your life in uncertain times.

Your Rebel Plans: 4 simple steps to getting unstuck and making progress today.

Your Rebel Life: Easy habit hacks to enhance happiness in the 10 key areas of your life.

Bust Your Fears: 3 simple tools to crush your anxieties and squash your stress.

✦———■———✦

Collaborations

The Boss Chick's Bodacious Destiny Nonfiction Bundle
Dark Shadows 2: Voodoo and Black Magic of New Orleans

Tikiri's novels and nonfiction books are available on all good bookstores around the world.

These books are also available in libraries everywhere. Just ask your friendly local librarian or your local bookstore to order a copy via Ingram Spark.

www.TikiriHerath.com

Happy reading.

Debate this Dozen

Twelve Book Club Questions

1. Who was your favorite character?
2. Which characters did you dislike?
3. Which scene has stuck with you the most? Why?
4. What scenes surprised you?
5. What was your favorite part of the book?
6. What was your least favorite part?
7. Did any part of this book strike a particular emotion in you? Which part and what emotion did the book make you feel?
8. Did you know the author has written an underlying message in this story? What theme or life lesson do you think this story tells?
9. What did you think of the author's writing?
10. How would you adapt this book into a movie? Who would you cast in the leading roles?
11. On a scale of one to ten, how would you rate this story?
12. Would you read another book by this author?

Tanya Stone FBI K9 Mystery Thrillers

*H*ow far would you go to avenge your family's brutal murder?

<u>Tanya Stone FBI K9 Serial Killer Thrillers</u>

Her Deadly End

Her Cold Blood

Her Last Lie

Her Secret Crime

Her Perfect Murder

Her Grisly Grave

A brand-new FBI K9 serial killer thriller series for a pulse-pounding, bone-chilling adventure from the comfort and warmth of your favorite reading chair at home.

Can you find the killer before Agent Tanya Stone?

www.TikiriHerath.com/thrillers

✦────╍────✦

Some small-town secrets will haunt your nightmares. Escape if you can...

FBI Special Agent Tanya Stone has a new assignment. Hunt down the serial killers prowling the idyllic West Coast resort towns.

An unspeakable and bone-chilling darkness seethes underneath these picturesque seaside suburbs. A string of violent abductions and gruesome murders wreak hysteria among the perfect lives of the towns' families.

But nothing is what it seems. The monsters wear masks and mingle with the townsfolk, spreading vicious lies.

With her K9 German Shepherd, Agent Stone goes on the warpath. She will fight her own demons as a trafficked survivor to make the perverted psychopaths pay.

But now, they're after her.

Small towns have dark deceptions and sealed lips. If they know you know the truth, they'll never let you leave...

✦────╍────✦

Each book is a standalone murder mystery thriller, featuring Tetyana from the Red Heeled Rebels as Agent Tanya Stone, and Max, her loyal German Shepherd. Red Heeled Rebels Asha Kade and Katy McCafferty and their found family make guest appearances when Tanya needs help.

There is no graphic violence, heavy cursing, or explicit sex in these books.

The dogs featured in this series are never harmed, but the villains are.

To learn more about this exciting new series and find out how to get early access to all the books in the Tanya Stone FBI K9 series, go to www.TikiriHerath.com/thrillers

Sign up to Tikiri's Rebel Reader Club to get the chance to win personalized paperback books, chat with the author and more.

Available in e-book, paperback, and hardback editions on all good bookstores around the world. Print books are available for free in libraries everywhere. Just ask your friendly local librarian or your local bookstore to order a copy via Ingram Spark.

Asha Kade Private Detective Murder Mysteries

How far would you go for a million-dollar payout?

<u>The Merciless Murder Mysteries</u>

Merciless Legacy

Merciless Games

Merciless Crimes

Merciless Lies

Merciless Past

Merciless Deaths

Each book is a standalone murder mystery thriller featuring the Red Heeled Rebel, Asha Kade, and her best friend Katy

McCafferty, as private detectives on the hunt for serial killers in small towns USA.

There is no graphic violence, heavy cursing, or explicit sex in these books. What you will find are a series of suspicious deaths, a closed circle of suspects, twists and turns, fast-paced action, and nail-biting suspense.

www.TikiriHerath.com/mysteries

A newly minted private investigator, Asha Kade, gets a million dollars from an eccentric client's estate every time she solves a cold case. Asha Kade accepts this bizarre challenge, but what she doesn't bargain for is to be drawn into the dark underworld of her past again.

The only thing that propels her forward now is a burning desire for justice.

What readers are saying on Amazon and Goodreads:

"My new favorite series!"

"Thrilling twists, unputdownable!"

"I was hooked right from the start!"

"A twisted whodunnit! Edge of your seat thriller that kept me up late, to finish it, unputdownable!! More, please!"

"Buckle up for a roller coaster of a ride. This one will keep you on the edge of your seat."

"A must read! A macabre start to an excellent book. It had me totally gripped from the start and just got better!"

"A great whodunit with a lot of twists and turns along the way. The story was amazing!"

"I could not stop reading it. It was as if I was there witnessing the murders myself. The characters had depth and personality and backgrounds that were explained nicely. It was awesome!"

"Nothing is more terrifying than the fear of the unknown. Do you have any nails left? Another NAIL-BITING story from a very talented master storyteller!"

⚜——·——⚜

A brand-new murder mystery series for a pulse-pounding, bone-chilling adventure from the comfort and warmth of your favorite reading chair at home.

Can you find the killer before Asha Kade does?

⚜——·——⚜

To learn more about this exciting series, go to www.TikiriHerath.com/mysteries.

Sign up to Tikiri's Rebel Reader Club to get the chance to win personalized paperback books, chat with the author and more.

⚜——·——⚜

Available in e-book, paperback, and hardback editions on all good bookstores around the world. Print books are available for free in libraries everywhere. Just ask your friendly local librarian or your local bookstore to order a copy via Ingram Spark.

The Red Heeled Rebels International Mystery & Crime

The Origin Story

Would you like to know the origin story of your favorite characters in the Tanya Stone FBI K9 mystery thrillers and the Asha Kade Merciless murder mysteries?

In the award-winning Red Heeled Rebels international mystery & crime series—the origin story—you'll find out how Asha, Katy, and Tetyana (Tanya) banded together in their troubled youths to fight for freedom against all odds.

—※———※—

<u>**The complete Red Heeled Rebels international crime collection:**</u>

Prequel Novella: The Girl Who Crossed the Line

Book One: The Girl Who Ran Away
Book Two: The Girl Who Made Them Pay
Book Three: The Girl Who Fought to Kill
Book Four: The Girl Who Broke Free
Book Five: The Girl Who Knew Their Names
Book Six: The Girl Who Never Forgot
The series is now complete!

An epic, pulse-pounding, international crime thriller series that spans four continents featuring a group of spunky, sassy young misfits who have only each other for family.

A multiple-award-winning series which would be best read in order. There is no graphic violence, heavy cursing, or explicit sex in these books.

www.TikiriHerath.com/RedHeeledRebels

In a world where justice no longer prevails, six iron-willed young women rally to seek vengeance on those who stole their humanity.

If you like gripping thrillers with flawed but strong female leads, vigilante action in exotic locales and twists that leave you at the edge of your seat, you'll love these books by multiple award-winning Canadian novelist, Tikiri Herath.

Go on a heart-pounding international adventure without having to get a passport or even buy an airline ticket!

What readers are saying on Amazon and Goodreads:

"Fast-paced and exciting!"

"An exciting and thought-provoking book."

"A wonderful story! I didn't want to leave the characters."

"I couldn't put down this exciting road trip adventure with a powerful message."

"Another award-worthy adventure novel that keeps you on the edge of your seat."

"A heart-stopping adventure. I just couldn't put the book down till I finished reading it."

"Kept me mesmerized and captivated with the rich descriptions which made me feel like I was actually inside the story."

"This is a fantastic read that will have you traveling the globe. I absolutely loved this book. You won't be able to put it down!"

"A real page-turner and international thriller. Reminds me of why I've always loved to read. Because I can visit worlds and places, I wouldn't ordinarily get to see."

Literary Awards & Praise for The Red Heeled Rebels books:

- Grand Prize Award Finalist - 2019 Eric Hoffer Award, USA

- First Horizon Award Finalist - 2019 Eric Hoffer Award, USA

- Honorable Mention General Fiction - 2019 Eric Hoffer Award, USA

- Winner First-In-Category - 2019 Chanticleer Somerset Award, USA

- Semi-Finalist - 2020 Chanticleer Somerset Award, USA

- Winner in 2019 Readers' Favorite Book Awards, USA

- Winner of 2019 Silver Medal - Excellence E-Lit Award, USA

- Winner in Suspense Category - 2018 New York Big Book Award, USA

- Finalist in Suspense Category - 2018 & 2019 Silver Falchion Awards, USA

- Honorable Mention - 2018-19 Reader Views Literary Classics Award, USA

- Publisher's Weekly Booklife Prize - 2018, USA

To learn more about this addictive series, go to **www.TikiriHerath.com/RedHeeledRebels** and receive the prequel novella - **The Girl Who Crossed The Line** - as a gift.

Sign up to Tikiri's Rebel Reader club and get bonus stories, exotic recipes, the chance to win paperbacks, chat with the author and more.

Available in e-book, paperback, and hardback editions on all good bookstores around the world. Print books are available for free in libraries everywhere. Just ask your friendly local librarian or your local bookstore to order a copy via Ingram Spark.

Acknowledgments

To my amazing, talented, superstar editor, Stephanie Parent (USA), thank you, as always, for coming on this literary journey with me and for helping make these books the best they can be.

❖———❖

To my international club of beta readers who gave me their frank feedback, thank you. I truly value your thoughts.

In alphabetical order of first name:

Beaulah McLean, South Africa

Cyndi Wannamaker, Canada

Ellie Algiere, United States of America

Janet Yieh, United States of America

Kim Schup, United States of America

Kristen Harnish, United States of America

Laura Edwards, United States of America

Liz Shulman, United States of America

Michele Kapugi, United States of America

Wayne Burnop, United States of America

To all the kind and generous readers who take the time to review my novels and share their frank feedback, thank you so much. Your support is invaluable.

I'm immensely grateful to you all for your kind and generous support, and would love to invite you for a glass of British Columbian wine or a cup of Ceylon tea with chocolates when you come to Vancouver next!

Dedication

T his book is dedicated to all the brave women of Ukraine and all other war zones in the world today.

About the Author

Tikiri Herath is the multiple-award-winning author of international thriller and mystery novels and the Rebel Diva books.

⟡—••—⟡

Tikiri worked in risk management in the intelligence and defense sectors, including in the Canadian Federal Government and at NATO. She has a bachelor's degree from the University of Victoria, British Columbia, and a master's degree from the Solvay Business School in Brussels.

Born in Sri Lanka, Tikiri grew up in East Africa and has studied, worked, and lived in Europe, Southeast Asia, and North America throughout her adult life. An international nomad and fifth-culture kid, she now calls Canada home.

She's an adrenaline junkie who has rock climbed, bungee jumped, rode on the back of a motorcycle across Quebec, flown in an acrobatic airplane upside down, and parachuted solo.

When she's not plotting another thriller scene or planning another adrenaline-filled trip, you'll find her baking in her kitchen with a glass of red Shiraz in hand and vintage jazz playing in the background.

To say hello and get travel stories from around the world, go to www.Tikiriherath.com

9 781990 234163